The Metamorphosis of Becca

THE MARSTON SERIES - BOOK ONE

JOCELYN KRAEMER

Editing: Corina Douglas, Burning Legacies Publishing
Cover Design: Fresh Design
Formatting: Tapioca Press

ISBN: 979-8-9853331-0-7 (e-book)
ISBN: 979-8-9853331-1-4 (paperback)

Email: JocelynKraemerBooks@gmail.com
Website: https://www.jocelynkraemerbooks.com/
Facebook: https://www.facebook.com/JocelynKraemerBooks

In memory of my boss and mentor, Dr. Jim Buechler. You were a guiding light for me and so many others, and I still find your teachings lighting my path today. You paved the way for me to meet a myriad of amazing individuals who work tirelessly to advocate for people with cancer or who are fighting their own battle with this disease. I continue to draw on your wisdom daily, as this gives me renewed strength for my own daily journey through life—both the ups and the downs. You, and all of those who are a part of the battle against cancer, are my superheroes. I am grateful for you, each and every day.

A huge thank you to my husband, who supports me in everything I do, including the crazy stuff like triathlons. Thank you for supporting me just as I am.

PART ONE
Love is in the Air

CHAPTER 1

Luna's Pub

Two Years Ago

BECCA LAUGHED AT HER FRIEND'S DESCRIPTION OF THEIR recent camping trip, her hand clutching her stomach as she doubled over. "Stop, Carmen! I'm going to snort this margarita halfway across the table soon!"

As her best friend ignored her and continued with the story, Becca wiped the moisture away from her eyes and found her laughter turning into a happy sigh. They were sitting in their favorite Friday night happy hour spot at Luna's Restaurant and Pub, surrounded by their usual group of girlfriends, and everyone at their crowded table was now shaking with laughter. Becca knew some of that was a release from a stress-filled work week, not to mention the now almost empty pitchers of margaritas and beer that had helped them along.

It was a splendid start to the weekend. There were already five women crammed around their small barroom table; soon to be six, Becca noted, as she felt a light squeeze on her shoulder as Anna, the newest member of their group, leaned in beside her to greet everyone present before commandeering an empty chair and slipping in next to her. The conversation continued to flow with a bubbly hum, sending a flow of contentment through Becca's veins. She loved getting together with her friends. Friday nights were always a highlight, and she suddenly remembered that she wouldn't have them soon. A hint of melancholy accompanied the thought, but it was followed by a surge of excitement that she'd be fulfilling her father's wishes. Yes, she would miss them, but she was finally on the cusp of achieving the goal she'd set out for herself so long ago.

As if hearing her internal thoughts, Carmen said into the sudden lull in the conversation, "We're going to miss you, Becca. I'm sad you're leaving." Her lips turned into a pout as she added, "Can't you just stay right here in Pittsburgh?"

"Wait...what?" asked Anna. "You're moving? When?"

Becca turned to face her. "Yes. I'm in a leadership rotation program with Patterson Consulting here in Pittsburgh. My rotation ends next month and then I'll be transferring to the Washington, D.C. office. It's where I grew up before I moved here in middle school. I've always been meaning to go back."

"You're way too driven, Becca. I don't know anyone else who has marched toward their goal with such determination," Carmen said proudly. Turning toward Anna, she added, "She went straight through college, flew through graduate school, and now she's in this highfa-lutin leadership program. Even in high school, Becca had her plan all laid out, and she hasn't wavered from it one bit." Carmen's smile faltered.

Becca felt the reality of her situation hit her then, and she reached out to pat Carmen on the knee. Her best friend quickly ducked her head and reached for her margarita glass. When Carmen looked back up, her smile was firmly back in place, but her tone belied her emotions. "Cheers," she said, in a gravelly voice, lifting her glass. "I sure will miss you, Becca."

"I'll miss you too. I love you, Carmen," she whispered. Turning to look at all their friends, she added firmly, "I love all of you. For now, though, we still have lots of Fridays ahead of us before I leave. Cheers!" Becca raised her glass and coaxed Carmen and the others to once again do the same.

CHAPTER 2

I Don't Need the Ball Thingy

Two Years Later - Present Day

BECCA IGNORED THE DOOR'S SOFT CHIME THAT SOUNDED behind her as she tried once again to explain what she needed to the young boy standing in front of her. "I don't need the ball thingy. I need the hitch with the two-inch hole so the other piece with the thing that sticks out can fit into that hole." Becca's words came out in a rush, her forehead scrunching in frustration.

A flush crept up the boy's neck, and his hands fidgeted with a roll of packing tape sitting on the counter between them. Becca sighed because the boy's attention was no longer focused on her, but on the shop's front door. "Do you think you have the part I need?" she prodded.

He turned his eyes back to Becca, sweat now beading on his upper lip as he reached for the keyboard and began clicking away. After a moment, he said, "Is this the right part, Ma'am?" His voice squeaked as he turned the computer's screen toward her.

"Oh please, just call me Becca," she said, as she leaned in over the counter to get a closer look at the image on the screen. The boy's head jerked up, and he took a fumbling step backward, but Becca barely noticed as she scrutinized the product. Another sigh escaped her lips.

"No, I don't think that will work," she said, shaking her head. "It's for a bike rack. My bike is too big to fit into my car. I need to attach it to this." She lifted the contraption she'd carted into the shop. It was comprised of metal tubes and fabric straps.

"Yes, Ma'am—I mean, Becca. Um...so...I'm not sure what you need."

"Maybe I can help," said a deep, disembodied voice from behind her.

Becca stilled. She'd heard the door chime, alerting them to someone entering the store, but had ignored it, too intent on her goal of getting the boy to understand her plea. She looked directly at the boy now. His face registered relief at the man's offer of assistance. Taking in the scattering of pimples across his forehead and his ashen complexion, she suddenly wondered about his age. He looked barely out of puberty. Sixteen, maybe?

A wave of guilt washed over her as Becca realized how flustered he was. She'd been so intent on overcoming her fear on her first foray at getting back out into the world that she hadn't taken in what was going on around her. She now felt as flustered as the boy looked. Taking a deep breath, she then blew it out slowly, using a technique that had served her well over the past two years to steady her nerves, before turning to face the man behind her. "Thank you so much. I would appreciate your help."

She couldn't fail to notice that he was tall and good-looking as he offered a hand and said, "Hi, I'm Ben."

"Becca," she responded, shaking his proffered hand. "I'm sorry. I'm not doing a good job of explaining what I'm looking for. This whole bike thing is new to me." She smiled up at Ben, hoping her confident demeanor masked her internal turmoil.

"No problem at all; I'd be happy to help. I actually have a lot of experience with bikes." Ben quickly scanned the bike rack Becca held and then turned to speak to the boy, giving her a chance to take in his features surreptitiously.

The way his body moved and the tone of his voice fanned her curiosity. She watched, tongue darting out to moisten her lips, as his arm lifted in a fluid motion and gestured toward the bike rack while he spoke to the boy. The shirt he wore was a crisp, deep blue that complemented his dark auburn hair. Despite being neatly cut, unruly waves of hair tumbled down from the top of his head to nestle just below his ears. Becca had an urge to reach up and run her hand through those thick curls, wondering if, in contrast to his toned physique, they were as soft as they looked. The logo on his shirt advertised a bike shop out in California, giving credence to his earlier comment about his expertise with bikes.

"I think what Becca is looking to purchase is a two-inch hitch that is specific to that bike rack she's holding," Ben said, indicating the section of the bike rack in Becca's hands that needed to connect directly to the hitch. "She'll also need somebody to install it for her." As he pulled his hand back, he ran it through his hair in what looked like a practiced but subconscious gesture.

Becca smelled the scent of minty eucalyptus wafting through the air. It tickled her nose and prompted her to pull in an additional breath. The fresh scent caused a memory to arise. She remembered watching her father shave when she was a young girl, and it brought a reminiscent smile to her lips, helping to calm her nerves.

"Is that correct, Becca?" Ben now asked.

She hesitated, momentarily caught off guard. *What was the question?* "Ah, yes. Thank you." She smiled politely at Ben, hoping he hadn't noticed her prior scrutiny. Turning back to the boy and now fully cognizant of his young age and likely inexperience, she gently asked, "Do you have that hitch in stock, and would you be able to install it on my car?"

"I think so," the boy said hesitantly, looking to Ben for reassurance.

"Type the word 'hitch' into your system and see what comes up," Ben coached in a gentle, deep baritone. "We can go from there to see what next steps are necessary."

The boy turned back to the computer to type in the word. "Got it!" he said, looking up at Ben with a smile. "Here it is—a two-inch hitch."

"That's it. Good job, Nick," Ben said, his eyes dropping momentarily to read the boy's name tag pinned to his shirt. A shirt, Becca now noted, that was still creased with oddly placed folds, revealing it was only recently released from its packaging.

The boy's chest puffed up at Ben's kind words. "What type of car do you have?" Nick now asked her, attempting to mirror Ben's relaxed stance and deep tone.

Becca smiled at Nick and gave him the make, model, and year of her car. He typed the information into the store's computer and then looked up with a twinge of confidence showing in his eyes. "We have that in stock," he confirmed. "With tax and installation it will come to a little over two hundred dollars. Um, but..." Nick hesitated, then said in a rush, "I don't know how to install that for you. It's my first week working here. Joe, the manager, won't be back for another hour. He got called away to help with a truck that broke down. He could install it for you as soon as he gets back, though, if you don't mind waiting. Or I can make an appointment for you for another day."

Becca's smile wavered. Weren't she and the boy a pair? Maybe this wasn't such a good idea. Maybe she wasn't ready. Maybe work was enough for now. The clock on the wall thudded loudly in her ears as Nick and Ben waited silently for her answer. She absently reached up to rub the pendant at the end of the delicate silver chain she wore around her neck as she took in a deep breath, trying to focus on one of the exercises her doctor had shown her to help calm her nerves. Becca reminded herself that she was fine now. Her doctor had assured her just last month that she was officially in remission and had encouraged her to get back out into the world.

The clock ticked louder in her ears. She needed to decide, but her thoughts were swirling. It was as though she were looking into an Escher print, with her mind's eye unable to focus. Her thoughts continued to whirl out of control, not settling on a simple response to the straightforward question posed by the boy. She fumbled with the pendant as her mind continued to race. If her plans hadn't been so drastically derailed, this is exactly where she would have been standing two years ago, right here at this same U-Haul counter. She wouldn't have been asking for a car hitch, though. She would've been buying boxes for her move to Washington, D.C. At that thought, a bitter taste entered her mouth.

Stop! Becca chided herself. *Breathe in, breathe out, count to five.* She took in another deep gulp of air and blew it out slowly. She was here now, and her doctor was right. So was Carmen. Every time she and Carmen spoke, Carmen found some way of subtly—or not so subtly—

reminding her that it was time to 'get back in the saddle.' She knew Carmen didn't mean that she should cycle, but that she needed to get her life back on track—and not just her work life, either. But she'd promised Carmen she would start riding with her. It was such a little thing but it represented a big first step. It was time to find that strong, confident person she'd been just two short years ago—before her life was so unceremoniously derailed by her surprise diagnosis.

Finally making a decision, Becca said, "Yes, I'll stay. Is there a place in the store where I can wait?"

"We have a couple of chairs over by those shelves," Nick said. "You're welcome to hang out there until Joe gets back."

Becca looked to where Nick pointed. Two metal chairs, looking anything but comfortable, sat behind shelves overloaded with flat cardboard boxes waiting to be assembled and a multitude of packing tape. She could manage an hour. Besides, all she had waiting for her at home was a pile of unpaid health care bills. And if she didn't get this done today, she would have to wait until next Saturday. Even with Carmen pestering her, Becca wasn't sure she could maintain this momentum to get out into the world for another full week. Yes, it would be best if she waited this out—today.

Lifting her head, she looked directly at Nick and repeated in a tone laced with determination, "Okay, I'll wait."

CHAPTER 3
Rose-Colored Glasses

As Becca walked over to have a seat on one of the cold, metallic chairs, Nick turned back to Ben. "Can I help you with something?" he enquired.

"I hope so. I need to buy five medium boxes and rent a cargo trailer. I have a reservation for the trailer. It should be listed under the name Morgan, Ben Morgan."

Nick moved his fingers back to the computer keyboard and began typing. "Yes. Here it is. I can ring you up for the boxes. You'll need to wait for Joe to get the trailer, though. I'm sorry about that," Nick said, his voice faltering. "I don't know how to check them out yet."

Becca peeked from her location behind the shelves as Nick addressed Ben. Ben Morgan was a nice, solid name, she thought. She delighted in being able to eavesdrop on their conversation. From where she sat, Becca didn't have the luxury of observing his facial expressions, but what she could see from behind was enough to keep her happily occupied, lessening the discomfort of her hard metal perch. He was tall and slender, with an athlete's body—not bulky, but svelte and toned. Maybe a runner's physique? Or a biker's, as he'd alluded to. His butt filled out his jeans nicely and his biceps rippled under the t-shirt he was wearing.

As Ben spoke, his deep melodic baritone wafted back to her in that still-measured pace, sending a soothing warmth through her body. His voice was mesmerizing. Even Nick must have felt it. *How could anyone not?* Becca thought with a sigh. And how come she was suddenly noticing him? Her friends had been trying to set her up with an array of men for ages, and not one of them had interested her these last few years.

But it didn't matter how good he looked or sounded, she reminded herself with a shake of her head. She wasn't interested in a relationship—or even in a date. Biking with Carmen was enough of a social life for now. Yes, it had been about two years since she'd been out with a man. But dating had been a distraction two years ago and would be even more of one now. She needed to stay focused and put her career plans back into action. The job that had been lined up two years ago was gone, but she'd heard rumors just last week that a new opportunity was about to open up. The timing was perfect now she was in remission, and she didn't need the complications that dating would bring.

The thought came with a surprise pang of regret. Trying to bolster her resolve, she reminded herself that if she started dating, she'd need to explain about her cancer and, inevitably, endure the pitying looks she'd get. She didn't want to drown in those tedious details with anyone—not even with herself. What she wanted right now was to feel normal—and to be seen as normal. *But that didn't mean there was any harm in looking, or in listening,* she thought with a surge of defiance. Her lips quirked up into a mischievous smile. What else did she have to do for the next hour?

"I'll wait on Joe," she now heard Ben tell Nick affably. "But I'm going to head out to find a bite to eat rather than wait in the shop. I haven't stopped for lunch yet, and now seems as good a time as any. You can wait on ringing up the boxes. I'll pay for everything all together when I get back. While I'm gone, can you please get the paperwork for the trailer ready, along with whatever the cost will be for the boxes?"

"Sure thing, Mr. Morgan," Nick said with a smile and a nod of his head. "Thanks for being so understanding."

"Great, I'll see you in about an hour, Nick." Ben made his way toward the front door of the shop, but instead of heading straight for the door, he made his way straight toward her.

Becca could feel his approach, but she didn't dare look up. Instead, she quickly dropped her gaze to the shelf in front of her.

"Interested in packing tape in addition to a bike hitch?" Ben asked in that rich, soothing baritone. Becca pulled her eyes away from the shelf and looked up, feeling an embarrassing flush creep into her cheeks. "Oh no...just day-dreaming."

"It looks like we're both relegated to waiting on Joe. I'm on my way to get a late lunch. Would you care to join me?"

In response to his invitation, Becca felt the warmth flowing through her body heighten to a simmer, but she hesitated on a response.

As if sensing that she was on the cusp of indecision, Ben added, "I sure could use some company for lunch. I hate to eat alone, and there's a nice little diner only about six blocks from here that looks out on the Old Oaks Trail and the river. Have you been on that trail? It's great for both walkers and bikers. It's one of my favorite places around here, and it looks like you might be in the market for a place to ride that bike of yours soon."

It was just lunch to help pass the time, Becca rationalized. It wasn't like it was a date. And she certainly didn't need to share any details of her life with him. Making a decision, she said with false confidence, "That would be great, actually. I'll be needing a place to ride, and I could definitely use some lunch."

Internally, she cringed. Did she really just say yes to this stranger? The words had popped out of her mouth without her brain fully engaging...or had they? Maybe it was just the opposite—maybe her brain was engaging and the rest of her just hadn't quite caught up yet. Isn't this exactly what was supposed to be happening right now? According to her doctor, she was no longer sick. And isn't that just what Carmen had been trying to tell her? What was holding her back?

I can live a normal life again, Becca thought with a thrill. That meant she needed to have some semblance of a social life, and here was an opportunity right in front of her. Maybe it was fate, and this is exactly what she needed—a simple shared lunch on a beautiful Saturday afternoon. Why not? *Who was she to question fate?* she thought as she smiled up at Ben.

"Great," Ben said, smiling back at her warmly. "Hold on just a minute and I'll let Nick know where we'll be." Ben walked back to the counter and wrote something out on a scrap of paper. "Hey Nick, this is my cell phone number. We're going to get a bite to eat. Can you please call me when Joe returns so we'll know when to head back?"

"Absolutely, Mr. Morgan. Have a nice lunch, or dinner, or whatever," Nick stammered, clearly as enamored with Ben as she was.

Becca preceded Ben out of the U-Haul store as he held the door open for her and motioned her ahead. She rubbed her hands along the sides of her jeans, trying to wipe away the dampness pooling in her palms. She felt a slight sense of trepidation, but she also felt hopeful for the first time in a long time, especially as she crossed the threshold of the store and left its cool, gray, and utilitarian interior behind.

It was a beautiful spring day and the sun's rays shone down on her, further brightening Becca's mood and confidence. If nothing else, the walk to the diner would be a pleasant distraction from the mound of paperwork she'd been working on this morning. Besides, her friends—as well as her mother—would be thrilled that she was finally out doing something personal rather than just focusing on work. *And doctor's appointments,* she thought with an internal eye roll.

Ben looked over at her and their eyes momentarily met before Becca quickly looked away. "Are you cold?" he asked, his voice laced with concern. "I should have realized how cold it is out still."

"No, no, I'm fine. I left my sweatshirt in the car, but the walk will warm me up. It feels nice to get out and walk after being cooped up for most of the winter."

Ben seemed satisfied with her answer and turned his gaze back to the sidewalk in front of them. "I know this section of town looks bad," he said, as they made their way further away from the U-Haul store. "But there's so much possibility here."

Becca's gaze took in their surroundings as they walked. She'd never been to the town of Marston before. She hadn't even known it existed until she'd started looking for a place that could install a hitch on her car. And yet, Marston wasn't all that far from her apartment in downtown Pittsburgh. It was only about twenty miles away and it had taken her less than an hour to get here. It sure felt different here, though, even when compared with Viceroy, the little neighborhood just south of downtown Pittsburgh where her mother had unceremoniously moved them after her dad died.

She'd only been twelve when her father died. But it still felt like yesterday when her mother, only a few months after her father had passed, packed them up and moved them from Washington, D.C. to Viceroy. It was where her mother had grown up, and she'd said they needed to be back in familiar territory. Becca had been so angry with her mother. How could she move them away from the only home Becca had ever known—and away from her father? She'd promised herself she'd get back there one day. She'd fulfill her father's legacy and make him proud. He'd been a financial analyst for the Federal government and she had promised herself she would be too.

Now, as she and Ben continued their walk, Becca didn't know just what to make of Marston compared to all the places she'd previously lived. The U-Haul store was in a decent enough little strip mall in the middle of town, but as they walked further from the store, the surrounding area worsened. She could see nothing but blighted, vacant storefronts on either side of them, along with overgrown lots littered with trash. Becca was sure they were heading in the general direction of the river, but it was nowhere in sight. Glancing backward, she felt reassured that she could still see the U-Haul store in the distance behind them.

She bit her lip, wondering if maybe she'd taken on more than she'd bargained for. Somehow, though, she wasn't scared. Instead, she felt like she was on a grand adventure. She never would have stopped in the City of Marston if it weren't for their large U-Haul store that installed hitches, let alone walked through any of this little town. Yet, here she was, venturing through the wilds of Marston with an intrepid tour guide who was visually painting a picture using just his words of what this town could become. Instead of the decaying buildings and crumbling concrete sidewalks, Ben's descriptions helped her see a vibrant, thriving riverfront community.

"See those sharrows on the roadway? Those are shared lane markings," Ben was now saying, pointing to evenly spaced images in the right-hand lane of the four-lane boulevard running next to them.

Becca could see that each image consisted of two painted triangles and a bicycle.

"Those markings are new," Ben continued. "They denote a new section to the Old Oaks Trail that allows for bicycles as well as cars, with the sidewalk here reserved for walkers. They're just paint at this point but it's a good start to formalizing a trail through here. And if we follow these markings, they'll lead us to the off-road graveled section of the trail that allows for casual walkers, runners, and bicyclists. That portion of the trail has been here in Marston for decades. It's not very well kept, but it serves as low-hanging fruit for developing a trail through here that could help revitalize this riverfront town."

But as they passed an outdated mall, more decaying concrete buildings, and empty lots, Becca's mood wavered and her mind defaulted back to reality. A sign reading *Welcome to the Marston City Mall* swung haphazardly in the light spring breeze at the entrance to the almost empty shopping plaza. Concern etched its way into her brain, along with an image of a gust of wind whipping through that mall, knocking not only that sign down but also a couple of the buildings already leaning precariously at dangerous angles. Should she turn back?

"It really is a beautiful area," Ben said then.

Nervous giggles escaped Becca's lips. She looked around her, now seeing only peeling paint, collapsing roofs, overgrown vacant lots— and no river.

Ben stopped and looked at her more directly. He laughed at her expression. "Hey, I think I need to let you borrow my rose-colored glasses," he joked, pretending to reach into his pocket.

"I'm sorry," said Becca, smiling. "I'm sure you're right. I didn't mean to be rude. It's just, well…" She raised an eyebrow and swept her arm out in front of her. "I'm not sure I'll be boutique shopping here anytime soon."

"Just you wait," said Ben. "I'll make a believer out of you yet."

"If you say so," she said skeptically. "And about that diner, do I need rose-colored glasses for that too? Is there really a diner along here somewhere, or are we fishing for our lunch?"

"Real funny. Yes, there really is a diner right off this trail, and it has a great view of the water. I promise. And the food is delicious. I found the place while exploring out on my bike. I've had a craving all week for one of their burgers—and for one of their world-famous salted caramel pretzel milkshakes," he added with a grin. "But work has been so busy, I haven't had time to stop in. You've given me the perfect excuse to do just that. You, Nick, and Joe, that is."

Before she could come up with a witty comeback, the trail they were walking on veered off to the right onto a crushed limestone path —and Becca gasped.

CHAPTER 4

The Old Oaks Trail and Diner

"This is amazing," Becca said, feeling her eyes widen in surprise and a grin quirk up on her lips.

"Told ya so." Ben chuckled, clearly pleased with her response.

The river glistened on her left, and an expansive patio just up ahead and off to the right enticed them forward. To either side were signs of spring. Purple crocuses and yellow daffodils stood tall. Blades of newly emerging grasses carpeted the area to either side of the path, still bright green in their infancy. A family of four further up the trail cycled into the distance, the smallest riding a bike with training wheels and wearing a bright pink helmet.

A pair of walkers holding hands ambled their way toward them. At the diner up ahead, two bicycles leaned jauntily against the diner's patio railing. Just beyond the railing were about ten tables, half of them filled with customers enjoying the beautiful mid-April afternoon. The patio beckoned, as it must have the other diners, to come and sit for a while and enjoy the warmth streaming down.

Ben placed his hand lightly on her back, gently steering her toward the diner. His touch felt comforting, and the warmth from his hand lessened the chill from the cool spring afternoon. But Becca also felt a tremor of disquiet, and she reminded herself that she didn't know this man. She looked up at his face. He was looking toward the diner and not at her, giving her a moment to take in his features. As of yet, he seemed unaware of his effect on her and was more interested in simply showing her what could be in this dilapidated and yet somehow charming community.

Ben looked relaxed and comfortable in his own skin. Becca had a yearning to feel that way too. It had been a long time since she'd felt any sense of...of what? Contentment? Confidence? Purpose? She wasn't sure what it was, and she couldn't quite grasp what she was searching for or how to fill the hole inside of her. But today, finally, here with this stranger, she felt fully ready to put her illness behind her.

It's time for a new beginning, Becca thought with an adrenaline-infused burst of happiness. She would be cool, confident, and collected—just like Ben. Maybe if she mimicked his stance, as young Nick had at the U-Haul store, she could absorb those traits until they became her new reality, and she was back to the person she used to be.

Ben looked down at her with a smile, and she openly smiled back, feeling herself let go in the unguarded moment. But the occasion was interrupted by a voice.

"Hey, Ben. It's great to see you. Are you having lunch with us today?"

Becca turned to see it was the hostess.

"I hope so, Sondra," Ben said to the woman. "Do you have a spot for us?"

The hostess beamed. "For you, of course. Inside or outside?"

Ben looked toward her, silently asking her preference.

Becca shrugged then suggested, "Outside?"

"Perfect! And preferably a table looking out toward the river," he said to Sondra.

"Sure thing. Follow me." Sondra led them to a table tucked away in the corner with a cushion-covered bench seat that faced the river.

"This is great," said Ben. "Thank you."

He motioned Becca to take a seat first, and she slid onto the bench, scooting over so he could slide in next to her. As he did so, his arm brushed against her.

"Excuse me," he said politely.

"No problem," she said, testing out a flirtatious smile and pushing a wisp of honey-blonde hair away from her face.

Ben returned her smile just as an attractive young woman advanced toward their table with an order pad and pen in hand. Becca could almost hear a purr in the woman's voice as her eyes moved with laser focus over Ben. He didn't seem to notice and turned toward her, encouraging her to place her order first. Becca ordered the famous oaks diner burger that Ben had recommended but declined the milk-shake, despite Ben's tempting description.

As the waitress turned to leave, an older woman wearing an apron came up behind her. The woman's dark hair was streaked with beau-tiful gray highlights and pulled back into a bun. She was slender and couldn't be much over five feet tall. Yet, somehow, she exuded a powerful presence and assurance that filled the room, belying her height. Her smile was warm and friendly, and Becca found herself smiling at her in return.

"Ben! How are you? Sondra told me you were here," said the older woman, motioning toward the hostess. "By the way, have you met Candy yet?" she asked, placing a hand on the shoulder of the waitress. "Candy is our new server. Her family has lived in Marston forever. She left several years ago but recently moved back to town—something I love to see, our young people moving back. Or, better yet, never leaving."

Ben slid out from behind the table and shook Candy's hand. "Nice to meet you, Candy. And it's good to see you, Rose," he said, leaning in to give the older woman a friendly hug. "We came in for your wonderful burgers. I told Becca they're the best." He motioned toward Becca to include her in the conversation.

Becca began to slide out from behind the table.

"Oh, please, don't get up," Rose said, motioning for her to stay seated. "It's nice to meet you and welcome. It's a beautiful day to sit out on the patio, isn't it?"

"It sure is," said Becca. "This is a beautiful spot."

"And hopefully you'll love our burgers just as much as Ben here does," she said, giving him a motherly pat on the shoulder. "And if you do like them, please tell all your friends. We're trying to get more people into this town. It's a great place, but not everyone has figured that out yet. Ben's one of the best, though. He's got so many great ideas. If anyone can help us get this place on the map, it's Ben," she said proudly.

Ben's cheeks colored slightly at the compliment, making him look younger and even more approachable than he had a moment ago.

"Rose is not only the owner of this diner but also the Mayor of Marston," Ben explained. "And, as you can see, she's a strong advocate for Marston and full of energy. Marston is lucky to have her in their corner."

"Ah, Ben, you say the sweetest things," Rose teased.

"All well deserved," said Ben, looking at Rose with admiration.

"Flattery will get you everywhere," she said. "But enough of that. Have a seat with your friend here and enjoy the view. We'll get your burgers out in just a minute."

As Candy and Rose left, Ben slid back in beside Becca.

"Rose? Is that seriously her name?" Becca asked with a giggle. "Is she the one passing out the rose-colored glasses?"

"She sure is," Ben said with a laugh. "Is it working?"

Becca felt an unrestrained giggle bubble up in response, and all the residual tension she'd held in her limbs from this morning flittered away as the two of them continued to exchange broad, silly grins.

"So," Ben started, "what has you wanting to start biking?"

"My friend has been bugging me for months now to get out on some trails in Pittsburgh. She just bought a new bike and is itching for me to join her. Although, if you ask me, I think she's more interested in the cute biking clothes. I expect she'll want me to go shopping with her just as much as biking." Becca chuckled at the thought. "Either way, she's always got some new scheme up her sleeve. I should probably say no to her...at least sometimes, but I have to admit, her schemes usually have a way of working out. They're usually what end up giving us our best memories...and we've got lots of them. We've been friends for ages—since middle school."

"Your friend sounds wonderful."

"She is, actually. I'm lucky to be able to call her my friend."

"I expect she'd probably say the same about you," Ben said sweetly, sending another tingle of happiness up Becca's spine.

After sending him another smile, she asked, "What about you,

Ben? How come you know so much about bike racks? Is that what you do for a living—something to do with biking?" Becca pointed to the t-shirt he sported, which had the bike logo on it.

He shook his head. "It's just a hobby. I'm a pretty avid biker, though, and I started back in college out in California. I stopped for a while when I started my company in Los Angeles about six years ago. I was just too busy. But when I moved to Pittsburgh a couple of years ago, I found I missed it. So, I picked it back up, and not only did I find lots of great bike trails around here, but it gave me a great way to explore the area. You'd be amazed at how much you can discover by bike versus by car. Exploring the trails on my bike is how I found this diner. And I've found lots of other great places to bike around here too. There's a good community of bikers in the Pittsburgh region who know where all the best trails are. Although, most of them don't know about this one in Marston. It's a pretty well-kept secret, much to Rose's dismay," he added with a smirk.

"I actually found a house near here too," he continued easily. "I found it on the same day that I found this trail. I don't know what came over me when I saw it, but I bought the house that very next week. It's an old 1896 mansion and a major fixer-upper," he said with a mock grimace.

"Wow, 1896? That's awesome! I didn't know there was anything that old around here. Do you live in that house here in Marston or somewhere in Pittsburgh?"

"When I first came to Pittsburgh, I bought a condominium that I could work from as well as live in. But as I started hiring staff, that space just became too limited. I'm sure Jason and Connie—my staff—would tell you the same thing," he said with a smile. "As a result, almost as soon as I bought the house, I moved in. Like I said, though, it's a major fixer-upper—not posh by any means. Not yet, anyway."

"And does Rose know you're here not just to save the town but also that house?" Becca teased.

"Shhh...don't tell her. She might get jealous."

"I won't tell if you won't," Becca stage whispered with a chuckle, and eliciting a hearty laugh from Ben.

When he sobered, Ben said, "Seriously, though, I've met lots of great people through biking since moving here. I'd be happy to connect you with some of them if you like." He added teasingly, "I'm sure they'd also be happy to clue your friend in to where the best bike clothes are."

"You might want to keep that last part to yourself. We don't want to give Carmen too much intel. She'll have you out shopping, too, if you aren't careful!"

Ben's dark brown eyes sparkled as he let out another hearty laugh.

This was fun, she thought. She was enjoying their banter—and the burger. She leaned in to take another bite. It was delicious, but huge! She'd never be able to eat the whole thing.

"What about you? Do you live in Marston?" Ben asked, as he put his own burger down on his plate.

Becca swallowed her bite and wiped her hands on her napkin before answering, "Actually, today is the first time I've ever been to Marston. I live in downtown Pittsburgh, but I hope to be moving back to Washington, D.C. soon."

"Oh...that's too bad. Well, bad for me, I guess. Just when I thought I'd found a new friend to go biking with—and maybe shopping with too," he added, quirking his lip up in a half grin. "Do you have family there still? In Washington, D.C., I mean?"

"No...well...sort of," Becca replied hesitantly, thinking of her dad. "Actually, I'm planning to take a job out there. I just don't know when yet. I was going to go a couple of years ago, but, well...it got postponed. It looks like a new opportunity is about to open up within the next few months, although that's not completely settled yet. What about you?" Becca asked, diverting the conversation back to Ben. "Why did you leave California?"

"I came to Pittsburgh to set up a second location for my design and development company. My headquarters are in California. I hadn't intended to come here, but one of my mentors from graduate school who helped me to set up my company, really wanted me to take on some work out here to help some of his former colleagues. I wasn't going to do it at first. I didn't want to spread myself or my staff too thin. But he kept on me and even helped me hire some additional staff for my California office. It's been great, actually. I've got more business than I can handle in both California and now here. And now he's trying to talk me into setting up a third location in New York."

"Are you going to?"

"That's a good question," he answered thoughtfully. "I just don't know yet. I may. Or maybe I'll just get this Pittsburgh office further established and then move back to California. I guess I just haven't settled on where I want to be yet." He gave an embarrassed shrug.

"What about staying in Pittsburgh—or would it be Marston? It seems like you've got some people counting on you here. It also sounds like Rose would be hard-pressed to give you up—"

"Looks like you enjoyed that burger," Candy interrupted her, sashaying up to their table and picking up the empty plate in front of Ben. She gave him a wink, but when she turned to Becca, there was no sign of that wink anywhere in sight. "I'll give you a little more time to finish," she said vaguely over her shoulder as she walked away.

Whatever, thought Becca, feeling an unexpected stab of jealousy.

As Becca turned her attention back to her burger, Ben picked up on the thread of their conversation that the waitress's appearance had so abruptly interrupted. "There is a lot that could be done here in Marston," Ben said thoughtfully, and he continued to share his ideas. His words came slowly at first, but then picked up speed, fueled by his clear passion for enhancing the area. He described the town and how this small section of trail had come to be. Today, the trail ran just a few short miles along the edge of the City of Marston, but he hoped it would run much further in the future. His deep voice was soothing and it felt as though it cocooned around her, putting Becca further at ease.

"The river running through here gives this community a wonderful opportunity," he said. "If we develop this area strategically, we can make it a place where people want to live, work, and play. As Rose alluded to, and as I'm sure you've noticed,"—he gave her a self-depre-cating smile—"there's a lot of blight here now, both in terms of the buildings and the overgrown vacant lots. That's not a simple thing to turn around, but the opportunity's here, especially with all that the river offers in terms of leisure activities. Not to mention all that Marston, being in such proximity to Pittsburgh, could offer in terms of housing, eateries, shopping, and jobs. The City of Marston is a mess right now; but the bones are here. There's this diner and the start of a trail. There's even a small marina just a few miles downriver. It needs a lot of work to bring it back to life, but it was enticing enough that I bought a boat and have it docked at that marina over there."

As Ben continued to describe how he'd biked along the old trail that ran in front of them and the days he'd spent boating on the river, Becca realized how much of a central part the river played, and could continue to play, in making the area a great place to live. As Ben explained it, not only did the river run through Marston, but it also carried a sub-culture of river dwellers, boaters, and businesses. And even as Ben spoke, Becca saw a pontoon boat float slowly by in the distance. She could hear voices and music wafting on the breeze and counted about eight people on the boat, two of them swaying in time to the music and singing into empty bottles in place of microphones. She imagined Ben out on his boat, just like those early spring revelers, with his melodious voice carrying her along on a gentle current, just like the river carried the boat that was drifting by in front of them.

"I love being out on my boat," Ben continued. "I've had so much fun exploring the waterways around here. Just like with the bike, getting to see the land from the river has given me a better feel of how this area could be revitalized. There's the trail expansion that could run further along the river, but there's so much more that could be done to improve people's access to the river and their enjoyment of it —with more opportunities for shops and eateries. All of that becomes a great opportunity to improve people's quality of life and—" Ben abruptly stopped mid-sentence and ran his hand through his hair. Becca watched a flush of crimson climb into his cheeks as he said, "I'm sorry. I'm getting carried away. I don't usually go on and on like this."

"Oh, please, don't apologize," said Becca. "What you're describing sounds incredible. I, well...I just had no idea that such opportunity existed here. I haven't ever really thought about the river much before. It's always just been a backdrop to my life."

Ben's smile returned at her words. It was that same subtle boyish grin he'd given Rose after she'd complimented him, and it tugged at Becca's heartstrings. His demeanor was still confident and composed, but she also sensed a slight vulnerability behind those cool and easy-going features. Becca found herself wanting to reassure him by letting him know that she genuinely meant what she said—as well as to encourage him to continue describing his vision for the future of Marston. It inspired a sense of hope in her that she hadn't felt in a long time, and it was something that she desperately wanted to hold on to. Her reality hadn't been all that rosy lately; she much preferred his.

"You are a wonder," he said, that boyish grin still in place as well as the crimson in his cheeks. "Thank you for listening to me go on and on. You've been very patient. And I'm really glad you joined me for lunch—" Ben's cell phone rang, halting his next words. He pulled out his phone and looked at the screen. With an apologetic face, he said, "Sorry, do you mind if I get this? It's work."

Becca shook her head. "Of course, go for it!"

With a "sorry," mouthed in apology, Ben lifted the device and said into the phone, "Hello."

Becca listened, as after a pause, he said, "That's terrific news, Jason! Excellent. I'll get the contract language completed with those numbers so we can get moving toward closing. How about we regroup first thing Monday morning? In the meantime, go enjoy the rest of your weekend. You deserve it. And, Jason, great job!"

Becca looked at her watch as Ben finished up his work call, realizing it was already after 3:00 p.m. How had that happened?

Before Ben set his phone down, it rang again.

"Excuse me," said Ben, with another apologetic look. He pressed it to his ear again. "Ah, Nick. It's great to hear from you. Are you ready for us to head on back?" Ben paused, listening to the voice on the other end of the line. "Thanks for following up to let us know. We can be back there in about twenty minutes. Do you think Joe will have that hitch installed by then? ...Great! And how about that trailer? Can Joe have the paperwork ready for me and the trailer ready to pick up?"

Ben hung up the phone and turned his attention back to Becca. "It looks like we're good to go. Nick said Joe can have us both ready within the hour. No rush though; I'm happy hanging out here with you for as long as you like," he said, giving Becca a smile.

He had that same gleam in his eyes that she'd seen in the store when he'd been teasing her about the packing tape. Becca sighed. She knew this lunch with Ben was only a temporary reprieve from the real world. *It must be this beautiful spring day and the calming view of the river meandering in the distance,* she thought. After all, spring always brought with it the hope of a new beginning. Unfortunately, that didn't mean it always delivered. She reminded herself this man in front of her was a stranger, and someone she didn't know existed a mere hour ago. This had just been a simple lunch shared to pass the time.

Conscious that Ben was still waiting for her answer, she said, "That's okay. I'm ready to go whenever you are. The burger was delicious, and I loved hearing about Marston." She realized that she meant those words sincerely, and added, "I hope they get the trail finished, and this town revitalized. It would be amazing to see that continued progress."

He smiled. "I hope I get to show it to you one day."

As they readied to leave the restaurant, Becca felt her mood plummet on what seemed to be a roller-coaster ride kind of day. When she'd first entered the U-Haul store and stood at the counter trying to get Nick to comprehend what she needed, she'd felt drained, knowing that was where she should have been two years ago, readying herself to move to Washington, D.C. But then Ben had offered his assistance, helping her achieve her goal for today—getting a hitch for her car. And then he'd brought her here, to this diner, and filled her head with fantastical images of a town reimagined.

She wanted him to do that for her, not just for the town. She wanted him to help her see herself through those proverbial rose-colored glasses that he virtually carried in his pocket. But they were about to head back to the interior of the dark U-Haul store—back to reality.

Ben made eye contact with Candy to let her know they were ready for the check. Becca reached for her wallet. "Oh, no you don't," said Ben. "I'm happy to treat you to lunch. You did me a huge favor keeping me company while we waited for Joe."

Candy dropped the check off at the table, as well as two to-go cups. "Two salted caramel pretzel milkshakes, compliments of Rose," Candy said, giving Ben a big smile and an eye flutter. *Really?* Couldn't she see Ben had someone with him? Not that she was jealous or anything....

CHAPTER 5

To Hell With Reason

"Hmm...this is good," said Becca, taking a sip of the milkshake Rose had given them, as she and Ben ambled their way back from the diner to the U-Haul store. Just like the entire afternoon had been—in fact, the afternoon had been better than good. So much so that she didn't want her time with Ben to end, she thought, taking another sip of the milkshake.

No, that's not right, of course I do. I need to think about my career again. Their time together was up. They would walk back to the U-Haul store, she would get her car, he would get his trailer, and then they would go their separate ways.

"There are fireworks over the river tonight," Ben said, interrupting her thoughts.

"What?" she asked, confused but also intrigued.

"There are fireworks over the river tonight down in Pittsburgh," he repeated. "I keep meaning to take my boat out to see them, but I never get around to it. Would you be interested in helping me get my boat out on the water tonight to work the kinks out for the start of boating season? It would be great to have some company. I enjoyed our time together at lunch, and I'd love to show you more of the river, especially the section where Rose and I were talking about adding to the trail. I can guess that what you've seen of Marston isn't enough of a place you'd think about spending a lot of time. But it's actually a great little hidden gem, especially the river section. Or, at least, it has the potential to be." They had now reached the U-Haul store, and as he held the door open for her, ushering her in ahead of him, he added, "Just think about it."

Becca felt excitement rise in her chest at Ben's invitation. Maybe she could spend a little more time with him…. She wanted to hold on to that sense of hope and contentment she'd felt ever since meeting him. Even though she knew it was crazy, she wanted to hear more of Ben's soothing baritone describing to her what Marston could be—as if she needed to hear it in order to understand that it was possible for *her* life to become revitalized.

And maybe this would get Carmen off her back…at least a little bit. Becca knew Carmen would be proud of her actions today. Her best friend had been pushing her to go out more often, and not only had she sorted out the bike on her car, but she was considering going out with this wonderful man on his boat. …Okay, so maybe Carmen wouldn't be pushing her to go out at night with a stranger on a boat on the river, but at least she was trying. Then, on reflection, that thought made her angry—and not at Carmen, but at life. *Why couldn't I just forget about being careful and cautious? To hell with reason!*

She turned to peek at Ben again as they walked up to the counter. Besides, he was clearly well-known and well-liked in town, including by the mayor. And life was short; she knew that better than anyone. And who better to spend an evening with than Ben? Becca couldn't deny she wanted to go out with him tonight. And, if Ben wanted her to go half as much as she wanted to come along, well, she was going to put everything else out of her mind and not think on it anymore— and that included the past and the future. She could always go back to being a basket-case tomorrow, because tonight, she just wanted to feel normal.

"What do you say?" asked Ben. "Want to see the fireworks and what Marston has to offer from the river tonight?"

They were standing in the parking lot next to the U-Haul trucks and trailers. Ben's well-used Ford truck now had a trailer attached to it, and Becca's car had a hitch installed.

"The fireworks start at nine thirty. I could pick you up at six thirty," Ben continued without waiting for her response. "That would give us time to enjoy the sunset and pilot down the river along the proposed trail route before the fireworks start."

Becca hesitated. She'd thought she'd made up her mind before, but now she felt as though she was getting cold feet. Was she asking too much of her first foray out into the wide world again? Should she just go home to her apartment and work her way through that pile of bills she'd left sitting by her computer? No, that didn't sound or look as desirable as the thought of being one of those carefree boat revelers she'd seen earlier today at lunch. Nope, she was going to remain firm on her decision. When else would she get this opportunity, and right when she needed it? She was going on that boat ride.

"It sounds amazing, Ben. And yes, I'd love to come along." Even as she said the words, she told herself that she just needed to keep it light. She wouldn't have to say anything about her cancer; there was no reason for him to know about it. Besides, he said he would probably be leaving for California soon, or even New York. And she'd be leaving for Washington, D.C.

Tonight, she could be a normal woman—who did not have cancer —out on a fantasy-filled trip on the river. She could wear her rose-colored glasses as she imagined the trail along the river that didn't yet exist. And why not? There was no harm in getting back up to the top of that roller coaster—just for tonight. She could bask there for a moment before sliding back down into her normal life tomorrow... where complications abounded. Yes, she needed this; tonight was for her. And somehow, she would have to keep her life secret from Ben. Thinking quickly, she added, "Can I meet you at the docks? I still have a couple of errands to run this afternoon."

His smile stretched wide across his face at her acceptance. "Sure. Do you know how to find the marina? It's just down from the little park off Sutter Street."

She nodded. "Yes, I remember passing Sutter on my way to the U-Haul. I had no idea there was a marina down that road! I'm excited to see it."

"Why don't we exchange cell phone numbers just in case," Ben suggested, and he handed her his business card.

"Oh...um...thanks. I'll call you if I need directions or anything." She took the proffered card and rushed out, "I'd better get going if I'm going to get my errands done on time. I'm looking forward to seeing your boat and more of Marston." With that, Becca turned toward her little Mazda and quickly climbed in, shut the door, and started her engine almost all in one movement. Then she drove off without looking back—before she could change her mind.

Becca drove to her one-bedroom apartment at the southern end of downtown Pittsburgh. It was only about a forty-five minute trip, but it was an emotionally tumultuous voyage. Her mind was in chaos. What was it about Ben that made her want to grab onto life again? Confusion raced through her. One minute she wanted to hide under the covers and the next she wanted to...well, go out on a boat ride with a stranger.

As Becca pulled into an empty spot in the parking lot of her apartment complex and turned off her engine, she pushed herself to also turn off her thoughts of Ben. She needed to focus instead on the more practical items on her agenda—like what she should wear tonight. She'd never been out on a boat on the river. What did one wear on a boat in April? It was a warm day but the afternoon air still had a chill to it, and they would be out on the water until well into the evening. She needed something that would take her from a warm spring afternoon into a cool evening, and then into a chilly spring night.

"Carmen, it's me," Becca said into the phone when her friend picked up on the first ring. "I need your help."

Becca outlined to Carmen how she had met Ben at the U-Haul counter and how they'd then gone out for lunch. She finished with how she'd accepted his invitation to go out on the river later that afternoon.

"*You're going to do what?*" Carmen said into the phone when she finished. "Okay, I know I've been pushing you to go out on a few dates, but do you even know this guy? Where does he live? Do you know any of his friends? What does he do for a living?"

Becca chose that moment to jump into Carmen's rant. "Yes, I know where he lives. He lives in Marston and works in Pittsburgh. And he's a developer," she added, reading the title on Ben's business card, still clutched in her hand. "It says on his business card: *Ben Morgan, President, Morgan Designs and Development, Inc.* And there are a lot of letters after his name."

"You know anyone can get business cards printed up for next to nothing in no time these days, right? And developer of what? Software? Buildings? What kind of developer is he? And what letters? You mean like a doctor? Like MD? That doesn't sound like a developer."

"Well...um...I guess I don't know," Becca muttered under her breath.

"What was that? I couldn't hear you?"

"I don't know what kind of developer he is. A developer of bike trails, maybe," Becca answered uncertainly.

"If he's that kind of developer, shouldn't you know about him already?" Carmen asked, her voice now rising an octave. "I mean, isn't that what your company does—develop stuff?"

"Yes, but not trails," Becca answered, hearing her voice now laced with annoyance and rising an octave to match Carmen's. "We deal with big buildings and infrastructure. And I'm the finance guru; I don't go out and develop stuff, I run the numbers. Give me a spreadsheet and a pro forma and I'm good. I'm not the one who knows every developer in town. Besides, we were talking about other stuff," Becca added. Even though she was arguing with her friend, the thought of her and Ben's lunch-time conversation brought a tingle of pleasure deep inside her as those rose-colored glasses he'd provided her with came top of mind.

"Anyhow," she said more gently now. "You're the one who's been telling me to get out there and take a chance on life. So that's what I'm doing, Carmen." Then she added as the thought came to her, "And he has to be legit if he knows the Mayor of Marston. He introduced me to her today. Her name is Rose...." Becca faltered, realizing she didn't know Rose's last name. And was she really the mayor?

"Where the heck is Marston?" Carmen asked. Becca could hear

typing as Carmen's voice trailed off on the other end of the line. "Here she is. Rose Magnum, Mayor. Hmm.... And you said his name is Ben Morgan?"

"Yes," answered Becca, and she heard more typing in the background.

"Here he is—I've got him! At least, I think this must be him. He's got a website, and it's got pictures of projects he's done. They're big projects too. Wow! There's also a picture of him. This guy is gorgeous and impressive! And you said you met him at the U-Haul counter? How in the world did you manage that? I've been trying to set you up for months with no luck, and then you just go wandering off to the U-Haul store and meet a hunk. How come I never meet anyone interesting? No fair!"

Becca smiled into the phone. "So, does this mean you approve of my proposed adventure tonight? Because, if you do, I need to know what to wear. I am so out of practice when it comes to going out for an evening that I have no idea what I'm doing right now. Help!"

"Don't worry, I'll be right over," Carmen said, and because Becca could hear her moving around in the background, she knew Carmen meant it legitimately. She pictured her friend walking through the house, grabbing her purse and keys.

"How about your cute capris pants?" Carmen continued. "You know, those soft, shimmery black ones? They say casual, but not too casual. Oh, and maybe that new top I just bought. It would look great with those pants. Hold on, I'm going back to get it." There was some shuffling and running footsteps, and then Carmen came back on the line. "Here it is! I'm on my way. This is so exciting!"

As the line went dead, Becca held her phone in her hand for another moment. There was no going back now. Carmen would see to that.

CHAPTER 6

Mending Fences

BEN

BEN CLIMBED INTO HIS TRUCK AS BECCA LEFT THE U-HAUL parking lot and headed toward the Marston Marina, wondering what he'd just done. His heart pounded. He was supposed to be helping his brother move tonight. But he'd gone and invited Becca to the boat. Now what? He didn't even have a way to contact her to cancel. *Not that I want to,* he thought, with a disgusted shake of his head.

What was he thinking, blowing Adam off? And for a woman? He knew better than that. It was just more evidence that he was no good at relationships—not with women, or with his family. He wanted to mend his relationship with his brother. Why had he risked that for a night out with a stranger? He shook his head again at his own stupidity.

Something about Becca had erased all coherent thoughts from his brain. She'd seemed so vulnerable one minute and so determined and strong the next. He wanted to delve into that conundrum and know everything about her, because he sure hadn't learned much about her today. He realized suddenly that Becca hadn't even given him her last name or her phone number. Would she even show up? Maybe he shouldn't cancel on his brother. He could forget this afternoon had ever happened and go back to his original plan of focusing on Adam.

It had only been four weeks ago when Adam had called out of the blue to let him know Carnegie Mellon University (CMU), located just minutes from Ben's office condo in downtown Pittsburgh, had accepted him into their summer program. Ben hadn't seen his younger brother in years. There'd been a handful of phone calls here and there, usually with Ben calling Adam to say happy birthday. But those were always awkward conversations, and Ben hadn't tried to take them further. This time, though, Adam had called Ben and proposed that maybe the two of them could get together during the summer. Adam said he would be moving into a small apartment just a few blocks from the university—minutes from Ben's condo and less than twenty miles from his new house in Marston.

Ben had jumped at the chance and invited his brother to stay with him for the entire summer. Adam had refused the invitation but had agreed to stay with him for a couple of weeks before moving into his new apartment. However, as soon as Ben had hung up after the call, he'd started second-guessing his invitation. What would Adam think of the trash heap that was his house? He'd bought it back in September, and even though it was already April, the house was still an eyesore.

He'd meant to jump right in and start renovating it, but he'd been so busy getting the new arm of his company up and running that he'd put most of the renovations on the back burner, only fixing up what he absolutely needed to in order to get moved in. That included patching the roof; clearing out all the debris—both inside and out; fixing the front steps; and getting the kitchen, one bathroom, and one bedroom into working order. That had been enough, and while Ben enjoyed the work, it took up too much of his time...and it also brought up memories of his childhood when he'd helped his father with building projects. Those thoughts left a sour taste in his mouth. So, he'd pushed the renovations aside. But, with Adam's visit spurring him on, he'd doubled down and redone a second bedroom and bathroom and gotten the living room into at least a small semblance of order.

It felt good to work directly with his hands again, and he was grateful to Adam for being his motivator. And, just like Marston, the bones of the house were good. The more progress he made, the more

Ben saw beyond the mess to the house's past glory, even past the Red X placard nailed to the front door by the Fire Department as a warning to first responders that if they got called to his house, they shouldn't step foot across the threshold.

Before Ben had bought the property and started renovating, the front steps had been rotted all the way through, and a portion of the roof had collapsed, which had allowed water to seep in, making other sections inside the house dangerous. Before he'd bought it, the City had plans to tear the house down. But, luckily, they didn't have enough money in their coffers to get all the Red X buildings in town demolished. So, it had sat, untended, including by the owner of the house. He hadn't stepped up at all to care for it, despite citations posted on the front of the house warning him of his responsibility.

Ben didn't know what had possessed him to think he could save the house. He had no reason apart from the fact that it had called to him. So, he'd tracked down the owner and made him an offer.

The owner had laughed at him. "Sure thing, you can have the house. You're gonna be on the hook for the overdue taxes, though, as soon as you buy it. No skin off my nose, though."

Ben hadn't hesitated and they'd closed the deal within a week. And now, here he was, living there with his brother...which would soon come to an end this weekend. He sighed, understanding that he couldn't put this call off.

He dialed Adam's number and waited nervously for him to pick up. When the line clicked, and Adam picked up his call, he did his best to infuse an air of confidence into his tone. "Hi, Adam, what's happening?"

"I'm glad you called, Ben," Adam said. "I just got back from the store with a few more supplies for my apartment. Did you get the trailer? I've got just about everything ready to load."

"Ah, about that," said Ben. "I was wondering, what do you think about us holding off until tomorrow for the move? It took me longer than I expected to get everything picked up and um...actually, I've ended up with some unexpected plans for tonight," he finished evasively.

"That's awesome," said Adam.

"It is?" Ben said with a little bit of surprise and a lot of apprehension.

"Yeah. I met a few people while I was on campus today who will be in my summer program. I told them I'd meet up with them tonight for some beers. I'm sorry, Ben, I know I shouldn't have said yes. I can cancel if you want me to. But I'd really like to go. It'd be great to start my new program with some friends already in my corner. If you really are fine putting the move off until tomorrow, I sure am too. What do you think?"

"I think that sounds perfect," said Ben with a silent sigh of relief. "I'm still planning to stay on the boat tonight, so how about I come home with coffee and breakfast sandwiches about 10:00 a.m. to help you load up the trailer?"

"Yes and yes! I think you've already figured out by now that I'm always up for caffeine and food—doesn't matter what time of day."

Ben could hear the grin in Adam's voice, and he felt his own lips twitch up into a smile. "Are you sure you're okay in that house all by yourself tonight? I know you told me it's those old pipes creaking and groaning in the night but, I'm telling you, there are ghosts flitting about inside that old monstrosity."

"If I recall correctly, it was you running up and down the stairs last night looking for the source of those bumps in the night. While I, on the other hand, was snoozing away contentedly when you barged into my room."

Ben laughed at his brother's good-natured teasing. "Yeah, yeah. We'll see how that goes when you're there all by yourself tonight. Seriously, though, I would like to stay on the boat tonight. I've got all my riverfront ideas scattered around on little scraps of paper and on every surface below deck. I need to get them in better order, especially since I'm going to have to put those ideas on the back burner."

"Why in the world would you do that?" asked Adam. "I thought you were excited about fleshing those plans out and using them to jump-start another line of business."

"Maybe someday," said Ben, feeling conflicted. "It's an uphill battle if I can't get Ethan Trapp to play nice. He's the guy wanting to put an amphitheater in near the marina. If he has his way, it's going to block a large portion of the area needed to get that trail project through. I tried to meet with him, but he was a real jerk about it. Wouldn't even listen over the phone, let alone meet up. Anyway, it's probably for the best. I need to make sure I don't lose focus and let some crazy, impractical dreaming take me off course. At least not until I get this new company on solid ground. Annnnnddddd," Ben said, deliberately drawing out his voice, "there's a very good reason for abandoning that community development project, beyond it being some pie-in-the-sky stuff. Remember I pitched to a potential client last week called Fischer Industries? About a large new office development? Well, I got news today that we landed the project! This will go a long way toward putting my new Pittsburgh office on the map. Fischer Industries is a heavy-hitter. Adding them to our portfolio is quite a coup. It's going to keep me and everyone else at my office on overload, but the extra work will be worth it."

"If you say so," Adam said hesitantly. "I guess if you're happy, I'm happy."

"Thank you. Well, I'll see you tomorrow at 10:00 a.m. sharp with caffeine in hand." Ben ended their call just as he pulled into the marina parking lot.

It was true. If Becca did show, he needed to tidy up all the paperwork he'd left lying around. The revitalization project was just in the idea stage and it was probably never going to happen despite what Rose had said at the diner today. And especially now that his company had landed another large downtown project. Besides, even if he could add the Marston community revitalization and the trail development to his portfolio, he'd need to plan it out much more fully in his own mind before presenting it to the world.

He'd only let some of his ideas slip out to Rose because he'd needed to sweet-talk both her and the City's Code Enforcement officer into issuing him the needed permits for his house renovations. At first, they'd been reluctant to give him the permits, but as they'd gotten to talking, they'd warmed up to his ideas—especially the City's revitalization project. He'd probably already let it go way too far, he thought with a pang of guilt. He didn't want to disappoint the mayor or anyone else in town if it didn't come to fruition, but he needed to direct his focus on what kept his company afloat and growing. That meant high-rises and large city-center developments with clients who had deep pockets, not small Rust Belt communities like Marston with no resources or in-house expertise. Why had he even taken the idea any further this past week by broaching the subject with Adam and then Becca? They were two of the last people he'd expect to share such things with—an estranged brother and a complete stranger.

CHAPTER 7

A River Cruise

BECCA MADE HER WAY ALONG THE DOCK AT THE MARSTON Marina. Ben hadn't given her a description of his boat, but she had no trouble making out the nice outline of Ben's rear end. He had his back to her and was wiping down the cushioned seats in the main compartment of the cockpit. Becca's heartbeat quickened as she caught sight of him. He was wearing faded jeans, a polo shirt, and docksiders, looking very much like what she imagined a boater should look like— casual but in command.

His dark hair fluttered in the light breeze. It was just long enough that little waves—not quite curls—softened the edges of the strands that danced near his face. The dark brown locks held sun-kissed streaks that made her wonder just how much time he spent outdoors. She was sure that the tanned skin and rippling muscle of his arms didn't come from the inside of a gym. Was it from bike riding? Or was it from developing? And just what did he develop? They hadn't delved into what he actually did at lunch earlier today. She kicked herself now for not taking the time to look at the website Carmen found. But she'd been in too much of a tizzy trying to figure out what to wear.

It doesn't really matter, she told herself. She didn't need to know everything about him right now—just like he didn't need to know everything about her. This was not a date. This was just a continuation of their fantasy lunch—and what a great fantasy it was. No matter where those muscles came from, Becca no longer felt the chill in the air. Instead, a zip of electricity ran through her, warming her body and quickening her breath.

Ben seemed to sense her approach and turned toward her, calling out a greeting. The smile he sent her way did nothing to bring down her body heat. In fact, she felt her temperature spike higher.

"Welcome aboard," Ben crooned in that sensuous, deep voice as she stepped aboard. She caught a momentary intensity flare in his eyes and when their gazes locked, his gave away that he liked what he saw. It only escalated the pleasure Becca felt.

Dropping her gaze, she looked around her. "Wow! I don't know a lot about boats, but I'm sure this is much more than any old boat."

"It's a forty-foot cruiser yacht," said Ben with pride in his voice. "I wanted to spend weekends on the river, not just sit next to it. But this is only my second season with the boat; I bought it last July in Cincinnati. A friend helped me pilot it up the Ohio River here to Pittsburgh. Would you like a tour?"

"Sure."

"It will be a pretty quick tour," he said with a smile. "You're standing in the living room, and right through here, as you can see, is the cockpit. Off the back here is a swim platform and ladder—although, I'd recommend we wait a couple more months for warmer weather before we brave a river swim!"

Ben pointed to the various areas as he named them. The 'living room' consisted of a circular cushioned seat that could easily hold about five or six people. There was also a small table and an outdoor sink and refrigerator. Ben proceeded to show her through to the central area of the boat and then onto the cockpit. There were various instruments, along with lots of levers, and what Becca thought of as a steering wheel. Was that the right term? That probably wasn't quite right; she'd need to brush up on her boating jargon. There was also additional seating next to the steering wheel. The seats faced forward and over the front of the boat to the river.

"There's also a walk-through here to the bow of the boat," Ben continued. "One thing I like about this boat is that you can get from the helm to the front of the boat without having to walk along the gunnels."

"The what?" asked Becca.

"Sorry, the gunnels. That's the ledge that runs along either side of the boat. You can walk along those, but they're pretty narrow, so it makes it tricky, especially when underway. When the fireworks start, we'll be able to use this pass-through to get onto the bow of the boat. We'll be able to sit and watch the fireworks there without anything obstructing our view. It's also the perfect location for stargazing, or just to watch the river go by. For now, though, since we'll be up there later tonight, I'll show you the cabin."

Ben led Becca down three steps into the lower area of the boat where there was a creamy latte-colored couch and two matching stools encircling an elegantly shaped dining table of polished wood. There was even a full kitchen, although all in miniature.

Becca felt as though she'd walked into a doll house. *Yes, perhaps this was a continuation of their fantasy lunch,* she mused.

Ben interrupted her thoughts, pointing to the forward and aft areas of the boat. "There are two bedrooms through there, each with their own bathroom. They're small, but it's all I need for weekends—more even."

Becca looked up at Ben as he spoke. He was clearly proud of this boat and was enjoying being able to share it with her. She loved being transported on that melodic voice through his proverbial rose-colored glasses, both earlier today and now. How had she not known that Marston and this river existed right outside her door? A fleeting, bothersome question flitted through her brain. Was she so focused on her goal of stepping into her father's shoes that she'd missed the wider world around her? *Of course not,* came her brain's quick response to her own infantile speculation. That had been her dream—her goal—ever since middle school. The cancer had derailed her, that was all. But she was in remission now; she could get back on that train—right to D.C. and that job that had her name on it. She would be a financial analyst in Washington, D.C. just as her father had been.

Ben suddenly turned to look at her. "I hope I'm not boring you. I love my boat, but I can understand if it's not your cup of tea."

"No way," said Becca, immediately dismissing her thoughts about work. "This is amazing, Ben!"

Ben's gaze intensified, and his mouth opened as though he were about to say something. She could see the question forming in his eyes and a spark of...? No, this wasn't a date, she reminded herself, tilting her head and lifting her brow in confusion.

At her expression, Ben closed his mouth and quickly looked away. "Anyhow," he said, looking a little flustered, "it's somewhat of a tight space in those bedrooms, so I will let you explore those at your leisure." Without waiting for her reply, he turned to head back up the steps to the cockpit.

What had he been about to say? Becca wondered. Her brain explored the possibilities as she peered in at each of the staterooms. The boat swayed gently under her feet as she both heard—and felt—Ben walking around above. A wave of disappointment washed over her. It was just as well, she thought, knowing full well she wasn't ready for whatever *that* was—and neither, apparently, was he.

"Are you hungry?" Ben asked, poking his head in from above. "I had some pizza delivered. I've also got wine, beer, sodas, and water. Does any of that sound good right now? Maybe some wine? I've got a great bottle of red that definitely should not be drunk alone."

"That sounds great except I'm not all that hungry yet. I think it was that caramel-pretzel milkshake that did me in. Can we wait on the pizza?"

"Absolutely. I'll get that bottle opened and pour us some wine and then we can get out on the water to enjoy the sunset from there rather than from the dock." He came back down below and joined her in the kitchen area of the boat.

"Can I help?" asked Becca.

"Sure. There are wine glasses in that cabinet to the left," he said, as he pulled out a bottle of Cabernet Sauvignon and a corkscrew.

She watched Ben expertly open the bottle of wine. He then turned to face her when she found two plastic wineglasses. Ben filled each glass while Becca held them in place. After deftly re-corking the bottle and tucking it into a protected section of the counter where it wouldn't slide around once they were underway, Ben motioned Becca to precede him back up topside.

Once on the deck, Ben pointed to two elegantly styled and curved metal cup holders next to the bench seat by the helm. "There are holders here we can use for our wineglasses."

Becca couldn't help thinking that it all felt so surreal and so perfect.

"Are you ready to head out?" Ben asked. He had set his wineglass into a cup holder to his right and was now standing over the wheel at the helm.

When Becca nodded in response, Ben ran his hands along the cockpit console, deftly adjusting levers and pushing buttons. The engines hummed to life at his touch, and the boat gently vibrated under their power. Becca watched Ben caress the controls at the helm, his excitement palpable. He looked like a kid, happy and carefree, who'd just been told he could run out and join his friends on the playground. Her smile returned, and she found herself wanting to wrap her arms around this night with Ben and hold it in for as long as she could.

"Go ahead and settle in," Ben urged her. "I'm going to untie us. Once we get closer to where the fireworks will be, we can anchor and then enjoy our pizza up on the bow."

Becca smiled at Ben's quick bursts of childlike energy as he readied to hop from the swim platform to the dock to handle the lines, picturing the boy he must have been in the man now before her.

During his ministrations, Ben brushed past her, sending a tingle racing up her spine. The tingle quickly shifted into excited jitters because they were about to head out into the middle of the river.

Ben now stood with one foot on the dock and the other on the back platform of the boat as he leaned over to unplug a thick, yellow electric cord. He coiled the cord and stored it neatly on the boat before walking along the side of the boat to untie each of the three dock lines. He then nimbly stepped back on the boat and moved to the helm, gently pushing two levers forward to the right of the wheel. In response, Becca felt the boat move slowly forward out of its slip.

There was still plenty of light, and Becca took in all the sights along the riverbank as they made their way out into the middle of the river. The trees were a vibrant mixture of greens, the early spring sun and warm rains coaxing out new life. Bright spring flowers dotted the shoreline, just beginning to pop up through the soil. As they meandered along, Ben explained the markers they were seeing on the river.

"And is that where the trail would go?" Becca asked, pointing to the riverbank as they floated along parallel to it.

"Yes, exactly. All along that shoreline to our right."

"Starboard?" asked Becca, testing out her boating jargon.

"Right! I mean, you're correct," he said with a laugh. "It is starboard. You've been hiding your expertise from me, haven't you?" he teased. "Wait, you aren't some sort of boating guru, are you? Cause you haven't told me what you actually do yet, ya know? Wait, wait, don't tell me—I know! You own a cruise ship line and you're humoring me on this little ole boat ride tonight, right?"

Becca smiled. "You got me. That's me—an heiress to an international shipping line."

He turned his head to look at her, still smiling, but with wide eyes and a slight crack in his usual perfectly composed demeanor.

Becca laughed and found herself wanting to put him at ease now, just like he'd been doing for her all day long. "No, silly. I really know nothing about boats. That word just popped into my head—maybe from some movie or book I read that I don't even remember now."

"Hmm, I'm still thinking you must know more than you're letting on." With another huge grin, he asked, "Want to try out your hidden knowledge and have a go at driving the boat?"

"Nope—no way. I'll stick to finance, that's my bailiwick and I'm good at that. What I want right now is for you to tell me more about all of this boating stuff."

"I aim to please, Ma'am," he said, winking at her.

Becca knew it wasn't coincidence that it was the word Nick had used on her earlier today that she'd taken exception to. She responded with a playful punch to his arm. "Go on then, Cap'n. I want to dream about this river, just like you had me dreaming along with you about that trail. Put on those rose-colored glasses again for me, will you?"

"Sure thing," he said while chuckling and dramatically rubbing his arm where she'd punched him.

As they made their way downriver, the sky took on a soft orange glow. Becca sat next to Ben on the cockpit bench that faced the console. She tilted her head up toward the setting sun and let her eyes drift closed. She could feel the wind in her hair, cool but not cold. The breeze blew her hair away from her face, and she felt the spray from the river lightly touch her cheeks. She sensed an aliveness she hadn't felt in ages as words sped through her mind that hadn't lodged there anytime recently: *calm, joy, hope, life—a future.*

Becca opened her eyes and glanced at Ben. Was this sense of hope coming from being out on the water, or was it solely because of him? Or was this just her working her way through her grief? The doctors told her this would be part of her journey. They'd said she would travel through the five stages of grief on her journey back to life. She could recite those stages without even having to engage her brain— denial, anger, bargaining, depression, and finally, acceptance. The words had become rote but working through them had not. Life did not always have a happy ending. She knew that from experience, and she didn't really believe in those words. But right now, in this moment, she felt happy, and no matter what the reason or what the eventual outcome of her life, Becca liked this feeling—a lot. And she was grateful to Ben for this evening.

CHAPTER 8
Fantasy and Fireworks

BEN GLANCED AWAY FROM THE HELM AND SMILED AT BECCA as he said, "We're headed down the Allegheny River toward The Point in Pittsburgh. That's where the three rivers meet—the Ohio, Allegheny, and Monongahela. We're going to anchor just before we reach the spot where the three rivers join because that's where the fireworks will be tonight. They'll be shooting them off just outside PNC Park, where the Pittsburgh Pirates play baseball. There's a game tonight, so we'll be able to watch a bit of it on the Jumbotron. We won't be able to see the field from the river, though, but they'll show replays and some highlights on the big screen, and the fireworks will start right after the game."

The boat slid under one of the many bridges that spanned the three rivers. The orange glow was across the entire sky now and set off the yellow of the painted bridge they were heading under for a picture-perfect evening. The bow of the boat, with its steel-colored railing, smoothly cut through the water and pointed toward more bridges up ahead. Off the stern, their boat left a gentle wake behind them, the ripples spreading from the back of the boat to the edges on either side of the river. A clipper ship ferrying tourists and Pittsburghers alike passed them going upriver, causing their boat to sway in the ship's wake.

As the sun set, the lights from the city took on more prominence, their reflection likening the river to a Monet painting with shimmers of yellow, white, blue, green, and red melting all together into what looked like an oil painting rather than a river. How had she not known this side of Pittsburgh existed?

Becca realized now that she'd rarely ventured away from the little neighborhood of Viceroy where she'd grown up and where her mother still lived. Once she'd gotten her job at Patterson Consulting right after graduating from college, she'd managed to find a small apartment near the center of downtown Pittsburgh. She kept to her apartment, work, and doctors' offices these days and by doing so, she realized then that she'd been missing out. There was a whole waterway here where a boater could travel from Marston right into the heart of Pittsburgh. How could she be so blind? This night and this river were so beautiful. What else was she missing that was right in front of her?

"We can throw our anchor out here," said Ben. "Once we're secure, we can relax with pizza and the rest of that bottle of wine. It's a beautiful evening, so we should be able to sit up on the bow without getting too cold. It will give us a bird's-eye view of the fireworks."

Ben nuanced the controls at the helm, and Becca heard the rattling of the anchor chain as it worked its way down toward the bottom of the river. She watched as Ben easily maneuvered the boat until it was secure and then he shut off the engines. A quiet came over the night that Becca hadn't even realized was missing. As he stood and turned toward her, she realized she was in the way of the passage from the helm to the kitchen and where the pizza sat on the cream-colored granite countertop. Becca stood as well, but didn't move away from him. A sweet tension filled the cockpit. Becca looked up at Ben and felt an ache of desire. He didn't move his arms, but he leaned his head toward her. Their lips were inches apart and she could feel his warm breath on her cheeks. He didn't move to close the gap. Did he want to kiss her as much as she wanted to be kissed? She could feel him holding back, but she could see the desire in his eyes.

"Becca," he said, his voice thick. "I want to kiss you...." He reached out his hand and touched her cheek, pushing a tendril of hair away from her face.

She reached up to touch his hand, feeling its warmth on her cheek. "I...I want you to kiss me. But..."

"I'm sorry. Don't say anything," he said, gently pulling his hand away. "You don't need to say anything. I don't want to make you uncomfortable."

Becca stared, mesmerized, into his conflicted dark brown eyes as they melted from mocha to a deep molten espresso. He closed them, hooding the look of desire she'd seen sparking in their depths. She wanted to reach out and reassure him, just as she had this afternoon. But...but....

Before she could finish her thought, Ben took in a deep gulp of air, opened his eyes, and stepped away from her. "So, how about that pizza? Want to help me with the plates and all?" he asked, moving to slide an arm around her and guide her into the kitchen.

Aware that he was now back in full control, she took his lead and told herself to do the same. "Sure," she said, as she followed him down into the kitchen.

BOOM, BOOM, BOOM! Becca and Ben both jumped at the sound and then burst into fits of laughter.

"It's the fireworks," said Ben. "We don't want to miss them. I'll grab the pizza if you grab the wine." He picked up the pizza box that sat on the counter along with a blanket from the nearby couch.

As Becca reached topside, wine bottle in hand, a splash of colors hit the night sky, soon followed by shimmers of sparkles falling like water from a fountain. "It's beautiful," she gasped. "It reminds me of when I was a kid on the 4th of July! All the neighborhood kids would head over to Mr. Santos's house. He put on the best display. It was magical. But this, over the river, is even better!"

Becca reached for Ben's wineglass that was now sitting next to hers in a nearby cup holder on the bow of the boat, but Ben held up his hand, motioning her not to fill it. "I'll stick with what I've still got for now. I'll save my second glass for when we're safely back at the dock."

"Oh," said Becca. "I'll hold off as well then."

"No need," said Ben, gently taking the bottle from her hands and topping off her glass of wine.

She hesitated, but then took the glass. Becca took a small sip before setting it down in the holder next to her and moving to settle next to Ben on the embedded cushion. He held up the blanket in a silent offering. Becca nodded her head, and he draped it around her shoulders. He pointed to the pizza box, also in silent offering. She shook her head and snuggled further into the warm blanket draped around her, lifting her face to the night sky.

She felt a child-like grin spread across her face. She felt so incredibly carefree right then as she watched the inky black sky being sprinkled with periodic streams of colorful lights. The only sound other than the fireworks were their own "oohs" and "ahhs" as they voiced their admiration from their little cocoon out on the river.

The fireworks ended with a dazzling finale, followed by a blanket of silence. It was a calm, clear night, the only sound now coming from the ripples along the river as the water bounced off the boat's hull.

Becca turned to Ben, her heart bursting. "That was amazing, Ben. Thank you. I couldn't have asked for a better night."

"You're very welcome. Although, as with lunch, I think I'm the one who should thank you. I couldn't have asked for a better night, either. But I guess I should get us back to the dock now, as much as I'd love to stay out here all night." He sighed. "You ready?"

"Sure. What can I do to help?"

"We just need to take these things below," Ben said, sweeping a hand toward the pizza and wine, "so they don't end up overboard once we start up."

Ben helped Becca up, and they both started back through the pass-through from the bow to the cockpit, their arms full of wine glasses, pizza, and the blanket. Becca stayed below to put things away as best she could while Ben headed up to the cockpit. Becca soon heard the now-familiar sound of the boat engines roaring to life, then the clank of a chain as Ben pulled the anchor back up into the boat.

She rejoined Ben in the cockpit just as he turned on the boat's navigation lights.

"Are you ready?" he asked.

Becca settled in next to Ben, where he sat on the bench seat at the helm. "Absolutely," she said with a smile. But she couldn't deny that she held a twinge of regret. She'd love to stay out here all night, too.

Ben turned to face her. As their eyes met, she saw that the desire in his eyes was no longer conflicted but clear as day, and it sent a sizzle of desire coursing through her. Ben let out an almost inaudible grumble from deep within his throat. "Let me get you a blanket," he said, sliding past her and down the stairs into the belly of the boat. He quickly returned with the blanket in hand. "Here you go. This will keep you warm." He draped the blanket around her just as he had on the bow, but this time, his hands rested just a touch longer than necessary on her shoulders, sending another round of shivers up her spine. She heard him let out another brief huff of air before he quickly turned his attention to steering the boat back up the Allegheny River to the Marston Marina.

Becca sat quietly while Ben guided the boat slowly through the water. His full attention was now on the river. Becca knew he was watching for the markers he'd shown her earlier in the day, now hidden in the shadows of the night.

"That's a barge to our left coming toward us. See it?" asked Ben.

She didn't see a thing and said so.

"It's hard to see if you don't know what you're looking for. There's a red light on the port side, the left side, of that first barge coming toward us. On the right side there will be a green light, which as you know," he said, turning to give her a quick smile, "is the starboard side. But as we can only see the red light right now, that's how we know we're coming to that barge with its left side coming toward us. Further out, you can see the white lights from the tugboat that's guiding those barges downriver. The barges are one of the main things we need to keep an eye out for. But their captains are very attentive and they have radar. So, even though it's dark out, they'll see us well before we see them."

Not long after Ben's explanation, the boats slid easily past each other. After it passed, the barge's wake sent their boat swaying from side to side again. Ben grinned at Becca's momentary squeak. "Good thing we put the pizza and wine below or they would be overboard by now."

Becca felt a slight rush of adrenaline as the boat rocked. She felt secure, though, with Ben in command of the helm, and the panicked feeling quickly faded back to enjoyment. The memory of being a kid again seeped into her as she remembered swaying on a swing in her neighborhood playground, feeling safe even though her father pushed her higher and higher. There was that comforting reminder of her father again, she thought, now having an urge to lean in and smell Ben's hair to see if it still smelled like eucalyptus. *Yeah, that wouldn't weird him out or anything,* she thought, laughing at herself.

"I love the rocking of the boat. Are we passing another barge soon?" she asked hopefully.

Ben chuckled with that sensuous melodic tone she was already coming to crave, sending another sensation of warmth through her body.

When they docked, Becca felt a wave of sadness splash over her for it meant back to reality. She knew it was late and she needed to get home and get some sleep. She was meeting her mother in the morning for brunch. They had a standing Sunday morning ritual at her childhood home. It was supposed to be a weekly thing, but Becca had called off for the last two Sundays. She knew her recent absence had disappointed her mother. She also knew her mother was careful about trying not to let that show and was doing her best to give Becca her space. Becca had made it clear she needed everyone to back off for now, and they were trying—really, they were. But Becca knew she couldn't let her mother down for yet another Sunday. Besides, she was kind of looking forward to brunch with her mother tomorrow, she thought with surprise.

She turned to Ben as he tied the boat to the dock. "I should get going. This was an amazing evening, Ben. Thank you so much for giving me this night," she said shyly, as emotions she had never felt before welled up from deep within her.

"Oh, don't go just yet," said Ben. "There's still plenty of time for another glass of wine. We've hardly even touched that one bottle. That wine and this evening are too good to let go to waste, and now that I'm done captaining for the night, I'm ready for a second glass."

Becca hesitated.

Ben came forward and reached out a hand, cupping her chin. She couldn't help but look up at him. Becca knew her gaze gave her away.

It told him that she didn't want to part ways yet, either. Ben leaned his face closer to hers, that gleam back in his eyes, and that silky, smooth, mesmerizing tone back in his voice. "Don't go, Becca," he whispered, just before he leaned closer and touched his lips to hers.

Becca leaned into the kiss, and he wrapped his arms around her, pulling her closer and sending a molten flare of heat up her spine and through her limbs. She ran her hands up his arms and over his biceps, and then up into that wavy dark hair that she'd been wanting so badly to touch. It felt silky smooth and, sure enough, a scent of minty eucalyptus once again wafted up to tickle her nose.

"Becca," Ben choked out in a voice thick with emotion. He pulled his lips away and rested his forehead against hers. "You taste so sweet but I don't want to move too quickly for you."

"Ben..." she started. And then her stomach let out a loud, low growl.

Ben stopped short and let out a hearty chortle. Becca's cheeks turned from a creamy peach to a bright red.

"What kind of host am I?" he laughed, now rubbing his hands up and down her arms. It did nothing to lessen her desire. "We never got to that pizza. You must be starving. Come on, let's get some food." He held his hand out.

"I guess maybe it is time for that pizza," Becca said with a grin, patting her empty stomach with some exaggeration. She then reached out and took his hand, allowing him to lead her back down below.

He pointed to the pizza boxes sitting on the kitchen counter. "Ham and pineapple or pepperoni?" he asked.

"Definitely ham and pineapple. How did you know that's my favorite?"

"It's mine too," Ben said with a laugh. "I was just hedging my bets with the pepperoni. It's lukewarm, though. Do you want me to warm it up?" While waiting on her answer, he reached into the cabinet above the sink and pulled two plates out.

"Sure," she said. "But how do you do that on a boat?"

"In this microwave right here." Ben pointed to a recessed area on the counter to the right of the sink and then turned to look at her with a drop-dead gorgeous smile—a smile that revealed a scar along his jaw line she hadn't noticed before. Becca wanted to reach up and run her fingers along that scar. She gave herself a slight shake to dismiss the thought just as he slid a plate with two slices of pizza on it into the microwave and set it to run.

Becca watched Ben as he prepared their plates and refilled their wine glasses. If she was honest with herself, she wanted to touch more than that scar. *Was she crazy?* She'd only just met him. And he was already a distraction—exactly what she didn't need...but exactly what she found herself so uncharacteristically wanting in this moment.

The microwave beeped, halting her thoughts, and Ben turned to hand her a plate and a newly-filled glass of wine.

"Thank you. This looks and smells amazing; just what I'm craving." *But not all I'm craving,* came the silent unwanted words that followed, flitting through her brain. Becca forced herself to turn her attention to the pizza in front of her and took a bite. "This is so good," she mumbled, as the taste of oozing mozzarella covered in marinara sauce, ham, and pineapple filled her mouth.

Before Ben sat down with his own plate, she'd already polished off her first piece of pizza and started on her second. The boat ride and the fireworks had definitely worked up her appetite...*but for more than pizza.* Ugh! There were those betraying thoughts again. She needed to get her mind off of Ben. She should go home, get some sleep, and use this night to get herself back on track. Life was good again, wasn't it? She was officially now in remission and she felt great—both physically and mentally—for the first time in forever, and it was time to go.

Ben set a second plate down beside her and slid in next to her. His thigh touched up against hers, sending sparks through her entire body and fully reminding her of what she craved—which was no longer pizza. She felt him tense, but she didn't pull away as she knew she should. Instead, Becca pushed her own thigh closer to his, stoking the fire in herself as well as the one she knew brewed inside of him.

He turned to look at her and she had the feeling he bit off another groan as he said, "Please, Becca, go ahead and eat." He picked up his wine glass and took a large gulp.

Becca didn't need the encouragement and they polished off the entire ham and pineapple pizza, as well as the first bottle of wine, before starting on the pepperoni pizza and opening a second bottle. As they ate, Ben entertained her with some of the many mishaps he and his friend had experienced on their trip up the Ohio River from Cincinnati to Pittsburgh.

"We just spun around in circles in that Lock," he continued. "The Lock Master had his eyes trained on us the whole time. I was afraid he was filming us and was going to post the clip on some social media site. We looked like idiots. So far, so good, though. No video has surfaced...at least not yet."

"What made you and your friend decide to brave that trip in the first place?" Becca asked in amazement. "I would have been afraid to tackle that trip knowing there were dams to navigate the entire way up river. What if you missed getting into one of those Locks before you came to the actual dam?"

Ben took another bite of pizza before answering her question.

"I hate to tell you this kind sir," Becca said, cocking her head at Ben with a grin. "But you've got cheese dripping down your chin."

Ben swiped a napkin off the table and wiped at his chin.

"Nope," she said. "Still there."

He wiped at his chin again and then quirked an eyebrow up at her.

"Sorry, still there," she laughed, taking the napkin from him and reaching over to wipe away the dangling string of cheese.

As Becca pulled her hand away, Ben gently caught her wrist and pulled her toward him. "Can I kiss you, Becca? I've been wanting to kiss you again."

She looked into his eyes. "Yes," she breathed. "I want you to kiss me." She reached up and touched his cheek. "I can't stay, though. We've only just met and I need to get going," she added, trying to convince herself as much as him.

He leaned in and kissed her tenderly and then ran his lips down her collarbone, sending shivers down Becca's spine. He exhaled in a faint sigh, leaving a warm trace of breath tingling across her neck as he pulled away. "At least let me drive you home, Becca. It's already after midnight. I don't want you out there on the road alone this late."

"Thank you, but I can't let you do that. It's almost an hour's drive to my apartment and then an hour back. You wouldn't get back here until almost 3:00 a.m. Besides, I need my car tomorrow and I'll be fine."

"Are you saying I need my beauty sleep?" he teased.

"Not hardly," she said, smiling up at him.

"It's so late, though. Why don't you just stay here? You can take my room and I'll take the back bedroom. Have you ever slept on a boat before?"

"Nope, never." And Becca couldn't deny that she was intrigued by the idea.

"You'll get the best sleep of your life," Ben said with a twinkle in his eye. "You enjoyed getting rocked by those barges, remember? Just think how wonderful it will be to get rocked to sleep by the gentle flow of the river. I've even got a clean set of sheets here on the boat. Let me make up the bed for you. You can leave in the morning—refreshed after a good night's sleep."

"Do you even fit in that back bedroom?" she asked hesitantly. "I can't imagine all six feet of you can fit on that bed. It looks to be only about five feet long."

"Don't worry about me; I've slept just fine on that bed before. And I want you to get the full boating experience. Trust me, you'll love it. You can have that whole master suite to yourself—bedroom and bathroom," Ben said, as he moved away from her to pull a clean set of sheets from a nearby cabinet. "I promise. I'll leave you completely alone for the rest of the night...unless you don't want me to?" he asked with a hopeful grin.

There's that sweet boyish grin again, Becca thought, and she felt her resolve begin to melt away. She didn't answer but instead picked up the other side of the top sheet he was now holding and helped him lay it over the fitted sheet he'd already secured over the mattress. She then leaned down to pick up the blanket to help lay it over the top sheet. It was a soft dark navy color, decorated with imprints of anchors. Very nautical, she thought with a smile. Just as her hand grabbed for one corner of the blanket, Ben reached for the same corner, and her hand fell instead to rest over his.

"Sorry," she said, looking up at him and feeling a flush run up her cheeks.

His eyes met hers once again, and the world around her drifted into the background. Even the subtle sway of the boat ceased to exist. She felt her eyes swirling with indecision as they met his.

"Don't go, Becca. It's so late, and I don't want to have to worry about you. I'll be a perfect gentleman, I promise," he said in that deep measured baritone, putting her once again at ease. He pulled the blanket the rest of the way up over the bed and then stepped out of the bedroom and back into the living room area of the boat. She watched him, worrying her bottom lip with her teeth as he reached for the door handle.

"I promise," he said again, as he pulled the door shut, leaving her alone in the boat's miniature master suite.

CHAPTER 9

Blueberry Pancakes and Lattes

BECCA WOKE UP TO A STREAM OF SUNLIGHT COMING IN through the porthole in the boat ceiling's master bedroom. She lay quietly for a moment, enjoying the sway of the boat. Was Ben still asleep? She slid off the bed, still wearing her pants and blouse from last night and slid on her shoes before going into the attached bathroom to freshen up.

Feeling more presentable, Becca quietly opened the door and peeked out into the living area. No one was about. She traversed to the other side of the boat and found that the door to the second bedroom was open. She leaned in, allowing her eyes a moment to adjust to the darkness. Ben lay on the bed, sleeping soundly. Sure enough, his bare feet comically dangled off the end of the bed. Becca felt a wave of tenderness run through her as she gazed at him. He had been the perfect captain last night—and the perfect gentleman.

A blanket lay across his middle. But he'd removed his shirt, leaving his tone and tanned torso exposed on the bed. His chest rose and fell with each breath and she couldn't help but note that his stomach was flat and muscled. She wanted to run her hands along those muscles, but knew she needed to pull herself away. Even if Ben was ready for that, she wasn't. She needed to get home, get washed up, and head over to her mother's house. Becca quietly leaned away, careful not to wake him, and picked up a notepad and pen from a basket on the floor next to the couch.

Thank you for a magical evening.
Becca

She left the note on the kitchen counter and headed topside and into the sun. The sky was a pure blue with billowing white clouds scattered across it. Despite it being spring, the day promised to be one without rain. Becca took in a deep breath, stepped off the boat, and made her way to her little blue Mazda Miata in the parking lot of the marina.

∼

"Hi, Mom," Becca called out as she pushed open the front door to her childhood home. "Oh, and hi, Buster," she added, as she reached down to pet her dog. "I've missed you, boy."

Buster barked happily and ran around the entryway in circles, tripping over his paws and coming back after each round for another greeting. While the graying around his muzzle should be a dead giveaway, his rambunctiousness often had people thinking he was still a puppy. And no matter how long she was away, every time she came home, Buster gave her a rock star greeting that always brought a smile to her face.

"In here," her mother called out. "In the kitchen."

"Okay, Buster, out of the way. Let's get this over with."

As Becca walked into the kitchen under the archway that separated it from the living room, Becca's mother looked up at her with a startled exclamation. "Wow! You look fantastic. I love that color on you. You haven't worn pink in ages."

Becca had gone home to change after leaving the boat, choosing a bright pink blouse from the back of her closet. She usually stuck with dark shades these days, but her mood called for something brighter.

Becca's mother stepped toward her and wrapped her arms around her. "I've missed you. Where have you been all these Sundays?"

"Just busy with work," Becca said offhandedly. She felt her mother's back stiffen before she pulled away and turned back to the kitchen counter to finish preparing their breakfast. It left Becca to her own thoughts in the now awkward silence.

She sat down at the kitchen table, feeling a twinge of guilt. Becca knew her mother wanted more information to go with her sorry excuse, but she didn't want to delve into the details of her life. Her mother had already dealt with enough. She reached down to pet Buster, who now sat at her feet, to distract herself from the usual awkward silence that followed whenever she and her mother were together.

Like her daughter, Becca's mother, Joan, was about five feet, four inches tall, with light brown eyes and dark honey-blonde hair. But her mother's hair now included subtle highlights of gray, one of the few things that hinted at her age. Joan was still slender and toned from her three-days-per-week exercise routine, which she'd kept up even through their rockiest of times. Becca remembered her mother disappearing for hours during those first months after her father's death, always with her exercise clothes in hand. Becca had never known exactly what to do with herself while her mother was away. She had often slipped into her father's study where the familiar scent of eucalyptus from his aftershave still lingered. It had calmed her. She'd even taken to pulling an old shirt out of his closet and wrapping it around herself as she walked through his study, running her hands along his possessions. Her favorite item in the room had been a picture of the two of them eating ice cream. In the photo, it was her twelfth birthday, the year her father had given her the necklace she wore around her neck today, and the last birthday she'd seen him alive. They'd just come from the playground and had stopped at a nearby ice cream store. As they sat outside, each with an ice cream cone in hand, her father had asked a passerby if he would take their picture. The man had gotten them laughing and snapped their picture just as he told them the punchline on some silly, adolescent joke. She still wished she could remember that joke.

Her father had only been forty-two years old when he'd died. It was an aneurysm, they said. He'd been doing paperwork one moment and slumped over his desk the next. His colleagues found him with the report he'd been working on still in hand.

After her father died, it was just Becca and her mother, just as it still was. They'd left Washington, D.C. shortly after that. She supposed if her mother had really wanted to, she could have found a way for them to stay in D.C. But Joan had said she wanted nothing more to do with that home so, just a few short months after her father's funeral, her mother had put the house up for sale, packed up all their belongings, and moved them to Viceroy. It was the summer before Junior High for Becca. She'd gone from being in an elementary school where her mother taught and from a father who doted on her, to a new city where she entered junior high not knowing a soul. *Until I met Carmen,* she thought, now with a smile.

Becca felt her mother's approach, and she halted her musing as her mother set two perfect lattes down on the kitchen table where Becca sat. She followed that up with a perfect plate of pancakes. Every one of those pancakes on that large stack was golden brown, fluffy in the middle, and crispy around the edges. Her mother then placed a bowl of freshly whipped cream and a bowl of blueberries in the middle of the table, along with a plate of butter and a jar of fresh maple syrup. Finally, her mother set down two empty plates with a fork on each; one for Becca, and one for herself.

"These look amazing, Mom. I don't know how you do it every time. What do you think for today? Some of everything on top or just syrup and blueberries?" Becca asked, garnering a smile from her mother.

"I always recommend a bit of everything. If you're going to eat pancakes, you might as well do it well."

Becca dressed her first pancake up and took her first bite. "Yum! These are delicious, Mom. I've missed your pancakes."

"I've missed having you here to share them with," said her Mom, as she took a bite of her own. When she swallowed, her mother asked, "Anything new to report?"

"Not really," Becca said, while continuing to eat.

"Are you feeling okay these days?"

"Yes, I'm good," she said, polishing off her fourth blueberry pancake while Buster dozed comfortably at her feet. Her latte sat enticingly next to her plate. Her mother had steamed the milk just so, with the froth now resting—almost floating—on top of the coffee in a perfect little peak in the center of the cup. A sprinkle of cinnamon dotted the top of the foamy white cloud, making the coffee look as though it had come off the page of a *Better Homes and Gardens* magazine. Her mother had always made their home seem perfect. But like that cup of coffee, there were hidden depths waiting to be explored under that perfect mountain of foam.

"Mom..." Becca started, wanting to burst out with the news of her night with Ben rather than drone on with their usual surface-level banter. But she stopped herself short, quickly filing that impulsive thought away. Her mother would think she was crazy. And just how would that conversation go, anyway? *Her mom: So, you're telling me you met a man at the U-Haul store yesterday and then went and spent the night out in the middle of the river with him—alone?* Yeah, no, never mind. Besides, she didn't want to burst that shimmery bubble cocooning her. Better to keep the fantasy of last night to herself, she thought with a quiver of delight.

Shutting that thought down, she started again. "Thanks for the brunch, Mom. It was delicious as always. I don't know how you get those pancakes so perfect. They're better than any I've had anywhere else. I'll get these dishes done and then I've got to get going."

"Don't worry about the dishes, Becca. Let's take our coffee into the living room and talk a bit more. Please?"

Becca hesitated at the request. Was her mother lonely? Was she happy? And how was Becca to even know? She'd rarely seen her mother as anything less than perfect. But maybe that was a shell, just like the one she'd built around herself after her father died? The one she had fortified with impenetrable iron girders over these past couple of years, she thought with an internal eye-roll. Maybe it was time she started trying to be there more for her mother, and explored beyond that wall—just like she had last night with Ben?

She released a breath and gave her mom a smile. "I guess I can stay longer. Just for a bit, though."

Becca and her mother picked up their coffee cups and made their way into the living room, Buster following close behind. Joan settled onto the couch, but Becca set her cup down on the coffee table and took a few moments to peruse the photos and artwork neatly arranged across the fireplace mantle, the bookshelves, and the side tables. As

Becca wandered through the living room, Buster followed. There were still lots of photos of Becca's father, Noah. He'd been the love of her mother's life. He'd also been everything to Becca.

Yes, they'd moved on by moving from Washington, D.C. to Viceroy. Her mother had made a nice life for them here, but they clearly both still missed him. Becca felt a pang in her gut, but let the feeling pass as she continued to take in the photos and other memorabilia. It had been fourteen years since her father died. She was twenty-seven now and finished with college and even graduate school. Yet the pain was still there, just as real as the childhood drawings that Becca had made for her mother over the years, still carefully placed throughout the living room and now in front of the older photos of her father. Unlike in Becca's apartment where most of her photos of her father were stuffed away in a drawer, hidden from view—just like her grief. There were also plenty of new art pieces on display from budding young artists that usurped the pictures of Noah and Becca.

Becca could feel her mother's presence behind her, watching her as she scanned the items on the shelves. Did her mother want to have a conversation about her father? She didn't think her mother would brave starting that conversation with her. She'd tried so many times before and every time it had happened, Becca had steered the conversation in another direction, withdrawing into pleasantries about the weather or some recipe she wanted to try. In junior high and high school, she'd also used homework as an excuse to retreat.

Becca turned her attention back to the more recent artwork prominently displayed and this time she smiled. It was sweet that her mother still held on to Becca's rudimentary attempts at art from elementary school, middle school, and high school. But she was most happy to see the newer works of art.

"Isn't that a cute one, Becca?" her mother asked, commenting on the colorful crayon drawing Becca had just run her hand over. "Little Eddie Parker made that. He's such a sweet boy. His family just moved here, so he's new to my classroom. Anyhow, that's a picture he drew of himself with his dog. He talks about that dog incessantly." She laughed.

Becca was grateful her mother had the elementary school community surrounding her. Her mom had made friends with many of the teachers and staff and was never short of an anecdote about a lunch date or shopping trip with one of those friends. But Becca knew her mother still pined for her father. Joan had a sadness about her lying beneath those perfect surface-level anecdotes and artwork. Becca had already learned life was short. She wanted her mother to be happy. Was she?

For the first time, Becca wanted to delve into that question. It had been natural during her teenage years to push her mother away. And later, she'd kept her mother at arm's length, not wanting anything to interfere with her own memories of her father or hamper her goal of stepping into his shoes to honor his memory. Her mother had finally quit trying to have any deep, meaningful conversations about her father's death, and they'd fallen into a stilted understanding that allowed only for sharing of surface-level pleasantries.

"Mom, do you think about Dad still?" she finally asked while running a finger over the top of one of the frames holding a picture of her father. Becca pulled her finger away and examined it, still with her back to her mother. No dust coated the smooth ball of her index finger, despite the frame being at the back of that shelf.

"Of course, Becca," her mother said in a soft but firm, hushed whisper. "They're all happy memories now, though."

"They are? All of them?" asked Becca. She turned sharply back to look at her mother, even more curious than just a moment ago. "What do you think about?" As she waited for her mother's response, Becca instinctively pulled the picture of her father to her breast, holding it in place with her arms gently crossed over her chest.

"I often think about how the two of you were together. That always makes me smile even now—especially now. You two had a special bond, and sometimes I felt jealous of that connection. But mostly, I just felt lucky to be surrounded by so much love.

"Do you remember how he would often take you one place or another on Saturday afternoons? Your dad would come up with new ideas each week and then present them to you, letting you choose your favorite. The two of you would chatter all week long about your upcoming adventure, and you would wake up on Saturday humming with excitement."

"Yes." Becca smiled. "But you two always teamed up to require that we first sit and eat breakfast together before we left the house. It drove me crazy," she said with a melancholy chuckle.

"You always tried to convince us you didn't need breakfast," her mother said with a laugh.

"I don't remember ever winning that argument. You also insisted we be back in time for dinner and that we come home with a good appetite. We usually had to do some pretending on that front. Ice cream was our favorite and, I have to admit, it was never hard to get Dad to cave. He always reminded me that those ice cream cones were our secret, though, and that I was not to spill the beans. He said you worked hard to make us a good meal, and we needed to make sure we appreciated that. You always knew, though, right?"

"Oh yes!" Her mother laughed again. "I tried not to let on, though. I didn't want to spoil your secret, and I really didn't mind. It was just a part of our game. Your dad knew that what I enjoyed most about those Saturday evening meals was listening to the two of you go on and on about what you'd seen and where you'd gone. Truth be told, the food wasn't what was most important. And I rarely made anything difficult. Those Saturday afternoons were not just about you getting time alone with your dad. They were about me getting to have a little quiet time. Your dad would whisk you away and bring you back, happy and tired.

"I think one of my favorite stories of your adventures was after you and your dad visited the Smithsonian's Botanical Garden. You gushed about the mix of flowers and plants and the secret paths that ran through those gardens. You'd got lost among them and found some new creature or other surprise around every twist and turn. You went on and on about how one minute you were in downtown D.C. surrounded by traffic, and the next, you were in a secret garden. I don't think your dad got a word in edge-wise that night.

"I also remember you two would often bring me some sort of trinket from your excursion. Usually it was just something small, like a single flower or some special cookies for our dessert. Do you remember these?" her mother asked, now moving her hand to lift one of the earrings she was wearing away from her face.

"I guess I don't," said Becca hesitantly. "Did we bring those back for you?"

Her mother caressed the earring she held between her thumb and forefinger. The earrings were crafted to look like tiny little butterflies, their wings lightly shaded in orange as they rested on a small, gold fili-greed leaf. "You may not have seen them then. Your father gave them to me later that night. This is one of those good memories, Becca. That was a special day, and it was one among many. We were lucky to have those good years."

Becca finally moved to join her mother on the couch, with Buster settling again at her feet as she and her mother went back to talking in surface-level pleasantries, akin to the foam on the top of their perfect lattes rather than about what lay beneath that rich murky liquid. But Becca was glad she'd come today and knew they'd at least put a dent in that foam.

"Next Sunday—do we have a date?" asked Becca.

"Of course," responded her mother. "You're always welcome—any day of the week, not just Sundays."

"Thanks, Mom." Becca turned away from her mother to set the picture she still held of her father back on the shelf. "I'm sorry we haven't had more conversations like this one. That's my fault," she said, as she surreptitiously wiped a wayward tear from her cheek.

"Oh, Becca, it's not your fault! It was difficult to know how to process your father's death and it still is. I think both of us just settled into not talking about it at all until it finally became a habit. And the last two years have given you even more on your plate to think through. I'm here for you for whatever you need whenever you're ready. In the meantime, please don't worry about me. I don't want to push you until you're ready. Goodness knows, you push yourself hard enough. But if you do ever want to change things up, please know I'm absolutely fine with that."

Becca's phone rang then, pulling her attention away from her mother. She pulled her phone from her front jeans pocket and glanced at the screen. A profile picture of Carmen popped up. Becca smiled. Carmen had texted her several times this morning, impatient for a report on last night. After the first text, Becca had sent off a quick response, letting Carmen know she was fine and on her way to brunch with her mother. Becca let the call go to voice mail, but she knew Carmen would not be denied for much longer.

"I'd better get going, Mom," Becca said, as she leaned in to give her mother a hug.

Her mother hugged her back and, for the first time in years, Becca didn't hurry to pull away, instead allowing her long pent-up emotions begin to seep through the newly emerging cracks in the shell she'd built around herself. "I love you, Mom. Thanks for the brunch and for the reminiscing. It was nice," Becca said, meaning it.

"I love you too, Becca. Now get going and get whatever it is you need done finished up so you can come back next week," her mother teasingly admonished. "I need to have someone to make pancakes for, and Buster and I are counting on that being you."

CHAPTER 10
Feelin' My World Start to Turn

As soon as Becca left her mother's house, she let her mind wander back to her magical night with Ben, and a wide smile spread across her face—a smile that stayed with her all the way home. Even the radio played along. What was that song, anyway? It was one of her favorites. As she began singing, the title popped into her head, David Cook's *The Time of My Life*.

As she continued to hum the tune now pleasurably stuck in her head, Becca glided into her apartment and headed for the shower, mentally going over what she needed to get done today. The tune served as a pleasant backdrop to her list making. She wanted to get to the grocery store and then review the hodge-podge of numbers on some of her team's back-logged projects. They had a new project starting tomorrow, something about a new amphitheater, and she wanted to get some of the older projects put to bed so she could better focus on the new one. She hated being caught short or causing any slowdowns, which meant her Sunday evenings almost always included her doing catch-up work and reviewing her schedule for the work week ahead—just as she'd seen her father do every Sunday evening before he'd passed away.

However, she didn't have as much interest in her work lately. The nagging worry that had been growing inside of her over the past several months seeped back in, usurping the song's place that had only moments ago filled her head. That sense of interest—of purpose —was the driver she used to stay focused on reaching her goals. What if she couldn't get back on track? How would she make her father proud? What would become of her dreams, her goals—of her?

Becca reached for the body wash on the shelf built into the shower wall, anxiety clouding her thoughts. She absent-mindedly poured a generous amount of soap into her hands and rubbed it into a lather. As she rubbed the rich lotion across her body, memories of Ben's touch returned, sending a tingling awareness flowing through her veins. All thoughts of work vanished as she succumbed to intense sensations that soon had her calling Ben's name out loud inside those shower walls. Her body pulsed with pleasure, even as her limbs relaxed.

She leaned her forehead against the cool shower wall, allowing some of the heat from her body to escape, and sighed with pleasure. As she stepped out of the shower, she crooned the lyrics to the song that had so recently been playing in her car—and in her head—and smiled.

～

On her way to the grocery store, Becca finally dialed Carmen's number.

"Where have you been? I've been dying to hear from you. I want every detail. But first, are you okay?"

"I'm fine," Becca said with a chuckle. "You got my text, didn't you, telling you I was fine?"

"Not enough, sweetie-pie. How was I supposed to be sure that was you texting me? What if it had been him? For all I know, he could have stolen your phone and texted me himself to put me off the scent of the dastardly deeds he had planned for you."

Becca laughed. "Okay, okay, I'll do better next time, *Scarlet*," she teased, using the name she always did when Carmen went into one of her dramatic soliloquies—which was often. "You are such a drama queen."

"And you love me for it," Carmen teased right back. "So, what happened? Do tell, please. I'm trying to be patient here, but it's high time you spilled."

"That's actually why I called. I'm on my way to the grocery store. You want to come over for dinner? I'll cook up something good to make up for being such a terrible friend and not texting you back after every one of your texts."

"And don't forget the lack of a phone call, too! But YES! You know I hate to cook. I'm already thinking I might forgive you. What are we having for dinner? Of course, I already know what we're having for dessert...."

"Ice cream!" Becca and Carmen sing-songed out in unison.

They planned their dinner menu while Becca drove to the store and Carmen continually interjected questions designed to steer the conversation toward Ben.

"I'm here now," Becca said, as she pulled into a parking space at the grocery store. "You're just going to have to wait until dinner to hear more...and I can't wait to tell you all about it." She grinned at the memory.

"You are such a tease! Bye, Becca. See you tonight."

"That was an amazing dinner," said Carmen.

They sat contentedly on Becca's couch, full from dinner, but none-theless indulging in a bowl of ice cream for dessert.

"I'm so happy to see you smiling again, Becca," Carmen continued. "You deserve it. Keep me posted on what you plan to do. But, for the record, you already know what I think you should do. I say you contact that man as soon as possible and keep this thing going. I know it's scary, but I haven't seen you this happy in an eternity. Just let it happen. It doesn't have to lead to anything deep or long-term. It also doesn't need to derail your plans. Just have some fun and enjoy it while it lasts."

Both their cell phones buzzed with an emergency notification, the sound encouraging them to turn their attention to their cell phone screens.

"Weather alert," said Carmen, reading the text on her phone. "It looks like our beautiful days are over. Storm's a comin'. I guess I'd better get home before the rain starts."

After Carmen left, Becca jumped into preparing for tomorrow's meetings. With little left of her evening, the pressure was on to get everything done that she'd planned. Thank goodness for that because she needed that pressure to focus! Every time she thought of Ben— yes, constantly—and their night on the boat, she felt like Cinderella and found herself drifting away into a far-off fantasy land....

It was a magical evening, but the clock struck midnight, she mused. Okay, so in her case, it had struck midnight and she'd ignored it. Luckily, she didn't turn back into a waif dressed in rags, and neither her car nor the boat had turned into a pumpkin. Unlike Cinderella, though, she'd been lucky enough to get some extra hours of bliss past that midnight hour. *But I need to move on now,* she reminded herself as she opened one of her project folders from her lap. She began running through the numbers. *Stay focused,* she reminded herself. The numbers swam in front of her eyes and sparkled like the night sky over the river....

Maybe she should call him. Would he want to hear from her? Was last night just a one-time thing for him? He didn't seem like that type of guy. He'd been so thoughtful during their time together and had never pressured her. Nonetheless, Becca couldn't believe she'd allowed herself to stay the night on the boat. Embarrassment coursed through her, sending shivers along her spine, as though someone had dumped a bucket of ice water over her head. What must he think of her? She didn't want to dwell on that thought right now; she didn't have time for it. *And thank God for that!* She turned her attention to the folder once again and attempted to create clarity out of the fuzzy numbers floating in front of her on the page. With now even less time left in her evening, Becca finally took control of her brain and focused, like a marksman, on stabilizing those numbers in her sights so she could slay them. The pressure was on, requiring her to push every-thing else out of her mind—at least for now.

Becca finally settled in and worked for the next two hours, reviewing notes and numbers and preparing a list of questions she'd need answers to from her team members before she could do more. Finally satisfied, she neatly put the papers she'd been working on into the bag she carried back and forth to work each day and set it on the table by her front door, ready to be picked up and carried out to the car tomorrow morning.

Next up on her mental list? Bills. Becca sighed. Several more piles of papers still sat lined up on the credenza next to her computer work-table, demanding her attention. She was too drained to deal with those stacks tonight; they'd just have to wait. She needed to get to bed, and she still had to lay her clothes out for tomorrow, something she did every night before work. It satisfied her need to feel prepared and maximized the time she had for sleep in the mornings, as she was not a fan of getting up at dawn if she didn't have to.

Becca turned her back on the stacks of bills and began examining the contents of her closet. She pushed all the black, brown, and dark blue clothes she'd been wearing to work over the past couple of years out of the way. She wanted something more upbeat for tomorrow. She had tons of pink in her closet, but it was all now hidden from view. She reached around behind all those dark colors and found a soft pink dress. It was a simple, straight line design, nothing frilly or too over the top for work. She selected a tailored, dark blue, flowered blazer to pair with it, giving it a sophisticated 'I'm at work now' vibe. She added navy blue heels, delicate small silver hoops for her ears, and she was done. Becca laid the items she'd selected over the bench at the foot of her bed, ready to be donned first thing in the morning and crawled into bed.

As soon as her head hit the pillow, her mind drifted back to Ben, and then to her mother's and Carmen's words from earlier today. Becca had expected the conversation with her mother to leave her feeling bruised, battered, and guilty about not being able to make things better for her mother—about not being able to *fix* her mother's life after her father's death. But her mother had surprised her. What were the words she'd used? *"They are all happy memories now...we were lucky to have those good years...Goodness knows, you push yourself hard enough...you don't need more of that."* Becca had left her mother's house feeling better—better about her life, and about her mother's life.

And what had Carmen said? *"I haven't seen you this happy in an eterni-*

ty...*I say you contact the man and keep this thing going...*" Should she call Ben? She was finally at a place where she could start getting her life back on track. But she didn't want to get derailed again, and Ben was certainly a distraction. But Becca had to admit that even before meeting him, she'd been having trouble focusing as much as she used to on her work and the future she'd so carefully plotted out for herself. Maybe it was time for a distraction?

Had she allowed too much to happen on their first meeting? No; she'd held herself in check, even though she had wanted more that night. Did she regret the evening? Not one ounce—so there! She'd chalk last night up to being one of the best of her life, and she wouldn't change a thing about it. But should she leave it at that? Ben didn't have any way to contact her, so the ball was in her court. He'd certainly been a willing partner, asking her to lunch and then on the boat. And he'd asked her not to leave that night, but rather to stay. Should she call him tomorrow? *Yes, yes, yes*, her mind screamed. Definitely, yes!

CHAPTER 11

The Great Stink

BECCA EASED HER CAR INTO THE DOWNTOWN PARKING garage closest to her work, leaving her just two blocks to walk to the office. The heavy rains that had poured down during the night had finally let up, but puddles remained in every indent and crevice of the sidewalk. She did her best to sidestep the largest of them, hoping not to arrive at her desk with her shoes soaked through.

She arrived at the entrance of the thirty-floor level office high-rise that housed Patterson Consulting, and the place where she'd worked for almost six years. She paused, hesitant to leave the outdoors despite the overcast day. Taking in one last breath of freely circulating air, Becca pulled open the heavy glass and metal door, crossed the threshold, and made her way past the central area of the lobby to the bank of elevators. The cab would take her up to the fifteenth floor where her office cubicle was located. Despite her hesitation at the door, she found comfort in this morning ritual. Over the past couple of years, she'd only been able to work in the office intermittently and had missed what once had been a familiar and inevitable part of her morning routine.

She was fortunate to work at Patterson. They were a large, well-known, and well-respected company with multiple locations across the country. They also had a deep client list that included the U.S.

government, which is precisely why Becca had set her sights on working at Patterson after she graduated from college.

Her elevator arrived, and she crowded into the tiny metal box with her colleagues and rode up to her six-by-six-foot cubicle on the fifteenth floor. It was small, but at least she had a space to call her own. Becca would prefer a little more square footage—and a little more privacy, especially for phone calls. She was fortunate, though, to have a wonderful group of co-workers, including Jenn, whose cubicle was right next to hers. Not only did she and Jenn work well together, but they'd also quickly developed a friendship beyond work, despite Jenn being a rung above Becca in the pecking order at Patterson.

"Morning," Jenn mumbled, as she continued to clack away at her keyboard.

Becca set her work bag down and pulled off her light raincoat before situating herself in front of her computer.

Jenn finished typing and turned to look at Becca. "How was your weekend? Anything fun happen?"

"It was great," Becca said, trying to hide her smile.

Jenn leaned in and eyed Becca more closely. "I think you're glowing. What happened? And what are you wearing? You look great! I love that color on you." Jenn motioned to Becca's pink dress and flowered blue blazer. "I was thinking all you owned was black."

"Thanks. You don't look so bad yourself," Becca said, motioning to Jenn's ensemble. "Did you have a good weekend?" she asked next, deftly deflecting Jenn's focus away from her.

"It was great. My little sister is visiting from Manhattan. I haven't seen her in almost a year. She's working for a theater company and hoping to get her big break in acting."

"Wow, glamorous!"

"It is! Except, the pay for a theater assistant is bare bones, and the cost of living in Manhattan is insane—probably what you'll experience when you move to D.C. She's sharing an apartment with four other women in a space about the size of a postage stamp. She kept walking around my tiny apartment, telling me how lucky I was to have so much space. I invited her to come live with me if she ever tires of her big city adventure. Wouldn't that be awesome? I really miss her. I guess it's kinda selfish, though, me wanting her to move here. But it would be nice to have more family nearby."

At the sound of her phone ringing, Jenn turned back to her desk. "Sorry, Becca. Gotta go.... Hello, Patterson Consulting, Jenn speaking, how may I help you?..."

The morning remained busy, curtailing any opportunity to revisit their discussion. That was just as well, thought Becca. She still found it all a bit confusing—a lot confusing. Even if she were ready to share, she didn't know exactly what she would say or how to describe her weekend to Jenn.

"I'm ravenous," said Jenn. "Are you ready for lunch? We're going to need some sustenance before our afternoon meetings."

"The usual?" asked Becca.

"Perfect," Jenn replied.

They grabbed their wallets and headed for the central bank of elevators. As the elevator doors opened onto the second floor, Becca and Jenn crossed over into the building's *Courtyard Cafe*. Unlike the rest of the building, the cafe was lush and green and evocative of the botanical garden Becca's mother had reminded her about during their weekend brunch date.

The garden area in the very center of the cafe rose from the interior of the ground floor of the building. It was open to the outside elements and included beds of fauna and flora intertwined with cafe seating. Becca and Jenn headed for the indoor section of the cafe on the second floor. It was enclosed by massive sets of windows that looked out onto the garden below, affording an almost completely uninterrupted view of the garden from every seat.

"Hi, Becca! Hi, Jenn!" called Tony from behind the counter. "The usual?" When they both nodded, he said, "Great, we'll get you started. Find your seats; we've got you covered."

Becca and Jenn called out a thank you.

"I love coming here," said Jenn.

"Me too," said Becca. "It sure makes for a nice break in the middle of the day, especially the getting to go outside part when sometimes we aren't even really outside."

As they seated themselves at a table next to one of the oversized windows, Becca delighted in the view of the garden below. Multiple colors dotted every section—yellow, purple, pink, orange, and, of course, green. Becca's eyes stalled on an array of purple tulips. Their stems were bent, their petals closed in upon themselves in response to the night's heavy deluge. A tinge of foreboding shivered through her brain, momentarily darkening her otherwise cheerful mood.

"Can you believe that email from Nathan this morning?" asked Roger, sliding into one of the empty seats at Becca and Jenn's lunch table. "It looks like we'll be talking about sewage this afternoon instead of amphitheaters. Better enjoy that lunch while you can, because what's on our plate after lunch doesn't sound too appetizing."

"I've already had to change my shoes once today," said Becca with a laugh. "Please don't tell me I'm going to have to slog through more crap this afternoon."

They continued to laugh and joke their way through lunch. The occasion offered Becca a nice break before their afternoon meeting, which promised to be a good one—or at least an interesting one.

"We'd better get moving," Jenn said just under an hour later, twisting her wrist around in front of Roger and Becca so they could get a good look at the time showing on her watch face.

The sound of their chairs scraped across the floor as they simultaneously rushed to pick up their trash and hurry back to the steel encased bank of elevators. As the elevator doors slid open, they eyeballed each other, silently asking if they should wait for the next car. Jenn subtly lifted her watch and raised her eyebrows. Roger shrugged his shoulders and led the way into the already over-crowded elevator car. As they stood silent, Roger twitched his eyebrows at Becca and quirked his lips up. She rolled her eyes, straightened her spine, and pursed her lips, silently attempting to show her disapproval—and keep from laughing. No way was she going to let Roger send her into a fit of giggles in this crowded elevator full of her colleagues from other unknown areas of the building. As the elevator doors slid open and they exited, she smirked at Roger in silent triumph.

"Hey, Becca, I didn't get to hear about your weekend," Jenn huffed.

"See what you did there, Roger? You sabotaged our lunch break with talk of sewage. Now I'm gonna have to wait until after our meeting to get an update on Becca's weekend."

"Hm...was it a good one?" Roger asked. "I'm all ears."

"Too late now, Roger. We've got to get into that conference room," Becca said, waving her hand at them to hurry and effectively halting their conversation. They split off to their respective cubicles to put down their personal belongings and grab their meeting fodder, which included notebooks, folders, and pens, and then made their way into one of the conference rooms.

"Welcome everyone," said Nathan Winslow, Becca's boss. "A big thank you to Jenn for pulling this team together. I know you all know each other, but I don't think you've all worked directly together yet. We'll get to an introduction of roles in a moment. I can guarantee you, though, that you're gonna be getting to know each other well in short order. This team's going to be diving in to more than we bargained for, starting right now. Should be fun, though," he said, raising his eyebrows with a smirk. "After all, there's never a dull day here at Patterson. I trust you all got my email this morning about our change of plans?" He rubbed his hands together, a mischievous smile twitching on his lips.

When everyone nodded, Nathan said in his usual powerful and no nonsense tone, "Good, then let's get on it. Patterson Consulting got a call from the mayor of Allison City this morning. You know those heavy rains we had last night? Those rains hit Allison City hard and, unfortunately, their infrastructure. Like so many of the small towns around here, it's in terrible shape and just couldn't hold against the storm. A pipe gave way in the middle of the night and sent raw sewage flooding right down the center of town. They were able to get emergency crews and their facility employees working on it right away. But all they could do was patch it to stop the hemorrhaging. They're going to need more than patches; they're going to need solutions," said Nathan emphatically.

"And that's where we come in," he continued. "The City is

engaging Patterson to help find and craft that solution as well as implement it. I know you all were thinking we were going to dive into our new amphitheater project today, but we're about to dive into something else entirely." He raised his eyebrows, getting a laugh out of everyone.

"After lots of back-and-forth calls this morning, we've decided to go with the team Jenn pulled together for the amphitheater project. She's put together an excellent team that is already prepared to hit the ground running. We're going to need that head start if we're to catch up to what's already flowing into basements and storefronts along Allison City's main street. That doesn't mean we're putting the amphitheater project on hold, though. This team will work on both projects simultaneously. I know you all are up for the challenge, and I'll be looking to add reinforcements as we get a better idea of what's needed and where the gaps are. So, without further ado, Jenn, I trust I can hand this over to you now to lead us off?"

"Thanks, Nathan. Welcome everyone. This is our team kickoff. I'll briefly go over how the team is structured, and then I'll turn it back over to Nathan to provide more baseline information and answer questions specific to the Allison City project. As Nathan said, this team, and your roles, will be the same for the amphitheater project.

"I'll be serving as Project Manager. So, any questions, ideas, or concerns, let me know and we'll work through them. My job is to make sure this project goes as smoothly as possible. Please let me know of anything you may need along the way to make your job easier. We don't have much information to work with yet, but the mayor has already started gathering information to send to Nathan. This includes maps of the sewage and water systems, draft plans for upgrades, funding they already have in place, and information about their funding shortfalls. Nathan will start getting that information to me later today. I'll be going through it and then getting it out to each of you in line with your role on the team. I'll also start putting together our team meeting schedule and set up a shared folder to facilitate collaboration. But, first things first.

"In terms of our team, there are six of us, seven if you count Nathan. Becca will be point on anything financial. If you've got numbers, get them to Becca. Roger is serving as lead on anything engineering related, including environmental. We might need a bit more than usual on that front," Jenn said, smiling at Roger. "Bob will head up anything related to construction. Patty will research funding opportunities, including federal, state, local, and private. Patty will also be our liaison with funders. Samantha's our grant writer; she'll start drafting the project language and gathering information specific to Allison City, so we'll be able to get any and all proposals written and submitted that turn out to be a good fit. Finally, Abbie is here for anything legal."

"Thanks, Jenn," said Nathan. "Any questions before I fill you all in a bit more on specifics?"

"Any thought of adding Joe to the team?" asked Roger. "He's got a lot of experience dealing with the state folks at the Department of Environmental Protection and with a lot of the surrounding water authorities."

"Good point, Roger. Jenn, please look into that and see if we can borrow him from the environmental team for this project. He'll probably be able to foresee a lot of the policy hoops we'll have to jump through."

"Do we know yet who is officially working on this from the state's Department of Transportation?" asked Bob. "There'll be lots of roadway issues on this project. If we can find out who it is, I can give that person a call sooner rather than later to see if they have any insights for us?"

"Good question, Bob. I'll look into that and get that information to Jenn. As soon as she's got that info, she can pass it along to you and the rest of the team. Jenn, if you don't get that from me within the next twenty-four hours, please remind me."

"Just a reminder to everyone," interjected Patty. "While you're all out there gathering information and meeting with folks, please be sure to ask if they know of any outside funding for this type of project. Just send me a quick note if you hear of anything, and I'll add it to my list of funding opportunities to research."

"Thanks, Patty," said Nathan. "Good reminder. Anyone else?"

There were general head shakes from around the room.

"Okay. Thanks everyone, I think we're off to a good start. As I'm sure you're aware, though, this will not be an easy process. It'll start slow but within the next twenty-four hours, it's going to be fast and furious. So don't wait for info to come to you before you start looking into solutions. You may think this is a first but, I assure you, there are plenty of examples of these types of failures beyond Allison City to pull from, going back centuries even. Take the Great Stink of 1858, for example."

As Nathan spoke with his usual flair and booming voice, every member of the team sat, enthralled at his ability to bring to life an example from history to inform their thinking about their current-day dilemma.

"Their lead, Sir Bazalgette," Nathan continued, "was a genius and a hard worker who came up with an innovative solution that is still in operation today. And that's what we're going to do here at Patterson. This isn't the first sewage infrastructure disaster, and it won't be the last. Look at some of those historical solutions and then at today's best practices. But I also want you thinking outside the box. What innovations could we incorporate? I want this team to come up with a solution for Allison City that will make them a model for this area. There are lots more communities all around us like Allison City—Rust Belt communities that are on the brink of similar infrastructure catastrophes. You'll learn a lot on this project, and I know you'll be able to put that knowledge to good use on similar projects going forward.

"Ideally, we'll be able to help some of those communities before disaster strikes. But with resources being strained and local political realities being what they are, we're more likely to get called in after the fact. Let's hope that isn't the case, but it is the most likely scenario —unless we do a great job on this project and word gets out that we're the ones to come to for great, innovative, and proactive solutions. Questions?"

Shortly into the barrage of questions that followed, Frank, Nathan's assistant, poked his head into the conference room. "Mr. Winslow, Ethan Trapp is here. Should I send him in?"

"Yes, bring him in," Nathan said to Frank, before turning his focus back to the team. "Okay everyone, we're going to have to switch gears. I want to introduce you all to our client on the amphitheater project before letting you get back to the Allison City project. I expect you to get to Ethan's amphitheater project today too, even if just briefly."

Frank returned to the conference room and ushered in a man who looked to be about ten or fifteen years older than Becca, the highlights of gray in his dark brown beard giving his age away despite his tall, lean stature and lack of wrinkles. As he entered, his translucent blue eyes swept the room, piercing but friendly.

"Ethan, welcome," said Nathan, standing to shake the man's hand. "Let me introduce you to your team. You'll be in expert hands with this group. They are deep into the middle of another project right now," Nathan said, as he turned to give them all a wink. "But I know you and I still have some basics to go over. So, I'll just briefly introduce you all to each other so you have faces to put with names."

Nathan quickly dispensed with the introductions and then whooshed out the door with Ethan in tow, leaving Becca's team to their own devices.

CHAPTER 12

Tulips in the Storm

"THE GREAT STINK?" ASKED BOB. "WE'RE GONNA NEED A team name for this one," he said with a laugh.

"How about we call ourselves 'The Stinkers?'" laughed Roger.

"Not exactly imaginative," said Bob. "What else ya got?"

"Hey, at least it's descriptive," Roger said, pretending to be offended.

"Okay, everyone," said Jenn. "We don't have a lot of time left in our day. We need to move on to the amphitheater project."

"So, what's our team's name for that project?" asked Bob. "We can't call ourselves 'The Stinkers' for that one. Isn't it supposed to be more than just an amphitheater? Isn't it supposed to be a full concert venue? Ohhh...maybe we need a band name too?"

As jokes and wisecracking continued to fly around the room, Becca's phone, sitting next to her on the conference room table, vibrated, alerting her to her next appointment. She reached over to silence the alarm. The time showed 4:00 p.m. and the words *Doctor's Appt* appeared on her screen. She really wanted to stay and listen in on the meeting; she liked to soak up as much information on a project as she could early on, as it made it a lot easier to know how to plug in the numbers when the time came. At this rate, it looked like she wasn't going to miss much, though, as proposals for band names now flew around the room.

"I'm so sorry, Jenn," Becca said, gathering up her belongings and pushing back from the table. "But I have to get going. I have a 4:30 p.m. appointment, and it's going to take me about thirty minutes to get across town. Can I catch up with you tomorrow?"

"Of course," Jenn said. "You don't need all of this up-front detail, anyway. And we can fill you in on whatever team name we decide on later." She laughed. "Go on—no worries."

Becca hurried back to her desk to grab her coat and work bag and headed to the elevator. She arrived at the Midtown Medical Center at 4:35 p.m., agitated about running late. She settled her thoughts by reminding herself this was just a general follow-up. She didn't have questions today, so she wouldn't need a lot of time with the doctor, and no one was going to mind her being just a few minutes late. *Quit worrying,* she chastised herself. It was exhausting—just as exhausting as having to watch her time so closely and run from one appointment to another.

Maybe that was the question she should ask her doctor today— could she reduce the frequency of her visits to the lab? Becca still routinely went to get her blood work done and then had a follow-up visit with the doctor about a week later to go over the results and any symptoms or questions. As everything had been going like clockwork for almost a full year now, maybe she didn't need all these visits anymore. Not having to attend these appointments would give her more time in her day—*including events like nights out on the boat with Ben.* There were those traitorous thoughts infiltrating her brain again! She felt the grin on her face turn into a full-on smile. At least this time, they weren't negative thoughts. And she'd already made up her mind —she was going to call Ben as soon as she got home tonight.

"Becca?" the receptionist called out.

"Right here," Becca responded.

"It's great to see you. Dr. Murtha is expecting you. Go on into her office," Carly said, gesturing toward Dr. Murtha's office down the hall.

"Thanks, Carly," Becca said, as she made her way down the familiar hallway. Becca knocked lightly on Dr. Murtha's open door.

"Hi, Dr. Murtha. Sorry I'm late, I got held up at work. I hope I didn't keep you waiting."

"No problem, Becca. Come on in. Go ahead and shut the door and have a seat."

Becca closed the door and moved across the carpeted entryway to the chair that sat opposite her doctor.

Dr. Murtha got up from her seat and moved around to the same side of the desk as Becca, taking the seat opposite her, and turning her chair to face Becca. "I'm afraid I have some bad news...."

Becca's body tensed and her vision blurred as Dr. Murtha's words hit her. She knew Dr. Murtha was speaking, but she couldn't make heads or tails of the words. They sounded like they were coming from underwater—garbled, thick, and undecipherable.

"Becca? Do you understand?"

Becca looked at Dr. Murtha, confused. "I'm sorry. I missed what you said."

"Your latest blood work came back from the lab. It's positive, I'm afraid." Dr. Murtha reached over and took Becca's hand. "We do sometimes get false positives, so I want you to relax and remain calm. But the lab work is showing that the cancer has returned, so we need to do some re-testing to be sure."

Becca's mind reeled out of control. She flashed back to sitting in this very seat two years ago, and to Dr. Murtha informing her she had leukemia. Becca hadn't heard Dr. Murtha's words then, either. She'd been in shock, then in denial, and then—her mind went blank.

As Dr. Murtha continued speaking, Becca worked to focus her mind on her question. She had asked her if anyone had come with her to the appointment. Was there anyone who could drive her home? Becca hated being so needy. She'd leaned on her friends, family, and colleagues enough over the past two years. She didn't want to keep burdening everyone with appointments. She'd asked no one to accompany her today because this was just a routine follow-up appointment —or so she'd thought.

~

Becca entered her apartment in a daze. She wasn't sure how she'd gotten there. Her brain felt foggy, her vision clouded. She wanted to rage against the world. This couldn't be happening! It wasn't real! But she knew, deep down, that this was her real life. It was the night on the boat and her fantasy boat ride that wasn't real.

A surge of anger ran through her. Her right arm flailed out as if of its own volition and pushed over the hallway table that stood just inside her doorway. Shards of pottery flew through the air as the table fell onto its side, and the vase that had sat upon that table only moments ago evoking a sense of calm, shattered with a satisfying crash. Becca propelled herself through to her bedroom, kicked off her shoes, and stripped off her dress. Why in the world had she worn pink today, she thought angrily, as she dropped onto her bed, bending to the will of her internal storm, not unlike the purple tulips she'd seen earlier today had crumpled under yesterday's drenching rain.

PART TWO
The Aftermath

CHAPTER 13

Adam's Move

BEN

BEN WOKE UP SUNDAY MORNING WITH LIGHT STREAMING in through the boat's back bedroom window. He stretched and smiled. It had been a fantastic evening, and he wanted to do it all again today. Maybe there was more to that movie, *Groundhog Day*, than he'd first realized. He could relive yesterday repeatedly, and he didn't think he'd ever tire of it.

He hoped Becca had slept well and wondered what her preferences were for breakfast. He had coffee on the boat, as well as eggs and some other ingredients for omelets—one of the few things he was good at making. Deciding to make a move, Ben slid on his shirt and quietly made his way into the living area of the boat, not wanting to wake Becca if she was still asleep. But the door to the master bedroom was open, and he immediately realized she wasn't in there. It was still quite early. She couldn't have left already, surely?

"Becca?" he called out. Maybe she'd gone topside? He went into the bathroom and brushed his teeth, catching a glimpse of himself in the mirror. Ben ran his hands through his hair to tame his curls and then climbed barefoot up the steps to the deck, only to find she wasn't on the boat.

Maybe she'd gone for a walk along the dock? He went back down the steps to retrieve his shoes and that was when he saw the note sitting on the countertop.

Thank you for a magical evening.
Becca.

Ben smiled. Magical was good. But, clearly, she was gone. He would call her later today to make sure she'd made it home okay.

"And just how am I going to do that?" he muttered out loud to himself. *I don't have her number or even know where she lives. But it was too good of an evening for her not to contact me. I know the night got away from us —not that anyone on the boat was complaining.* Ben smiled as a sizzle of desire ran through his veins, remembering the way Becca's eyes had shone so brightly as she'd looked directly into his when he'd kissed her—multiple times.

Her pure enjoyment of the evening had delighted him, as well as her willingness to stay the night. She'd been so shy at the U-Haul store and almost uncertain. But then, at lunch and on the boat last night, she'd been willing to take things further. Not too far, but far enough for a first date—if he could call it that. Sure he could, Ben thought with a broad smile. He couldn't wait to see her again. He was positive she would call. She had his business card after all. In the meantime, he had a lot to do today.

Ben stepped into the small bathroom on the boat for a quick shower, aware that he needed to help Adam with his move this morning. Too bad Adam wasn't willing to stay with him longer. But at least his brother had reached out to him, despite their not being close anymore. That was partly because of their age difference, but also because of so much more, Ben thought with a stab of pain.

Ben, at thirty-two, was six years older than his brother, and Adam had only been twelve years old when Ben moved out to attend UCLA. The university was only about two hours from his childhood home, but he'd rarely made it back and, when he did, he'd spent little time bonding with his brother. There were brief, stiff hugs, a family meal, and then Ben had always found a reason to hasten his return to school. He felt a familiar pang of guilt, remembering that Adam had floundered through middle school and high school, spending more time getting high than on his studies. His younger brother had subsequently dropped out before getting his high school diploma.

Their parents had been of little help to Adam. Their father was away much of the time in one foreign country or another, and their mother seemed only to be going through the motions of living and parenting. She was too absorbed in her own thoughts to think much about Ben or Adam. Ben had been angry with his parents. Looking back on it now, he knew he was being unfair. They clearly loved their boys and had done their best. He'd had a happy childhood in his younger years. It was only later that things fell apart. And Adam hadn't exactly made it easy for any of them. But he'd been the youngest. It shouldn't have fallen to him to have to take care of them; it was their job to take care of Adam, and none of them had been able to do that—not he or his parents.

Ben slid into his truck and headed toward Java's Coffee House to pick up the coffee and breakfast sandwiches he'd promised Adam. "Hi, Tammy. Two large coffees and four bacon and egg breakfast sandwiches to go please."

"Big appetite today, Ben," she teased. "I'd be happy to help you polish those off if you like."

"Appreciate that," he said with a chuckle. "But I think I've got it covered this morning. My little brother's in town, and he's got a pretty enormous appetite."

Ben drummed his fingers on the edge of his truck's open window as he waited for Tammy to return with his order. He used the opportunity to sort through the list of things he needed to get accomplished today and over the rest of this week.

Tammy arrived soon after. "Here you go, Ben. And if you change your mind about needing someone to share that with, just let me know."

"Thanks, Tammy," Ben said, handing her some bills. He also dropped a generous tip in the jar sitting on the ledge next to the drive-through window before pulling away.

Ben turned his attention away from the myriad of thoughts flitting through his mind—his childhood, Becca, work, food, coffee—and focused on making sure he had everything he needed to help Adam get the rest of his packing done and moved into his new apartment. If only he had a bit more time to bond with his younger brother before the move. He'd tried to talk Adam into staying with him through the entire summer, but not even free room and board had enticed him to stay longer. Adam said he needed to be near campus to give himself added focus for his studies. He couldn't fault his brother's logic. So, instead of badgering him, Ben had opted to support Adam in his decision. And at least he could help his brother with the move—including bringing him food and caffeine. Maybe that was enough considering how much Adam could shovel into that bottomless pit of his, Ben thought with a smile.

Gravel crunched under the tires of Ben's pickup truck as he drove up the long drive to the front of his 'dilapidated mansion,' as Adam liked to call it. Ben parked his truck at the top of the drive, with the now-added trailer connected to it. As soon as he got out, Manky and Mel approached, quacking and wagging their backsides. "Hi, Manky. Hi, Mel. So nice of you to welcome me home," he said, laughing at the two ducks who'd mysteriously shown up at his house about a month ago. They almost always greeted him whenever he entered or left the house now. "Did you miss me?" he crooned, giving them a pat.

After giving them sufficient attention, Ben stood and reached back into his truck for the coffee and breakfast sandwiches, calling out to Adam as he entered through the side door of the house and into the kitchen. "I come bearing sustenance," Ben yelled. He set the food down on the 1950s style cracked Formica countertop that hid the former elegance of the circa 1896 home.

Adam's heavy footsteps beat a quick rhythm on the stairwell treads and across the cracking linoleum at the base of the stairs and into the kitchen. "Ahhh...coffee! Just what I need," Adam said, as he grabbed one cup off the counter. He held the coffee cup up in both hands and moved his nose to hover just over the lid, inhaling deeply. "Mmmm...this is the good stuff. Did you get the extra boxes?"

"The boxes are in the truck. Get them whenever you're ready. I'm going to head upstairs to change. I'll be right back down to help with whatever you need."

~

Fortified and ready for action, Adam and Ben now sat on the floor of the bedroom Adam had occupied for his brief stay with Ben. Each sat with a partially filled box in front of him. Adam haphazardly folded the rest of his clothes and stuffed them into his box as Ben neatly filled the box in front of him with Adam's books.

"Are you sure you don't want to stay for the rest of the summer? I've got plenty of room," he asked his brother again.

"I have to agree with you there," Adam said with a laugh. "I thought I'd be cramming in with you in your condo-slash-office. I didn't expect a sprawling mansion on an estate—even though it is so last century," he wise-cracked.

"You and me both. You would have been sleeping in the bathtub, though, at the condo-slash-office," Ben joked. "That place was enough when it was just me starting up the office, but we've already more than run out of space now that Jason and Connie also work there. They didn't need me still living there too. But this monstrosity wasn't at all what I had in mind when I decided to look for a new place to live." Ben chuckled. "I just couldn't resist it. I knew there was something under its surface still worth saving. And who would have thought there would be this much land still available so near the river and so close to downtown Pittsburgh?"

"I'm thinking you have more of Mom and Dad in you than I'd thought," joked Adam. "I wouldn't put it past them to live in a place like this that has yet to have fully functioning plumbing. I thought you only went in for gold-plated pipes and granite countertops these days."

Ben's body stiffened. Should he be offended? Probably. But to be honest, Adam was right. Ben had long since left behind those days spent with his dad overseas, working on water and sewage upgrades in small, remote villages. Those projects just didn't pay. And look where it'd gotten his parents—nowhere. When problems had arisen for their family, they didn't have any funds in reserve or any foundation for their young family to fall back on—even paying for groceries became a struggle.

"Earth to Ben," Adam said, as he closed the box of clothes he'd just finished packing and pushed it next to the other already packed boxes. "Ready to load these?"

Ben heard the amiable tone in Adam's voice and the pit that had formed in his stomach eased. "You're not far off there," he said. "Don't write off the gold-plated pipes just yet, though. It's early days still, and I fully intend to turn this place into a modern palace—with hot water no less, not just tepid trickles dripping from the shower heads."

∿

"That's all of it," said Adam, as they did one last look around Ben's living room for any forgotten items. "Thanks for helping with all of this, Ben, including getting the U-Haul and that couch and table and chairs. I think my apartment-mate and I would have been sitting on the floor to eat our meals without that furniture. He didn't realize his ex-housemate was going to take all the furniture with him when he left."

"No problem. My friends are happy their old stuff is being put to good use. It was just sitting in their garage waiting for someone to love it so they could get their two-car garage back."

"Just one more thing," Adam said shyly, holding a package out to Ben. "I brought you something from home. I hope you like it."

"You didn't need to get me anything," Ben said, pulling back the wrapping paper to reveal a framed photo of three young children smiling into the camera. He swallowed, trying to ease the lump that had formed in his throat.

"Do you recognize it? It's of us in—"

"I recognize it," Ben interrupted. "The flamingos in the background are a dead giveaway. It's Lake Nakuru in the Rift Valley in Kenya...." Ben's voice trailed off as he spoke.

"It was the last time we were all overseas together," said Adam. "Remember how much Sophia loved those flamingos? They covered the entire lake until all you could see was a sea of pink. The flamingos stood on one leg with their heads stuck in the mud. It was before Sophia—"

"You keep it," interrupted Ben. "No need to give it to me." He held the gift out toward Adam, feeling as though the framed photo were burning the tips of his fingers. "I'm sure you'll want to have it with you."

"Oh no, I've got one too. I made that copy for you. I thought you might like to have it...something from home...." Adam's voice trailed off, his face falling.

Ben pursed his lips. He felt like all kinds of a jackass. "Yeah, of course. It's great. Thanks," he said, his expression twitching into what he hoped was a smile but probably showed up as a grimace. Ben set the framed photo on the bookcase next to him then lightly clapped Adam on the shoulder to cover the awkwardness of the moment, and asked, "You ready? We'd better get this move done before we run out of daylight."

"Sure," Adam said, preceding Ben to the door.

Ben followed behind and shook his head, disgusted with himself. He had his brother with him now, and he had a chance to set things right. He didn't want to blow that by over-reacting to an off-hand comment and a stupid photo. And maybe Adam had meant that comment about him being like Mom and Dad as a compliment...and the framed picture as nothing more than a gift. Was he misreading everything? That would be just like him, he thought derisively.

CHAPTER 14
So Many Questions

Becca's alarm blared, waking her from a deep sleep. She'd tossed and turned all night, continuously glancing over at her clock, hoping she was at least getting a bit of sleep. No such luck. Last she'd looked, her clock read 5:00 a.m.

She reached over and pressed the button on top of the clock, stopping the alarm's incessant chiming. She felt groggy and confused. What day was it? She glanced again at the clock, which told her it was Tuesday and 7:00 a.m. on a workday. She needed to get up and get ready for work. But all she wanted to do was disappear. Becca didn't want any part of it; she just wanted to stay in bed and escape into oblivion.

She rolled over and pulled the covers up under her chin and thought about calling in sick, just like she had so many times in that first year after being diagnosed. Staying in bed and hiding under the covers would not do it, though. She needed to do more than that to escape the jumbled confusion emanating from her brain. Maybe she could crawl under her kitchen table and pull a tablecloth over it? She sighed. That wouldn't solve anything either. Her lip curled up in a sneer at her inane thoughts. But rational thinking was far from her reach right now. Instead, her thoughts tumbled around in her brain, like clothes in a dryer, jumbling together in an unending cycle, never settling.

A barrage of thoughts pummeled her brain. But it was the feelings that were unbearable—that same intense fear, anger, and frustration she'd felt two years ago assaulted her senses. Only this time, she knew what to expect. Was knowing better—or worse? Either way, the questions were still endless and the answers far too few. Would she have to go through chemo again? Would she lose all her hair again? Would she be so fatigued that the thought of moving even her pinky finger would be daunting? Would she need to keep a barf bag by her side for hours—even days—at a time? Could she beat this? How could she go through it all again? And how could she make her colleagues, family, and friends ride with her again on that grief-infused roller-coaster?

But there was one new question—*was she willing to go through this fight again?* Becca knew that last question would devastate her mother. She didn't want to hurt her family or her friends and colleagues. She knew they cared about her and would want her to fight. But, in this moment, she couldn't fathom going through it all again, and she knew she didn't want to bring anyone—especially those she loved—along with her for another terror-filled ride. It was too much to ask. Climbing under that dining room table—and never coming out— seemed like a much better option.

Becca's mind continued to race, and her head throbbed with the beginnings of a headache. She hadn't spoken to anyone after her doctor's appointment yesterday. She hadn't even bothered to eat dinner, brush her teeth, or lay her clothes out for work. Maybe she should just stay in bed. That would give her time to process Dr. Murtha's words before bringing anyone else into her newfound chaos. It was all such a shock. She'd finally been getting back on track at work, once again putting in full days and preparing for a potential transfer to Patterson's D.C. office. Would this news now derail that move? Becca didn't want to risk the opportunity. She'd need to pretend everything was okay, at least until she knew more. But they'd probably see right through her at work.

She gritted her teeth and growled out her frustration, then pulled her covers up past her chin and over her head, as she shut her eyes and willed herself back to sleep.

~

Becca lay in bed...waiting. Was she asleep yet? Obviously not. She sighed. Probably a good thing, because if she were going to stay home, she needed to call her boss. She dreaded making that call. He would want to know what was wrong. Did she have a cold? The flu? Something else? She wasn't ready to share those positive test results with anyone—not her boss, not even herself. But she didn't want to lie to him. Nathan had been so good to her during her treatments in that first year. He'd reduced her workload and told her she could work on a flexible schedule, including working from home when she needed to.

He'd also contacted Human Resources and asked them to keep her on board. HR, at his direction, set her up on a leave program that allowed her to take time off whenever needed, even on short notice. And it wasn't just her boss. Everyone at work had been good to her while she'd crawled her way back to fully functioning. She was lucky to have their support and her job. But she'd hated feeling like a burden. She'd prided herself on being someone willing and able to pitch in whenever someone else needed help. Instead, she'd become the one needing the help. If Becca told anyone about her recent test results, they'd start tiptoeing around her again. She couldn't bear that right now.

Becca's stomach grumbled, interrupting her thoughts, and making her aware that she hadn't eaten dinner last night. She needed to get up and face her day. "Up and at 'em, sweetheart," she said out loud. That's what her father would have done. She remembered him getting up every day and going off to work. He wouldn't want her to hide away in bed—or under the kitchen table.

Becca rolled out of bed and shuffled into the bathroom. She looked at herself in the mirror. She didn't look any different from yesterday. Maybe she could pull this off without attracting any unwanted questions? *Smile*, she told herself, as she grimaced back at her reflection. *Time to put on your happy face.*

CHAPTER 15

No Answers

BECCA ARRIVED AT HER DESK IN PLENTY OF TIME TO MEET her 9:00 a.m. start time, with no one the wiser about her struggles over the past twenty-four hours. Jenn hadn't even arrived yet. Becca removed her coat and draped it over the back of her chair. She turned on her computer and then went down the hall to get herself a much-needed cup of coffee. She was in luck. Someone had already prepared a full, fresh pot. She poured herself a cup, added some milk and sugar and made her way back to her desk. She kept her eyes down and her face hovering over the cup, breathing in the fortifying smell emanating from the creamy, mocha-colored liquid. She sat down at her desk and opened the folder with the latest project budget she'd been working on from yesterday—one of Jenn's projects, and one that should wrap up soon. She moved from hiding her face in that cup of coffee to hiding it in that comforting budget spreadsheet. At least the numbers still made sense.

"Morning, Becca," Jenn said as she blew in. She dumped her purse on her desk, shrugged off her coat, and set it around the back of her chair. "How's everything?" she asked cheerily.

Becca, with her head still bent over her work, plastered a smile on her face, then looked up to respond. "Morning. Good; everything's fine. How are you?"

"Great," Jenn said, not looking at Becca as she focused on getting her computer turned on and settling into her chair. "Do you think anyone noticed that I'm late? It's only a little after nine, but I know it stresses Nathan out whenever anyone is late. Well, except you maybe," she said with a smile as she now focused on her illuminated computer monitor. "He knows better than to ask for a reason from you if you're late. Rightly so, too, Becca," Jenn prattled on without turning to look at her as she continued to get herself settled in. "You're never late or absent, unless there's an excellent reason. My reason...yeah...not so great, actually. I couldn't find anything clean to wear this morning. Nothing I wanted to wear, anyway, and I didn't get around to doing laundry last weekend. Can you tell I pulled this blouse off the dirty clothes pile? I'm thinking it's okay. What do you think?" Jenn discretely lifted her arm, sniffed, and then turned her gaze finally to Becca. "No smell anyway. At least, I don't think there is," she said, and a slight blush crept into her cheeks.

Becca snorted out an unexpected laugh. She pulled her hand up to cover her mouth, her shoulders shaking and her body leaning forward as she edged toward an almost hysterical laugh. Pulling herself together, Becca removed her hand from her face and, still smiling, said, "You're the best, Jenn. Thank you for that this morning. And I think you look great—no worries on the clothes. No one will notice. You look—and smell—wonderful, as always."

Jenn smiled and took a slight bow. "Well, I'm glad to be of comic relief this morning," she said. "Now, what're ya workin' on?"

"Your project, actually. It's looking good. The ROI looks solid, not too much risk. I think we need to beef up the comparisons, though, to be sure your margins on the various product lines your client is proposing are really there and not just assumed. Not having that solid back-up data is always a danger. No worries, though. We should be able to pull the data together, and then I can run the risk scenarios. We can mock-up some graphics, too, to show the expected range regarding profit and loss for each product singly as well as in aggregate. You're not meeting with them again for a couple of weeks, right? That'll give us plenty of time. It always helps to have graphics in addition to a written summary. What do you think?"

"That sounds awesome. But, ya know, Becca, you are way outside my area of expertise now, so can you help me with all that?"

"Of course! That's what I'm here for. That's kind of the fun stuff, anyway."

"If you say so." Jenn laughed.

Becca smiled. "I do say so. When do you want to get started? I have a project call with one of my older clients, Henderson Dynamics, at 11:00 a.m. that I need to get ready for right now. But it shouldn't go for more than an hour. Do you want to do our usual lunch thing and then get started right after?"

"Perfect. Thanks, Becca, you're the best."

"No problem." Becca turned back to her pile of folders and pulled the Henderson file from the middle of the stack. She wanted to review their most recent project details, especially the numbers, to make sure she was well-prepared for her call with their innovation team this morning.

"Ready for lunch?" Jenn asked.

"Is it noon already?" Becca asked, looking up with surprise. She'd been inputting her notes from the Henderson call, making sure she documented the next steps before she forgot what they were.

"No. It's twelve thirty already. Are you still okay going to lunch? I'm starving."

"Me too. Yes, now is perfect. Let me just enter this one last item. There, all done. Lead the way."

Becca and Jenn made their way to the Courtyard Café on the second floor, as usual. As they entered, Tony called out his typical greeting, which Becca and Jenn returned as they made their way to the cash register. Becca reached into her purse for her wallet, readying to pay for her salad.

"Uh oh, you dropped something," Jenn said, as she reached down to pick up a slip of paper from the floor. She handed the paper to Becca, and then she reached for her own wallet.

Becca's face blanched. It was the lab work order from Dr. Murtha.

"That will be seven dollars and eighty-five cents, as usual," the cashier said, smiling at Becca. But then her brows furrowed with concern. "Are you okay? Is something wrong?"

"No...not at all. Here you go." Becca maneuvered her face into a stiff smile as she handed the cashier a ten dollar bill. "You know what, Jenn, as I think about it, I really probably shouldn't take time to sit for lunch today. If you don't mind, I'm just going to eat this at my desk. I really have a lot to take care of, and I think it's stressing me out a bit. Would you mind if I just head up to my desk with my salad today?"

"Of course not. Is anything wrong? Is there anything I can help you with?"

"No, it's all good...I just have lots of work to get done. I'll see you up there," Becca said.

"Hey Jenn, Becca," called a voice from across the cafe. "Want to join us?"

Becca sent a quick wave in the general direction of the voice before saying to Jenn, "You go ahead, Jenn. I'll see you back upstairs later."

Then, with her head down, she headed straight for the elevators. Upon arriving at her cubicle, Becca set her salad and drink down on her desk before going to the bathroom down the hall. She shut the stall door, sat down on the toilet seat, and put her hands over her face. A tear slipped out from behind her hands. She should not do be doing this. She didn't want her face to get all puffy from crying. That was sure to get noticed. She needed a good cry, though.

Becca didn't even remember Dr. Murtha handing her that slip of paper. But as she'd held it in her hands, Dr. Murtha's words came flooding back to her, telling her she needed to go to the lab and get her blood drawn again. She didn't want to face another round of blood work. What if it confirmed the cancer was back? *But what if I don't get the blood work done? I don't want to remain here in limbo, wondering if I'm heading to D.C.—or back to the cancer ward.*

Becca left the stall and went to the sink where she washed her face and then dabbed a touch of makeup over the dark smudges beneath her eyes. Then she straightened her shoulders, smoothed out her skirt, and headed back to her desk.

"Do you mind if we hold off on going over your project this afternoon?" Becca asked Jenn when she arrived back from lunch. "I've got way more to get done than I'd realized. I'm thinking your next client meeting isn't for a couple of weeks, so maybe we could wait a bit. Would that be okay?"

"Of course. But is anything wrong? Is there anything I can help with?" Jenn asked again, this time giving Becca a searching look.

"No. I just have more to do than I realized. Stupid of me to lose sight of that."

"No problem, Becca. Just let me know whenever there's a good time for you. I really appreciate you being willing to help me so much. It is my project after all and not really your problem."

"Oh, please, I want to help, Jenn! I just want to do it after I clear a little of what I've got going on off my plate first." Becca turned away and tried to focus on the blurring paperwork sitting on her desk. She felt Jenn hesitate, but then she turned away, seemingly satisfied. Hopefully, thought Becca, Jenn couldn't see the depth of the turmoil running through her brain. She sighed and turned back to the papers in front of her, doing her best to focus on work for the rest of the afternoon.

Four hours of silent, companionable work later, Becca stood and pulled on her coat right at 5:00 p.m. on the dot. "I'm going to head out, Jenn," she said. "I've got an errand to run, and I want to be sure to get there before they close."

Jenn started to ask a question, but Becca quickly interrupted. "Sorry, Jenn, gotta run. See you tomorrow," she said as she headed toward the door.

"Okay. See you tomorrow," Jenn called out, her voice sounding slightly confused.

There went the alarm. Becca glanced over at her clock to confirm that it really was 7:00 a.m. on Friday. *One more day to get through this week,* she told herself. She'd gotten her blood work done Tuesday after work. Still no word, though, from Dr. Murtha's office on the results. She reached over and pushed the top button on the clock and rolled out of bed, shuffling her way to the bathroom while rubbing the sleep out of her eyes. At least she'd been sleeping okay; not great, but good enough to get her to Friday.

Becca brushed her teeth, took her shower, and then went to her closet to figure out what to wear. She grabbed a black pair of slacks, a blazer, and a plain gray blouse. She then pulled out her low wedge, black work heels and then headed into the kitchen for some breakfast. A to-go yogurt would do, she thought, grabbing the container out of the refrigerator.

Becca's phone beeped with a new text message from Carmen. What was she even doing up? Carmen rarely got up any earlier than she had to, and she still had plenty of time before she had to leave for work. But she knew why. Carmen had been texting her all week and Becca hadn't really responded. It wasn't like she was ignoring Carmen. She'd been replying, just with only one- or two-word responses. But Carmen wanted more than that and she couldn't blame her friend—so would she. Becca just didn't have any answers right now, or even the energy to think about anything beyond work. Work she could cope with; numbers and spreadsheets made sense. Everything else was just a confused, scary jumble. But Carmen would not be denied, as right then, her phone chimed again, alerting her to yet another incoming text:

Carmen: What the heck, Becca? Did you contact Ben? How did it go? I want details. Call me. And let me know what time we are meeting tomorrow for our bike ride. No excuses. It's supposed to be beautiful on Saturday, and I know your car is ready for your bike. Does 2:00 p.m. work? Love you. CALL ME!

Becca: Sorry, rushing to work early today. My boss added extra projects. Not sure Saturday will work. I will keep you posted.

Pushing send on the text, Becca chose not to think any more of it as she quickly finished her yogurt, locked up her apartment, and headed for her car. The drive to work was a blur and the rest of the day even more so as she continued to plaster a smile on her face and pretend that everything was okay in her world. When the end of the day finally rolled around, Becca sighed with relief.

She pulled into her parking spot at her apartment complex shortly after 5:00 p.m., not even remembering her drive home. Her limbs felt heavy and her brain fuzzy. Another deep sigh escaped her lips. She'd made it to the end of the work week—barely. Now what? She still didn't have her test results back, and her mind kept see-sawing from one 'what if' to the next. What if the cancer wasn't back? What if the cancer was back? It was exhausting. Maybe that exhaustion was the cancer? If it weren't, would she call Ben? What was he doing right now? Was he on his boat? She couldn't stop thinking about him, which was ridiculous. They'd only just met. It was a much nicer place to be in her head, though, than wondering if her cancer was back.

Becca sighed again. Even if the blood work came back negative, she knew she wouldn't contact Ben. He was just her fantasy—and a well worth it one at that. She smiled sadly. But who was to say the next, or the next, or the next blood work wouldn't come back positive? Even if this last test turned out only to be a false positive? Becca couldn't force that kind of painful roller coaster ride on anyone, including Ben. *Just face it, relationships are out for you.*

Work she could still do. She liked her work, and she was good at it —even when she wasn't at her best. And they had a team of people, so if she needed to take a back seat at times, others could step up. That's what teams were for.

As Becca forced her heavy limbs to activate, she climbed out of her car, wondering what to have for dinner. Maybe a can of soup, a mind-less movie, and bed. *That's about as much as I can manage for tonight.*

The elevator doors slid open on the third floor, and Becca made her way down the hall to her apartment—only to find a familiar figure standing out front. "What are you doing here?!" Becca asked, startled.

CHAPTER 16

Wigs, Hair Ties, and Promises

"OKAY, FESS UP. WHAT'S GOING ON?" CARMEN ASKED AS she handed Becca a bag from Five Guys Burgers and Fries. Becca's mouth watered. Yum—greasy, fattening fast food. Just what she didn't need—but wanted. She spied a bottle of red wine in Carmen's other hand. Carmen knew her too well.

"What are you doing here?" Becca asked, leaning in to give Carmen a hug.

"You didn't answer my calls or texts," Carmen replied.

"Yes, I did. Well, the texts, anyway."

"I do not consider *Talk Soon* to count as a text. That's more like a brush off if you ask me."

Becca put her key in the lock and opened the door to her apartment. She walked into the kitchen and grabbed some plates while Carmen went straight to the cabinet that held Becca's wine glasses and made herself right at home opening the wine.

"Here," Carmen said, handing Becca a glass of wine before grabbing the bag of food and another glass of wine off the counter and motioning for Becca to follow her.

Becca followed Carmen into the living room with the plates and sat opposite her on the couch, as she knew Carmen meant her to.

"What's going on, Becca? When we last had a proper conversation, you were excited about your date with Ben. And you were going to contact him, right? Did you? What happened? And how come you haven't given me a time for our bike ride tomorrow? I know you got your car hitch, so you can't give me that excuse anymore. And what's with the all black outfits again? Way too dreary. You deserve better; you deserve pink. Spill," Carmen demanded.

Becca sighed. She was so confused. She didn't know how to begin. "It's been busy at work..."

"Nope, not good enough."

"I...I..." Becca's mind scrambled to explain. Instead, tears leaked from her eyes, and then sobs emerged, along with hiccups. "The night with Ben was amazing, Carmen. I wanted to contact him. But I'm sure he thinks I'm some sort of crazy woman. He doesn't really know me. What must he think of me? How is he supposed to know I haven't been out with a man on a proper date in almost two years? I was going to contact him. I was going to be brave and just see what could happen. But then...then..." More hiccups and sobs wracked Becca's body. "It's back...."

"What's back? Wait...do you mean...? Oh, sweetie!" Carmen leaned in and put her arms around Becca and let her sob.

Becca pulled away from Carmen and nodded her head. "Yes. Maybe. I'm not sure. I don't know if it is or isn't. But maybe it is."

"Um, Becca, that's about as clear as mud. Go on...but take your time. I'm here as long as you need me."

Becca took a deep breath, trying to reclaim her voice. "I found out on Monday, but I went to work all week. I didn't say anything because I didn't know what to say. I just don't know what's happening yet."

Carmen pulled Becca back into her arms and stroked her hair. "Oh, Becca. I wish you'd let me know so I could have been here for you. You must be exhausted from keeping that inside all week. Put that shield down, would you?" Carmen scolded. "You don't need to go through this alone. We'll figure it out together. Okay? Look at me, Becca. Can you tell me exactly what happened? What makes you think the cancer is back?"

"But I don't want to dump this on you," Becca whined. "You need to spend time on your own life and—"

"Are you saying I'm too much of a mess to talk to about this?" Carmen gently teased.

"Of course not.... You know I don't mean that." Becca sniffled. "I just hate being such a burden. I'm supposed to be strong and focused —like my father was, and like my mother needs me to be."

"Don't you talk about my best friend like that! You are *not* a burden. Never have been and never will be. You are one of the strongest people I know. It's a privilege to help you if I can. In fact, you are being a terrible friend by not letting me help you—you're denying me that pleasure. So, stop that thinking right now! Deal?"

"Deal," Becca murmured.

"Good. Now let's eat this crap I brought you tonight that is absolutely no good for us, and let's drink that entire bottle of wine and see if we can talk this thing through to make some sense of it. We might need some ice cream later too. We can't trouble shoot without that helpful tool in our toolbox—or freezer, as the case may be," Carmen said in mock-seriousness. "Do you have ice cream?"

"Of course," Becca said, sniffling and wiping her eyes on her sleeve. "Thanks, Carmen. Now hand me that plate. I need some of that horribly wonderful greasy food. It's been a long week, and I need to blow off some steam. Why not do that by doing something terribly unwise, just like last weekend with Ben? Cause that felt really good, and I expect this food will too—at least temporarily," she added, finally smiling.

"Are you sure you'll be fine tonight, Becca?"

"Mmm hmm. Thanks, Carmen. I am completely drained, but at least it's a good drained now. I think I cried the whole week out on your shoulder. Do you want to borrow a shirt for your trip home?" Becca asked, her cheeks tinged with pink.

"Nope. I'm just glad you got some of that negativity out of you and onto this shirt. I'm wearing this shirt home as a badge of honor that I finally got you to open up a bit. And when I get home, I'm throwing it into the wash to get rid of that negativity that was inside of you. And no changing your mind about tomorrow. I'll see you at the downtown South Entrance Trailhead. No excuses, right?"

"No excuses," Becca said, giving Carmen a hug. "See you tomorrow."

Becca closed the front door behind Carmen and carried their used dinner plates into the kitchen, loading them into the sink. She'd get to those tomorrow. It was funny, though, how much more energy she had now than when she'd first arrived home from work. She meandered into her bedroom and began gathering items she'd need for tomorrow's bike ride. She pulled a black pair of leggings from the bottom drawer of her dresser and then reached for a black t-shirt to match, but then hesitated. Carmen said she deserved to wear pink. Maybe. It was really Carmen who deserved the pink, though, she thought, pushing the black t-shirt to the back of the drawer and grabbing a pink shirt instead.

She laid the shirt on the bench at the foot of her bed next to the leggings. Pink it is. *This one's for you, Carmen.* She hesitated. But, what if...? *No. No more what if's!* she told herself. She forced her mind back to gathering more items for their bike ride tomorrow—and leaving the pink t-shirt right where it was.

Helmet, check. Water bottle, check. Windbreaker, check. Hair tie... hair tie? *Where in the world had she put those?* She rummaged through the drawers in her bathroom vanity to no avail. Her gaze swiveled around her bathroom and then around her bedroom, her eyes finally landing on the tiny drawer in the top of her dresser. She rarely remembered that drawer was there. It was designed to hold valuables and as such, it was tucked well out of sight. *Yep, here they are.* As she reached for one of her hair ties, she remembered the last time she'd reached into that drawer. It was just a few weeks after her cancer diagnosis two years ago. Her doctor had been talking about chemotherapy. One of the side effects was hair loss. She'd gone into the drawer looking for an old scarf. She'd found the scarf, but she'd never ended up using it. Her friends had taken her wig shopping instead.

How ironic. Here I am two years later looking for a hair tie instead of a scarf to cover a bald head. Becca lifted the pendant at her neck, remembering what else she'd found in that drawer two years ago. While looking for the scarf, she'd angrily yanked out the contents of that little hidden drawer. As she'd harshly pulled the scarf from the drawer, a box had fallen to the ground at her feet. She'd leaned down to pick up the box, and memories of her father had flooded her mind. Inside the box was the necklace her father had given her on her twelfth birthday, just months before he'd died. It was not an expensive piece of jewelry, but the words from her father on that day were invaluable.

Becca remembered being hopeful as she'd taken the necklace out of its box that day, despite her cancer diagnosis. She'd thought the necklace had been lost in the move from Washington, D.C. to Pittsburgh. It spoke to her that she'd found it when she'd needed it most. Her father had told Becca when he'd given it to her how proud he was of her and how she was growing into a strong young woman with powers beyond her understanding. Wisdom, kindness, compassion, strength. She'd put the necklace on that day, along with a smile on her face, and had gone out to have a wonderful day with her friends—doing of all things, wig shopping. It had been a day full of friendship and laughter. Would she need that strength again now to get through another round of cancer treatments? Did she have that strength within her?

Becca looked out the window, up at the sky in response. *She would fight—and she planned to win,* she silently promised her father, as she subconsciously rubbed the pendant's etchings between her thumb and forefinger.

CHAPTER 17

Sparkling Water

CARMEN

CARMEN SAT AT THE TRAILHEAD WITH HER BIKE, WAITING for Becca. Her thoughts turned to the cancer support group she'd reached out to shortly after Becca had first been diagnosed. They'd been a big help to her. She hadn't known what to do or say, or how to help when Becca had first been diagnosed. And she'd been scared—both for Becca and for herself. She and Becca had been best friends forever. She couldn't imagine life without her.

Carmen hadn't told Becca about the group. She was glad she'd reached out to them, though. She'd met some amazing people, and they'd given her a good understanding of what to expect. Who knew, for example, that wig shopping could be an outing, and that there were places that catered to people who were going to lose their hair from chemo?

Carmen had found a great place for that outing, and some of their happy hour friends had joined them. They'd actually had a great time joking and laughing with the staff at the Mastectomy Boutique, where they'd spent a couple of hours trying on wigs while sipping berry-flavored sparkling water out of champagne flutes. The staff had been so helpful; they asked good questions and provided a lot of information. After purchasing two wigs that day, they had all gone to lunch afterward.

Carmen never let on that she got the idea for this outing from her new buddies from the cancer support group she'd joined. The idea for bike riding had come from that group as well. They'd talked about the importance of getting out and getting exercise. Carmen had told them she was a runner and that she and Becca had done a lot of running during their junior high and high school days. The consensus, though, was that running could be hard on the body and maybe something like swimming or biking would be better. Carmen had loved the idea. She hadn't biked since she was a kid, but she'd been thinking about getting back into it as there were some very good trails in Pittsburgh they could start with. Plus, she was always up for something new.

At first, Becca gave her a firm, "No way." But she'd worn Becca down, and they were finally ready to go biking—today actually. But should she call it off? After all of that nagging and convincing and finally getting a yes from Becca, maybe it wasn't such a good idea after all. What if Becca's cancer really was back? Should Becca be resting instead of biking? As much as she wanted to go today, she didn't want to do wrong by her friend.

Maybe she should call Liane. She would know what to do; she always had excellent advice and good ideas. Liane was the one who came up with that wig shopping idea and that had gone great. Carmen dialed Liane's number, who answered almost immediately.

"Liane, it's Carmen. I'm so glad you're there. Can you please give me some advice?" Even Carmen could hear a hint of panic in her voice.

After ending her call with Liane, Carmen felt much better. Why had she even worried? Liane told her, "Of course, you should go!" And she'd reminded Carmen that Becca's doctor had supported the idea. Becca's doctor had even said yes to the running if Becca paid attention to how she was feeling and reported any symptoms to her doctor immediately.

Carmen knew Becca wasn't feeling sick right now, and no one knew for sure if the cancer was back. And even if it were back, exercise was still a good thing. They could just keep it light today; they didn't need to go crazy. Just a short and meandering bike ride would be fine.

CHAPTER 18

Back in the Saddle

BECCA PULLED INTO THE TRAIL PARKING LOT ALONG THE riverfront on the south side of Pittsburgh. Carmen was already waiting for her with her bike off her rack and her helmet on. Carmen wasn't usually the first one to arrive, but she knew how excited Carmen was about their new bicycling ventures, and it made her feel good to do something for her friend. Becca couldn't help but feel that she'd been taking and taking from everyone around her—at least, that's how it felt.

Pushing the cancer thoughts out of her head, Becca stepped out of her compact little Mazda Miata and walked over to give Carmen a hug. "Hi, Carmen."

"Ready?" Carmen said, with excitement in her voice. "This is going to be great."

"Yep. Let me just get my bike ready. This bike has seen better days, but I think it'll be fine. I'm not sure I've got the tires where they need to be, though."

"No worries," said Carmen. "I've brought some tools with me, including a pump. I've been practicing with my new bike. I even went to a bike class a couple of months ago. They went through a list of everything we should have on hand. I've got extra tubes for our tires in case we get a flat, CO_2 cartridges, a mini pump, tire levers, and a rag in case we end up covered in grease." She smiled sheepishly at the list. "They even had us practice changing a tire. I'm not sure I can actually do it in the real world, though. But I don't think we have to worry about that too much. There are plenty of people out on this trail, so I'm sure we'll be able to get some help if we need it. We'll just have to bat our eyelashes and smile," she joked. "Make sure you have your cell phone with you, though, and your ID. At that class, they also beat it in to us that we really need to wear our helmets. You've got yours with you, right?"

"Yep, right here in my back seat," Becca said, as she reached in and grabbed an old looking helmet.

Becca and Carmen spent the next twenty minutes fussing over their bikes, helmets, and other accessories. It was still chilly out despite the beautiful sunny day. But better days were on the horizon. She would not let herself think otherwise today and was happy she'd chosen the pink shirt, not so much for herself, but for Carmen—who was, of course, wearing an incredibly cute, turquoise bike jersey that set off her olive skin to perfection. She also had on a pair of trendy new bike shorts that fit tight around her slight frame and that had her behind poofing out from the padding interwoven into the shorts.

"I love the new enhanced behind, Carmen. Very flattering."

"I can't wait to get you outfitted too," Carmen said with a laugh. "Part of this whole thing has got to be about shopping and new clothes. You know how much I love being a fashionista," she said, eyes twinkling.

"I'm going to have to stick with my old sneakers and t-shirts. I'm still trying to wade through that mountain of health care bills. I know I'm supposed to be a financial expert, but that stuff is mind boggling. It's hard to make heads or tails of it. I am getting lots of help, though, from the social services department at the hospital. Dr. Murtha's office has been great about getting me connected. But, enough of that. Let's not talk about anything cancer related today. I'm sorry I even brought it up."

"Agreed. Today is about enjoying this beautiful spring day and getting to have some girlfriend time. I definitely want to talk more about Ben, though," Carmen warned, waggling her eyebrows.

"Carmen," Becca said in a warning tone. "You know I don't want to add anyone into my complicated mess of a world right now. That weekend with Ben was one of the best of my life, but it was just a fantasy, a much needed one at just the right time. But it couldn't have been more than that. We don't even know each other. And I can't even imagine what he thinks of me. I stayed the night on his boat with him —on the first day we met!"

"Okay, not now...but soon. Fair warning! So, are you ready? I think we've stalled enough getting set up. Let's get cycling!"

As they neared the end of their ride, Becca pulled up beside Carmen, pedaling gently. "You were right. I should have said yes to you a long time ago. It feels good to be out here. I'm not sure how that can be, but I'll take it. I'm not going to look a gift-horse in the mouth right now, that's for sure."

"Thanks for saying that, Becca. You've made my day. And I agree— this is awesome," Carmen said, smiling. "We're almost back to our cars. What do you say we stop at that restaurant coming up? This ride has made me hungry, and it's getting close to dinner time. Look at that great patio they have looking over the river. That looks too perfect to pass up. And look, there are already a couple of bikes parked up against that patio railing. They probably wouldn't mind if we set our bikes there too. That way we can keep an eye on them while we eat.... Becca? Did you hear me? What do you think about stopping at that restaurant for an early dinner?"

Becca's body tingled with thoughts of Ben. This was not the same diner where they'd first had lunch together, but it sure brought back memories of that day. "Sure," said Becca finally. "Maybe they'll have a good salad to balance out those greasy burgers and fries you had me eating last night—and, of course, that ice cream and wine. You *are* a bad influence."

"Hey, this bike ride today was good influencing, wasn't it?"

"You've got me there." Becca smiled.

"No promises I won't get a chocolate milkshake with my salad, though," said Carmen.

≈

Becca spent Sunday regrouping for the week ahead while thinking about her afternoon with Carmen yesterday. It had been a great afternoon. She hadn't felt sick or weak, but she'd felt out of shape. They'd kept the ride to under eight miles and had lolly-gagged the whole way, keeping the pace slow enough that they could chat as they pedaled. That part wasn't exactly the smartest, she knew. They were supposed to go single file so as not to hog the trail, or worse, cause an accident. But they couldn't resist taking some time to talk while they pedaled.

Most of it had been in short bursts when no one was coming at them from the other direction. They had kept their conversation light given they couldn't very well get into in-depth conversations while pedaling single file and yelling back and forth to each other. Most of the conversation had centered on the sun shining down on them and the emerging spring flowers. It was mostly still just daffodils and crocuses and other early spring flowers, but it was still a sign that spring was upon them, and summer would soon bring with it not just sunshine but warmer weather.

She'd enjoyed the day. Becca hadn't thought about cancer, or health care bills, or her potential job transfer to Washington, D.C.—or even Ben. Well, maybe that wasn't exactly accurate. To be honest, she'd thought a lot about Ben. It made little sense to contact him, though. She had too much going on in her life right now, and if the cancer were truly back, as much as she wanted that tingly, floating on a cloud feeling again, Becca knew she couldn't be that selfish.

She continued with her chores, preparing for the week ahead while trying to sort through her thoughts. Except she wasn't making much progress. Her thoughts were still jumbled and confused. Of course they were—she needed to get those test results back. How else could she know how to proceed? Maybe she should call Dr. Murtha's office tomorrow. It won't even have been a full week yet, though, since she'd had her blood drawn. *I might just need to get through another week before I have my answer,* she thought, as she pulled clothes out of the dryer, setting some aside for Monday morning.

CHAPTER 19
Margarita Time

BECCA HAD SOMEHOW FOUND HER WAY BACK TO A RHYTHM at work. She closed out the Henderson Dynamics project and then helped Jenn with her latest project. She was proud of the graphics they'd come up with, especially after the positive feedback they'd received from Jenn's client.

Her phone rang on her desk, halting her musings. Nathan's assistant's name popped up on the screen. She picked up the phone. "Hi, Frank. What's up?"

"You got a minute? Nathan asked if you could come to his office."

"Sure, I'll be right there. I'm not in trouble, am I?"

Frank's laughter came through the phone. "Girl, you are never in trouble. See you in a minute," he said, hanging up.

Becca walked down the hall and peeked her head in through Nathan's doorway. Frank waved her forward. "You wanted to see me?"

"Yes. Come in, Becca," Nathan boomed out in his usual high-volume but affable voice.

As Becca walked in and shut the door, Nathan continued, "Oscar Singleton from our D.C. office called. He asked if I was ready to let you go now that things are back on track with your health. Of course, the opening you were shooting for a couple of years ago has long-since been filled. But he's got another opening coming up for someone with your type of financial expertise. He said if you're interested, the job's yours. If not, once HR officially approves the position, he'll start looking for someone outside of Patterson. As you know, I'm not excited about you leaving. But, if you want to, I'll put the transfer through when the time comes."

Becca's mind raced momentarily. She still wanted to fulfill her goal of working in Patterson's D.C. office, didn't she? Her father would be proud of her for achieving that goal. But, what if her cancer really was back? She couldn't very well commit to a new job if she were about to end up back on that miserable health care treadmill. "Um, do you have any details on the job yet?"

Nathan shook his head. "Not much. Once HR approves the job description, Oscar said he'd send it to me. Once I get it, I'll send it to you. In the meantime, I promised Oscar I'd let you know—as much as I don't want that weasel to steal you away from me," he groused. "What do you say? You still wanting to go?"

"Um, yes," she said uncertainly. "Is it okay if we wait until the job description comes through, though, so I can get a better idea of the specifics?"

"Sure. Smart of you, actually. I'll let you know when I know more. I really don't want to lose you, though, Becca. If there's something I can do from my end to convince you to stay, let me know. That said, I don't want to be the killer of your dreams—or, at least, I won't let myself be."

"Thank you, Nathan. I'll watch for that write-up. I really appreciate you and Mr. Singleton keeping me posted."

Nathan's phone beeped, and he hit a button on the phone in response, allowing Frank's voice to come through. "Nathan, you have a call from Ethan on line one. Should I put it through?"

"Yeah, go ahead," he said, nodding his head at Becca to let her know they were done and she was free to go. He then turned his focus back to his phone, punching another button on the console. "Hi, Ethan. What can I do ya for?"

Becca indicated her thanks and kept her head down as she left Nathan's office. Was she being unfair to Nathan by not telling him about her positive test results? *There's nothing to tell yet*, she rationalized. She didn't want to lose this opportunity. But, she also didn't want to mislead Nathan or Oscar. Her gut clenched. Becca knew it was more than that. She couldn't put her finger on what was nagging at her. It was probably just the not knowing. Whichever way those results came out, waiting was torturous.

Just as Becca reached her desk, her cell phone rang. She glanced down at the screen. Dr. Murtha's office. She veered away from her desk and toward the stairwell, answering the phone as she began her descent to the first floor, aiming for the privacy of the outdoors. She was hoping for good news. Either way, she didn't want to take this call where anyone could overhear her. And, if it were bad news, she knew she'd need some time to compose herself before facing anyone.

"Becca." Dr. Murtha's voice came through over the line. Becca's heart dropped into her stomach. If it were negative, wouldn't it just be one of the nurses giving her a call? "I'm so glad I caught you. I wanted to call myself and tell you the great news! The test came back negative. It looks like we got a false positive on that last test. I'm so sorry to have worried you. As you know, none of this is an exact science, so we get false positives at times. It's unfortunate, but it's a reality."

Becca stepped out onto the sidewalk. As she struggled with the door, her cell phone slipped from her fingers. She scrambled to pick up the phone. "Dr. Murtha? Dr. Murtha? Are you there still? I'm so sorry, I dropped the phone. What did you say?" Becca had heard Dr. Murtha's words, but her heart was beating out of her chest, and she was afraid that she'd just heard what she wanted to.

"The test is negative, Becca. I'm so happy to be able to give you this news. Are you okay, Becca? Are you still there?"

"Yes. I'm here. Thank you so much for calling me yourself. I really appreciate that. What happens next? Do we need to do more testing? What if it's actually this test that's wrong?"

"Let's not get ahead of ourselves. You've gotten lots of negative tests back with only the one positive. I really don't think this is wrong, Becca. You're doing really well right now, and your numbers overall look good. You're looking strong; I don't think the cancer is back. This last round of tests confirms that. So, in terms of what's next, we stay the course. Get back to your life. Enjoy it. We'll continue to monitor your numbers as we have been. But I don't think you need to stress about this one."

"Thank you, Dr. Murtha," Becca said in a shaky voice.

"Becca, I am officially considering you to still be in remission. That's what I want you to get into your head right now. Can you do that for me?"

"Yes. Yes, I can. Thank you!"

"You're welcome. I'll see you back in my office soon, but not too soon. You're doing great, Becca!"

Becca floated back up to her desk, bursting with the news. She picked up the phone to call Carmen, but immediately put it back down again. They only called each other at work in a true emergency, opting instead for texts as much as possible to be sure they didn't get each other in trouble. Was this an emergency? She didn't think she could wait to let the news spill from her chest. Maybe her mother? No, that was a bad idea. She hadn't told her mother about the positive test. She would be upset with Becca for keeping her in the dark. Better to keep that door closed for now.

She itched to call Carmen but, instead, took a big gulp of air and practiced one of her breathing exercises—this time simply trying to summon patience. She decided to text Carmen to ask her if she could meet her for drinks, or even drinks and dinner. She would tell her best friend then and they could celebrate. They rarely went out on a work night, but this was a special occasion. With rising excitement, Becca picked up her phone and began typing.

Becca: *Carmen! Can you meet for drinks after work?*

Becca sat down at her desk. She squirmed in her chair, trying to get settled. She couldn't sit still, and she certainly couldn't concentrate. It was already 4:30 p.m. Hopefully, Carmen could meet her. Then, she'd just have to get through the next half hour before skipping out to celebrate.

Carmen: *Yes. When and where?*

Becca: *Luna's asap? 5:15?*

A thumbs up appeared in response.

Thank goodness, Becca thought, as she started putting her desk in order to prepare for an escape to Luna's. A margarita was in order!

CHAPTER 20

Yes!

"PLEASE," BEGGED CARMEN. "PRETTY PLEASE. PRETTY please with a cherry on top—and sprinkles?"

Becca and Carmen were sitting at a high-top table at Luna's Pub, their old happy hour favorite, contentedly sipping margaritas.

Becca had practically leaped up off her bar stool when she saw Carmen enter the pub. She'd beckoned her over to the table and given her a big hug, then with a huge grin, the words had tumbled from her lips as she related the call from Dr. Murtha earlier that afternoon. They'd ordered a round of drinks and toasted in celebration. But now, Carmen was onto something new. She was trying to convince Becca to go along with another crazy idea. No surprise there, Becca thought with a smile. This was how it should be; all was right with the world again.

While Carmen chattered on, Becca's mind wandered. It felt good to be back here at Luna's Pub. Becca hadn't taken part in any happy hours for ages now. After her diagnosis, Carmen had tried to get her to continue with their almost every Friday night get-togethers. At first, Becca had felt too beaten up to come. She'd been trying to juggle work with her cancer treatments and was just too exhausted to fathom showing up. Plus, it wasn't like she was keeping cocktails and appetizer-type food down in that first year, anyway. Even if it weren't for the exhaustion, her falling out hair and constant barfing wasn't exactly great fodder for a cheerful, happy hour.

Carmen had somehow figured out how to balance keeping Becca in the loop while also supporting her in her new reality. While the frequency of the happy hours had significantly fallen off, whenever they did have them, Carmen would make a point of following up with Becca to give her a blow-by-blow of what everyone was up to. Carmen always seemed to get some laughter and smiles out of her with her post-happy hour stories. Thank goodness for Carmen. Becca didn't know what she would have done without her. She hadn't been happy, though, about how much Becca had pushed her and all their friends away, saying Becca needed to stay connected so her friends could be there for her, especially to help her keep her spirits up, which was good for healing.

In fairness, Becca did make time to take part in some of the support counseling groups Dr. Murtha's office set up for her. Carmen had wanted to go with her, but Becca never relented on subjecting her best friend to that, and Carmen had finally left her alone about it. She wasn't sure why Carmen had backed off. But Becca certainly wasn't going to question it, happy that Carmen had allowed her to get away with erecting a wall of sorts between herself and her friends, and even between herself and her mother.

She'd told Carmen the reason was because she didn't want her friends to go through this painful cancer journey on a day-to-day basis. They had their own lives to think about. But what she hadn't told Carmen was that, in her imaginings, she pictured herself standing tall with a shield in her hand. She wanted her friends and family behind that shield, protected. It sounded ludicrous, of course it did—way too ludicrous to share, even with Carmen. Nonetheless, that's how she pictured it. So, yes, Becca had done her socializing of sorts, with most of it—the crying, the bargaining, the rationalizing—through patient support groups and with people already immersed in this cancer-filled world. It wasn't fair to them to be in this world either, but at least it hadn't been Becca who'd pulled them into it. Carmen had heard Becca out. She hadn't been happy about the decision, but she'd backed off.

Becca took another sip of her margarita, feeling a flush creeping into her cheeks. Geez, she was such a lightweight, especially since she hadn't been drinking much at all these days. Well, except for that bottle of wine she drank with Carmen on Friday night...and that bottle of wine she and Ben had on the boat. Hmm...maybe she was back to her old life. Better not push it too much—starting tomorrow. Today was a special day.

"It's just an information session," Carmen continued. "You only need to come to hear what they have to say. Are you listening, Becca? Once you hear what it's all about, then you can see what you think. If you still don't want to sign up after you've heard the info spiel, you don't need to. No pressure."

Becca laughed. "No pressure?" she smiled. "Now that's an oxymoron when it comes to my best friend."

"Well, okay, you got me there. Maybe just a wee bit of pressure. You've got to see it too, though. This would be so cool!"

Carmen was trying to talk her into coming to an information session held by the Leukemia Society tomorrow night. Carmen wanted them to sign up and help with fundraising. But that wasn't so much the crazy part. The crazy part was that this fundraiser would require them to run a half marathon, 13.1 miles. Yes, they'd done lots of running together during their junior high and high school days, but the furthest they'd ever run—at least in a race—was a 10K, 6.2 miles. This would have them running more than twice that. Was her body strong enough for that? Maybe the more pertinent question was whether she was strong enough to say no to Carmen?

Becca knew Carmen had her best interests at heart. Carmen wanted her to get back out into the world and have some fun. But, 13.1 miles? Sure, it would be fun to run alongside her friend again. She missed their long chats and the easy camaraderie that came with being out on the trail with Carmen. Those had been some of her favorite days back in school. And she'd had a great time biking on Saturday. With biking, though, it was harder to chat. Of course, Becca remembered with a smile, their coach during their school days had often yelled at them about their chats. He'd told them that if they could talk, they weren't running fast enough, and he'd said pointedly to get on with their run. The draw to chat, though, had been stronger than their desire to please their coach, much to his dismay.

She decided to go the route of caution. Turning to her friend, she said, "Let me think about it, Carmen. I really did like going out on the trail with you last week, but signing up to run a half marathon is another thing."

"But there's no time left to think about it, Becca. Thursday is the last info session. That's tomorrow! They've already had three of them, and the training officially starts on Saturday."

"You know you are absolutely crazy, Carmen, right?"

"Of course, but that's what you love about me," Carmen said, giving Becca a pair of pleading, sad eyes that she somehow knew how to match with a begging smile.

How did Carmen do that? Becca could never resist that face. She took another sip of her margarita, aware that she was feeling so happy right now. It felt like an enormous weight had been lifted off her shoulders this afternoon when Dr. Murtha had told her to go forth and live her life. And now Carmen was trying to coax her into doing just that. This wasn't such a big deal, right? Becca and Carmen had lots of running experience; plenty of 5Ks and even 10Ks. And they didn't need to win the race; they just needed to finish it.

Their server swished by their table, giving them a questioning look while turning his finger in a circular motion, silently asking them if they wanted another round of drinks.

Becca nodded her head. "Yes," she said aloud. "Yes to going to the info night and yes to a second margarita."

CHAPTER 21

You've Got to be Kidding

"WAIT—WHAT? A TRIATHLON? YOU'VE GOT TO BE KIDDING me. What happened to the whole half marathon thing? What even is a triathlon?" Becca asked, as she leaned over and whispered the question to Carmen.

Becca and Carmen sat in the back of the local library's meeting room. Two speakers from the Leukemia Society stood at the front of the room explaining how their endurance event fundraisers worked.

"We've added a new option this year," one of the women at the front of the room explained. "We've actually never had this as an offering before. It's not our usual, but we're really excited about it. A lot of things just started coming together, and we felt we couldn't pass this up; maybe it was fate." She gave a small laugh and a shrug of her shoulders. "Who knows. What we do know is that a new triathlon race has been added just a couple of hours north of here, and one of our past participants came to us excited about this new event. He offered to coach the event for us if we added it as a fundraising option. At first, we thought he was crazy. But he offered not only to coach but also to help with logistics. It's really an amazing opportunity. He really knows what he's doing, and he's been a great supporter of the Leukemia Society. I think he's done at least five of our marathon fundraisers, and he has a lot of experience competing in triathlons.

He's very well-versed on every front, including with the Leukemia Society, marathons, and triathlons."

"Are you still signing people up for the half marathon event too?" interrupted someone hesitantly from one of the seats in the front row. "I'm really interested in running the half marathon. I've been thinking about doing it for a couple of years now, and I've finally gotten up my courage. I'm just not ready to brave more than the running at this point."

"Oh yes, of course. The marathon or half-marathon, whichever you prefer, is really our biggest event. This is an additional offering this year. It might be the only year we do it. We'll have to see how well it goes. It's not only a new event for us, but also for the organizers. We think it will be a lot of fun and another good way to raise awareness and funds to support our mission."

The top half of Carmen's body was literally undulating, thought Becca. She might as well have been dancing despite her butt still touching the seat of her chair. Carmen leaned over toward Becca, shielding her mouth from the front of the room so as not to disrupt the speaker. "This is way better than the half marathon! We know how to run already. Think how awesome this will be! It fits right in with our biking, and you loved our Saturday ride. I know you did. Don't tell me you didn't because that was one of the biggest grins I've seen on your face in two years—well, except for the Ben weekend thing, now that was a grin," she said, wiggling her eyebrows. "Think about it, Becca; we'll get to join a group of people who actually understand the biking world. They can teach us how to fix a flat, what clothes to wear, where to ride. Did I say clothes? I can't wait to see how this all works. It's going to be amazing!"

"Are you kidding, Carmen? Run, bike, and swim? You're crazy." The person sitting right in front of Becca turned to look at her, shaking his head up and down in agreement. A blush bloomed in her cheeks at the realization she was being rude. Luckily, the person in front of her had already turned back around to face the speaker and didn't seem to be offended, just in agreement with her that Carmen was crazy—which she already knew. Becca lowered her voice as she said, "Good grief Carmen, I'm still not even sure what a triathlon is."

Carmen whispered back, still undulating in her chair with excitement, "She just told us it includes a short swim, bike, then a run. We've already got the running and biking thing going for us. And I know you know how to swim. We went to the community pool enough summers together to know we can handle a short swim. It can't be that hard."

She must be kidding, thought Becca. How in the world had they gone from a simple 'getting back in the saddle' bike ride to signing up for the half marathon—which was already crazy enough—to now signing up for a triathlon? Becca had to admit she did love that Saturday ride, though. And, she thought, as the fiscal side of her brain nagged at her, she'd put a chunk of money into getting that car hitch and bike rack. She might as well get some good use out of those. Maybe she was as crazy as Carmen. Was that why they were friends?

But no, she couldn't do it. She was still reeling from the supposed return of her cancer. And she hadn't been working out at all lately. Did she have the strength to work up to even the run portion of a triathlon, let alone the swim and bike portions? She shook her head. "It's too much, Carmen. We should start smaller."

"Come on, Becca, you heard her. This might be the only year they offer this. Do you want to miss out?" Without waiting for a response, Carmen turned to face the speaker and raised her hand.

"Yes? In the back—you have a question?"

"Yes. I'm sorry. I'm just really excited about the idea of this triathlon. I think you explained it already, but can you please go over the distances again and how that works? My friend and I might actually be interested in doing the triathlon," Carmen said, while trying, unsuccessfully, to keep her body still.

The speaker smiled. "Sure thing. I'm so pleased to hear you're excited about it. We are too. It's a swim-bike-run all in one race. This is a sprint distance race. The swim is less than a half mile. So, think about thirty-three laps in a twenty-five-yard pool. That's followed immediately by the bike ride, which is about 12 miles. That's then followed by the run, which is a 5k, which is 3.1 miles. The course is perfect for beginners because it's mostly flat—no hills at all. I know for someone new at this, it can sound a bit intimidating. That's what we were concerned about at first. But we spoke with the organizers, and they assured us it's going to be a small field of participants and very low-key. They, along with their partner organization, a local triathlon club, want to introduce more people to triathlons. And, because this is the first year for this specific event, they're keeping it small on purpose. They want to make it as fun and as laid-back as possible. After the event there will also be a barbecue and an awards ceremony where people can just hang out and enjoy the day."

"That sounds amazing," said Carmen. "Thank you." Leaning back over toward her, Carmen whispered, "Oh yes, Becca, this is awesome. We just have to do this!"

"This is the last of our information sessions," the speaker continued, "as the Triathlon training starts Saturday. So, if you do plan to sign up, we'll need all your paperwork in before then."

Carmen gave Becca a 'let's-do-this' look while waiting expectantly for her answer....

PART THREE
Proximity

CHAPTER 22

Emotional IQ

BEN

"WHAT THE HELL?" MUTTERED BEN. HE STILL HADN'T heard from Becca, and he had no way of contacting her. At least not without literally hunting her down. If she hadn't called yet, she must not want to be found. It had already been thirteen days since the night they'd spent together on his boat—*not that he was counting*. He'd been sure she would contact him.

Ben shook his head at his delusional thinking. He shouldn't have assumed he knew what Becca was thinking or feeling. He already knew his emotional IQ was abysmal. He'd seen that throughout his entire life. First with Adam, and then with Lindsay, whom he'd dated in college. And then again with Debbie, whom he'd started dating shortly after starting his company in Los Angeles.

He'd dated Lindsay for almost two years. It'd been great at first. But she'd dumped him when he'd said he intended to go to graduate school to get a degree in architecture. She'd wanted the finer things in life right then and there and, as soon as someone else with sufficient money in his back pocket came along, Lindsay had dumped him.

With Debbie, Ben had thought maybe it would be different. They'd started dating shortly after he'd started his company. He'd tried to make it work, but she'd wanted more from him emotionally than he could give. He'd been so focused on getting his company off the ground that he just didn't have the time or the energy to give Debbie what she'd craved. They'd finally parted ways amicably enough, but not before it had become too messy for his liking, and not before both of them had experienced a lot of pain from their breakup. Since then, Ben had kept his relationships solely casual. And that suited him just fine. If he were honest with himself, he was embarrassed at how gullible he was when it came to people and relationships. He liked helping people, but he'd learned to keep it at a professional level.

That I can do, Ben thought. He tried to push all thoughts of Becca aside. If he didn't get back to focusing on getting his new Pittsburgh office off the ground, he might end up blowing that part of his life as well.

He pulled into the marina parking lot. It had been a long week, and he still had a lot of work to get done—he just couldn't stomach doing any more of it from his cramped condo office. Hopefully a change of scenery would help.

As Ben started down the dock toward his boat, unwelcome memories flooded his mind. It was a beautiful night out, just like that night with Becca. A slight breeze tickled his nose. He could smell spring in the air and the coming of summer, reminding him even more of Becca. He wanted to share another night—this night—with her.

Ben stepped onto the boat, and it swayed gently under his feet. He remembered Becca stepping onto the boat with him, her hair fluttering in the evening breeze. Her smiles had been shy at first, but later, she'd opened up, clearly delighting in their adventure out on the river as well as in their molten kisses that had flared his and her desire —or so he'd thought. Ben was sure there had been a connection between them and beyond just the physical. She'd called the night 'magical.' How could he have been so off-base with her emotions— and why in the world did he care? Maybe it was the turmoil of Adam showing up? That must be it. It would pass as soon as things settled in with Adam, he told himself.

Despite his attempts to push the memories aside, Ben's eyes seemed to close of their own accord as he stood in the boat's stern, remembering. *I can't stand here forever waiting for her to contact me,* he derided himself. *She clearly doesn't want to see me. And I'm certainly not going to stalk her down. What would be the point?*

Anyway, there are plenty of other women out there who would be happy to spend the day—and the night—with him on his boat. His chest puffed up at the thought. But then it immediately deflated, leaving him feeling rudderless. Apart from Becca, he'd never invited a woman onto his boat before. This was a special place, a place where he felt more himself than anywhere else—until he had lunch with Becca. What was it about her that had gotten him talking about his ridiculous dreams? What had made him open up to her? Why had he invited her on to the boat, even going so far as to ask her to spend the night?

Ben shook his head, trying to dampen the questions and the hurt that had been haunting him over the past thirteen days. *Not that I'm counting.* He opened his eyes and let out an enormous sigh at the lie before moving into the cabin of his boat. He set his bag, crammed full with his computer and mounds of paperwork, onto the table, determined to get back to work. His thoughts and memories of Becca were pushed to the side as he worked diligently, almost obsessively, into the night.

Early the next morning, Ben woke up to his alarm. He'd finally called it a night at about midnight, knowing he still had a lot to do but also knowing he needed to build up a reserve of energy for today. Adam would be here soon. They were meeting at the boat for breakfast, but then planned to spend the day together at a training event, something Ben was looking forward to, and something that would hopefully get his mind off work—and Becca. *How stupid could he be with women?* he scolded himself with one last angry shake of his head.

"Permission to come aboard, Captain?" called Adam from above.

"Come on down. I've just finished making a pot of coffee, and I've got some eggs and bacon going. You interested?"

"You know it. Thanks."

"Sure thing. We're going to need a good breakfast for today. We'll be fueling for our workout."

Adam sat down and tucked into the eggs Ben set before him. "Looks like you've got the perfect love nest going here, Ben," Adam teased. "How come you've got papers everywhere instead of a woman?"

"Some of us have to work, you know," Ben responded with annoyance, immediately chastising himself for his unwarranted, terse reply.

"Ohh-kaayy... You know I'm just kidding, right?"

"Yeah...sure. Sorry. Eat up. We've got to get moving; I don't want to be late," Ben said, embarrassed at his own outburst but somehow not having the energy to pull it back as much as he knew he should.

"So...maybe this isn't such a good idea today, Ben. I've got a lot I still need to get done before classes start. Do you mind if I call off? Maybe we can catch up later after I'm feeling a bit more on solid ground with this CMU stuff. You could show me another time some of that biking stuff you're into."

"Yeah, that sounds good. It'd be great if you could come, but I understand if you don't want to—can't, I mean." Was he screwing it up again? Ben wanted to get to know his brother better and get back to how it was when they were little kids. But maybe he just wasn't destined to figure out these relationship things. He'd screwed up enough relationships—first with his brother, and most recently with Becca. He tried again. "It's your choice, Adam. Whatever works for you is okay by me," he said, more gently this time.

"Um...yeah, sure." Adam gave Ben a puzzled look. "So, I guess I'll get out of your hair today and let you get on your way. Thanks for the breakfast. Much appreciated." Adam headed up the stairs and back to the dock, calling over his shoulder, "Let me know how it goes this morning!"

Ben began moving. "Wait! Adam...."

But Adam was too far ahead and didn't hear him. "I'd love to hear about today's event when you get a chance," Adam called back over his shoulder, his voice quickly dissipating as the spring air caught his words, breezing them away—right along with Adam.

"What is wrong with me?!" Ben said aloud, running his hand through his hair. It was already starting out to be a bad day, and it was his own fault. *How stupid could he be?* He slammed the dirty breakfast dishes into the sink. But he couldn't think about how he'd just screwed up, and he couldn't deal with those dishes now either. He needed to get a move on or else he was going to be late for this training event, and he certainly didn't want to let anyone else down today. And, anyhow, what he needed most right now was to get off this boat.

Ben grabbed his gym bag and stomped his way up to his truck. Maybe some exercise and a change of scenery would turn things around.

CHAPTER 23

Orientation

"I can't believe you talked me into this, Carmen," Becca whispered.

It was early Saturday morning, and Becca and Carmen sat on a set of bleachers next to a high school track just like the one where they'd first met in middle school. Memories of that first meeting flashed through Becca's mind. Her nerves jangled, and a shiver of fear snaked its way up her spine. This was just like in junior high when she'd ended up trying out for the cross-country team. Then, she'd been running away from her fear of her new surroundings and from those ginormous—or at least seemingly ginormous—kids in her new junior high. That ended well, though, she thought, smiling. Maybe this would too. After all, that's where she and Carmen first started their friendship—on bleachers just like these.

"Hello," said a couple of women as they moved past Becca and Carmen to an empty spot on the bench next to them. "Are we in the right place?" asked one of the women. "We're here for the orientation and the run being held today for the Leukemia Society."

"Hello," chorused Becca and Carmen.

"Yes, you're in the right place. My name is Carmen, and this is my friend, Becca."

While Carmen struck up a friendly conversation, Becca surveyed their surroundings, intent on people-watching as more participants filtered in. It was amazing to see the eclectic nature of the group. It was made up almost equally of men and women who spanned a broad age range, with some of them young—maybe in their twenties like she and Carmen—and some of them older, maybe even into their sixties. They certainly didn't all look physically toned or athletic. They just looked...what? thought Becca. *Normal,* came the answer in her head. They just looked like average, normal people. That was reassuring, because that was exactly what she wanted to be—*normal.*

Maybe it was also okay that she wasn't in shape right now, Becca thought. And maybe that was a part of the journey they were all about to go on together. During the information session, the speaker had told them they would have several months to prepare for the race. She'd also said they would be in good hands throughout their training to ensure they were well-prepared for race day.... Maybe that would truly be the case.

About twenty-five people now sat on the bleachers talking in quiet but excited voices. It was nearing 8:00 a.m., the start time for their orientation. A man sitting on one of the front bleachers stood up and turned to face the group. He had a clipboard in hand, just as their track coach had that fateful day in junior high. But this time was different—at least he didn't have a whistle and wasn't yelling at them.

Becca watched him as he cleared his throat to get their attention. When the murmurs died away, he gave them an encouraging smile and began talking.

"Hi, I'm Sam. I'll be your coach for the next couple of months. We'll also have another coach joining us shortly. This is because I've been offered a job out in California, and I won't be able to train with you in your final month as originally planned. Not to worry, though. You'll be in expert hands all the way through your training as well as on race day.

"I won't go into too much on my background right now, as we'll have plenty of time to get to know each other better as we work through the miles. What I will tell you is that I've done a lot of endurance events over the years, so I'll be able to share lots of tips and tricks with all of you about what to expect. When race day comes, you'll be well-prepared to tackle, and hopefully enjoy, your race.

"I've also been involved with the Leukemia Society for many years. It's a great organization. They do a lot to support patients and families through some of the most challenging times in their lives. They also provide millions of dollars in funding to researchers working to improve treatment options and find cures for blood-related cancers. You've now become an important part of that effort. Thank you for that! You'll be hearing more about those efforts in furtherance of our mission throughout your training. Today, though, is mostly about getting you oriented and launched on the training aspect of your journey. So, let's dive right in!"

Sam paused to ensure he still had everyone's attention. When a few gave reassuring smiles, he continued, "I know at the info session you got an overview of what's in store. Today, I'm going to go into a little more depth. I'll give you your full training schedule—always exciting, I think. I've got those here now. Can someone please help me pass these out?"

Two hands went up, and Sam handed a large stack of spiral bound books to each volunteer.

"While those are being passed out, let's go around and have everyone introduce themselves. Please just tell us your name and as much as you're comfortable sharing today, including your reason for being here, if you would like."

The group went round-robin style, giving their names. Some provided a brief sentence about their reason for joining. Most though, including Becca, just quickly provided their name, a smile, and a "hello."

"Thank you everyone. And, again, welcome," said Sam. "I'm also pleased to introduce Tom to you today. Tom is a physical therapist—physical therapist extraordinaire," Sam said, gesturing at Tom as he gave him a smile. "He'll be leading us through some important stretching exercises before we start our run today. And, as you'll hear, Tom is happy to answer your questions about any aches or pains that may develop as a part of your training along the way. You have his email address listed in your orientation packet, so please be sure to reach out to him with questions. Do what Tom says and, I assure you, you'll be happy you did."

As Becca focused on Tom's demonstration, following along easily since the stretches he demonstrated mostly mimicked what had become rote during her junior high and high school days, her mind ran onto a different track to her earlier days of running. Back in high school, she'd run many miles and multiple times per week. How many 5K runs had she completed—and not just completed but competed in? Those 3.1 mile races were along country trails with hills and valleys and other runners trying to push by her, often with a rough—supposedly unintentional—push as they jockeyed past her. She remembered the body blows those otherwise sweet looking girls could dole out once they rounded a corner or ran through the wooded areas of the course away from the course marshal's eyes. Many times, she'd come out of the woods with little droplets of blood sliding down her shins from the cleats the other runners wore to kick her with. They'd done it to slow her down and psych her out when passing her by.

At that reminder, a wave of apprehension washed over her. Becca gave her head a quick shake to clear the sensation. This would be nothing like that, she reassured herself. This was only a one-mile fun run around a fully visible high school track. Plus, she felt the support of everyone out here today, not just in what was said, but also in their eagerness to be a part of something bigger than themselves. No one seemed to care how fast her time was going to be or whether she would be faster or slower than they were. It was good to feel that support from everyone here—not just from Carmen, who had never cared if she ran fast, slow, or somewhere in between.

She and Carman had always enjoyed each other's company and the sharing of secrets that came along with eating up the miles. Not to mention that endorphin spike from the feel-good chemicals their bodies produced, she thought with a smirk. Yes, she could do this one-mile run today. Sam had even said it was okay if they interspersed that run with some walking. In fact, he'd encouraged it if they were new to running or hadn't done any recently. She was ready for this, excited for it, in fact. Today, all she had to do was eek out one slow mile.

"Thanks, Tom," said Sam, pulling her back into the briefing. "Okay, let's get started! The idea today is to keep it very low-key; no trying to prove anything. And no injuries allowed, especially on day one," he said with a smile. "Today it's a one-mile run—that's four times around this track. And, again, don't push yourselves. The race isn't until mid-July, so we have plenty of time to work up to the full run distance, and you'll have plenty of help to get you there..." Sam's voice trailed off as his gaze moved beyond the group to the parking lot. "Speaking of help, here comes some now."

Everyone turned to follow Sam's gaze. A man was purposefully walking toward them. He looked fit, toned, and handsome—but he also had a scowl on his face and was walking with intimidating determination. Becca's heart started to thud. Surely not? But Sam's next words confirmed her fears.

"You're just in time," said Sam. "We're about to start the run. Everyone, meet Ben. Ben, meet everyone."

CHAPTER 24

First Run

BEN

BEN QUICKLY MOVED TOWARD SAM'S SIDE, FORCING HIS facial expression into a smile. "Nice to meet you... " Ben faltered in his greeting. He felt more than saw Becca as an intense heat ran through him. He pictured her soft brown eyes staring into his as he leaned in to kiss her—both above and below deck on his boat. Their easy banter, including her interest and quick comebacks as they'd fed off each other's words throughout the day and then into the night had him wanting to put those proverbial rose-colored glasses back on, pull her toward him, and drag her back to his boat.

For God's sake, he thought with frustration. He needed to remember Becca hadn't contacted him after what he'd thought—and she'd said— was a magical night. Ben visibly sighed, not sure whether to be pleased or miserable at this turn of events. Either way, if she truly was one of the participants, they were in for a bumpy ride.

Suck it up dude, he told himself, hoping no one had noticed his momentary lapse. He needed to keep his cool and remain professional. He could like her—or not. And she could like him—or not. Either way, it didn't matter now. Ben took in a deep breath and started his greeting again on the exhale. "Nice to meet you all," he began again. "Sorry to be late. I don't want to delay anything. So, if you all are

141

ready, let's get started. I'll see you out there on the track. Sound good, Sam?"

Sam simply nodded, giving Ben a quizzical look.

As the group started their run, they slowly began to space out, as some moved forward at a quick pace while others moved more slowly.

"So glad you could be here, buddy," Sam said, giving Ben a friendly clap on the back. "You good? Is something going on?"

"Nope, just sorry I'm a little late," Ben said, not meeting Sam's eyes.

"No problem. You're just in time. And I appreciate you being here. You're savin' my butt, ya know."

"Happy to do it." Ben looked directly at Sam, now giving him a smile he genuinely felt in his gut.

"You know what to do—go for it!" Sam smiled, and with a nod of his head, he ran ahead to catch up with a couple of participants.

Ben stood stock still for a moment. He could see Becca just a short distance away, running alongside a dark-haired woman of about her age. Leave it to her to be running away from him again, he thought with a frown. That look on her face, though... When he'd first turned to face the group and their eyes had locked, she'd looked like a scared rabbit peeking out from behind that dark-haired woman she was now running with. Where was the woman who'd spent the day and then the night with him on his boat? The woman who'd delighted in everything about their trip on the river? She now seemed shy and unsure of herself.

Becca was certainly a puzzle—and one that he wanted to solve if she'd let him. He shook his head and turned away from the enigma that was Becca to focus on the other participants. He needed to get to know these folks, as he would be spending a lot of time with them over the next several months—including Becca, it seemed.

"Your stride looks great," he said to a blonde-haired woman who looked to be somewhere in her forties as he caught up to her on the running track. "Do you have running experience?"

"Yes, just casual, though. I've done a few 5K races, and I try to get in a couple of runs per week around my neighborhood. No big race stuff, though."

"I'm sure you'll do great," he said encouragingly. "You already look like you're having no trouble at all handling this track—and it's only day one. My name is Ben, by the way."

"I'm Elora. Nice to meet you."

Ben ran beside Elora for a short distance, chatting amiably. After a while he said, "You're doing great, Elora. No pointers needed for you. I'm going to go on ahead and check in with some of the others to make sure they're doing okay. If you have questions or need anything, please be sure to let me or Sam know. Keep up the good work." He flashed her a smile.

"Will do. Thanks, Ben."

Ben moved toward the next group, looking around to see if anyone was struggling or needed some one-on-one guidance or reassurance. Unfortunately, his eyes betrayed him as he went searching for one woman—and one woman only.

He found her immediately. Becca was no longer running with the dark-haired woman, but alongside an older woman, who had elegant gray streaks running through her shoulder-length hair. Ben watched them as they ran at a slow pace; almost a walk, actually. They seemed to be in an intense but amiable conversation. Did they know each other? They must, he thought, for they stopped momentarily and gave each other a hug before picking back up with their slow but steady run.

Ben pulled his gaze away from Becca and told himself to focus on his coaching duties. He spent the rest of the next thirty minutes or so introducing himself to some of the other participants as he ran or walked with them around the track.

Before Ben knew it, he was walking side-by-side with Matt, one of the last participants to finish up the fourth and final lap that would complete today's one mile goal. "Great job, Matt! Don't worry, you'll get this. It's only day one. It's absolutely fine today to include some walking. In fact, it's wise. You're going to want to work slowly up to the distances and your pace. If you don't, you're likely to get injured. That can affect your race more than just about anything else, as well as your enjoyment of the process of getting to that race. So, for now, you're very much on the right track—pun intended," Ben said with a wink.

As Matt left his side to grab some water, Ben lifted his gaze to see if there was anyone else left out on the track. Only one person remained, and Sam was with her, so she was in expert hands. He looked back toward the bleachers, and his body immediately stiffened. There was Becca, sitting on those bleachers—and Adam was with her.

Ben was shocked. He'd stupidly pushed Adam away this morning and didn't think he'd show. So why was he here? Ben froze, confused and unsure, before his limbs reignited and his hesitation turned into determination. He quickened his pace toward the two, feeling conflicted. He was thrilled Adam was here, but why was he talking to Becca? And why was Becca talking to his little brother—and not to him?

A fissure of hurt ran through him. Ben knew he was thinking irrationally. Nonetheless, his thoughts drove him at an even faster pace toward the two.

As Ben passed one of the participants on his way toward Becca and Adam, he noticed the woman flinch and realized he must look like he was on a tear. Thoughts of Becca, and then seeing her here in person today, and now with his brother of all people, were making him crazy. He owed that woman he'd just passed a thank you. Her look of concern had forced him to take note of his own demeanor, giving him a chance to get a hold of himself before he reached Becca and his brother.

Taking his own advice, Ben turned back toward the woman he'd just passed and smiled. "Good run?" he asked, trying to compose himself.

"Yes, thanks. All good." She smiled back at Ben, albeit a bit hesitantly.

"Great," said Ben, as he continued forward, consciously shifting his gait into what he hoped would come across as a relaxed, purposeful stride. First things first, Ben told himself, I need to find out why Adam has shown up and see if I can get things back on track with him. Then I can delve into what to do about Becca.

When he came up to them, Ben forced himself to say casually, "Adam, it's great to see you. I'm glad you could make it. Is everything going okay?" He then gave Becca an awkward nod as she looked up at him from where she sat next to his little brother.

"Absolutely. Sorry about earlier," Adam responded awkwardly. "I didn't think I should come because of the required pre-course work I still need to complete before my program officially launches. But I realized I've got all weekend; no need to spend every minute studying. I hope it's okay that I came?"

"Of course! And I'm glad you did," Ben said, gently clapping Adam on the back. "It's a great surprise."

Ben was pleased to see a smile creep up Adam's face.

"Oh, sorry," said Adam. "Where are my manners? Becca, this is Ben. Ben, this is Becca. Although maybe you two already know each other?"

Ben's eyes locked onto Becca's as he grappled with how to answer Adam's question. Becca looked just as flustered as he felt.

Luckily, Adam didn't seem to notice their hesitation and continued on. "Oh, actually, I'm sure you two have already met. Sorry I was late this morning. I'm guessing I missed earlier introductions?"

"Yes, yes, we already met—earlier today," both answered, almost in unison.

"Great," said Adam. "Well, it looks like all went well with the training today. Ben, I'm happy to hang around until you're done. We could—"

"Becca!" called out Carmen as she skipped up to the group. "How did it go? Sorry I went on ahead. You good?" Carmen paused, looking hesitantly at the rigid faces in the group. "Sorry, I didn't mean to interrupt."

"No worries. You didn't interrupt anything," Ben said, putting his hand out. "Hi, I'm Ben, one of the coaches, and this is Adam."

"Carmen," she said, reaching out to shake Ben's hand and then Adam's.

"Can everyone please gather round?" called out Sam then, distracting them from their introductions. As one, they turned to obey Sam.

When everyone was assembled, Sam smiled and addressed the group. "Great job today! Please make sure you all get something to drink. Help yourselves to whatever you find on this picnic table. There's Gatorade, water, and snacks. Hydrating and fueling is an important part of your training, so be sure you don't shirk on that. And while you're getting hydrated, any questions about the run today?

It looked like it went really well for everyone, but I don't think Ben and I had a chance to touch base with every one of you."

Sam paused to answer a handful of questions about things like running shoes, blisters, and preferences on types of sports drinks before he continued, "It looks like there are no more questions. So, we're ready to move on to our next item of importance for today. Ben, can you please go over what's in store for everyone at our next training?"

Ben nodded and stepped forward. "Sure thing. As Sam said, and as you'll see in your training schedule, we'll usually just meet as a group on Saturdays. But this week, we'll also be meeting tomorrow. We want to get you off to a good start with not just the running, but with all the triathlon disciplines. So next up, tomorrow, is biking."

CHAPTER 25

First Group Bike Ride —Or Not

BEN

HOW HAD HE GOTTEN ROPED INTO BEING THE ONE TO HELP BECCA WITH BIKING *today?* Ben asked himself. Most of the participants were in good shape and seemed comfortable with their bikes. Sam was already out on the trail with that group. There were just two people who needed extra help, with Becca being one of them.

He saw Adam start toward her, but he wasn't having any of that. He didn't want his little brother anywhere near Becca. Things were already complicated enough. He'd handle her himself.

Ben called out, "Hey Adam, I'll help her out. You see if you can help that other woman, would ya?" *Yeah*, he told himself, as he dragged his hand through his hair, it was his own fault he was the one having to help Becca out—or getting to help her out. Ben just wished he knew which it was.

"Sure, Ben," Adam said with a shrug.

Ben made his way toward Becca while also keeping an eye on his brother, hoping he hadn't sent Adam into a situation he wasn't ready for. Just as the thought crossed his mind, he saw Adam and the woman he'd gone to help give each other a smile, climb on their bikes, and head off down the trail. A satisfied smile crossed Ben's lips, proud that his brother had so adeptly been able to help that woman with whatever bike woe she'd been having. Now, he just needed to see what was up with Becca.

He approached her. "Becca," he said in as neutral of a tone as he could muster, "I didn't expect to see you here. How are you?"

"Good... Great... It's good to see you, Ben," she stammered.

"Is it?" he asked carefully. "It's been a while since our boat trip. I was surprised you didn't get back in touch." He pressed his lips together and shrugged nonchalantly. "I thought maybe you'd already jet-setted off to Washington, D.C."

"No...not yet," she said, worrying her bottom lip with her teeth. "I'm...I'm not sure yet when I'll be going. I just, well, it got pretty busy with...well, with work and all, I guess. But, I do want to thank you again for lunch...and for the boat ride. It was a wonderful day and....um...."

"Look, Becca," Ben finally said, knowing he needed to put her out of her misery. He couldn't let her stammer on awkwardly forever. If she wasn't interested, she wasn't interested. "You don't owe me an explanation. It was a great day, but we've both got busy lives. We're here now to train for a triathlon. So, how about we stick to that?"

"Sure...yeah. I guess so."

Ben gave her a brief smile. "So, tell me what's going on? Why aren't you out on your bike on the trail yet? Is there something I can help you with?"

"Yes," she said, not making eye contact with him, but instead looking down at her bike. "My chain has fallen off. See, right back here," she said, touching her finger to the chain. "It's not all the way around this circle-thing anymore."

She finally looked at him, her forehead creased with worry. A lock of hair blew across her face and as she lifted her hand to brush it away, it left a streak of bike grease on her cheek.

Ben chuckled and reached a hand out to her cheek but then pulled it back in quickly, taking a rigid stance while schooling his features. *What the hell was he doing? Hadn't he already learned his lesson?* Releasing a breath, he said, "Here, let me help you." He leaned over the bike and deftly slipped the chain back over the derailleur. He then held up the back of the bike and gave the wheel a spin. "There, all fixed."

"Thank you," Becca said, carefully taking the bike back from him and setting her leg over the top, ready to start her ride.

Ben hesitated, not wanting to prolong her agony—or his, but knowing he'd be remiss if he let her ride off on this bike. "Before you get started, Becca, I should tell you that this bike probably isn't going to be a good idea for you for this triathlon."

"What do you mean?" she asked, her voice rising an octave and her eyes tightening with concern.

"This bike is way too small for you. Plus, the derailleur is corroded. You also don't have any gears on this thing. The race course is mostly flat so that's probably not a big deal, but it won't make for a great ride. This bike is going to be a challenge for you. It could even cause you to get some posture-related injuries because of sizing. Have you thought about getting a new bike? I know you recently got your car set up to transport a bike. Does it have to be this one?" he asked gently now, knowing these words were not what she wanted to hear.

"How much does a new bike cost?" Becca asked, anxiously shifting from foot to foot.

"That really depends," Ben said truthfully. "Ideally, you would spend somewhere between five hundred to one thousand dollars for a decent bike for this type of race. They can get a lot more expensive than that; but you won't need anything real high end. You should be able to keep it at that lower end of the price spectrum. Although, if you need to get a new bike anyway, you might as well make it one you're going to love, and one that you can grow into if you decide to move up to more challenging races down the road."

"Oh...well, I'm thinking I can make do with this bike," Becca said, worrying her bottom lip between her teeth again. "Is there something I can do to get by with this one?"

"Maybe. It's going to cost you something, though. And it may cost more to fix this one than to just buy a new bike. You'll need some new parts, and then there's the cost of labor. No matter how much you spend, though, there's no way to fix this fit. This frame is expanded as far as it can go, and it's simply way too small for you."

Becca stood silently, cocking her head.

"I can give you some pointers on what to look for in a bike if you'd like. Would that help?" Ben suggested. He waited expectantly for her answer. Was this really that hard of a question? Did she want his help, or not?

He waited for what felt like an eternity. But she still said nothing. She just stood there, now rigid, and no longer with any hint of emotion. *What was going through that pretty little head of hers?* he thought with rising frustration.

"Look, Becca, it's up to you. If you want my help, just let me know. If you don't, there's not really much I can do about it." He knew his words had come out harsh. He hadn't meant them to, but she needed a new bike—this one was a mess. And he could help her...if she'd just let him. "Which is it, Becca? Do you want my help or not?"

Becca's lower lip quivered.

Oh crap, thought Ben. He took a good look at her face, noting the flush caused by his words now rushing into her cheeks, and felt a pang of guilt in the pit of his stomach. He much preferred when there was no emotion showing on her face. What had he done? He felt like a complete heel. He knew he wouldn't have used such a harsh tone with any of the other participants. And now she had that same lost and broken look she'd had when he first met her at the U-Haul counter. The frustration he'd felt only moments ago morphed into him now wanting to shield her from whatever hardship she seemed to be dealing with. He wanted to see that light come back into her eyes—the one he'd been able to coax out of her during their lunch.

Enough, he scolded himself. He'd already tried that, and where had it gotten him? All Becca had done so far was serve as a distraction. Unfortunately, that thought sent images racing through his brain of her soft lips willingly parting for his kisses, and her eyes smoldering with desire as he'd stroked her peaches and cream-colored skin....

Ugh! Ben shook his head and blew out a heavy gust of air, trying desperately to refocus. He needed to keep this professional. He needed to make this coach-trainee thing work—for both of them. Becca had made her choice already on the personal front when she hadn't gotten back in touch with him after their night on his boat. If he'd known this is how that night would turn out, and that she'd then turn up as one of the participants in this triathlon training to add another layer of complication to his already confused emotions, he never would have let that night happen, and he certainly wouldn't have agreed to help

Sam with the coaching. But it was too late for second-guessing now. She might've bailed on him after their night on the boat, but he couldn't bail on Sam. He deserved better than that—and so did all of the other participants. They were here for more than just themselves. They were here for people like his sister.

The pain in Ben's stomach intensified, and he quickly tossed that thought aside. He'd better get his head on straight. He had a responsibility to Sam and to Adam and to his company. And yes, to this team —a team that included Becca. He just needed to remember that she was just one of its members—and not someone to be treated any differently than any of the others.

"It's okay, Becca. Don't worry," he said, gently now, resigned to his fate and now determined to help her in whatever way he could, whether or not she wanted him to. "We can see about fixing up this bike or I can help you get another one. There's no need to decide today. We'll see what we can do to get this one into good enough shape so you can get in some riding while you think about it. And if you decide you want to look at new bikes, just let me know. I'll go with you and help you. Okay?"

Becca kept her head down, but nodded her head briefly.

"I know a great bike shop," he continued, now just wanting to see her smile again. "They'll let us spend as much time as we want looking without pressuring you to buy. That way you can get more information so you can do whatever you decide works best for you. We'll figure this out."

Despite Becca's lowered head, Ben could see a tear hanging at the lower lid of her right eye, threatening to slide down her cheek at any moment. His hand twitched. He wanted to reach up and wipe that tear away....

Voices came to them, floating softly on the breeze from down the trail. The first group of riders was coming back in, followed closely by Sam and Carmen. Becca quickly reached up and wiped the tear away as the riders approached.

"Woohoo!" yelled Carmen. "That was so much fun!"

Three other participants were right behind them, also whooping and hollering and with big grins on their faces. Adam brought up the rear, laughing at everyone's enthusiasm and clearly enjoying himself.

Becca sniffed and pulled herself up straighter. "Thanks, Ben. I'll think about it. I really appreciate your help—again."

Carmen pulled up next to the picnic table where Becca and Ben were standing. "That was awesome! Becca, did you get out for a ride? How's your bike?" Carmen paused and looked more intently at Becca's face. "Are you okay?" she asked.

She turned to look at Ben with what he was sure was suspicion. Did this woman know about his and Becca's weekend? She was clearly Becca's friend. And if she knew about it, how had Becca portrayed it? Ben tried to school his features and wipe away any remnant of what he was sure looked like guilt. But why was he the bad guy here? He hadn't been the one to disappear into the early morning mist, never to be heard from again.

"All good, Carmen." Becca jumped in quickly, giving Ben a moment to better compose his features. "It just turns out my bike is more far gone than I'd realized. Ben is going to help me figure it out."

Carmen turned her gaze away from Becca to give him a thoughtful look. Ben felt a flush creep into his cheeks, and he ran his hand through his hair in a nervous gesture. If Carmen knew about their night on the boat together, that was going to make his goal of keeping everything professional a lot more difficult.

CHAPTER 26
Calories and Quesadillas

BECCA AND CARMEN MADE THEIR WAY BACK TO THE parking lot with their bicycles in tow.

"That's him, isn't it? That's Ben Morgan—the architect and developer, the guy from the boat?" Carmen asked.

"Shhhh...." Becca said, indicating, with a tilt of her head, the other participants who were walking toward the parking lot alongside them.

Carmen sighed and looked over her shoulder to where Ben, Sam, and Adam stood in conversation near the picnic table, which was still loaded with snacks.

"Carmen, don't look!" Becca said in a worried whisper. "Hurry. Unlock the door!" Becca pleaded, now standing next to the passenger side door of Carmen's old beat up Honda.

"Are you forgetting the bikes? We've got to get them onto the bike rack. We can't just drive away—or run away—without them," Carmen said, as she lifted her bike onto the rack attached to the back of her car. She then held her hand out for Becca's.

Becca's bike began to swerve out of her control in her rush to guide it by its seat with just one hand toward Carmen. She grabbed the handlebar with her other hand to catch it just before it fell. With some relief, she transferred the bike into Carmen's control. She then bobbled almost imperceptibly from one foot to the other as Carmen strapped her bike onto the rack next. Becca nervously flitted her eyes to where the three men still stood.

"Now who's looking?" asked Carmen. "What happened back there, anyway?"

"Carmen... just hurry... *please*."

Carmen pushed the button on her car's key fob, eliciting a soft beep as the car's doors unlocked. Becca's body stiffened at the sound, and she quickly glanced back toward the picnic table to see if the group of coaches had heard the noise. Just as Becca's eyes landed on the three men, Ben swiveled his head toward her. He nodded his head briefly in acknowledgement before spinning his attention back to Sam and Adam.

"Oh. My. God! Carmen—can we just get out of here! Please?" Becca said, as she pulled the car door open and slid into the passenger seat. "That man must hate me."

"He does not hate you," Carmen said, as she slid into the driver's seat and started the car. "How can he hate you? You don't even know each other? It was one night, Becca. Now who's being dramatic?" she admonished. "I get that it's awkward. But that'll pass. What did you tell him, anyway, about not contacting him? Did he ask?"

"Yes. And I didn't tell him anything."

"Becca..."

"Carmen, no! I couldn't bear the pitying looks he'd give me. I couldn't stand that. And I don't want you to tell him either. Okay?"

"But Becca..."

"Promise me, Carmen. Please."

"Okay, okay. I promise," Carmen said, as she guided her car toward the parking lot exit and out onto the larger roadway beyond. "So...want to get lunch? Pretzels and Gatorade are great, but I'm starving. And you heard Sam, we're supposed to *fuel up*. Do you think that means we get to eat whatever we want? This is going to be great! How about a burger?"

A small smile escaped Becca's lips. "First, I don't think one mile gives us carte blanche on calories. Second, thanks for trying."

"Did it work?"

"No."

"It worked a little. I got a smile. Admit it." She grinned.

"Maybe I shouldn't be doing this triathlon," Becca said, ignoring Carmen's comment. "Maybe we could switch to the half marathon? We'd still be living up to our commitment. We'd just have a different coach. Let's do that...okay?"

"You are kidding, right, Becca? This is the coolest thing ever. Doesn't a half marathon sound boring now, compared with a triathlon?"

"You thought training for the half marathon was the coolest thing ever when we walked into that info session on Thursday night," Becca reminded her.

"That was before I knew about the triathlon. There's no going back now. The seed has been planted, and it's grown into a full-blown obsession. One that cannot be denied!"

"You are such a drama queen!" Becca sighed.

"And that bike ride today—that was amazing. It was so much fun. And just think, this was probably meant to be all along...us, doing a triathlon. It's fate! You got that bike hitch installed just in time. And Ben was there to help you get it! See, what did I tell you? It's fate."

"Except that my bike is apparently not what it needs to be."

"Yeah. What happened back there? How come you never got on your bike?" Carmen glanced over at Becca with a look of concern. "You looked like you were about to cry when I rode up. Was he being a jerk? Cause if he was, he's going to get a piece of my mind."

"Carmen! You wouldn't!"

"Yeah, I would. No one messes with my friends. Hey, where am I driving to? Are we getting a burger? How about we go to my house instead? That way we can save up for some new biking clothes. You definitely need to come shopping with me, because I found some great stuff." Carmen motioned toward the new bike jersey she was wearing. "I can make us quesadillas and show you the other new stuff I bought."

"Just how much did you buy? I thought you just bought the one outfit you're wearing now."

"Only one other," she answered sheepishly. "Wait till you see it, though. You're gonna love it! You should have come with me, Becca. There are so many cute biking clothes out there and all kinds of cool gear. Who knew? Enough about that, though, back to Ben," Carmen said, as she steered the car toward her own apartment, the decision already made apparently that they were going to Carmen's place.

Becca didn't complain. Carmen's quesadillas were amazing, and her mouth was already watering at the thought.

"What did happen back there?" Carmen pushed.

"He said I need a new bike."

"Well, your bike does kinda look like it's been sitting in a garage unloved for a decade, or a few decades... Oh, wait!" Carmen said sarcastically. "That's because it has."

"Carmen, you know I have to watch my finances."

Carmen glanced at her with an admonishing look on her face. "You should buy yourself a new bike, Becca. Those bills won't get paid off immediately, anyway, and you need to treat yourself to something. A bike would be a good present to commemorate the start of your new cancer-free life. You don't have to buy the Taj Mahal, it's just a bike. How expensive can that be? I've got to give it to Ben on this one, that bike you have sure doesn't look like it should be racing in a triathlon. Oooohhh, a triathlon!" she squealed. "Can you believe we're doing a triathlon? How cool is that? You aren't going to bail on me, are you? You can't bail on me. And switching to the half-marathon just won't cut it now that we know what's out there waiting for us. It would be like eating diet ice-cream when we could eat a pint of Ben & Jerry's. And I need you out there with me. It's kinda scary, right?" Carmen said, this time with a hint of nervousness. "Scary-good, though. And I want my best friend there beside me for this grand adventure."

Becca sighed and looked at Carmen. How could she let her best friend down? Carmen was so excited, and she'd said *yes* to the triathlon. She couldn't back out now. They'd been on so many adventures together, and she knew Carmen missed that. Becca missed it too. And, if she were honest with herself, she really wanted to do this triathlon. She wanted to feel strong again and ready to face the world —as well as new challenges. "I'm still in, Carmen," she assured her. "But how am I going to deal with the Ben thing? He must think I'm a horrible person. And he was kinda harsh with me today."

"He was? What do you mean? He has no right to be harsh with you!"

"I think, maybe, he hates me. I can't even imagine what he must think of me. I walked off with a perfect stranger, spent the night on his boat with him, and then disappeared."

"Maybe you should be mad at him for not tracking you down."

"And how was he supposed to do that? I never even gave him my phone number—even after spending the entire night on his boat." Becca felt her cheeks flame, no doubt into the color of ripe tomatoes.

"I am so proud of you," Carmen said in a dreamy voice with a hand over her heart. "You grabbed him by those hunky muscles of his and had your way with him—well, almost," she teased. "Just like I now want you to grab onto this new lease on life you've been given," she added in a more serious tone. "It's time to get back into the game, Becca. Step one is this triathlon. And, who knows, maybe you can enjoy the coach too—not just the coaching," she said with a wicked grin.

"Carmen! Even if he does forgive me for disappearing without a trace, he's off limits now. He's our coach."

"So? It's not like you're a schoolgirl. You're an adult and so is he, and this is just a fun diversion, not some formal classroom setting. Ohhh, that's it! This can be your coming out summer fling. Can you picture it? There we are on our new streamlined racing bikes, wearing our cute, new bike jerseys with the padded shorts that puff up our tushes, our hair flying behind us as we fly through the course."

Becca burst out laughing, failing miserably at all attempts to look stern. "What am I going to do with you? Didn't I just say he's our coach and he's off limits? The bike thing sounds awesome, though. I'll give you that."

"He is not off-limits. And did you see his face? When I rode up to you two—both of you still standing next to that picnic table—you should have seen him. He looked as flustered as a schoolboy with a crush on the most beautiful girl in school. Whoops—wait," Carmen said with a tinge of embarrassment. "Forget that; let me come up with another analogy. To your point about him being your coach, maybe a schoolgirl comparison is not such a good one. Anyhow, this could be a fantastical summer fling—you know, between two grown up and consenting adults." She flashed Becca a grin.

"Oh, geez. See what I mean, Carmen? This is not a good idea; it's just plain old awkward all around."

"No it's not! You said it was a magical night. Maybe that's what he thinks too. He's probably just as unsure about exactly what happened between the two of you as you are. Let's just take it one step at a time and see what happens. So, first question: what are you going to do about your bike?"

"Good question." Becca sighed. "I have no idea."

CHAPTER 27

Work, Work, Work

IT WAS ALREADY FRIDAY AND ALMOST LUNCH TIME. THE week had gone quickly for Becca. She got her bike training ride done during the week, but she'd done it by herself at her office's on-site gym on a stationary bike. Luckily, tomorrow's group training didn't include a bike ride, so she had a little more time to decide on whether she needed a new bike by pushing the decision back another week. She felt frustrated at her lack of ability to make decisions when it came to her personal life. Was it because she was just out of practice? Had she put her personal life on hold for so long that she no longer knew how to have one? It was something Becca knew she needed to take care of in order to embrace what being cancer-free felt like.

It had been a pretty good week all-in-all. She'd gotten a lot done at work this week, despite her many lapses in concentration. When it came to her job, Becca usually had no trouble concentrating or on making decisions. But this week had been different. She attempted to pull her mind away from her bike dilemma—and away from thoughts of Ben—and tried to focus on the spreadsheet in front of her. But it was no use. It was Friday, and she wanted to think about her weekend.

I don't want to self-exile myself to my apartment tonight, Becca thought with a wave of loneliness. All that was in store for her there was the pile of mail that had accumulated over the week, mostly consisting of bills. Where were the interesting pieces of mail? Where were her friends tonight? Were they missing their old happy hours? It would be so much fun to see them all again, she thought wistfully.

Despite formally being in remission and feeling the best she'd felt in a long time, Becca hadn't pushed to restart the Friday night happy hour events. She'd been afraid to jump back in. She wasn't sure there was solid ground anywhere around her yet—at least not enough to land that jump. *Did any of her friends get together anymore?* Becca couldn't seem to let the thought go. She looked at her computer screen and tried to focus, but the numbers just floated across the screen in front of her. So, instead, she pulled out her cell phone and texted Carmen.

Becca: It's Friday. Are we on for happy hour tonight?

No response. Becca looked at her phone again...and again. Still no response. Carmen usually had her cell phone always at the ready. How come it was taking her so long to respond? Maybe she was in a meeting. Although, even when in a meeting, it wasn't unlike Carmen to respond quickly. Instead of unnecessarily panicking, Becca went back to working on the spreadsheet sitting open on her computer screen. She'd give Carmen a little more time to respond.

One hour later, almost to the minute, Becca looked at her cell phone screen again. Still no answer.

Becca: Are you there? Did you get my text? Where are you? What do you think? Happy hour tonight?

This time, a response came back almost immediately.

Carmen: Our spot. Now? Need a walk. Okay?

Becca quickly typed a reply as she simultaneously stood up from her desk and grabbed her purse.

Becca: Yes! On my way.

Becca turned to Jenn. "I'm just going for a quick walk to clear my head. Be right back."

When Jenn gave a nod of acknowledgment, Becca headed toward the bank of elevators that would take her down to the lobby and to her and Carmen's usual work-day emergency meeting place. When Becca arrived, Carmen was already standing next to the small fountain in front of the building where Becca worked.

Carmen looked more agitated than Becca had seen her in a long time. "What's up, Carmen? Is everything okay? Did something happen?"

Carmen nodded, and in a stream of words that just kept coming, she shared, "In our staff meeting this morning, my boss said our company is going to be laying people off. We've got several marketing-related departments in the company, and my boss said they're going to streamline them all into one and won't need as many people. I know they'll still need layout artists, like me, but there are three creative teams that include that function. I'm freaking out. Do you think I could lose my job? I know this isn't my dream job, but I have a great boss, and I like my colleagues. It's interesting work, and I know I'm lucky to have this job."

Becca held her hand up, palm out, urging Carmen to slow down. "Hold on, let's think this through. Did your boss say you are getting laid off or that the company is just generally considering laying people off?"

"Well,...he said it isn't a sure thing yet when or how many people will be laid off. They expect to begin laying off next week. He did say he didn't think it would be anyone from our department—at least not yet. You know I'm not a good saver like you, Becca. I have some money set aside but not enough to last very long. What if I get laid off next week?"

"Take a deep breath, sweetie. Now let it out slowly. You know the drill; you've walked me through de-stressing many times over the past two years." Becca softened the advice with a small smile. "First, it sounds like you are not immediately at risk. And often, companies provide some sort of severance package when they lay people off. Sometimes they even offer career counseling to help people find new jobs. There could also be an unemployment package available. So, for right now, I wouldn't panic. Just let it play out, and we can keep talking it through to make sure you're ready *if* it happens. You'll be fine, Carmen. You know we're all here for you no matter what happens, right?"

Carmen's shoulders fell as she let out another deep breath, and she reached over to give Becca a hug. "Thanks, you're right—it's going to be okay, no matter what happens." Taking and releasing another breath, Carmen switched gears, already seemingly over the crisis for now and said, "So, about that happy hour—do you really want to go tonight? It's been ages since we've all met up. And, selfishly, I admit, I can't think of a better way to decompress from the day I've had. How about I send out a group text to see if we get any takers? I know it's last minute, but you never know. Maybe everyone else had a stressful week, too, and would love to get together to decompress. And even if they can't come, you and I could still go."

"That sounds perfect. Do you want me to help contact anyone?"

Carmen shook her head. "No, I'll send a group text to our usuals. If you think of anyone additional you want to invite, don't hesitate."

"Great!" said Becca with a smile. "See you tonight at 5:30 p.m., no matter what. For now, though, I guess we'd better get back to work so we can pay for those drinks. And, Carmen, just remember you're going to be just fine."

CHAPTER 28

Happy Hour

BECCA RUSHED ALONG THE SIDEWALK TOWARD LUNA'S PUB. She'd been anxious but excited all afternoon, waiting for the clock to get to 5:00 p.m. Then, somehow, she'd gotten her head back in the game and lost track of time. It was now 5:20 p.m.; she needed to get moving. It would probably only be Carmen tonight, and after the news she'd been delivered, Becca didn't want to leave her best friend alone at the bar. Although, she thought with a wry grin, she knew better than to worry about Carmen. She'd probably be surrounded by a group of strangers within minutes of arriving, whether or not Becca showed up. No doubt that group of strangers would be best friends by now and chortling with laughter from one of Carmen's stories.

Ten minutes later, Becca opened the door to Luna's Pub, her eyes searching the bar area for Carmen. When she spotted her, she gasped and put a hand to her chest, feeling her mouth drop open. Carmen was sitting at a large, round bar table at the back of the room. There were four others already at the table with her—Eileen, Anna, Stacey, and Natalie.

Carmen lifted her head and looked around the room as she picked up her beer glass to take a sip. A smile lit up her face as she saw Becca in the doorway. Carmen stood up and waved excitedly for Becca to come and join them. As she did so, all eyes around the table lifted to see what Carmen was waving at. When the other women saw Becca, they also started waving excitedly.

Becca felt her lips turn up in a gigantic smile. It felt like she was coming home. Before she even reached the table, her friends were jumping up to give her hugs, everyone talking at once in a bubbly hum.

The group eventually settled in to update each other on their lives and share stories, just as they had on so many past Friday evenings. Then the focus shifted to Becca and Carmen's newest crazy adventure.

"I can't believe you and Carmen are going to do a triathlon, Becca!" exclaimed Eileen. "You are truly the most amazing person I know!"

"I see Carmen is already telling tales," Becca said with a smile.

"Is it true?" asked Eileen. "I mean, I know Carmen's good at story-telling, but the thing that makes them so good is that they're pretty much always true. You two are always doing something crazy—or, at least, you were before..." Eileen ducked her head in embarrassment as her voice trailed off.

"Not only is it true," said Carmen, quickly stepping in to pick up the conversation, "but we have two—not one, but two—hunky coaches!"

"Ohhhh...now we get it. Is it too late for me to join?" Stacey laughed.

"I don't know. We're only one week into it, so I bet you could. What do you all say? Anyone else keen to get in with us?" Carmen asked. "I hadn't really thought that you all might want to do this, but that would be fantastic. Any takers?"

There was a moment of awkwardness where they all remained silent in the face of Carmen's pleading eyes. Then everyone burst into laughter.

When the giggles died down, Anna said, "Not me. I don't even run, let alone bike or swim. You're on your own for this one. I'll be cheering you both on, though. Hey, how does that work? Can we go on race day? I could be your statistician."

"I don't think we need a statistician for this race," said Carmen gently.

"Oh..." Anna's face fell, then she asked hesitantly, "Do you maybe need a cheering section?"

"I would think so. We'll definitely be needing you for something, Anna," Carmen said kindly. "Now, how about we get these happy hours back on track so we can keep everyone updated as we work our way through to race day. We're only just starting out, so we really aren't sure what we need yet, or even what to expect."

"Now we're talking!" said Stacey. "I'm not in for swimming, biking, or running, but I'm definitely in for our Friday happy hours. I've missed seeing all of you and hearing about your crazy endeavors." She lifted her glass, and everyone answered by lifting her own glass and joining in to clink them all together.

"So, tell us about these coaches," said Stacey, wiggling her eyebrows. "Just how hunky are they, and is there an extra one for me?"

Becca tucked her chin to her chest and lowered her eyes as she felt a flush creep up her face.

"Ohhh! I saw that, Becca. Do tell," said Natalie.

"There's really nothing to tell," Becca stammered.

"I wouldn't be so sure," said Carmen. "One of those two coaches can't seem to take his eyes off Becca."

"I think he's just trying to make sure he knows where I am so he can keep his distance," Becca scoffed.

"No way," said Carmen. "I saw those glances he kept sending your way when he thought no one was watching. That guy is definitely into you."

"Why in the world would he want to keep his distance from you, Becca?" asked Eileen. "Didn't this training just start last weekend? You can't have done anything to cross him already. And anyhow, it wouldn't be you who would do anything wrong. Carmen, on the other hand..." She trailed off with a grin before sobering and adding to Becca, "But not you. You're too sweet and straight on perfect. No one could ever be mad at you."

Carmen and Becca exchanged glances.

"They have a bit of a history from before this whole triathlon thing started," said Carmen.

"Carmen!" admonished Becca with a stern look.

"It's no big deal," Carmen continued cautiously. Turning back to the group, she elaborated, "They just happened to meet about a month ago when Becca was getting a hitch for her car so she could transport her bike around. They went to lunch and..." Becca looked at Carmen nervously, catching her eye again before Carmen finished her sentence. "...Ya know. It's no big deal. I think he wanted Becca to get back in touch with him after that, but she never did, and he may not be too happy with her about that. That guy definitely has the hots for you, Becca."

Becca's face turned from pink to crimson, which clearly did not go unnoticed based on her friends' pointed looks.

"Are you going to go out with him, Becca?" asked Stacey.

"Of course not. For one thing, he's my coach. And, for another, it doesn't make sense to start anything. I'm finally ready to get back on track. You know that involves moving to Washington, D.C."

"Since when does moving to D.C. mean you can't hook up with a hunky looking guy?" asked Stacey. "I say go for it. You don't have to commit your life to him—just try him on for size and take him out for a spin...get it? Bike riding. Spin." She winked, smiling. "Just have fun!"

Everyone laughed as Becca rolled her eyes at Stacey.

"Speaking of rides, didn't Ben say you need to replace that old junker of a bike of yours?" Carmen asked pointedly.

Becca sighed. "Yes, he thinks I need a new bike," she told her friends. "He said the one I have is too far gone and that it's also too small for me. I'm thinking I can probably make do, though. It sounds like it could get pricey, and I've got mountains of health care bills to deal with. I can't deny I'm a little nervous, though. I need to make sure I can actually do this whole race thing. I don't want to fail because of the bike. That would be a bummer. I just don't know yet what I'm going to do."

"What about the cancer, Becca? Have you looked at the science? Did your doctor say you're cleared for this much exercise?" asked Anna with concern.

A palpable hush came over the group, and all eyes looked to Becca, waiting for her answer. Leave it to Anna to point out the elephant in the room with an innocent but well-placed question. *How could you not love that about Anna?* Becca thought with a smile.

Becca considered her response carefully before answering, "Well, this is actually a good thing." At her answer, she felt a bolt of surprise, and she suddenly realized she was glad Anna had asked the question. "I'm really out of shape. But Dr. Murtha says exercise is important from both a physical and a mental standpoint. It's an important part of the healing process right now. This training comes at a good time. It will keep me focused and force me to get out and exercise. And I'll have a support group there to help keep me on track, especially since Carmen will be there with me the whole way." Becca looked toward Carmen. "I have to thank Carmen for finding this opportunity and for encouraging us to sign up." She felt her eyes tear up with emotion.

Carmen's face melted and answering tears shimmered in her eyes as Becca continued, "It's hard to step into this after everything that's happened. But, I think the timing is good. I know I haven't kept you all in the loop through the whole treatment journey. It just felt too all-consuming, and I really didn't want you all to have to delve into that mud pit with me. But I did join a patient support group during the treatment portion. And Dr. Murtha says I'm in remission now, and it would be good to get out and get some exercise. She said it will make the transition from treatment and into this new phase—where I'm in remission and getting back to *normal* life—a lot better and a lot easier. Of course, just walking is probably enough." Becca gave Carmen a sideways glance. "Maybe going into training for a triathlon—even a short, low-key one as we're assured by the Leukemia Society and the coaches this one will be—is a bit of overkill. You all know Carmen, though. If it isn't something new, she probably isn't interested. And how can I refuse that face over there?" Becca waved her hand at Carmen and chuckled at her best friend's shining eyes and hopeful expression. "So, this is a good thing, a very good thing—I hope." Becca ended with a shrug.

"Have I told you all lately how wise Becca is?" Carmen said, adding levity to her voice. She was always up for trying to help lighten the mood. Carmen gave her a big grin. "Yep, she knows it's always best to listen to her best friend. Love you, Becca."

"Love you right back," said Becca with a smile.

With concerns allayed, the conversation turned to other things, including, eventually, to jobs—and to potential layoffs. Becca was relieved to have the focus move off her. But that conversation had been a good one. It made her realize just how much she really wanted to do this triathlon—and just how great it was to have her friends around her again to help process life's ups and downs. Hopefully their conversation would now do the same for Carmen and help her come to terms with her concerns over her job security.

Becca looked around the table at all her friends, feeling more relaxed and hopeful than she had all week. She felt a tingle of excitement about tomorrow's training, suddenly realizing she was looking forward to it.

CHAPTER 29

First Swim

"Ask him, Becca."

"Shhh!" she answered, jabbing her elbow into Carmen's side.

"Ow!"

"Do you two have a question?" asked Ben, as he came up behind them.

"Ummmm..." said Becca.

"Not sure how to answer that one," Ben said with a smile.

Was he teasing her? Or was he making fun of her? Becca felt unsettled at his nearness. "No, no questions. Um...aren't we needing to get started?"

"Okay, listen up!" Sam called from across the pool deck. "Everyone gather round please. It's time to get started on our first group swim training."

Thank goodness, thought Becca. She followed along with the rest of the participants as they moved toward Sam, who was now standing at the shallow end of the pool. It was a reprieve from her conversation with Ben—at least a temporary one.

"As with our first run and bike group trainings," Sam continued, "this first group swim is mostly about getting acclimated and getting a better understanding of what's included in the swim portion of your event. We'll go over things like goggles and swim caps. We'll also go over distances and get in some laps. No hard-core training today. Just getting started and getting acclimated is enough. In later weeks we'll go over some of the really fun stuff, like alligator eyes and open water swim starts." Sam gave them a mischievous grin before adding, "More on that in coming weeks. For now, we're just going to start out in the shallow end of the pool and then get some laps in to make sure everyone has a comfort level with the water. Go ahead and pick a lane and jump in."

The next hour was taken up with getting acclimated to the pool and learning swim drills. The activity required almost all of Becca's attention. She'd been okay at swimming as a kid and was comfortable in a swimming pool, but all of her swimming had always been focused on play, never on competition.

"Great job today, everyone," said Sam, after he'd called everyone back to the wall at the shallow end of the pool. "As you know, our next group training isn't until Saturday, one week from today. Please be sure to follow your training schedule either on your own or with friends throughout the week. We'll see you again next weekend. In the meantime, if any of you have questions or concerns, please be sure to let either me or Ben know. You all have our email addresses in your training books."

As the group dissipated toward the locker room, Becca approached Ben. She'd decided before she arrived today that she needed help with this bike decision. Ben was her coach and the expert and he'd offered to help. And it didn't need to be awkward between them anymore, she admonished herself. He'd told her straight out she didn't owe him any explanations, and they could leave it at that. And she'd agreed. He was now simply her coach, nothing more, and she needed her coach's help.

Becca had no idea what was needed in a bike for a triathlon. She also didn't know if she was ready to spend money on a new bike right now, but she did at least want to see what her options were. Just before the swim session, Becca had concluded that she just had to take him up on his offer but make it clear that that's all it was—a trainee asking a coach for an expert opinion and assistance in purchasing a new bike. As a result, she'd been screwing up her courage during their whole swim session today. It was now or never, she thought, as she saw him heading for the exit.

"Um...Ben?" Becca called out, quickening her step to catch up with him. "I was wondering about what you said last week and..."

"Yes?"

Becca hesitated. Ben now stood in front of her, giving her his full attention and patiently waiting for her to continue. He stood tall and composed, the exact opposite of what Becca was feeling.

"Well,...um..." she stammered, kicking herself for her lack of composure, "...if you're still willing to help me look at bikes...I mean...if you're too busy, that's okay. I don't want to take up too much of your time. I know you're really busy with work...."

Ben raised an eyebrow. "Do you mean you want help finding a new bike?"

"Yes...maybe. Uh, I'm not sure if I can get a new bike. But I recognize I need to see what my options are in terms of getting my bike fixed or getting a new one."

Ben pursed his lips and gave her a thoughtful look.

Becca's insides twisted into knots. She shouldn't have asked. This wasn't going well. Maybe he wouldn't even agree to help her now.

But then Ben said gently, "I'd be happy to help you, Becca."

A tingle of excitement went through her; however, the knots in her stomach tightened even further. But this time, a traitorous sizzle of longing accompanied the growing queasiness in her stomach.

"How about tomorrow?" asked Ben. "I'm meeting some contractors later today, and I have some work to do in the morning, but I can help you in the afternoon. Does that work?"

Becca felt her insides melt with relief. "Are you sure?" She immediately derided herself at the stupid question. Why would she ask him if he was sure, when he was probably already on the fence about being willing to help her out? She didn't want to give him a reason to say no. Had she just given him that opening?

"Absolutely sure. How about 3:00 p.m. at Chad's Bike Shop? I'll text you the address. That is, if you're okay with me contacting you on your cell phone?" he asked with a slight challenge in his voice.

"Of course. No problem," said Becca. "I can give it to you now."

"Okay, let me go grab my phone."

As Becca watched him walk across the pool deck to where his clothes, bag, and other belongings were laid out on a bench, she couldn't help but notice how his body moved in his tight-fitting racing swimsuit. She remembered running her hands up his arms and over those biceps. She'd wanted more that night on the boat, and she knew he did too. But she hadn't been ready for more, and he'd respected that.

Becca sighed, now more confused than ever. Ben had been a perfect gentleman, never pressuring her. It had truly been a magical night. She'd told him so, and she'd meant it…and then she'd never contacted him again. No wonder he was running hot and cold with her. Maybe she owed it to him to let him know why she hadn't given him her contact information. And then what? Could she just have something casual—try him on for size, as Stacey advised? She'd done some dating back in college, none of it ever very serious, but she'd never gone into a relationship thinking it would be casual. Maybe that would be just fine with Ben, a temporary fling with no strings attached?

But she knew she didn't want that. And even if Ben wanted something more, Becca wouldn't allow for any more complications that could derail her from achieving her goal. *And Ben would be more than a complication,* she thought. She ran her arms down her sides trying to dampen down the sensations tingling across her now highly sensitized skin.

So, why tell him? There was no point. He already had enough reason to treat her differently from her teammates. Becca didn't want to give him another one. She wanted to be seen as *normal* during this whole triathlon experience—not as *the woman with cancer.* Which is exactly why she hadn't told him about it and why she'd sworn all of her friends, not just Carmen, to secrecy during happy hour last night. None of them had been thrilled about making that promise, but at least they'd agreed.

"What's your cell number?" Ben asked, now standing in front of her with cell phone in hand.

Becca gave him her number, and they agreed to meet at Chad's Bike Shop at 3:00 p.m.

"Be sure to bring your current bike with you tomorrow," Ben recommended. "Chad's the owner of the shop. He'll be able to take a quick look at your bike and give you a better assessment than me of what's involved to get it back into shape."

"No problem—now that I have that hitch and bike rack set up on my car," said Becca with a shy smile. She knew she was playing with fire by throwing in a reminder of the day they'd met but somehow wasn't able to stop herself. "See you tomorrow."

CHAPTER 30

Butterflies

BEN

As Becca turned to walk away, Ben thought of the smile that had just crossed her face. He felt a thrill go through him at the knowledge that he'd been the one to coax that out of her by agreeing to help her out tomorrow. He must be crazy. But it sure felt worth it right now.

Had he read her wrong all this time? They hadn't known each other from Adam, he thought with a laugh at his own unintended pun, before that fateful weekend meeting in—of all places—a U-Haul store. *That's the last place he ever expected to be hitching up with a woman.* He laughed to himself again at the pun. Well, at least he could laugh at the situation, if nothing else.

Ben knew it was dangerous to think of Becca as anything other than a trainee. He'd be better served to remember she was just another woman who would want more than he could give. Although, what exactly did she want? At the thought, he felt even more baffled, because the truth was, she hadn't even contacted him after their weekend together. Usually, his interactions with women included them hounding him. Ben scratched his head. Had she known he was going to be the coach for this triathlon? Is that why she was here? No. He remembered the look on her face when he'd appeared on that first day of training. She'd looked just as surprised as he'd felt.

Ben just couldn't figure her out. One moment she was delightfully shy and the next, she was confident and determined. He'd seen that complex character at the U-Haul store, and he'd seen it again today. He'd also seen it during their *magical* night. Becca had been shy, hesitant, and sweet at first. But she'd clearly delighted in their boating adventure—even to the point of staying the night.

Hmm, who was she really? And could he afford to find out? Ben felt the need to be cautious. He didn't want to tee up some emotional mess that spilled over and sidetracked his goal of reconnecting with Adam or of building up the new Pittsburgh arm of his company. But as he headed toward his truck, Ben realized it was already too late for that, because he was supposed to be meeting Jason at the condo-office right now. They needed to get ready for their first meeting with a couple of Fischer Industries' lead contractors tomorrow morning. It was a huge account, and both he and Jason didn't want to mess this up. They still had to hone the first draft of their building design documents if they were to have them in tip-top shape and ready for the discussion at tomorrow morning's meeting.

CHAPTER 31
Chad's Bike Shop

"Hi," said Becca, as Ben approached her where she stood outside Chad's Bike shop.

"Hi. Ready to check out some bikes?"

"Absolutely. I'm actually pretty excited about it. I'm not sure about those price tags you were talking about, though. I don't think—no, let me rephrase that. I didn't know what I didn't know when Carmen talked me into signing up for this triathlon. I'm glad she did. But I think a new bike is going to be a little pricier than I'd realized."

"Don't worry about that just yet. Let's see what Chad has to say about your current bike first." Ben held the door open for her and gestured her to go on ahead of him into the shop.

As Becca wheeled her bike in, she was immediately greeted by a nice-looking man who looked as though he was in his early thirties, the same age as Ben.

"Hi, I'm Chad. It's great to meet you, Becca. Ben called me yesterday and let me know you'd be in today. He said you're interested in looking at your options regarding your existing bike versus potentially a new bike for the tri in July. Is that correct?"

"Yes, exactly," said Becca.

"Great. First thing then is for me to look at your current bike. I'll also want to get some of your measurements so we can get you a good

176

fit, either with your existing bike or with a new one. Where do you want to start? With measurements, looking at your current bike, or looking at new bikes?"

"Maybe we can start by looking at my current bike?"

"Sure. I'll take that off your hands right now then," Chad said, as he reached for the bike Becca was holding. "Why don't you and Ben check things out. Ben knows his way around a bike really well, so he can provide some expert advice to get you started."

After Chad disappeared into a back room with Becca's bike, Ben ushered her around the shop, pointing out all sorts of cycling paraphernalia she'd never known existed.

"Ideally, you'll want something light and streamlined. Like this one here." Ben pointed to a bike amidst a long line of others located against the back wall of the shop. "Go ahead and pick it up," he urged.

Becca reached over and lifted the bike off the ground. "Oh my gosh. This is so much lighter than my bike," she said in amazement.

"Bikes have come a long way since someone initially bought that bike of yours. But this one's not really a fair comparison. It's top of the line and one a professional racer would look at. But you can get that same feel to a certain extent in a lower end model. That's what we'll try to target today. I'll show you some options that would give you great performance in a realistically priced model. Let's head over to the other end of the shop. We don't need to be looking in this crazy high-priced section."

Becca slowed as they walked through a section of cycling attire. "This is cute," she said, reaching out to run her hand along a brightly colored top. "It's like the top Carmen just bought. It's got the longer length and pockets in the back. She called it a jersey."

"Yes," said Ben. "There's more to those jerseys than you might think. They're designed to reduce wind drag while you ride, and they're made of wicking material to help keep you dry. They're also cut differently than a regular shirt, especially in the shoulders and in the back, to give you a better fit while leaning forward over your bike in a riding position. They usually have pockets in the back where you can store things like food or gloves that you can easily reach while riding." Ben paused for a moment, then asked, "Carmen—that's your friend from middle school?"

His tone was thoughtful but held no other inflections, leaving Becca wondering at his reference to their lunch conversation on that first day they'd met. She'd thought they were going to leave any discussion of that weekend alone. It was inevitable, though, wasn't it? It wasn't like they could just erase that day or that night. And she truly didn't want to. She just...she just needed them to move on from it.

"Yes," Becca said awkwardly. "She's my friend from middle school."

Two men entered the shop, drawing both her and Ben's attention away from their awkward conversation.

"Papa! Regarde! Look at this," said the younger man in a thick European accent. "These wheels are only five thousand! I know they're used, but this is a great deal. I wonder why Chad's got such a good price on them? These could help shave off some significant time and make the difference between winning or not winning the prize money."

"Je concur. I agree," answered the older man, picking up one of the wheels. "They look to be in great shape. It would be hard to pass them up at this price. Let's ask Chad."

Becca's mouth hung open as she watched the interaction between the two men. "Ben," she whispered. "Five thousand? Really? They're just looking at a set of bicycle wheels. Where's the bike?" she asked incredulously.

Ben chuckled. "There's no bike. That's just for the wheels."

"You've got to be kidding me," she hissed out. "Who would pay five thousand for two old, used bicycle wheels and no bike?"

"A professional racer," he whispered back. "I don't recognize those two, but the younger man looks familiar. If you start watching some bicycle racing footage, I wouldn't be surprised if you see him some-where. He looks like a racer, doesn't he?"

"Yes, he does." And so does Ben, Becca thought, noting the younger man's svelte physique was similar to the man beside her.

Chad emerged from the back of the shop, and the two men approached him about the set of bicycle wheels.

"I'll be right with you Becca, Ben. Are you okay if I take a moment with these two before we get into more bike specifics, Becca?"

"Of course. No rush. Please take your time, Chad," said Becca.

Becca and Ben continued to watch the two men surreptitiously as they interacted with Chad. They clearly already knew each other. Within five minutes the sale was complete, and the father and son departed the shop with the set of wheels in hand, clearly ecstatic with their find.

"So, Becca," Chad said, approaching Becca and Ben with a serious look on his face, "I'm sorry to be delivering bad news, but your bike has a cracked frame. You're going to need a new one. It would be dangerous to use this one any longer. It will also be more expensive to fix than it's worth. Do you want me to show you some of your options?"

"Sure," said Becca hesitantly.

As Chad showed her various bikes, explaining their features, she felt more and more deflated. They were so expensive. Chad wasn't specifically pointing out cost just yet, but she couldn't help but note the prices. The least expensive bike she'd seen so far was about five hundred dollars, and they went up sharply from there. Who knew you could buy a ten thousand dollar bike? Luckily, Chad wasn't showing her the more expensive models, but even five hundred dollars was more than she had in mind.

If she'd had the time to think about this tri thing before they'd signed up for the race, it likely would have occurred to her that she could be getting in over her head—both in terms of the training and the financials. She should have known.

Financials were supposed to be her area of expertise, Becca thought with a scoff. And Carmen always had a way of getting them in over their heads. But…Carmen also had a way of pulling her into stuff she never would have dreamed of doing—fun stuff. And it always seemed to work out. *This was going to be fun and a good thing,* she reminded herself. Everyone around her was telling her to relax and enjoy the ride, even her doctor. And she didn't need to win the race for this to be fun. Maybe her best option was to borrow a bike… But how did she go about telling Chad and Ben that? Ben was doing something nice for her, and here she was again, wanting to walk away without an explanation.

"Here's one option that would be a good one for you, Becca," said

Chad. "This is a great brand with a spectrum of options in terms of price and size. They can get quite expensive, but you wouldn't need any of those higher-end models. Check this one out. Isn't she a beauty? Here, pick up your bike and then this one," he said, pushing her current bike toward her, then the new bike so she could test the difference for herself. "The reduced weight of this newer model can make a big difference in your race time and enjoyment of the ride."

"Wow," said Ben. "That's a beauty. Carbon fiber frame and Shimano parts!"

"And check out these wheels, Ben. Aren't they sweet?" Chad said, joining in on Ben's excitement—and veering off course.

Becca had no idea what their words even meant, but she was enjoying watching the men act like kids in a candy shop. They were so excited about each little nuance. An unintended giggle escaped her lips.

Ben and Chad stopped and looked at her.

Oops. She hadn't meant to stop their banter and garner their attention back to her—or make them feel like she was laughing at them for that matter.

"Sorry," said Ben sheepishly. "I guess we got a little carried away. As you were saying, Chad, this one here would be a good fit for Becca, wouldn't it?"

"Yes. Sorry, Becca. We promise we'll try to focus. It's just that having a great bike makes for a great ride. When you get a good fit on a good bike and get into the zone, it can feel like you have wings and like no one can stop you. We get a bit carried away with it sometimes," he said with a grin. "What I can tell you is that no matter what bike you end up with, you're going to love this triathlon journey. You're going to meet lots of amazing people and learn lots, and not just about triathlons. The event isn't just about race day, it's about the journey to get there. And it's very much a mental thing, not just physical. You're in the best of hands here with Ben. He knows how to mentor someone through a journey like that, and he's a great teacher too."

Becca looked at them both a little nervously. She was determined to get to race day. She'd made the commitment to Carmen and to herself. But she was aware this would not be an easy goal to meet.

Ben must have seen something in her face. "What's wrong, Becca?" he asked.

"Well, I am excited to get to be a part of it all. I guess it's just a bit daunting and more than I'm really wanting to spend."

"Hmm, do you have any loaners or used bikes that might work, Chad?" asked Ben.

"I don't generally do loaners or rentals," Chad said, tilting his head in thought. "But I do have someone looking at doing a trade-in right now. She's about your size, Becca. I haven't seen her old bike yet, but from how she's described it, it could be a good option. I could make an inquiry if you like, and I'd be willing to make an exception if she does decide to trade in since Ben's involved."

"Sounds like it might be a good option. Thanks, Chad," said Becca.

He nodded. "I'll follow up with her tomorrow. For now, let's get some measurements so I know what we're aiming for. Go ahead over to that bike stand. I'll bring over a bike that should be about right for you."

Becca moved toward the bike stand where Chad was now securing a sleek-looking, midnight blue bike. It sparkled under the candescent lights in the showroom ceiling. *It's gorgeous*, thought Becca. It was magical, just like her night with Ben on the boat. This was not good, she thought nervously, aware that she was in way over her head—and not just with the bike.

"Climb on, Becca, and peddle slowly to see how it feels. It's on the stand so you won't tip over," Chad said, pulling out a tape measure.

Becca moved this way and that at Chad's direction as he measured her from multiple angles. "You've got great femur length, Becca."

"Is that a good thing?" she asked, blushing.

"Oh yes, those long femurs will give you more power for your cycling," Chad replied without looking up as he reached around her for another measurement. "Okay, I've got all the measurements I need. A few more questions, though. Are you going to be riding with clip-less pedals?"

"Umm...I'm not sure," Becca said, turning to look at Ben. "Ben and our other coach, Sam, mentioned clip-less pedals in our training. But I don't actually know what those are."

"They can be tricky," said Chad. "But they can also be well worth

the effort to learn how to use them. You would wear cleats like these."
He lifted a pair of shoes and showed her the cleats on the underside of
the sole. You get a lot more power with your pedaling with these
shoes. The sole of your shoe locks onto the pedal. This connection
gives you more power not just when you're pushing your foot down,
but also when you're pulling your foot up, making them power effi-
cient. I'd be happy to help you try them out. There's definitely a bit of
a learning curve, but I've trained lots of people to use these."

"I've got her there," said Ben sharply, causing Becca and Chad to
turn and look at him.

"Okkaay," Chad said. "So, back to the bike. What do you think,
Ben? Does it look like a good fit?"

Ben stepped forward, his features now exuding his usual cool
competence that had Becca and everyone else around him relaxing.
"Can you pedal for me one more time, Becca?" he asked. "I want to
see the angle of your leg when your pedal and foot are at their
lowest."

Becca complied, but felt self-conscious as Ben's eyes followed her
thigh, calf, and foot as it moved in a circular motion, following the
pedal stroke.

"And how about your arm position? Does it feel comfortable when
you're leaning over the handlebars?"

"I think so," answered Becca, catching Ben's eye before quickly
averting her gaze. But not before catching a glimpse of his pursed lips,
reminding her of those same lips sensuously caressing her collarbone.
Her neck tilted to the side of its own accord, her body traitorously
remembering his lips and hands trailing along her neck. Ben's next
words had her jolting from her reverie.

"It looks like a perfect fit. And it's a beauty. I'm impressed, Chad,
as always. Do you like it, Becca?"

Swallowing, and hoping she wasn't blushing, Becca said, "Well,
yes. But remember, guys, you were going to see if you might have a
loaner or a used bike for me. This is just a stand in for sizing, right?"

"Yes," said Chad. "Hopefully, we'll get that trade-in, giving you a
good less expensive option. I'll follow up with it and keep you posted.
How about I try to call you tomorrow? In the meantime, I wouldn't
ride that bike of yours. It could crack all the way when you're out

riding and leave you sitting on the ground. I don't want to see you getting hurt."

"If that trade-in doesn't work out," said Ben, "we're going to need to think through some other options. I want to be sure you've got something to train with sooner rather than later so you'll be ready on race day. It's important for you to work up slowly to your race on the equipment you'll be racing in. I don't want you trying to catch up because that is usually what leads to injury."

"I'll do my best," piped up Chad. He handed Becca a piece of paper. "Here, I've written your measurements down for you in case you want to try to find a loaner. If you do and you want to bring it in to have me help fit it out for you, I'm happy to do that. But hopefully, I will be calling you tomorrow with good news about a trade-in."

CHAPTER 32

Lasagna

BEN

"THANKS AGAIN, BEN, FOR SETTING UP THAT MEETING with Chad. I enjoyed looking at the different bikes."

"You're welcome," Ben said, as he helped her secure her bike to her car. Then he hesitated before adding, "You know, Becca, I'm sure Chad could work out some sort of payment plan if you need him to."

Becca waved her hand dismissively. "It's not that. It's just that I have some other financial obligations that I need to make a priority. Anyhow, it sounds like Chad might have a good option for me with that trade-in."

Was that meant to dissuade him from asking more questions? Or was that simply a 'it's no big deal' dismissive wave? Ben cocked his head thoughtfully as another shadow crossed Becca's features. He just could not figure this woman out and it was driving him crazy. Maybe the whole obligation thing had to do with her mother? He wanted answers and couldn't seem to keep himself from digging deeper.

"Do you want to get a bite to eat before you go?" he asked her. "That Italian restaurant across the street is really good. It's one of my favorites, and it's been a while since I've been there."

Becca hesitated, and Ben was sure she was about to turn him down, but then she looked across the street to where he pointed. "Oh," she said with surprise. "I've been there before. My mom and I ate there...but that was ages ago," she added wistfully. "I'd forgotten all about that place."

"Was it a special occasion—a celebration?" he asked with an air of innocence as he continued to probe.

Becca hesitated. "I wouldn't exactly call it a celebration. More of a commemoration. It was on the anniversary of my dad's death. It was about three years ago now. We haven't been back since. There were just too many other...things that got in the way." He watched Becca agitatedly rub the pendant hanging from the chain around her neck. "Anyhow," she said, now changing the subject, "I'd better get going. I've got to get some things done before my work week starts up again tomorrow. Thanks again for helping me today."

"Are you sure you couldn't use some food before you go?" Ben asked, knowing he was pushing them into territory they'd agreed to leave alone but somehow not being able to help himself.

Becca hesitated again, taking another long look at the restaurant, and then a small smile quirked her lips. "It would be great to go there again," she said, her fingers now dragging the pendant that hung around her neck from left to right along its chain. Her small smile grew bigger as she teased, "But I don't know. I've got this slave driver of a coach. He's given us all these workouts we need to get in. He's so demanding." She rolled her eyes dramatically and, shaking her head, she said with a smirk, "Swim, bike, run, you name it, he's got us doing it. Can you believe it?"

Ben was surprised and delighted at her teasing. "Sounds like a horrible guy," he responded. "What did he say about fueling, though? I'm guessing he said something about getting in some extra carbs and protein. I'd be happy to help you with that. I wouldn't want you to get cross-wise with that villainous slave driver."

"Hmm...I thought I was supposed to be doing most of this training on my own. Is this a part of the group training now? The fueling?"

"Only for those who need extra energy to figure out their bike situation," he teased. "Seriously, though, we could debrief over lunch, and I could give you some ideas on how to translate what's in your training manual from outside biking to inside biking. Where do you work, anyway? Didn't you say you have a gym at work with spin bikes?"

"Nosy, aren't you, coach? But, yes, we have a very good gym. And I work at Patterson Consulting."

"Whoa," Ben said. "I'm impressed. I'm sure they have a good setup. What do you do there?"

"Again with the questions?"

"Sorry. You're right; no more questions, I promise. Just some help with carbo-loading. Italian restaurants are great for that. What do you say? I'm starving, and I would love some company."

Becca hesitated.

"Just as friends," Ben added. "No questions and no pressure—on the bike or on anything else."

Becca looked up at him with a smile. *There it was—that smile,* Ben thought, suddenly feeling very pleased with himself. He knew it shouldn't matter to him. Who cares why those shadows cross her face? Who cares if she pulls herself back into her cocoon like a butterfly afraid to face the world? And who cares if she gets a new bike or does the training...or ever goes for another boat ride with him again? But that smile was worth it, he thought, as he waited for her response. *Please say yes!* He wanted to bask in that smile of hers for just a bit longer today.

"Okay," said Becca finally. "Dinner would be great."

As soon as they crossed the threshold into the restaurant, a short, stout man with a thick Italian accent gave them a broad smile and called out a robust greeting. "Ben, it's great to see you! Where have you been? I thought maybe you didn't like us anymore."

"You know I love you guys," Ben said, shaking the man's hand and giving him a friendly clap on the back. "It's just been really busy at work lately. But you know I'll always get back here at some point. Do you have room for two for dinner?"

"Of course. We can always make room for you."

"Thanks, Tony." Ben followed Becca's gaze out of the corner of his eye as it swiveled from him to Tony. He held out a hand toward her. "Tony, I want you to meet Becca. Becca, Tony. Tony is the owner of this restaurant. It's his family's restaurant," Ben explained.

"Nice to meet you, Tony," Becca said.

"You too, Becca. Give me a minute and I'll get a table ready for you two. Will you be wanting your usual, Ben? Lasagna?"

"Of course," said Ben. "It's the best. You okay with that, Becca?"

"Absolutely," she said. "My mouth is already watering."

As Tony moved away to clear off a table for them, Becca turned to Ben. "What in the world? How do you know that guy? Do you know every restaurant owner around these parts? First at the Oaks Diner and now here."

"Now who's asking questions?" Ben teased.

"Touché," said Becca.

"I'm just giving you a hard time," Ben said with a smile. "This is actually one of my favorite restaurants. I've spent many a time in that bike shop, even after out riding with friends. With this place just across the street, we often end up here for lunch or dinner afterward. Somehow, Tony and I just hit it off. I probably come here at least a couple of times per month, if not more. Sometimes I just call in and have Tony make me some of his famous lasagna that I can pick up and eat at home. Believe me, his cooking is a lot better than mine. He usually tries to get me to sit down and eat it here, though, instead of taking it home. On many occasions, I've acquiesced, and Tony, or one of his other family members, ends up sitting with me. It kinda feels like family here now. Pittsburgh really is a great city. It's been easy to get to know people.

"Take Tony's place, for example. I just started out by coming in here with friends after a bike ride and ended up with some extended family. Tony's place and Rose's place are good for a home-cooked meal. I'll probably be going back to California before too long, though. But we'll see...I would miss my boat, that's for sure." As soon as he said that, he chastised himself for dangerously pushing the envelope with her again.

"What about the trail you were showing me out in Marston?" asked Becca, adding fuel to the fire as she picked up on the thread he'd laid down.

Ben gave a shrug. "That small city revitalization stuff, the trails and all that..." Ben hesitated. "Well, that was just dreaming," he said with a dismissive wave of his hand.

"You mean the rose-colored glasses thing? Did you lose them?" She pretended to look through her purse. "Hmm...let me see. Maybe I can find a pair for you in here somewhere." With a grin, she lifted her head and caught his gaze. "But seriously, Ben, whether or not you do the trail development in Marston, I'm glad you showed it to me. I didn't really appreciate what's out here, both in the city and especially outside the city, until I saw the river and everything near it through your eyes—well, through your rose-colored glasses," she added. "Where I live now—right inside the city—is great for my commute, but there isn't a lot of wildlife to enjoy like there was on the trail you showed me. I guess I just haven't really explored much outside of school and work and…" Becca trailed off. "Well, outside of school and work," she finished abruptly.

There was that shadow again. Ben sighed. Something was up and he wanted to figure it out. He decided to move the conservation along. "Do you like your work, Becca? What do you do at Patterson?"

One of her brows lifted. "No questions, remember?"

"You're right," Ben said, holding his hands up toward Becca in apology. "I'm sorry, no questions. So…" Ben faltered, suddenly looking for a new topic.

Becca laughed, granting him mercy and answering his earlier question. "Yes, I like my job. I like it a lot. I'm a financial analyst, and I mostly put together the pro formas. I also help more broadly with the business plans and the overall proposals for various projects. Mostly, though, I'm the numbers person. It's really busy right now. We just had an infrastructure project unexpectedly fall into our laps." She gave a laugh, almost as if recognizing she'd said too much in an attempt to not share much at all.

There was that smile again. He could live in that smile, he thought, returning her grin. "So, what are we laughing at? Whoops! No more questions, right? I forgot already. No worries, you don't have to answer that. Either way, I'm enjoying the laughter."

Becca stopped laughing enough to share, "There was a sewage break after all the rain, and the city we're working with—or that we're about to be working with—had sewage running down main street." Becca's body shook with laughter, and she wiped her eyes, now wet with tears. "I'm sorry. It's not funny. Not funny at all. I really shouldn't be laughing." But her body doubled over with mirth despite her admonition to herself that this was not a laughing matter.

Becca's laughter was contagious, and Ben found himself also

bursting with uncontrollable laughter. "It's the Great Stink all over again," he said.

Becca looked at him in surprise. "How do you know about that?"

"I'm an architect, remember? I studied the Great Stink in school. Plus, in my earlier days, I spent a lot of time thinking about infrastructure." Ben stopped short of telling Becca about his younger years and about following his father around as a kid, helping him out with water and sewage projects in Kenya.

"You did? You worked on infrastructure projects? Is that what a big city, award-winning architect and high-rise developer does? I wouldn't think that would be within your scope."

"It's not anymore. That was a long time ago."

"Why did you give it up?" asked Becca.

"Now who's going on with the twenty questions?" he teased.

"You're right. Fair's fair; you don't have to answer that last question."

"It's not surprising, though—your story about sewage running down Main Street, I mean. There's a lot of decay across all the United States and it hasn't been dealt with in decades, especially in the smaller Rust Belt communities. It's not something that's going to go away or that can be ignored. If it's not addressed at some point, there will be a problem—like the one you just mentioned."

A server approached their table and cleared away the empty lasagna dishes. Tony followed just behind him, setting a plate with two forks on it down between them. The plate held a large and decadent-looking piece of chocolate cake. "For you and your girlfriend to share and enjoy," Tony said, winking and lighting the candle that sat in the middle of their table.

"Oh, we're not..." said Becca.

"No, we're not..." said Ben at the same time.

"Whatever you say," said Tony, winking at Ben. "It's great to see you having fun, Ben. Enjoy. And take your time."

Ben looked around the restaurant, realizing they were full on into the dinner hour now with every table filled and candles flickering on the tables all around them. He looked out the window, noticing the setting sun. How long had they been sitting here?

"Oh my gosh, Ben!" Becca exclaimed. "I didn't realize how late it's gotten. I really need to get going."

"Yeah, me too. We'd better finish this dessert first, though. I don't want to disappoint Tony."

"You're right. We can't disappoint Tony. I'm not sure I can fit in another bite, though. That lasagna was amazing; I ate way too much of it." But even as she said that, Becca took a bite of the dessert. "Oh my," she said, moaning, "this is so good. I take it back. Maybe just a few more bites!" She dipped her fork back in for another bite.

Ben smiled and reached in with his own fork just as Becca did, causing their forks to spar.

"Hey, watch it there, buster. You don't want to get between a girl and her chocolate," Becca teased.

"Definitely not," Ben said, smiling, as he reached in for another bite anyway and teasingly pushed her fork aside.

"Are you done with your dessert?" asked Tony, motioning to the now empty plate between them.

"Yes," said Ben. "Thank you. It was delicious." Tony cleared their dishes and turned back toward the kitchen, but not before giving Ben a sly smile.

An awkward silence followed, with neither of them saying a word. Ben noticed that Becca looked everywhere but at him.

"Becca?" he said hesitantly. "About that weekend. I know we're both focused on our careers right now, with you planning to move to D.C. and me probably moving back to California before too long, and the coach–trainee thing sort of complicates things as well. I know it was sort of an...unexpected thing...and just a one-time thing—that night on the boat," he stumbled out. "But I don't want you to feel pressured or awkward about it. I have to admit, I wanted to hear from you afterward...."

Becca winced. "I'm sorry about that, Ben."

"Don't be sorry. You didn't owe me a follow up and there were no commitments made. So, it really is okay, but it looks like we're going to be in close proximity for the next couple of months. And I want this training—the race, the whole thing—to be a good experience for you. I don't want there to be any tension between us. So, maybe we should just agree to move forward as friends?"

"Yeah, sure. Perfect," said Becca. "You're absolutely right. Friends." She put out her hand to shake on it.

"Friends," Ben said, shaking her hand. He knew he should let go. But his eyes locked on hers, and he enveloped her hand in his larger one, wanting to hold on just a bit longer. Finally, he pulled his hand away. But it hung there in the air momentarily, seemingly possessed, with his brain unable to make it move away from Becca. He forced his hand away and picked up his water glass and took a large gulp.

"I'd better get going," said Becca. "Thank you again for taking so much time helping me think through my bike options. I really appreciate it. I guess I'll see you at the next group coaching session on Saturday. It's a run coming up this Saturday, correct?"

"Yes," said Ben as they both stood up, readying to leave. "And hopefully you'll know by then whether Chad has a bike for you."

CHAPTER 33

Second Group Run

BECCA BUZZED WITH ANTICIPATION AS SHE PULLED ON HER running shoes. She hadn't seen Ben since their dinner at Farfalle, Tony's Italian restaurant, last Sunday.

She grabbed her Yeti filled with coffee, certainly an early morning necessity, and her peanut butter toast with banana and honey on top. It was finally Saturday morning and time for their second group training run. Over the course of the week, Chad had contacted her. But Ben had not. Not that she thought he would. Why should he? And she shouldn't want him to, anyway. Ben, like her health care bills, was something that threatened to get her off track—way off track. She knew how to right-size bills, but if she made a mess of things with Ben, Becca wasn't sure she'd know how to right-size that.

Nonetheless, she was looking forward to this morning's training. Becca tried to tell herself it was because she was excited about the triathlon. It was getting her back out into the world of the living. Not only had it taken her mind away from the painful, cancer-filled world she'd been in, but it had also gotten Becca off her behind and out of her office chair over three separate lunch hours this week alone. She'd done her swim at the YMCA near her office yesterday, her bike ride—on a spin bike as Ben had recommended—at her office gym on

Wednesday, and she'd gone out for a short run along the river walkway near her office on Tuesday.

It hadn't been easy to shift her mind from her computer screen at work. But after each training, she'd felt reinvigorated, and had also found it easier to refocus on her work. None of the trainings had been all that difficult once she'd gotten herself out the door. Sam had said that would be the case and had emphasized that these first weeks were just as much about getting into a routine as they were about upping their fitness levels.

Becca swung her car into the parking lot of Carmen's apartment complex. She'd offered to pick Carmen up for their training this morning so they'd have more time to catch up. It'd been a heads-down kind of work week for both of them and they hadn't had a chance to touch base with each other. Not surprisingly, Carmen wasn't waiting for her. She dialed Carmen's cell phone number to let her know she was downstairs, waiting. But just as the phone rang, she saw Carmen rushing through the apartment complex door, her hand lifted in a wave.

"Great job, Carmen," Becca said with a note of surprise as Carmen slid into the car's passenger seat. "I know early mornings are not your thing, but I didn't even have to rouse you out of bed this morning."

"Nope; I'm on it. Whoever would've thought we'd be doing a triathlon? I didn't even know what that was until we went to that info session. But this sure is a good thing to get out of bed for in the morning."

"I must say, I agree with you there." Becca smiled. "You've finally hit on a good one after all the crazy schemes you've dragged me into."

"Hey, look at you!" said Carmen. "Nice outfit. Love the bright pink with yellow flowers. I recognize that top, but I don't think I've seen that on you in ages."

"Yeah, I guess." Becca shrugged. "I thought I'd go for a little more color this morning. You know, with it being spring and all."

"Uh, huh..." Carmen said with a smile. "Are you sure it's not for Ben?"

"Of course not! We're now confirmed friends. We agreed there should be no awkwardness about that weekend and that we should go forward as friends through the rest of this training. All good there," Becca said, trying to convince herself just as much as Carmen.

"Wait a minute—when did all this happen? Did you two go out on another date to discuss this? Why didn't you tell me?"

"No, we did not go out on a date. You know I plan to leave for D.C. soon, and he's focused on his work too. Neither of us is looking for a relationship, so we agreed to call a truce and just be friends. And, anyhow, the work thing is just a part of it. With him being our coach, it wouldn't be right to see each other on anything but a professional level."

"That's not what Stacey said at happy hour," Carmen scoffed. "Remember? If I recall correctly, she said you should 'try him on for size' or 'take him out for a spin' or something like that. It's not like he's your teacher or your boss or anything. And neither of you is young and impressionable anymore. You're grown adults. No reason not to extend that to being grown, *consenting* adults," Carmen said, lifting her eyebrows and giving Becca a knowing smile.

"Not gonna happen," Becca said, as she pulled into a parking spot at one of the trail access lots near downtown Pittsburgh. "We're here. Time for a run with our new teammates."

"Okay, everyone, gather round," said Sam. "I'm so glad to see all of your smiling faces early on this beautiful Saturday morning. Are you all ready for a run?"

There were about fifteen participants gathered around this morning. As expected, not all of their twenty-plus team members were here today. But Becca was determined to make it to as many of the sessions as she could. She was enjoying the camaraderie, especially since no one knew about her cancer. There had been story sharing during 'mission moments,' but Becca had chosen not to share hers with the group yet, despite it being helpful to hear everyone else's stories.

On the other hand, she had shared her story with that one woman, Gwen, on their first day running around the track. Gwen had been so distressed about her friend's cancer and how to help support her that Becca's own story had just tumbled right out of her mouth. Becca hoped that she'd helped Gwen to some extent that day. It was hard to say, though, because Becca hadn't seen her since. She hoped she'd helped Gwen. There wasn't much to be done about it all now, though, other than hope that Gwen and her friend were doing well. They were in her thoughts, at least.

"We're going to try to get a better idea of your pace today," announced Sam, gaining Becca's attention and helping her to refocus on the goal for today. "If you know roughly what pace you run or run-walk, that's great. If you don't, no worries. You'll start getting a better feel for that as we continue over the coming weeks. But for those that do, please give me a show of hands if you think your pace is under ten minutes per mile?"

Three hands went up.

"Okay, great, let's have all of you stand over here by this bench. Next, who thinks their pace is between about ten to twelve minutes per mile?"

Five hands went up, including Becca's and Carmen's.

"Great, let's have you all stand over here by the water fountain." After gesturing to the fountain, Sam faced the remaining members of the group and asked, "How about over twelve minutes per mile?"

Two more hands went up.

"And, finally, who has absolutely no idea what their pace is or maybe even no idea what I'm talking about?" Sam softened the question with a smile.

Two final hands went up.

"I think I might just be a walker," said Matt, looking sheepish. "I did the distances listed in the training schedule, but I just wasn't all that comfortable running, so I ended up walking instead. Is that okay?"

"That's absolutely fine," said Sam. "We can assess your pace a bit more today. And if that's what you end up being most comfortable with, you can definitely walk that segment of the race. We'll just have to make sure we get you into a quick enough walk pace to meet the time cut-off. It's pretty generous for this race, so I don't think you'll have any problems. Plus, we still have plenty of time to work on ramping up our endurance levels, and that always helps with improving overall times."

"Thanks," said Matt, looking relieved.

"Okay, let's get started," said Sam. "We're fortunate to have Adam here with us again today, as well as Ben. And, luckily, Adam, just like his big brother, is an excellent runner, including in terms of knowing about running mechanics. That means you all get an extra coach today, which gives us a chance to give you each a little more one-on-one attention. For today's run, Adam is going to go with the faster group —that's all of you over by the bench. Ben is going with you mid-pacers, and I'm going to hang with the thirteen-minute-plus and not-sure groups. We're going to do our best to talk with each of you during the training today. Nonetheless, you may find yourselves on your own for some of your run because we'll be running on a trail, rather than on a track, where it isn't as easy to always keep an eye on everyone. It is just a simple out and back course, though.

"You'll know when you've hit the turnaround point because we've put a fuel stop at the turnaround, along with signs letting you know you're in the right place. At that fuel stop, you'll find Gatorade, water, pretzels, and fruit gummies. Please be sure to grab a bite of food and take a drink of something to stay hydrated. Since our run is short today and we've got a nice temperature going, you're not likely to have any problems, but you need to get used to incorporating fluids and food into your routine. You never want to do anything new on race day. So, part of our training is testing out what does and doesn't work for you in regard to food and hydration. Then, on race day, you'll run your race exactly as you've trained for it, and you'll know going into it that you won't likely run into anything you can't handle.

"Try to buddy up with someone, if you can. It's always nice to have a partner—or partners. It not only makes the training more fun, but it also makes it safer than going it alone. For today, if you want to slow your pace a bit to hang with another teammate, go for it. Slower is fine. Faster, though, is not necessarily okay. Please be sure not to push your pace faster than you're ready for, but do give yourself permission to drop back. Ultimately, though, you'll want to 'run your own race,' as they say, or you're likely to end up frustrated—or worse, injured."

Becca's thoughts had turned in on themselves at Sam's comment about Adam. He was Ben's brother? How had she not realized that? Didn't Ben just move here from California not all that long ago? How did Adam end up here too? She found her curiosity diverting her attention down a rabbit hole, distracting her from Sam's instructions.

"...Any final questions before we get started?" asked Sam.

Uh oh. I'd better pay attention and quit thinking about who's related to who here. It doesn't really matter, anyway.

"Okay, let's go!" said Sam. He waved his arm first toward the fast-paced group standing with Adam, then toward Ben with the mid-paced group before facing the slower runners and walkers.

Ben turned to face the five of them and asked, "Ready?" When they all nodded, he started them off.

Becca felt an exhilarating tension in her body at Ben's nearness. A surge of adrenaline pumped through her, like a spring wound so tight that it was ready to leap forward.

"Hi Becca," said Ben, sidling up beside her. "Are you sure you're a ten-to-twelve-minute pacer? You're looking pretty fast there."

Carmen laughed from her other side. "I can assure you, Becca and I are not speedsters, we're lolly-gaggers. At least, that's what our high school coach always accused us of being."

"What?" asked Ben, looking confused.

"Lolly-gaggers. You know—back of the packers."

Ben laughed as Carmen began telling him about her and Becca's junior high and high school running days.

"Our coach was always pushing us to go faster. It never worked," said Carmen. "We did okay; we just weren't the ones bringing in big wins or big points for our team."

"You're probably faster than you realize," said Ben. "One of the best measurements to help gauge pace is how easily you can talk while you're running. It seems to me you're running at an easy pace right now since you can talk with no difficulty."

"Are you saying I don't have to be a lolly-gagger or that I'm too much of a talker?" asked Carmen teasingly.

As Ben and Carmen carried on with their friendly banter, Becca adjusted her pace to fall back a bit, realizing the pace she'd initially set had been a bit too quick for her. The other three members of their pace group were also beginning to lag back behind Becca. As Becca found herself running on her own but still comfortably within her pace pod, her thoughts turned inward again. It was a beautiful day, just like that day she and Ben had walked to the diner by the river for lunch, and then later had gone out on that river for a romantic boat ride. As Carmen and Ben ran at the front of their pack, Becca's eyes focused on Ben's lithe body. His physique was sleek and powerful, and that gorgeous butt, encased in tight-fitting running shorts, moved with his every foot strike in sync with the rest of his body. She closed her eyes for just a moment as she ran, letting those visuals fully evolve inside her brain. Her body responded to an image of Ben running alongside a lion across a broad plain, the muscles in their bodies flexing and unflexing with every stride.

Becca quickly opened her eyes, wondering what she was thinking by risking a fall out here with her eyes closed. But the sensation of desire remained as her eyes refocused on Ben's lithe strides. He was graceful yet powerful, deferential yet in command.

Becca's thoughts were interrupted by the voices of the three women running just a short distance behind her. "I would go for that," said one woman. "He is hot, hot, hot. I wonder if he's single?"

"I'm with you," said another of the women. "Too bad I'm not single," she added jokingly.

"How are you two talking? I can't even breath," said the third woman, her voice coming out in short gasps. "I agree, though; he is hot."

All three laughed.

"We can slow up a bit," said the first woman.

As the three women slipped further behind, their words were no longer discernible, and Becca was able to return to her own musings. Which, of course, were about Ben, she thought with a measure of frustration. She couldn't seem to keep her mind off of him. What was wrong with her? She prided herself on being able to focus on her goals. She was always on track—no pun intended, she thought ruefully.

She'd already been derailed once. That had been out of her control. But this attraction to Ben—this she could control. And she'd decided she would not let her attraction to Ben ruin her plans. She needed to remind herself they were just friends. After all, they'd agreed to that and only that. Anyhow, he deserved better than she could give him. Getting involved with her would just embroil him unnecessarily in her painful world. She may be in remission now, but that cancer could return at any time. All the more reason to stay focused on her work. She was going to take that job in D.C. and fulfill her father's legacy.

Becca was jolted out of her musings by Ben's words, floating back to her on the breeze.

"I'd better check in on the others, Carmen," he was saying. "You're doing a great job. If you're feeling comfortable, keep on going ahead. You'll have no problem recognizing the turnaround when you get there." He then slowed his pace to let Becca and the other three behind her catch up to him.

"How's everyone doing?" Ben asked when they were all assembled.

"Good," panted one of the three women.

Ben ran alongside each woman in turn, checking on their pace and comfort level and giving them individualized pointers about their running mechanics. He ran easily but slowly next to the women. Becca knew he must be capable of significantly faster speeds with those toned core and calf muscles. Instead, he was connecting with each woman on their terms and at their pace. Becca could tell each of them was flattered by Ben's attention and appreciative of his kindness as he gently coaxed the best out of each of them.

This run was so different from her school days. When she was in junior high and high school, Becca had often felt intimidated by the faster runners and by her coaches. She'd fought feelings of inferiority and self-doubt to gain the confidence to compete, let alone run at all. She'd also had coaches who'd tried to motivate her by yelling. Ben, instead, thought Becca with admiration, coached through encouragement, confidence-building, and, most of all, kindness.

"You're doing great, Becca," Ben said, as he came up alongside her for her one-on-one time. "Are you feeling comfortable with this pace? Any discomfort at all?" Ben continued with questions and tips regarding things like mid-foot strikes and arm motion—things she now recalled more vividly from her earlier running days. As they settled into a comfortable pace and Ben seemed satisfied that Becca was doing just fine, he turned his attention to the non-running aspects of their training. "Any word from Chad, yet?"

"Yes. Chad called yesterday to let me know he hasn't heard about the trade-in. He's still hopeful, but for now, it looks like I'm stuck with my old bike."

Ben didn't respond. Becca turned to look at him to see if she could gauge what he was thinking. Was he upset with her about not getting a new bike, or was it a non-issue for him?

"Sticking with my old bike—or a loaner if I can find one—really seems like the best option for me," said Becca firmly, making it clear this was the way it was going to be regardless of whether he liked it or not.

There was a moment of silence.

"Aren't you going to say anything?" she asked with a tinge of uncertainty.

Ben gave her a small smile. "I'll support you in whatever you decide to do, Becca. I just want to make sure you're safe, that's all."

As they came to the end of their run, Carmen eagerly approached them. "Hi, guys. Good run?"

"Very good," they both answered in unison.

"So, I was telling Adam"—Carmen motioned at Adam, where he was speaking with another participant—"about our Friday night happy hours. He said he's in for this Friday. What about you, Ben? Do you want to join us too?"

Becca was standing behind Ben, giving her an opportunity to shoot Carmen a "what the heck are you thinking?" look.

Carmen just smiled at her sweetly as Adam came over to stand beside Carmen.

"Sounds great, doesn't it Ben?" he said with a grin. "What do you think? Are you free on Friday night?"

CHAPTER 34

Balance

BEN

"I CAN'T BELIEVE YOU TALKED ME INTO GOING TO A HAPPY hour on Friday," Ben said affably to Adam as they carted lumber from Ben's truck into his new 'dilapidated mansion,' as Adam referred to it.

"You can't just work all the time, Ben. There's more to life than that, ya know. And as my big brother, you owe it to me to help me get acclimated here," Adam razzed.

"Aren't you meeting lots of new people in your summer program? There must be some cute and very smart women in that program of yours."

"I am meeting new people. But, as I said, there's more to life than work—or studying for that matter. And that program is my work. It is awesome, though. The concepts they've got us learning are really cool. But it's all so new to me, and everyone there is so smart. It's intimidating. My thinking is that no one at that happy hour is going to want to quiz me on whether I understand every-thing that's being put down in front of me at CMU. At least, I hope they won't. I'm looking forward to just having some fun and relaxing with no pressure about whether I'm good enough or smart enough. Plus, you know they say it's important to shift gears at times to give your mind time to ruminate on what you're working on—or even forget about it all together. When you come back to it, it all just clicks into place, ya know? And that's what I'm hoping for with this happy hour—a little mental break from all the new concepts I'm learning."

"First, I don't know about that whole ruminating thing," Ben said. "I've found keeping my head down and focused on my work has been what's gotten me ahead. Second, what the heck are you talking about —not being good enough or smart enough? You're one of the smartest people I know and one of the most creative. Remember that time in second grade when Mom was trying to talk you into being Superman for Halloween?

"You were determined to make your own costume. You went off in a huff to the park across the street and came home dragging an old cardboard box with you. I'll never forget Mom's reaction." Ben laughed, coaxing a smile from Adam at the memory. "Mom finally let you put it in the garage, and next thing we knew, you had a full-on football player costume with a built-in bucket for candy. It was so cool! I was so jealous of that costume."

"That was a cool costume," Adam said, chuckling. "And as I recall, you're the one who ended up dressing up as Superman that year— even though you were kinda old for trick-or-treating."

"Hey, who ya callin' old?" Ben grinned.

"It sure is nice having my big brother around again." Adam sighed contentedly. "I've missed having my own personal cheerleader. I just wish I'd appreciated it more when you were home. I think I'm going to have to get a double dose of it while I'm here in Pittsburgh so I can really enjoy and soak it up this time. Go on...tell me more. What else am I great at?" Adam encouraged.

Ben laughed. "No problem. Just let me know anytime you need a pep talk. Of course, there's a price to pay. There's still a lot more wood to bring in. Ready for another load?"

"Happy to do it," said Adam.

"Seriously, though, I appreciate you helping me with this project, Adam. It's nice to have some company for the heavy lifting."

"No problem. It's nice to get in the exercise that comes with this as well as with the group trainings. Plus, it gives me an excuse to put aside the books for a while."

Ben and Adam continued in comfortable silence, carrying in load after load of oak boards for the new hardwood floor Ben was planning to install across the entire first level of his new house.

"How did you learn how to do this stuff?" Adam asked after an hour of labor.

"What stuff?"

"Fixing up an old house. Installing hardwood flooring. This is certainly not something we learned from Mom or Dad."

"Well, actually," Ben said. "I did learn some of this stuff from Dad. When I went with him on his trips overseas, he always made a point of including me in whatever project he was working on. They were water and sewage systems, mostly. And sometimes building projects—like that community health clinic he built. In some ways, it really wasn't so different from this. We weren't installing quartz countertops or new hardwood floors; we were thinking through what problems needed to be solved and how to solve them and then spent time on implementing the solutions. Most of the implementation required hands-on construction. Dad did a lot of that with his own hands. It went well beyond what he'd learned from a book." Ben shrugged. "And, I guess along the way, I learned a lot."

"Like what?" asked Adam.

Ben cocked his head. "Well, in one village, he helped put in a new water system. There was an enormous problem with dysentery from bacteria infested waters. The villagers used that water source for lots of things—washing clothes as well as for drinking. It wasn't the clothes washing, though, that was the biggest problem; it was mostly from human and agricultural waste and chemicals that ran into the water, especially during and after the hard rains. People didn't have a clean water source for drinking, so they turned to the polluted source.

"That led to serious health problems, which meant people were often too sick to work. They couldn't provide for their families or for the overall economy of the village. Improvements like that new water system that Dad designed and helped build, along with ensuring there was clean water for drinking, went a long way toward improving their quality of life—and saving their lives." Ben felt a stab of self-disappointment in terms of how he thought of his father these days. He'd forgotten how hard his Dad had worked back then and how proud he'd been of him.

"Wow," said Adam. "I guess I didn't realize all that. Everything changed so much after Sophia left us, including Mom and Dad."

Ben stiffened at Adam's vocalization of their sister's name, and then shook off the memories of working with his father in Kenya all those years ago. He needed to stay in the here and now, not in the past. He didn't want to forgive his parents for leaving so much of their upbringing in his and Adam's hands. It wasn't forgivable. He hadn't done much better, though, he thought. He'd really messed things up with Adam. That wasn't forgivable, either.

Ben sighed. "Anyhow, when I first graduated with my architecture degree, I worked on a number of construction sites. Beyond what I learned from Dad, those construction jobs are really what taught me about things like this flooring installation.

"There's still a lot more to do on the house, though, before we get to the surface improvements—the pretty stuff. It's the underlying foundation that's more important. So far, I've gotten the roof stabilized and the front steps rebuilt, so they're safe. But I've still got to get other things done like the utility upgrades before I jump into the cosmetics. I need to make sure all the pipes are in good shape for my small water project here." Ben laughed. "Getting this wood inside the house is one thing, but I won't be ready to get started on the installation until I have some of those 'below the surface' necessities further along."

"Good thing you haven't forgotten about the utilities," Adam teased. "Even my little apartment has better utilities than this house. But, I give you license to take a break from both this house and your development work to escort me to the happy hour. I need a wing-man if I'm going to jump into yet another new situation."

"You got it. I guess it wouldn't be right for me to leave you hanging. So, Friday it is. How about I pick you up at 5:00 p.m. outside your apartment building? That way we'll get there just a little after it starts, and you can make a grand entrance onto the social scene."

"Perfect," said Adam, and the two of them once again lapsed into a comfortable silence as they carried in more loads of lumber.

∾

After Adam left via an Uber, Ben continued to work on the house. He knew he needed to get some of his real work done. It was already Sunday evening, and he'd have people looking to him Monday morning for answers to both business and design questions. It was a lot. But it was more than a job for him. He loved designing and then getting to see his designs turn into actual buildings occupied by multitudes of people on a daily basis. And he'd been recognized and rewarded for those designs.

His eyes traveled toward the living room's built-in bookcases that held numerous awards—as well as the picture of him and Adam and Sophia. Ben sighed, feeling a hole in his heart and an ache in his chest. Lately, he'd been feeling more unsettled with his life as if something were missing. The results of his designs were also starting to leave him feeling cold. Was that how it felt to others who now worked or lived in those buildings he'd created? Did they feel a lack of warmth when they entered? Apparently not. He was now a sought-after architect, and his company was growing to the point where money was no longer the issue it had been when he and Adam were growing up.

So, why did he feel a need to change anything? Why not stay the course? How did that saying go? *Why mess with success?* Maybe it was just that he knew it was risky to keep all his eggs in one basket. Ben shook his head at yet another cliched saying. But it was true. If he wanted to be sure his company continued to grow, he really should diversify into additional lines of business.

He liked the idea of reaching out beyond city centers to help revitalize some of the Rust Belt communities in the outlying areas. They created a great opportunity for work-life balance, something Adam had referred to just today. It seemed like a no-brainer to intertwine the best of the city with the best of its outlying areas—like with the trails. And wouldn't making a name for himself here in Pittsburgh with that type of development serve as a good stepping stone for him and his company?

Ben knew he wanted to bring a lot more of the natural world into his daily life. Training for the triathlon was one way to do that. But that still left him with two separate worlds. He wanted to intertwine them. Were other people craving that balance as well? Is that why this old house had called to him? Because it had potential to balance the old with the new, the rural with the urban, and the river and the trail with up-to-date living space?

A nagging in his brain told him that just maybe he'd bought this place because his life—not just his business—needed a change. Ben shook his head in annoyance. It wasn't like him to lose his focus. He didn't like it. He needed to get back into that engineering mind-set that had made him a successful architect and developer. Yes, he wanted to get his own house in order and reconnect with his brother...and maybe even with his parents, he thought with a fissure of surprise.

He didn't need to be forgiven—or forgive his parents—for that to happen. Or did he? Why get all sentimental about it? Ben huffed out a derisive laugh at himself. It wasn't like that could happen. He would never be an emotional safe haven for his brother, or for his parents; that just wasn't a skillset he possessed. But maybe they could rebuild some trust, enough to be a small part of each other's lives again? He had a successful company now, and he wanted to share that success. There was no need for his family to struggle any longer, at least not financially. He wanted to help them, and he could help them. And that was enough.

CHAPTER 35

Happy Hour with Ben and Adam

CARMEN

Friday, May 20

"YOU'RE ALL IN FOR A TREAT TONIGHT," CARMEN SAID, AS she took a seat at the table she shared with Stacey, Eileen, Anna, and Natalie. The other girls were already comfortably in place, with drinks in hand and a plate of nachos in the middle of their usual table at Luna's.

"Oh? What is it?" said Stacey.

"Two of our coaches are joining us for happy hour tonight. Not only are they nice guys, but they are also gorrrrgeous. Although, I'm thinking Ben is already off-limits. Just an FYI for all of you. Believe me, the looks between Ben and Becca are nothing less than steamy. There's definitely a lot of heat there; you can almost see the flames! You don't want to get in the way of that or you're likely to get burned."

"Did Becca succumb to his charms like I told her to?" asked Stacey. "It would be about time that woman gave herself a break and let go a little. We all know she's amazing, but she's also more buttoned up than anyone else I know. That's not sustainable. And then getting hit with cancer before she was even fully ready to accept her Dad's death. It just isn't fair. She deserves a break and some real happiness for a change. Do you think this Ben guy can make that happen? Maybe I should have a talk with that boy. What do you think?"

"Hold on there, Ms. Matchmaker. If we go in with guns blazing, we're likely to scare them *both* away. Remember how hard she fought to keep us at arm's length? And I have no idea what's going on with Ben.... Well, maybe a bit of an idea," Carmen hedged, not wanting to divulge too much about Ben and Becca's weekend together. "But no matter what the reason, they both seem to be fighting this thing with all they've got. Becca has it in her head that she's still going to D.C., and now that her doctor told her she's officially in remission, she's determined to get back onto that train. I wish I knew for sure that's truly what would be best for her. I know none of us has a crystal ball, but I just don't see it. Everyone is here for her. Who is there still in D.C.? Just the ghost of her Father as far as I can tell. I get how important that is to her, making sure she does right by his memory. I just don't see why she has to go all the way to D.C. to do that."

"We've tried giving her as much space as she needed over the past two years," said Stacey. "Maybe enough is enough. Maybe it's time we butt in and make sure she knows we aren't going anywhere and that we don't want to just hang out in the background anymore. We want to be there for her, always have. What do you think, guys? How do we do that?"

"Maybe," said Carmen thoughtfully, "she's getting there on her own now that her doctor is assuring her she's in remission. And she said yes to this whole triathlon thing. I don't know whether that's because of the remission, our nagging, or Ben. If I had to wager, I'd say Ben has got more than a little to do with her shift in attitude. It wasn't until after she met him that she wanted to do happy hours again. Maybe we just keep doing what we're doing, and let it play out. She's only officially been in remission for a few months—actually, only a couple of weeks if you count that scare of a blood test. She's got to be in a pretty vulnerable place in terms of figuring out how to navigate this transition. I wouldn't want us to do anything to scare her back behind that shield she's been hiding behind. Before we do anything major, let me run things by Liane—that woman from the cancer support group—to make sure we're not pushing her too hard. Stacey, maybe if you..." Carmen trailed off as her eyes caught on the door.

The other women all swiveled their heads and saw it was Becca.

"Hi!" said Becca as she approached the table. But she was met with silence as all eyes quickly turned their focus to the drinks in front of them. "What's up?" asked Becca suspiciously. "Did I miss something?"

"No...not at all," said Eileen. "Carmen was just telling us that two of your triathlon coaches are coming tonight. I can't wait to meet them. Carmen says they're nothing less than smokin' hot. What do you say, Becca? Is Carmen right or is she telling tales again?"

"Oh, well, I hadn't really noticed," said Becca. "They're our coaches, so they're off-limits. I'm just focused on following our training plan to make sure I don't embarrass myself on race day. And just a reminder, no spilling the beans about the cancer. Promise?"

"Becca—" started Stacey.

"*Please!* I'm just not ready to share yet. Okay?"

"Fine," said Stacey with a huff. The others silently nodded their heads in agreement—albeit reluctantly.

"We won't spill the beans," continued Stacey, "but didn't we already go over this whole coach-trainee thing?" She gave an exasperated sigh. "Who cares if he's your coach? I'm telling you, just try him on for size. You don't have to decide to buy him."

A spitting laugh escaped Eileen, and her eyes started to water. "You are a hoot, Stacey!"

"Hey, you just spit on me!" said Anna. She gathered up some napkins from around the table and began blotting at her blouse.

A crimson blush crept up Eileen's cheeks. "Sorry, Anna, I promise it's just water. Just think how lucky you are that I wasn't taking a sip of beer when Stacey so eloquently explained to us how male-female courtship works." She burst out into a new round of laughter while turning an even brighter shade of red that closely matched the color of her hair.

Eileen's laughter was infectious and soon everyone at the table joined in, including Anna.

"You're all nuts," said Becca, grabbing a napkin off the tabletop to wipe the tears from her eyes. "Oh. My. God! —This napkin is soaking wet!"

"Whoops," said Anna. "I think that was my fault. Well, it was

Eileen's fault. She's the one who spit all over me." Anna looked up to search for their server to ask for more napkins and then paused. "Um, Becca, Carmen? I think your coaches have arrived," she said in a hushed whisper.

All eyes at the table shifted in search of what Anna was now looking at, and silence descended over the table once again as Ben and Adam approached. That silence was quickly broken as Eileen, unable to keep her fits of laughter under control, let out another snort, causing everyone at the table to burst out with another round of guffaws. Fortunately, none of these fits of laughter was accompanied by another snort of water—or beer—shooting across the table.

"It looks like we've arrived at exactly the right time and to the best table in the house," said Ben, as he stood looking over the group with a sexy look of affable confidence. "May we join you, ladies? It looks like you're having a great time."

"Absolutely," said Carmen. "Welcome! I'm so glad you could come." Carmen stood up and swept her arm in a clockwise motion that encompassed each person sitting around the table. "Everyone, meet Ben and Adam, two of our esteemed and amazing triathlon coaches."

"Nice to meet everyone," said Ben, and then Adam.

After introductions were made, Ben and Adam went in search of chairs.

"May I?" said Ben to Becca and Carmen, who were sitting next to each other.

"Certainly," said Carmen without hesitation. She scooted her chair away from Becca, making room for Ben to squeeze in between them.

CHAPTER 36

You Are Strong

Friday, May 20

AS BEN SAT DOWN NEXT TO BECCA, HIS LEG BRUSHED UP against hers, snatching her breath away. She tried to hold back from pushing her leg up closer to his as tingles ran from her toes to her face and everywhere in between. She not only wanted his leg pressing up more firmly against hers, but Becca also wanted to reach her hand over and caress his tightly toned thigh, and then she wanted to slide her hand up further to see if Ben was as hot and bothered as she was by their proximity.

Becca didn't dare look at him, but she could feel his eyes on her. What was he thinking? Why had he chosen to scoot in next to her? Was that just a coincidence, or was it purposeful? Was it simply because he already knew her and they had agreed to be friends? She wished she could read his thoughts. Not only did she know that was beyond her abilities, but Becca knew she also didn't even have the courage to lift her gaze to his to see what he might be thinking. She did not, however, make any move to pull her leg away. She told herself that was because there just wasn't enough room to pull away. *Whenever did I become so good at lying to myself?* thought Becca.

"So, Ben, are you from Pittsburgh?" asked Stacey.

Becca tried to concentrate on the conversation now flowing freely around the table. She could hear Ben's voice, as well as Adam's from time-to-time, amiably answering question after question from her group of friends. Ben's voice purred through her mind and her imagination—silky smooth, powerful, confident, and in control, very much in line with the images in her mind of his body moving through their run last week. If he was as flustered as she was, he certainly wasn't showing it. And that was a good thing, she reminded herself.

Ben then turned his attention to her. "So, Becca, any news on your bike situation? Are you ready for our group ride tomorrow?"

"Nothing yet. It's still just me and my old bike for now," Becca said, relieved to hear her voice coming out strong and stable rather than trembling. "I did the mid-week training ride on a stationary bike at Patterson's gym, like you recommended. I'm still hoping Chad will get me that trade-in or maybe even a loaner."

"Hmm," said Ben thoughtfully. "I'll check in with him on that."

"Oh, you don't have to do that," she said hurriedly. "I don't want to put you out."

"I don't mind. That's what I'm here for."

"Well...okay. If you're sure. It probably would be better for you and Chad to confer, as bikes are not exactly my specialty—as you probably already gathered when we first met," Becca added coyly.

Ben's leg tensed and pushed harder against hers, sending more heat through her body. She knew she shouldn't have stoked that fire. She was playing a dangerous game for someone who had made it clear she didn't want to be anything more than friends—or even more than just coach and trainee.

"I'll give you an update as soon as I can," said Ben in that controlled and confident no nonsense baritone that probably sounded to anyone and everyone—except her—as nothing but professional. "Right now, though, if you all wouldn't mind," Ben said aloud to the group, "I'm going to take my leave. It's been great meeting you all. I wish I could stay all night and hear more stories, but I've got a full day tomorrow. Adam, you about ready?"

Adam looked at him in surprise. "So soon? We just ordered another pitcher of beer," he said, gesturing toward the rest of the group. "Would you mind if I stay? You go ahead, and I'll just call for an Uber when I'm ready."

"Well, sure, no problem," said Ben. Becca saw a hint of curiosity cross his face as he took in Adam, surrounded by all the beautiful ladies. "Anyone else need a ride?"

"Becca, you don't have your car here tonight, do you?" asked Stacey. "You should *grab* that ride while it's there," she said, giving Becca a sideways glance out of Ben's view.

Becca pursed her lips and gave Stacey an answering eye roll right back. "I was actually just planning to *grab* an Uber home."

"Why would you do that?" Anna asked innocently, clearly missing the underlying nuanced meaning. "You've got a perfectly good offer on the table. Unless you aren't ready to leave yet. Are you wanting to stay longer?"

Leave it to Anna not to clue in to the big picture. She always got her science right—but not the social cues.

Becca hesitated before answering. She was ready to leave. It'd been a long work week, and she had a lot to get done this weekend, including that group ride tomorrow. But she felt a shiver of apprehension run through her at the thought of leaving alone with Ben. She'd done that before and where had it led? She wasn't worried about Ben. He had already proven he could be a perfect gentleman. No, she was afraid of herself. Could she be trusted around Ben? She needed to hold it together enough to keep her focus. And yet anytime she was around him, she felt herself melting into a puddle of irresolve that threatened to tempt her off her chosen track.

"I'd be happy to give you a ride," Ben said, interrupting her thoughts as he stood up and pulled her windbreaker from the back of the chair and held it out for her to slide into.

Becca looked at Carmen, not sure how to respond.

"Go ahead," said Carmen. "I'm planning to hang out a bit longer. Stacey still needs to give me an update...ya know, that thing, Stacey, that we were talking about earlier," Carmen said.

"Yeah...that thing," Stacey agreed. "You go ahead, Becca."

Becca gave them a discreet look and took the hint, turning to follow Ben out of the pub.

"Thanks for offering me a ride home," Becca said, as she and Ben walked the two blocks to the parking garage where Ben's truck was parked. "I'm not sure my friends gave you much of a choice, though. Are you sure you don't mind driving me home?"

"Of course not, I'm happy to do it. And your friends seem great. I enjoyed getting to meet them. I must admit, though, I was sure Carmen was going to be your most outspoken friend. But I'd say Stacey may have her beat. It's too early to tell yet, though." He chuckled.

"They are all amazing. I love getting together with them. I've missed them."

"What do you mean 'missed them?'" he asked curiously.

"Oh...um...nothing. This is your truck, right?" Becca asked, grateful their arrival had given her a reprieve from having to answer his question.

"Yes. Let me get the door for you," Ben said, opening the door and helping her up into the truck's passenger seat.

When she was settled, he moved around into the driver's seat. "You're going to need to give me directions; I don't know where you live." Ben turned slightly to give her a pointed look that held a hint of a sexy smirk before starting up his truck and pulling out of the parking garage.

"It's not far at all," she said, choosing to ignore that look for fear it would melt her resolve to keep her relationship with Ben at just friends. "It's down this road and then a few turns and we're there." She pointed ahead out the window. "At that next light, turn right."

For the next ten minutes, Becca focused on giving Ben directions to her apartment, curtailing any additional slips on her part. Not long after, she said, "This is it."

Ben pulled his truck into the parking lot of Becca's apartment complex and put the truck in park. He then quickly jumped out of the truck to come around and open her door for her before she'd even had time to gather her belongings. As she moved to slide out of the truck, Ben reached for her shoulder bag and purse with one hand and held out his other hand to assist her.

"Thank you," said Becca. She grasped Ben's hand and let him guide her down out of the truck. As soon as their hands touched, she felt that now familiar fission of heat. She stood in front of him, motionless, with the truck door still standing open. Ben didn't move. The world stood still. Becca felt herself standing on a precipice, together with Ben, where no one could touch them. What would happen next? Would they fall off a cliff together into an abyss of passion...or into despair? Or would they stand still in that moment forever, undecided on a direction?

"Becca," said Ben. "I..."

But no more words escaped his lips. Becca stood there, her insides in turmoil from desire and indecision. Then, her hands, now free of her belongings, reached up with a will of their own to cup Ben's chin gently as he stood there motionless, with nothing but their gazes touching. She could see desire in his eyes and knew it was mirrored in her own.

Using just his arm, Ben first gently set her bag down on the pavement without looking away from her, then slowly moved his arms to enfold her. He leaned forward in a gentle movement and his lips came down to meet hers. Becca did not hesitate to meet his kiss, feeling her own desire welling and tumbling over. The kiss became passionate, both clutching each other close, until eventually, Ben pulled back and rested his forehead against hers. "Becca," he said, "what are you doing to me?"

A sigh escaped her lips, and Ben tightened his grip, his hands caressing her down the full length of her spine, sending shivers of delight through her entire body.

"Becca, tell me what you want," Ben said, holding his lips a breath away from hers. She couldn't bear the absence and leaned back into him, reclaiming his lips with her own. Ben let out a groan and deepened the kiss, now running his hands up over her shoulders before caressing her neck, her cheeks, and then cupping her face. His tongue slid between her lips, exploring, and Becca succumbed to the sensations radiating through her.

Ben stopped suddenly and pulled away. Becca moaned, deeply feeling his absence. She wanted him back, back for more.

He placed his hands firmly on her shoulders and gently pushed her away from him and asked again, "What do you want, Becca? Tell me."

Becca felt the chill in the air wash over her, cooling her rebellious emotions. She stepped further away from him until his arms fell to his sides. The mantra she had been steeling herself with since middle school vibrated through her head just like the chill from the night, dampening the flames that threatened to engulf them both. *You will fulfill your goals and make your father proud.* She touched the charm that lay at her throat and rubbed it subconsciously as she recited the words her father had said to her when he'd given her the necklace on her twelfth birthday. That moment was so many years ago now but it still felt as though it were only yesterday. *You are strong. You are beautiful. You can do anything you set your mind to.* Ben, she reminded herself, was a distraction, and one that threatened to derail her. He could be her coach and even her friend for a short time; nothing more.

"I'm so sorry, Ben. I should not have let that happen," Becca said in a tone that left no room for discussion. "You said you only wanted to be friends, and we agreed to that. And you're right—you're my coach. I should have respected that." With a tone of formality, she finished with, "Thank you for driving me home. I'll see you tomorrow for the bike ride."

Ben looked slightly stunned. "Becca, we both know there's something here between us. You can't deny it and neither can I. Maybe we can give it a chance...?"

Becca began to shake her head. "I can't, Ben. I'm sorry. My life is a complicated mess. You deserve better than me. I can't give you what you need. I can't give anyone what they need. I'm so, so sorry." She picked up her bag with one hand and swiped at the tears that trickled down her cheeks with the other. "I have to go." She turned abruptly to make her way across the parking lot, feeling Ben's eyes on her back with every step.

Just before the door of her apartment complex closed behind her, she heard him say in that signature purr that carried a cool and confident power, "Goodnight, Becca."

CHAPTER 37

Midnight Blue Contessa

BEN

BEN DROVE AWAY FROM THEIR SECOND BIKE GROUP training in frustration. Becca had made it clear she wasn't planning to buy a new bike. He sighed. He didn't like it. Not one bit. That frame was old and battered and way too small for her.

It wasn't his call, though, he thought, pulling into a parking spot in front of Panera Bread. He wanted to pick up a sandwich before heading to the hardware store just down from Panera's, as he needed supplies for the renovations he'd planned for his house this afternoon. Thanks to Adam, he had finally gotten some momentum on those renovations, and he wanted to keep it going.

Ben reached for the door handle of Panera's but then stopped short, stepping back from the door. There was Becca. She was sitting inside the sandwich shop with an older woman. His heartbeat quickened. He reached for the door again, thinking he should go over and say hello before ordering his sandwich. But then he stopped short again. It looked like the two women were arguing. He stepped away from the door and into the shadow of a nearby pillar, hoping not to be spotted. Ben knew he should just leave. But he was curious. He still had so many questions. Becca was intriguing—and maddening.

He looked again through the window from his shadowed location. On the table between the two women was an envelope. He could see a stack of bills peeking out from it. Becca looked exasperated as she pushed the envelope toward the woman, who responded by adamantly shaking her head and pushing the envelope back toward Becca. He could see a flash of anger in Becca's eyes as she said something and then pushed the envelope back toward the woman. The woman lowered her head and sadly shook her head with seeming resignation as she picked up the envelope and put it in her purse.

Was this the 'obligation' Becca had referred to? Was this why she wasn't spending money on a bike? Was she giving money to this woman instead? Whatever it was, it was none of his business, Ben reminded himself. He started to turn away. He'd get his hardware supplies first and then come back for his sandwich later. But before he had fully turned, Becca looked up and spotted him. Her face lit up with a smile and she waved. He couldn't help but return her grin. It was infectious, he thought, resigned to the fact that when Becca smiled, he smiled. She stood up from the table and said something to the woman across from her. The woman stood up as well, and then they both made their way toward the door and Ben.

"Hi Ben! Let me introduce you. This is my mother, Joan. Mom, this is Ben. He's one of the triathlon coaches."

"It's so nice to meet you, Ben," Joan said, offering her hand. "Becca was just telling me over lunch all about the training. It sounds wonderful."

"It's nice to meet you as well," Ben said, shaking her hand. "And it's nice to have Becca on the team."

"Well, I certainly know it's doing wonders for her. It's getting her back out again after—"

"Mom!" Becca said curtly, interrupting whatever her mother was about to say. "We need to get going. Sorry, Ben, we hate to rush off but we're going to be late." Becca now had her hand on her mother's back and was steering her toward the parking lot.

"But...okay," her mother finally said with resignation. "I guess we need to rush off. Hopefully we can visit more another day."

"I hope so too," said Ben. "I guess I'd better get on with my errands as well. It was nice to meet you, Joan, and good to see you so soon again, Becca. Bye."

No wonder Becca didn't want to buy a bike, Ben thought, as he walked into Panera and up to the counter to order his sandwich. She was giving all her cash to her mother. He could relate to that. He'd sent plenty of money home to his parents after he'd left for college—money he really didn't have to spare at the time. He'd wanted to do it, though, and he wouldn't do it any differently now. What about Becca's safety, though? Didn't he have a responsibility to her as her coach to make sure her ride was safe? What if that frame ended up giving way while she rode that bike?

After leaving Panera's with his sandwich and purchasing supplies from the hardware store, Ben began loading his truck, realizing he'd been on auto-pilot the whole time he'd been doing his errands. Hopefully, he'd come away with the right items. He slid back into the driver's seat of his truck and started his engine. But before driving away, he hit the button on his steering wheel and spoke into the microphone when prompted. "Call Chad's Bike Shop."

"Dialing," responded the electronic voice coming out of his truck's speaker.

"Hello, Chad's Bike Shop. Chad speaking."

"Hey, Chad. It's Ben. I'm calling about the bike situation for Becca, the woman I had in last week."

"Oh sure," said Chad. "Sorry I couldn't accommodate her. I really thought I might end up with that trade-in, but it didn't come through. I know she wanted me to fix up that old bike of hers, but it just doesn't make sense to fix it. It's not worth it, not even a little bit."

"Yeah," said Ben. "That's what I'm calling about. I'm thinking it might be good to have an extra bike around for the team. I want to buy a bike that we can use as a loaner when needed. Do you still have that midnight blue Scott Contessa you fit her with?"

"Sure," said Chad. "It's kind of pricey for a general team loaner, though. And it's not gonna be a good fit for everyone. It's on the small side."

"Right," said Ben. "Yeah, I get that. I, ah, well, I'm still kinda liking the idea. Do you think I could come by today and buy that bike off you?"

"Sure. I'd be happy to get it ready for you—or her."

"Great, I'll be there in about thirty minutes. I'm already in my truck and nearby. Oh, and, I'd appreciate it if you just kept this to yourself. If anyone asks, just let them know it's a loaner we were able to make happen. Okay?"

"Ohh-kaayy," said Chad with a glimmer of curiosity in his voice. "I'll get her ready for ya. See you soon."

~

As Ben left Chad's Bike Shop, now with the midnight blue Scott Contessa loaded into his truck, he dialed Becca's number. At least I have her number now, he thought.

"Hello," answered a familiar voice.

"Hi, Becca. This is Ben. I hope you don't mind me calling your cell phone?"

"Of course not. What's up?"

"I have something I want to show you. Are you free tomorrow?"

"I have a standing brunch date with my mom in the morning. But I'm free tomorrow afternoon."

"Perfect. Can you meet me at 2:00 p.m. at the Old Oaks Trail next to the diner? And can you wear something you can bike in?"

"What's up, Ben? Did that woman decide to trade-in her old bike after all?"

"Not exactly. It's a surprise, one I think you'll like. Will you meet me?"

"Yeah, sure, of course. See you at 2:00 p.m. tomorrow," Becca said.

CHAPTER 38

Going Clip-Less

"SEE YOU NEXT WEEK, MOM," BECCA SAID, HURRYING OUT the front door. "Great brunch. Thank you!"

Her mom waved from the porch. "Great seeing you, Becca. Love you."

Becca backed her car out of the driveway, getting a glimpse as she did of her bike in her rearview mirror. Her fingers tightened on the steering wheel. Ben had sounded excited on the phone last night when he'd asked her to meet him today. He hadn't given her any details, though, except to wear something she could bike in. He hadn't said to bring her bike. But wouldn't she need it? Of course she should bring it.

Becca easily found the trailhead parking lot Ben had described. Thank goodness for GPS. But now she had about twenty minutes to kill before Ben was to arrive. Becca's bike slipped through her fingers and fell to the ground as she fumbled with getting it off her bike rack. *Great,* she thought, *why don't you just go and completely wreck this bike that needs to get you through.* She picked up the bike, brushed it off, and checked it over for additional dents. *As if I know what I'm looking for.* She sighed.

Becca rolled the bike over to a nearby picnic table and leaned it up against the bench, and then began to pace back and forth along the edge of the table. She was excited to see Ben, but she knew she needed to keep her emotions in check, even if the memory of their kiss on Friday still sizzled through her. And there he was.

Becca watched as Ben strode confidently toward her. She hadn't seen him pull into the parking lot. He had a smile on his face and a bike in hand that he was rolling toward her as he quickly approached.

She took a quick intake of breath, which then refused to be released, and she found herself momentarily holding her breath. When Ben was within reach, she exhaled the air she'd been holding from her now stressed lungs and asked worriedly, "What's that?"

Ben's eyes shifted away from her, and his smile faltered at her apprehensive tone. "This is the bike Chad showed you at the shop. We've got it until after the race. Ready to try it out?"

"Where's your bike?"

"We don't need it today. Today is about getting you acclimated to this new bike, including to the clip-less pedals. That is, if you're willing?" He held up a new pair of bike cleats. "What do you say? Are you game? If you're not up for going clip-less, we could just stick with getting used to the bike itself since this bike has more gears than you're used to."

Becca's arms came up around herself in a tight hug. She sucked in her bottom lip and took in another deep breath of air. She could feel herself outwardly beginning to panic but then watched, mesmerized, as Ben, in response, slowed the pace of his words and relaxed his large grin into a small, gentle smile. He spoke now in that soothing baritone Becca found so reassuring. Her body responded as though she were a lost animal being coaxed to safety by a compassionate and capable caregiver. His tone was kind, yet confident, powerful, yet reassuring. She let out a slow breath. Her arms dropped to her sides, and her shoulders relaxed. Her brain focused in on Ben's tone more than on his words, responding to them as though he were a hypnotist, coaxing her into a relaxed trance. The thought crossed her mind that she should feel apprehensive still, but it quickly flitted out of her head as Ben continued talking.

Then, Ben stood motionless. Now in front of her, he slowly and gently reached his arm out to set the shoes down on the bench next to where Becca was standing. He then gently pushed the bike forward toward her, akin to holding out a small offering of tuna to a skittish cat to coax it closer. "Would you like to check it out?"

His voice washed over her, like a drug designed to put her at ease. She reached out for the bike. It was so pretty; the color of a midnight sky on a calm night. It had subtle sparkles that shone through, just like stars peeking out from behind a cloud cover, only to be seen clearly when the fog lifted and the moon shone directly on them. Becca couldn't resist reaching out to take the bike from Ben. She held it steady with one hand and caressed the frame with her other.

Ben silently watched her, making no more moves toward her, as though knowing he needed to wait for a frightened animal to settle and trust. "Do you like it?" he asked in a hushed voice.

"I love it. Can I ride it?" she asked, finally looking up at him.

"Of course you can."

CHAPTER 39
Flying to California

BEN

"WHY ARE YOU GIVING ME THAT LOOK?" BEN ASKED suspiciously as he entered the office condo early Monday morning. He dropped his computer bag down on the desk in the back corner of the living room space that served as the office's main work area.

"Pat called from California," Jason said, referring to the manager of Ben's Los Angeles office. Jason looked at Ben with concern, his lips pursed with consternation, but said nothing further.

Ben raised an eyebrow at his expression. "Yeah? That good, huh? Come on, let me have it. That look you're giving me is making me nervous."

"It's the Cessair account."

Ben sighed. "Of course it is."

"Lucas Cessair is giving our team a hard time about the finishings for the new condos. He says our contractors painted them the wrong interior color—all of them. He says they're supposed to be pewter, not alabaster, and he wants them re-done at our expense."

"Haven't we already been through this? We have a recording of the videoconference where Lucas clearly picked the alabaster and gave us the go-ahead to get started. How can this still be a problem?"

"'Cause it's Lucas Cessair. And not only are our guys stressed, his are too. But Lucas won't listen to anyone. He just keeps ranting and bullying, determined to get his way. Why did we even take him on as a client? He's never happy."

"'Cause he's friends with the governor. And the governor, at Lucas' wife's fundraiser last year, told us clearly he thought we needed to take on this project."

"I guess that is kind of hard to say no to." Jason smirked.

"It's a good question, though, Jason," Ben said, sighing with resignation. "I should have known better and found a way to say no. And I should have insisted on a sign-off on the color. Lucas's got a horrible reputation for being a bully and a manipulator."

"What's done is done, I guess," said Jason. "We just need to figure out how to go forward. However, I'm out of answers. We've already spent a lot of time trying to placate him, but it doesn't seem to be working. I hate to say it, but I think you're gonna need to get out there in person to fix this one. I can handle the Fischer account while you're gone, but that Cessair account, not so much. Believe me, I've tried. I think this is one for the boss. Thank God I'm not the boss." Jason smirked while shrugging his shoulders and holding up his hands in defeat.

"You sure you don't want to play boss for this one?" Ben joked.

"Completely sure! Oh, and by the way, boss, our folks already have a meeting scheduled with Cessair's team on Wednesday morning. They asked if you could make it out for that meeting. They said they're pretty nervous about it."

Ben flicked a look at his wristwatch. "That's day after tomorrow. Can't we push it off another week so I can get some of these Fischer project sketches out the door? I'm also going to need to delve in a bit deeper into what's going on with Cessair before going out."

Jason shook his head. "If you're not gonna be there for that meeting, you're gonna have to tell them yourself. You know this has been coming, and they know it too. It'll go a long way for them to see the boss out there in person."

Ben sighed and ran his hand through his hair. "You're right. And I'm sorry I left you to deal with so much of this. I should have gone out a month or two ago when we first started seeing this new bout with Cessair rearing its ugly head."

Ben turned his head toward his assistant, who sat across the room at the large conference table in the middle of their meeting space. "Connie," Ben called, "can you please get me a flight out to California? Tomorrow afternoon, and direct if you can."

"On it," said Connie. "When do you want to return?"

Ben hesitated. How was he going to pull this off? He wanted to be back in time for the Friday night happy hour. Adam couldn't stop talking about getting to go again this coming Friday. And then there was the Saturday group training. Could he get back in time? He looked back at Jason. "I don't suppose there's any way I could get this back on track in time to be back here in Pittsburgh by Friday night?"

"You're funny," said Jason with a scoff. "Anyhow, I know they've also already got a meeting set up with Cessair himself on Monday. That means you probably need to stay out there at least through to that meeting."

Ben let out a growl of frustration. "All right, it can't be helped. Let's just hope I don't have to stay longer than that. Connie, go ahead and look for a return flight on Monday, preferably on the red-eye."

She nodded. "I'll see what I can find. Do you need me to work on getting any meetings set up for you too?"

"No, I'll work with Pat on that. It sounds like he's already got a couple of meetings on the books. I'll need to see where his head is on that. I'm sure we'll also need to do some strategizing before we set up any more meetings. I'll call him right now to see what he's thinking. In the meantime, just please get an idea of flight availability."

Ben turned back to Jason. "Can I push some of these refinements to our Fischer account sketches I've been working on over to you before I leave today—since it looks like I'll be pivoting this week?"

"No problem. Those I think I can handle. Give me what you've got. And you know, if I can't, I'll be coming right to you, boss—just maybe via coast-to-coast video."

"Thanks, Jason. You're the best, as always."

"Don't build up his head too much, boss," Connie joked from across the room. "And there are only two direct flights out of Pittsburgh to Los Angeles tomorrow. I can get you on the 6:00 a.m. flight or the 9:30 p.m. Not very decent of them, ya think? Do you want me to look for other times that take humans into account? It just wouldn't be a non-stop flight. I can get you on the Monday red-eye coming back, though, but it won't get you into Pittsburgh until 5:00 a.m. on Tuesday—another ungodly hour of the day."

"Book the 6:00 a.m. tomorrow and the Monday red-eye. I don't want to lose the time it would take to change planes in random airports across the country. I just hope taking that Monday red-eye back gives me enough time to get everything accomplished." Ben gave another sigh. "Better make it a changeable ticket, Connie—just in case."

Ben turned his focus back to the next order of business and dialed Pat's number. He needed to get up to speed on what Pat already had in play and see how he could help move things forward.

"Hey, Pat," Ben said into his cell phone as soon as Pat picked up. "I hear things are a bit tricky out there right now. What can I do to help?"

"Hold on, Ben. I'm glad you called. I'm going into the conference room. The entire team's gathered in there. Can I put you on speaker phone with all of us? We're pulling our hair out here and we need some help strategizing."

"Sure, no problem. Let's do it," said Ben.

Ben sat mostly listening with only occasional interjections for the next fifteen minutes as Pat and the rest of his Cessair team unloaded their frustrations along with some proposed solutions for all they'd been dealing with of late. Ben then spent the next half hour leading the team in pinpointing exactly what the issues were that needed to be dealt with to make sure the project stayed on track. They then worked through prioritizing those issues and laying out steps to mitigate the most dire of them, with the biggest hurdle—and the only real hurdle—clearly being Lucas Cessair himself.

"Okay, folks. I think we've got a good plan," Ben finally said. "Now we just need to see if we can execute on it. As promised, I'll see you all tomorrow. I'm gonna get home and pack and then put some more time into fleshing out these action steps we agreed upon. Call me if you need me before I get there tomorrow. I'm not looking forward to these meetings, but I sure am looking forward to seeing all of you in person. It's been a while since I've seen your faces on anything other than a video screen."

Ben hung up the phone and rubbed his fingers into his eyes. He yawned and stretched his arms over his head, trying to work out the kinks that had formed in his neck. Somehow it was already late afternoon, and he still had a lot more work to do. But he needed to pack, and if he were going to get any sleep at all, he'd need to get to bed sooner rather than later. He'd need to be up well before the crack of dawn to catch that 6:00 a.m. flight.

As Ben drove home, he ran through all he needed to do to get ready for his meetings out in California. It was good he was going out there, even though he dreaded having to deal with Cessair. He'd been meaning to pull in a couple of his California staff onto the Fischer account, anyway, and this trip would give him a good chance to do that. There was a need for more expertise on that account, and it looked like he'd need to pull some of that from his California team—who also were already stretched way too thin. But it couldn't be helped. He, Jason, and Connie also needed help, and not just with engineering, but across the board on everything. He'd been meaning to hire another person for his Pittsburgh office but just hadn't gotten around to it yet.

Ben took in a deep breath and exhaled it out in a forceful huff. He'd added too many distractions here in Pittsburgh—Adam, the Triathlon, the Marston revitalization project, and now, Becca. He'd let his personal life get in the way with his work goals, making his plate even worse. And now the Cessair project had become a potential liability. That was his fault; it was his job to make sure everything ran smoothly. And he was doing a piss-poor job of that right now. Something had to give.

Ben knew he certainly couldn't give up on Adam. He didn't even need to think about that one. Not to mention that he couldn't bail on Sam. But that was an easy fix—there were just six weeks left until race day, and Sam would still be here for another month of that. Ideally, both he and Sam should be at each training, but as long as at least one of them was present, the team would be fine. Ben just needed to make sure he let nothing impede those last two weeks of training after Sam left for his new job. And then, of course, he'd need to be—and wanted to be—at the actual race. Yes, he could do that and would enjoy committing to the task.

…But Marston—that would have to go. He just didn't have the

time for it. And he'd already found himself at odds with Ethan Trapp, the rising star of the development world in the Pittsburgh region. Ethan had made it clear to Ben that he didn't want anything or anyone messing with his new amphitheater project. He wouldn't even agree to meet with Ben to discuss ideas. But it didn't matter, Ben thought, shaking his head. He didn't have time to babysit Ethan's ego to get him to see how the amphitheater and Marston revitalization projects could be combined to ensure a better outcome for everyone. And why did he care, anyway? Marston was really no concern of his—it certainly wasn't *his* project. It wasn't even *a* project yet. Sure, he and the mayor and a couple of the City Council members had discussed the idea, but they hadn't solidified anything. His new home sat in Marston and he could live comfortably in that house whether or not Marston was revitalized, including whether or not the recreation trail materialized. His focus needed to be on his bread-and-butter projects and not on distractions like that trail—or Becca.

But as his mind turned to Becca, as it so often did these days, Ben thought about the look on her face when she'd mastered those clip-less pedals yesterday. She'd looked so proud of herself. He felt his lips turn up into a smile just thinking about it. He could give up the trail. But could he give up Becca?

What was he thinking? He felt his brow wrinkle at the thought, because there wasn't anything to give up. They had agreed to be nothing more than friends. But they weren't even that, were they? Hadn't Becca made that clear after he'd dropped her off at her apartment on Saturday night? He was just her coach, and she was just another participant on the team. Anyway, there were only six weeks left until race day. He and Becca would be out of each other's lives after that.

Ben's stomach scrunched up into a tight knot, and he shook his head in frustration. He couldn't think about that now. He needed to sort out his schedule so he could get on that plane tomorrow morning., He hit the phone button on his steering wheel and barked out a name on his contacts list.

"Hey, Ben. What's up?"

"Hey, Sam, I'm sorry to do this to you but I can't make Saturday's training."

"Is everything okay?"

"Yeah, sure. It's just that something's come up at work, and I need to go out to California. I have to stay through the weekend, but I should be back in time for the following training. Are you okay handling it on your own this coming weekend?"

"No problem. This Saturday is just a run. That's usually one of the easier ones, and the group is doing great so far. Do you think Adam will come? It's okay if he doesn't, but he sure is nice to have around. He's been a great help."

"Yes, he has." Ben smiled. "I don't know for sure, but he's next on my list of calls. I'll ask him to give you a follow-up call either way so you'll know what to expect."

"That would be great. Thanks, Ben."

"No worries, and thanks for understanding, Sam. Gotta go. I've got a lot to get done before I get on a 6:00 a.m. flight tomorrow."

"Hang in there, Ben. See you when you get back."

Ben hung up and turned his focus to Adam. Was he about to disappoint him yet again? He'd find out soon enough. He sighed as he hit the phone button on his steering wheel again.

"Hi, Ben. How's it going? Hey, that happy hour was awesome!" Adam said, without giving Ben a chance to respond. "We're going again on Friday, right? I can't wait. It was fun to get to meet some locals. Carmen and Becca's friends are great. Do you want to drive there together again? Or maybe that's not such a good idea," Adam added suggestively. "Maybe you want to go with Becca? That woman can't keep her eyes off you. Are you two a thing? Don't worry about me if you want to take her; I'll find my own way there. And after Saturday's group run, if you want help on your renovations again, I'd love to help. We could probably make a lot of progress on that hardwood floor for the living room. You can just pay me in food again. How about we order some of Tony's lasagna like you got for us last time? I've been craving it all day today—"

"I'm sorry, Adam," Ben finally interrupted. "I've got to go to Los Angeles this week and won't be back until Tuesday morning. There's a problem with one of our projects, and I've got to meet with some of our clients in person to smooth it over before it turns from a mole hill into a mountain of a problem. I'm really sorry, I didn't want to disappoint you."

"Oh..."

Ben waited anxiously for Adam to say more.

There was another beat of silence before Adam said, "I understand. What about happy hour, though? And Saturday's training? Should I go? Maybe that would be weird. I guess I can wait another week until you're back." Adam's happy chatter had turned sour.

"I think it would be great if you go, and, in fact, Sam asked about you. He's hoping you'll be there for the training on Saturday. He asked me to see if you would go even though I won't be there. You've been a great help so far. What do you think?"

"Yeah, sure, I'd love to help. I'll give Sam a call and make sure I know what he needs me to prepare for," Adam said, his voice brightening a little; but Ben could hear that it was still tinged with disappointment.

"I think you should definitely also go to happy hour," Ben now said. "I've got Becca's number. Do you want to call her to let her know I won't be there but that you will?"

"Nah, that's okay. We don't really know each other well enough yet. She might think it's weird that I'm calling."

Ben remembered Becca's hesitancy in giving him her number that first weekend they'd met. Maybe Adam was right. Maybe she wouldn't appreciate him sharing her number, even if it were just with Adam. His brother sounded so defeated, though. Again, his fault. Why could he not get his world on track—work and personal?

"How about I call her?" said Ben. "I want to check in with her anyway to let her know I won't be there." Wait—should he be calling her? He wasn't planning to call any of the other participants. But this was different, he told himself. He needed to call her—for Adam's sake.

"Well, if you're going to call her anyway, I guess you could just see if they're still on for happy hour. If I'm going to be a fifth wheel, though, it's no big deal."

"I'll check in with her and call you back."

"Thanks, Ben. No big deal, though, really," Adam said. But Ben knew Adam was lying.

"Hey, Ben, before you hang up—maybe while you're out in California, you could check in on Mom and Dad? I kinda feel like I deserted them by coming out here to Pittsburgh. I know they're worried about me...and I know they really miss you. You'd be surprised how different they are now. They're back pretty much to being their old selves."

Ben didn't answer.

"Anyhow, no pressure. Just think about it," said Adam.

"Gotta go, Adam. I'm going to call Becca. I'll keep you posted."

After his phone call with Becca, Ben immediately dialed Adam's number again. "Hi, Adam. I just talked with Becca, and she absolutely wants you at happy hour. I didn't even bring it up with her either. When I told her I was going to be out of town, she immediately asked me to relay to you you're still invited. She really wants you to go, and she asked me to give you her number in case you need it. I also gave her your number. But, you don't need to call her back unless something changes. She said to tell you just to show up anytime after 5:00 p.m. She also said to tell Sam he's welcome too."

"Thanks!" Adam said, and then he started to chatter on about who might be there again and about how much fun he'd had last week. "That Anna, though, she's a strange one, isn't she? It's all science to her. Not to the others, though, they're all a hoot! Anyway, thanks!"

Ben laughed at the happiness coming through in Adam's voice, and at his descriptions of the women they'd met last week, pleased that he could be the catalyst for some of that happiness. "You're very welcome. However, I think you're the one doing me a favor. Sam and Becca sounded pleased about seeing you and not a bit worried about me not being there. Sam is especially grateful to you for all your help with the participants, and I know you're better company at a happy hour than I could ever be. So, thank you."

"Ahh, you know me, I aim to please! Have a good trip, Ben. And don't forget about Mom and Dad...please?"

"I'll think about it. See ya, Adam. I've gotta go get ready for this trip."

CHAPTER 40
Happy Hour with Adam and Sam

ADAM

"Thanks for picking me up, Sam. I'm glad you were up for happy hour tonight. I really didn't want to go alone. The ride is a help, too. I've been taking a lot of Ubers lately, and it's kind of a drain on my pocketbook. Ben did loan me his car for whenever I need it since he's got his truck, too, but I don't know my way around very well yet. Plus, I don't want to take advantage."

"No problem. Thanks for inviting me. And for being willing to help out again tomorrow at the group run."

"It's been great for me too, actually. It's nice getting to meet people outside of my summer program. The program's great but it's intense. I'm not used to all of this college stuff. Plus, being a part of the group trainings has given me an opportunity to see another side of Ben."

"I didn't even realize Ben had a brother! Oh, sorry, I hope I didn't offend you. I probably just wasn't around him enough."

"No offense taken. I doubt he would have talked about me much—or our parents. It's a long story. We kind of lost touch actually for a lot of years in there—until I contacted him a couple of months ago to let him know I was coming to Pittsburgh."

"I'm sorry I didn't know."

"No way you would have. Ben's not exactly an open book with people. He's a good guy, though."

"That he is. He's always there for anyone who needs a hand. Take this training, for example. When I called to ask him if he would help—and I gave him a good enough reason to—he was right there for me. And back in college, I had a rough go of it at first. The transition from home to college for me was a real struggle. We met at a race early in our freshman year and somehow got to talking about school. He asked if I'd be interested in a study group to help each other out.

"It turned out he really didn't need any help. He's a smart guy and the academics were no problem for him, but me...well, I would have flunked my calculus class if it weren't for him, and maybe even a few other classes. We didn't even go to the same school, and we were fierce competitors during our college tri competitions. That didn't matter to him, though. Ben still helped me out. And others too. He was a sucker for anyone going through a hardship. Sometimes I think he kinda got taken advantage of, though. There were a couple of women along the way who didn't treat him so nice. But I'll always be grateful to him, and I'm sure there are lots of other people out there who would say the same."

Adam was fascinated to hear this story about his brother. He shared with Sam, "He was there for me when I was younger. It just kinda got really messed up, and we ended up losing touch. It wasn't anyone's fault, really. It was just a tough time. And we were just kids...." Adam turned to look straight ahead, but he felt Sam turn his head toward him to give him a quizzical look.

"Want to talk about it?" asked Sam.

"No, I guess not," Adam said hesitantly. "I'd better leave that to Ben—or not. Like I said, he's not exactly a communicator with his personal stuff, and I don't want to mess with that just when we're getting to know each other again."

"Understood," said Sam without hesitation. "If you need anything while you're out here, though, don't hesitate to come to me. I know you've got Ben here, but you've got me too."

"Thanks," said Adam, his voice thick with emotion. "Anyhow, thanks again for the ride to happy hour. I had a great time last week." Adam swiveled his head to make eye contact with Sam, and an air of excitement crept back into his voice as he added, "I'm sure you're gonna love it too."

~

"Hey, Adam! Sam! Welcome," said Carmen. "I'm so glad you two could make it tonight!"

"We wouldn't miss it for the world—unlike my big brother," Adam joked. "He's jetted off to California without us."

"Yes, Becca told me he couldn't come tonight. Not sure why she rated a call and I didn't, though," Carmen said, elbowing Becca.

Becca rolled her eyes. "I told you, Carmen. he just wanted to let me know he wouldn't be at happy hour. He also wanted to make sure Adam and I had each other's numbers in case Adam wanted to come tonight."

"He still could have called me instead of you," Carmen persisted. "Oh wait, I think I know the answer to that one!"

"Zip it, Carmen!" Becca said, her already crimson cheeks turning an even deeper shade of red.

"Aren't you going to introduce us?" interrupted Stacey. She leaned across the table and offered her hand to Sam. "Hi! You must be Sam. I'm Stacey. We heard a lot about you last week," she said as her gaze flicked over his physique. "All good stuff, and it looks like it was all true. Glad you could come tonight. And this is Anna..." she continued on with the introductions.

"Nice to meet all of you," Sam said with a grin while eyeing Stacey with a bit of trepidation.

"So, how are our girls faring through all of this training? Are they going to be able to finish the race?" Stacey asked, forthrightly forging ahead while continuing to ogle Sam.

"Absolutely. I have no doubt they'll do great. But what I want to know is why you all aren't doing this with them?"

Stacey nodded her head appreciatively at Sam's quick comeback, and he winked at her.

Anna snorted, clearly catching only the question and not the flirta-tious undercurrent of Sam and Stacey's exchange. "Not me, I'm the statistician," she said, pushing her glasses up higher on her nose.

Adam leaned back in his chair, glad he'd chosen the seat furthest away from Anna. That girl scared him. She was clearly wicked smart...but a bit odd. He felt like an out-of-place doofus around her as he had barely made it through high school. At least he'd finally gotten his GED, but not until several years after he should have graduated. He hoped to keep his distance from her at these happy hours. He was already surrounded by many smart and accomplished people at CMU —high school valedictorians and other over-achievers spawning from parental unit overachievers. He was the odd man out in that pod. He didn't want to feel like that in this group here too.

"Well, I'm sure we could use a statistician," Sam said politely. "What do you think, Adam?"

"Uh, yeah, sure. Or at least a cheering squad. You're all welcome to come join us on race day. The more spectators, the more fun."

"I'll be there," said Stacey. "I've already got it marked in red on my calendar."

"Me too," said Anna.

"We're all planning to be there," said Eileen. "We don't want to miss a chance to cheer on our besties here for this crazy ride they're on."

"Speaking of rides," said Carmen. "Did you see the loaner bike Ben gave Becca? It's a beauty. We went for a quick ride during the week after work—as we were supposed to, coach," she said, giving Sam a wink. "It's even got clip-less pedals! *And* Becca already knows how to use them! Kind of, anyway." Carmen turned her head toward Becca. "You fell that one time. She just tipped right over," Carmen said through a laugh.

"It was not funny," Becca said, but with a smile. "And it hurt. I have a skinned knee to prove it."

"You weren't even moving when you fell. She came to a stop and then just hung in the air upright for a moment before tipping right over and falling to the ground."

"That's pretty common," said Sam. But Adam could see that Sam was trying not to join in with Carmen in laughter. "I've seen it many a time. Been there myself, in fact. It's a part of learning to clip in and, more importantly, clip out. If you don't get your foot out in time, there's no way around it—you're going to fall."

"I want to learn how to do that too. Not the falling part, just the clipping in and out part," Carmen clarified with a smile. "Can you teach me, Sam? Ben taught Becca on Sunday when he brought her that loaner."

Adam and Sam exchanged a quizzical glance. Very interesting, thought Adam. He knew Becca desperately needed a new bike. But last he'd heard, she was sticking to her guns and was going to use the one she already had—broken or not. And Ben hadn't said a word to him about teaching Becca to ride, let alone ride clip-less.

"Sure," said Sam to Carmen. "I'd be happy to. Did you change out the pedals on your bike to clip-less yet? You'll need to do that before I can teach you."

"Oh," said Carmen with disappointment. "Maybe I could get that done later this week. Maybe for tomorrow, Becca and I can just practice with her bike after the group run? What do you think, Becca?"

"Yes!" said Becca. "I would love for you to go clip-less too. And practicing tomorrow sounds great. We don't want to put you out though, Sam. We can practice on our own."

"Actually," said Sam. "I'd like nothing more than to help you two. I would love to see Ben's face at the next group ride when you two both show up with clip-less pedals—and show up knowing how to ride with them. But,"—Sam paused momentarily before asking—"where exactly did that bike come from, Becca? I didn't know you had a handle on a loaner."

"Yeah, Becca. Just where did that bike come from?" asked Carmen.

"Ben said it's just a loaner for the team to use."

"Seems to me you and Ben are spending a good amount of time together," said Stacey, wiggling her eyebrows. "Don't forget what I told you, Becca."

Becca's face colored, and she ducked her head.

"What did you tell her?" asked Sam and Adam in unison.

"Nothing, nothing at all," Becca said, giving Stacey the stink eye. "Right, Stacey?"

Stacey leaned back in her chair with a heavy sigh. "Yeah, right, nothing at all. Nothing to see here. Move along, folks."

"So," said Sam, adroitly changing the subject, "tell me about this mansion Ben mentioned earlier. It sounds cool. How the heck did he end up buying in Marston, anyway? Isn't that place kind of a scary mess?"

CHAPTER 41
A Visit to Mom and Dad

BEN

THANK GOODNESS THE TEAM MEETINGS HAD GONE WELL this week, including through the weekend. Ben sighed at the effort he'd put into them. They were now well-positioned for the meeting coming up on Monday with Lucas Cessair. They'd fleshed out a succinct list of clear and viable solutions, along with talking points for each item. Everyone, both from his team and from Cessair's, was on board. In fact, Cessair's team was clearly grateful to Ben's team for picking up the mantle on strategizing ways to move the project to completion. It was obvious they were all tired of Lucas's bullying.

And on Friday, Ben had even been able to take a break from the Cessair project to meet with his two California engineers to delve into the Fischer project. They were now much better situated for the long-distance working relationship they'd need to employ going forward. That would take at least some of the pressure off of him and Jason.

However, although he was prepared, Ben couldn't deny that he was still nervous about Monday's meeting with Cessair. But he was even more nervous about tonight's dinner. He'd done what Adam had asked—he'd called his parents when he'd gotten into town. And they'd invited him to their house, the same house he and Adam had grown up in, for dinner tonight.

His mom had answered when he'd called. He'd been surprised at how happy she was to hear from him. And then his dad had picked up a landline handset from another room and had encouraged him to come as well. But what was up with the landline? Had they never progressed to cell phones? Maybe they hadn't progressed at all since...since his sister's passing. Maybe time just stood still for them from that day forward? But Adam had encouraged him to check in on them, and Ben would do it for Adam.

Ben stood at the door to his childhood home. Should he just walk in like he used to? That would be awkward, he thought. He forced himself to move his hand toward the doorbell and pushed the button. A chime sounded from within the house, and he heard voices and footsteps approach. He took a deep breath, trying to still his racing pulse.

His mother, Cindy, opened the door. "Ben!" she exclaimed with tears in her eyes as she cautiously reached toward him with open arms. "We're so glad you're here," she sniffled.

Ben awkwardly leaned in, reaching out with one arm to return the hug his mother offered. His dad, Henry, stood just behind her. He looked so much older, but he still wore the same glasses—or at least versions of them—that drooped off his nose as he peered over the top of them. His mouth pinched as he did so, giving his face a severe expression.

"Son, come on in. It's so good to see you," his father said, awkwardly taking a step back and ushering Ben into the house. As Ben moved forward, his mother reached around him to close the door, and then followed Ben and his Dad further into the house. There was no turning back now, thought Ben.

"Go on ahead into the living room. I've set some snacks out for us," said his mom. "Henry, go ahead and offer him something to drink. I'm just going to check on the roast. I remember how much you liked a good pot roast when you were a child, Ben. I hope you like it."

"That sounds great, Mom. I hope you didn't go to too much trouble," he answered politely.

"Not at all," she said, stepping away into the kitchen.

While his dad was busy at the sideboard fixing them each a drink and his mom was in the kitchen checking on dinner, Ben surveyed the living room from his perch on the couch. Memories flooded in, jumbling his thoughts. There was the ornamental pitcher that Adam had broken when they were kids. He'd tried to glue it back together before his parents found out but had failed miserably. Fortunately, neither of them had gotten into too much trouble over it. His parents had simply been impressed that they'd tried to fix it. They hadn't been as impressed about the glue they'd gotten on the living room sofa, though. Was this that same sofa? He shifted his weight to look at the spot just beneath where he sat. Yes, there was the discoloration on the cushion from that misadventure.

There were pictures on the bookcase in the corner as well as on the fireplace mantel of him and Adam...and of Sophia. Ben was surprised to see the pictures of his sister. When he'd left, none of those had remained on the shelves or anywhere else visible in the house. He wasn't sure where they'd gone, but it seemed they'd returned, now holding a place of prominence throughout the living room. There was even a copy of the picture Adam had given him when Adam had arrived in Pittsburgh—the one of the three of them in Kenya at Lake Nakuru. He wondered if Adam had been the impetus for that picture being included in the bunch on the mantel.

Ben's father approached from the sideboard and handed Ben a gin and tonic before taking a seat next to him on the couch. "We've been following your career, Ben. We're very proud of you. All those awards for your designs; it's impressive."

An awkward silence filled the room. The clock ticked and, finally, the floorboards creaked as his mother returned from the kitchen. She carried the flowers that Ben had brought, now in a vase with water, and set them on the coffee table in front of where he and his father sat on the sofa.

"Thank you for the flowers, Ben. They're beautiful. And for the wine. I've opened it up to let it breathe before dinner. It will go perfectly with the pot roast."

Another awkward silence filled the room.

"Dinner will be ready in about fifteen minutes," his mother said.

"In the meantime, hopefully we can do some catching up. We've missed so much. Are you doing okay, Ben? Are you happy?"

What an odd question to plop into the middle of the room, Ben thought. Am I happy? "Sure, Mom, I guess so," he replied awkwardly. "How about you two? Are you doing okay?"

"We are, actually," his dad finally answered. "It's been a long time coming, but we really can't complain. You and Adam are doing so well now. Adam called us after he got to Pittsburgh, and he's been keeping us updated. He's so happy to get reacquainted with you. He missed you—we all did. And, of course, we miss Sophia. But we know now that we were lucky to have had her in our lives as long as we did. What we miss most now is you, Ben," his father said in a choked voice, clearly struggling to hold back strong emotions.

"Yeah," said Ben awkwardly. "Are you going overseas anymore, Dad?"

"No, I haven't traveled in years, at least not for work. I have some friends who are still abroad, though, so I get to hear about various infrastructure initiatives, especially out in Kenya where we spent most of our time. There's still a lot of hardship out there and a lot to be done. Are you interested in any of that kind of work anymore? There's lots of it if you want it." His father coughed, covering his mouth with his hand and took a moment before continuing, "I'm sure you don't need that work or even want it anymore for that matter. Your designs are beautiful but more of a fit for big urban US cities than for far-off African villages."

Ben felt a shadow cross his face and wondered if his parents noticed. He'd wanted to do that kind of work when he was young and following his father around, supposedly helping but probably getting in the way more than anything. He'd steered clear of that type of work after he got his architecture degree, though. That's not where the money was—and he'd needed the money. And so had his family.

"I'll go ahead and serve dinner," his mother said, filling the now palpable silence at Ben's lack of a response.

"Do you need any help, Mom?" Ben asked stiffly.

"Yes. That would be nice."

Ben followed his mother into the kitchen and helped serve up the plates and carry them to the small dining room table just off the kitchen. The same dishes, the same table. There were good times here, Ben realized with a start. Not just devastation as he'd remembered it over these past many years. But then, he remembered that morning when Adam had thrown one of those dishes across the room, shattering it to pieces. His mother hadn't even noticed, and his father had been out of the country.

His mom walked over to the coffee table, halting his internal reminiscing, and picked up the vase of flowers he'd brought. She set them in the middle of the dining room table. "These are so beautiful. It'd be a shame not to have them front and center while we eat. Would you please do the honors and pour the wine you brought for us, Ben?"

Ben complied and settled in at the table, his feelings conflicted. The last time he'd sat at this table was when he was back in college. He'd come home for the weekend. His dad had been surly and noncommunicative, and his mom had spent almost the entire visit sitting in a large stuffed chair in the far corner of the living room. She'd clearly been medicated and had only mumbled vague responses to the few questions Ben had asked. Adam had been nowhere to be found. When he'd asked his parents where Adam was, his father had given only a short, brusque response: "Out. Don't know where."

Ben had brought takeout Chinese food that night. He'd filled their three plates with the food but hadn't stayed to eat it with them, giving some lame excuse about needing to get back to school to study for an exam. This differed from that night. His mother was not only alert, she was solicitous toward him. Overly solicitous, in fact, making him feel confused and unsure of himself.

"Ben, would you like another helping of pot roast? Or some pie? I bought an apple pie for dessert. And I have whipped cream...?"

"No thanks, Mom. That was delicious, though. Like the old days —" Ben stopped abruptly, not finishing his sentence.

"It's okay, Ben," his mother said in a hushed voice. "We can talk about those old days now. And we owe you an apology."

"No!" Ben said, more harshly than he'd intended. "You don't owe me anything. I'm doing fine now. It looks like you're both doing fine too," he added angrily.

His mother leaned back as though struck.

"Ben," his father started, "don't talk to your mother like—"

"Henry, stop!" said his mother. "We owe Ben an apology. You know it and I know it. And Ben has a right to be angry with us."

Ben's father slumped back in his chair and rubbed his eyes with his fists, pushing his glasses up and finally taking them off and setting them aside. He picked up the napkin next to his plate and wiped his eyes, the sweat now visible on his forehead. He cleared his throat, his eyes now fully shut, and gently rocked back and forth in his chair. "Your mother's right, Ben. I'm so sorry. I'm so, so sorry," he said, tears now streaming down his face. He wiped his eyes and cleared his throat again before looking back up at Ben. "There's no excuse. It was our job to take care of you and Adam. I'm sorry I left you two, and I'm sorry I left your mother on her own to fend for all of you alone. I hope someday you can forgive us...forgive me. But your mother's right; you have a right to be angry."

Ben sat there, stunned. His heart raced wildly. He wanted nothing more than to run from this house and never look back. And yet, he sat, rooted to his chair, his mouth hanging open. His parents remained in their seats...waiting. Waiting for what? Was he supposed to just forgive them? Just like that? He'd struggled to make his way through college, and Adam hadn't even made it through high school. Ben had sent money home. But not for his parents—for Adam. Had they even used it to buy food and clothing for Adam? Or had his father used it to fly off to Africa and his mother for some sort of drug to settle her nerves? He hadn't known what they'd done with the money back then. And he didn't know now. But it didn't matter anymore. He and Adam were fine. Weren't they?

Ben watched as his mother finally pushed her chair back. The only sound now was the scraping of the chair legs across the wooden floor.

"Ben," his Dad started, "when Sophia—"

"Don't! Just don't! Since when do you talk about...about *her*...in this house? It's okay. It'll be okay!" he yelled, trying to convince himself it would be. "I don't want to talk to you about her tonight, though."

Ben caught his parents exchanging a look. What did that look mean? He wasn't the one who required her name to be off-limits all those years ago. He wasn't the one who had taken all of the photos of her down. He had succumbed to his parents will and had never spoken her name in this house again after she died. Did they really want to change those rules now? Tonight? Ben pushed his chair back and started to stand.

"Ben—wait. Please. Let's talk about your work. Tell us about your work," encouraged his dad, pleadingly. "You're clearly good at it, and we're so proud of you. Of course, you can leave if you need to, but we hope you'll stay...at least for a piece of pie. Will you please stay? Just for a little while? You made the trip all the way out here. Please, at least tell us about your life. We want to hear about it. We want to know you're okay."

Ben, now standing next to the table, ran his hand through his hair and looked at his mother. She looked so...hopeful and so afraid. Of what? Of him? Afraid that he would leave? He felt a pit develop in his gut and wrenched his gaze away from his mother, not wanting to see the pain he was causing her. Didn't they deserve that pain, though? He swiveled his gaze to his father. His father's cheeks were stained with tears, and his face looked puffy and swollen. There was also pain in his father's eyes...and fear as well. They were old man eyes now, with wrinkles emanating from his eyelids across his face and down into his cheeks. His father shouldn't look that old. He wasn't that old. But the years had not been good to him. Did he deserve more pain? And from Ben? Ben didn't want to be that person. There'd been enough pain already.

But did his dad mean what he said? Could he trust him or would his dad lull him into a false sense of security and then, again, betray that trust? He didn't want to stick around for that. His indecision must have shown on his face, because his father finally spoke again, this time through obvious anguish.

"Ben," his dad choked out, "please stay. Cindy, can you please get my..." He never got to finish his request as his father was suddenly leaning forward, clutching his chest.

"Henry!" his mother cried. "Are you okay?! Hold on. I've got your medicine right here."

"Dad! What's wrong?!" Ben said, bewildered. "Are you okay? Mom, what's wrong with him?"

"He'll be okay. Don't worry, Ben. Just give him a minute, he'll be fine. Don't worry." But her voice was clearly laced with anxiety.

Ben moved to his father's side. "Do you need to lie down, Dad? Do you want me to help you to the couch?" Ben was ready to lift him or do whatever else was necessary to fix this...this situation—or whatever it was. "Should we call an ambulance?" he asked, turning to his mother, his own voice now rising in panic.

"No. I'm sorry, Ben. We didn't mean to worry you. It's just that...just that life has taken a toll on your father over the years. He's a good man, though, Ben. Remember? I know you probably don't think that right now. But he is. Please try to remember all those years the two of you...and then you and Adam...and then... Well—" she stopped abruptly and took a breath. "Well, all those years when the two of you were out in the field, building things together. You were so young, but you were born to do that kind of work. That's even more clear now. We're so proud of you, Ben, and we're so sorry we let you down."

"Mom, stop. It's okay. What's wrong with Dad? What does he need right now?"

"If you could help him to the couch, that would be very helpful. He just needs a moment to let his heart slow back down—and he needs to know that you, Ben, his son, and his other son, Adam, are okay."

Ben helped his Dad to the couch. His father's body felt small and frail in his arms. He was so light, and his face was ashen, with a new sheen of perspiration evident on his forehead. "Thank you, Ben. I'll be fine," his Dad said, the color now beginning to return to his face. "I just need to sit a minute. I didn't mean to scare you."

"Take your time, Dad. I'll stay as long as you need me to." Ben inhaled a massive amount of oxygen, hoping to slow his own racing pulse.

"Here, Henry. Take this glass of water. Ben, here's one for you too," his mother said, handing them each a glass of ice water.

"Thanks, Cindy," his Dad said, reaching up to clasp her hand, which was sitting on his shoulder. "I don't know what I would do without you. Your mother takes good care of me, Ben. I'm a lucky guy. So, Ben, how about you tell me about some of those awards you've won while I sit here a minute to catch my breath? I saw the latest one come through not too long ago—the American Institute of Architects Merit Award. I'd love to hear about that project."

Ben settled in next to his father's nearly prone figure on the couch and began to talk about his work—his designs, the awards he'd accumulated, and especially about his current projects as the pace for the evening fell back into a steady, more soothing rhythm.

"Anyhow, that's the project I'm out here for now," Ben said after regaling his Dad with story after story and finally ending with the details of Lucas Cessair's bullying and high-powered, irrational politicking.

"Can you please help me sit up, Ben? I feel so much better now. Thank you for telling me about your projects and your life. You've done well for yourself, and I'm so proud of you."

"Thanks, Dad," Ben said, as he helped his Dad into a sitting position. "I learned a lot of it from you...in those early days in Kenya."

"I still have some things from those days, Ben. Do you remember the model we made before we implemented the stormwater collection project in that small village in northern Kenya near Lake Nakuru? I've still got that. It's in the garage. Would you like to see it?"

"You still have it?" Ben said in amazement. He felt his lips twitch into a semblance of a smile for the first time that evening. "We spent hours, days, weeks—months, working on that model! And then seeing it come to life, giving life... That is...something I will never forget." A swell of pride bloomed in Ben's chest at the memory. "When that clean water started flowing from the taps we'd installed..." His voice trailed off as emotions choked off the rest of his words.

"Would you like to see it?" his father repeated.

"Are you sure you're up to it?" asked Ben, now itching to leave the house, but this time for a trip to the garage rather than to escape far and away.

"Absolutely," his father said, holding his hand out to Ben in a silent request to help him up.

Ben held his father's arm as he led them into the back corner of the garage, where a large table sat with a model of the water infrastructure system they'd built all those many years ago. Ben lifted his hand to touch it, but then turned to his father, silently looking to him for permission. His father solemnly nodded his head and gave Ben an encouraging smile. As Ben's hand made contact with the model, memories flooded him—good memories—and the two of them spent the next half hour in that garage, reminiscing about their overseas travel and his father's work, before heading back into the house.

"Anyhow," Ben said, as they approached the house, "that meeting with Cessair tomorrow is going to be a challenge."

His mother looked toward them as they entered, an anxious smile on her lips that turned up when she saw they were talking amiably now.

"We're hoping Cessair won't give us too much trouble," Ben continued, returning his mother's smile without breaking stride in his conversation with his Father. "But you can never be sure with him. We've put together a pretty good strategy I think, and both my and Cessair's teams are on board. Now we just need to get Lucas to step up and play nice."

"Your strategy sounds like a good one, son. And, ya know, I found in my working days that sometimes you just have to take a step back and tell someone to go to hell."

Ben startled and leaned back in surprise at the advice.

His dad grinned and added, "You just have to make sure you do it in a way that makes them look forward to the trip."

Ben felt a grin creep across his own face. "I like that. I may just try that with Cessair tomorrow. Speaking of work, I'd better get going. It's getting late."

"Wouldn't you like a piece of pie before you go, Ben?" asked his mother. "And, Henry, it looks like you're feeling much better. How about you? A piece of pie?"

"I will if he will," his dad said, pointing to Ben. "Whaddya say, son? Some pie?"

"Sure. How can I say no to a piece of apple pie with whipped cream?"

CHAPTER 42

African Muse

BEN

DURING THE TWO-HOUR DRIVE BACK TO HIS HOTEL ROOM, Ben had a lot to think about. His visit with his parents wasn't at all what he'd expected. It had gone well—ultimately, anyway. It was fun to see that old model he and his dad had created. And his mom had remembered what his favorite dinner was as a child. She was awake and aware—not exactly how he'd remembered her back in the days shortly after Sophia...passed. And there were pictures of Sophia displayed all around their house now. While he'd been living at home, Ben had known to tiptoe around that subject. Even Adam, while still so young, knew better than to bring up Sophia's name in front of his mother. And it wasn't like they could discuss it with their dad—he was rarely even in the country.

But tonight had been different. His dad was home. His mom was attentive. And they'd asked about his life and knew a lot about Adam's. And they'd truly seemed proud of his accomplishments. They'd also seemed content with each other—maybe even happy with each other. A flash of Becca's face ran through his mind, but he quickly brushed it aside. He'd seen first-hand what personal distractions could do to his life. And he didn't need more evidence about his inability to be a family man, just take tonight. His parents and Adam had all reconnected years ago, apparently. He'd been the odd man out.

The one who hadn't known how to rectify their family life. But...maybe...

Ben reached to hit the phone button on his steering wheel. Darn, he'd forgotten he was in a rental car. He dug into his pocket and pulled out his cell phone and then used a voice command to direct it to call Adam on speakerphone.

"Hey, Ben. Are you okay?" Adam asked in a sleepy voice.

"Oops, sorry Adam. I forgot about the time difference. What time is it out there?

"It's 1:00 a.m. here," Adam said with concern. "Are you okay?"

"Yeah, all good. Hey, I can call you back another time. I just wanted to tell you...that I just left Mom and Dad's house. I had dinner with them tonight."

"*No shit?*" Adam said in a surprised and now fully alert voice. "How did it go?"

"Good, actually," Ben said, just as surprised to say it as to hear himself say it. "How did happy hour go? And how was training this morning?"

"Good, really good. Sam came with me to happy hour, so you are now officially excused for leaving me hanging as my wingman," Adam teased.

"Good, hey, that's good. Was Becca there?" Ben asked, now getting more to the crux of the reason for his call.

"Yesss...she was there. And so were Sam, Carmen, Stacey, Eileen, Anna, and Natalie. Want to know how they are?"

"Yeah, sure...of course I do. I was just about to ask about them," Ben lied.

"Sure you were. Hey, what's up with you and Becca, anyway? Is there something you want to tell me?"

"No, why would there be anything to tell?"

"She has a new bike. Apparently, you got her a loaner. And apparently, you also started teaching her how to clip in."

"Yeah, I did. That was no big deal, though. I was just worried about that frame giving out on her old bike. I didn't want her to get hurt. I don't want any of our team members to get hurt."

"Well, just so you know, and in case you care, I think Becca is great. I think it would be cool if you two got together."

"That wouldn't be such a good idea."

"How come?"

"I'm her coach. And we're both focused on our careers. She's planning to move to D.C. soon. And who knows where I'll end up after I get this Pittsburgh office established. I may end up coming back to California. Or, I may go to New York to set up a third branch out there."

"None of those sound like show stoppers to me. What's really going on, Ben?"

"Well..." Ben hesitated.

"You still there, man?"

"Yeah, I'm here. You know I'm not good at relationships, Adam. It's better off if I just stay far away from dating. And Becca's not really the type of woman for just a fling. I mean...yeah, you know what I mean." Was Becca up for just a fling? He didn't think so. And neither was he. Not with Becca, anyway. And he obviously wasn't able to give her more than that. How could he when he couldn't even figure her out?

"Whatever you say," Adam said. "But, for the record, I know you're good with relationships. You were good to me when we were kids, and I sure didn't make it easy on you."

Ben didn't say anything.

"Ben?"

"Yeah, I'm here. There were a lot of pictures of us up around the house—including the picture of the three of us. The one you gave me a copy of. That was different. I didn't expect to see pictures of her all around the house."

"Yeah, it's kinda nice. Don't you think?"

"Yeah, sure, I guess."

"Hey, Ben, what do you think about me giving a 'mission moment' at the next training about Sophia? I kinda want to share with the group about her. That's what the group is about really. They would understand. I don't want to do it, though, unless you're okay with it. And I don't want to do it without you there. What do you say?"

"Can you let me think on it, Adam? I'm kind of drained after the week I've had with the Cessair project...and after the dinner with Mom and Dad."

"Sure. No pressure. We can talk about it when you get back."

"By the way, did you know Dad still has the model he and I built back when he did that water project in the little village near Lake Nakuru?" Ben asked. "Remember that project?"

"No way! I thought that would be long gone by now. You and Dad were really into that project."

"He took me out to the garage to see it. That would be a great model to use to stimulate some ideas for the Marston revitalization."

"Are you working on that project again?"

Ben could hear a tinge of hope in Adam's question. "Probably not," he hedged. "I've got way too much on my plate right now—everyone at my company does. I found someone during our meetings, though, who I think would be a great fit for our Pittsburgh office. We really need more staff. His name's Graham. He and I are going to talk more after we get through the Monday meeting with Cessair. Hopefully that will go well—and quickly—and we'll have time to talk about him coming out to Pittsburgh to work for me. But, hey, I'd better let you get some sleep. Sorry to wake you."

"I'm glad you did, Ben. Good luck tomorrow. Good night, sleep tight," Adam said, repeating the phrase Ben had said to Adam almost every night in that first year after Sophia died.

CHAPTER 43
Right of Way

BEN

BEN DROVE STRAIGHT FROM THE AIRPORT TO HIS OFFICE condo in downtown Pittsburgh. He'd slept well enough on the red-eye. There was nothing quite like jet lag to take the steam out of your pace, especially when going west to east. But Ben wanted to get right to work. He was energized from his meetings this past week. His dad's advice had paid off big time for his meeting with Cessair. He hadn't told Cessair to "go to hell" in those exact words. But, just like his father advised, Cessair had gotten the point when Ben had given him a choice of going forward, either with or without Ben's team. And meeting Graham through those meetings had been serendipity. They'd worked together during the week, and then through the weekend in the trenches, finishing up with dinner on Monday night, where they'd worked out the details for Graham to join Ben's Pittsburgh office in just six short weeks. He couldn't think of a better person to fill out his Pittsburgh team.

Ben couldn't deny that the evening he'd spent reminiscing with his dad about their early days in Africa had sparked something inside him. He really wanted to tackle the Marston revitalization project now, starting with the trail expansion. And with Graham coming on board, he'd have some time for that project after all. It wouldn't be easy—maybe it wouldn't even work. But he wanted to take a shot at it.

Ben couldn't wait to tell Becca about it. And that was another thing—why were he and Becca fighting this attraction they had for each other? Maybe they could make that work too....

At the office, he threw his bag down next to the desk he generally worked at and went into the kitchen to make a big pot of coffee. Ben didn't wait for it to finish brewing before tucking a cup under the stream and walking with it over to his desk. With Jason now working on the Fischer project with their two staff out of the California office and with the Cessair project back on track, he could pull out the files he'd started on the Marston revitalization project and set to work. It was only 7:00 a.m., so he still had at least an hour, maybe two, before Jason and Connie arrived.

First, he needed to lay out all the ideas in relation to the area. The house he'd bought in Marston included land that went to the river's edge. To the north of his house was the Old Oaks Trail and the diner where he and Becca had lunch the day they'd first met. To the south was the marina, where he kept his boat. He owned only the section of land straight down from his house. He'd already worked out a right of way for the trail going from his house to the Oaks Trail Diner and to the trail that was already there. That portion simply needed to be upgraded, and it wasn't a stretch.

It was the section of land that went from his house south that was the challenge. Ethan Trapp owned that land and it was where he planned to establish his amphitheater. If they worked together, they could sync up the two projects. But if he couldn't get Ethan on board, they'd need to route the trail up through the mountain. That just wouldn't work. The elevations were too steep. He'd contacted Ethan about the idea for the trail, but Ethan hadn't even been willing to give Ben the time of day. In fact, he'd been a real jackass about it, not even letting Ben present the ideas to him. What was that about? *Jerk*. That meant he was back to square one in terms of figuring out how to make this work. They'd need just a small portion of that land to make this feasible. Ben scratched his head and sighed. He couldn't figure a way around it.

～

Ben was deep into his drawings, head down, when Jason and then Connie arrived.

"Hey, boss," said Jason, coming over to clap him on the shoulder. "Welcome back, mister conquering hero. I knew you could do it. What are you working on?"

Ben looked up at Jason sheepishly and leaned away from the drawings to give Jason a better view.

Jason gave him a wry smile when he saw the project. "Hey, don't look at me like that," said Jason. "I'm completely on board with the idea. You're the one who's been dragging his feet. I'd love for us to branch out into Rust Belt community revitalizations. And I'd especially love to see it start with Marston. Is there anything I can help with?"

"Not unless you can sweet-talk Ethan Trapp," Ben said. "I'm not sure why I'm even wasting time on these drawings. When I tried to speak to him about this project, he pretty much told me to get lost." A memory of his dad's advice popped into his head. Maybe he needed to figure out how to tell Ethan to go to hell while making sure Ethan looked forward to the trip. It had worked with Lucas Cessair.

"If anyone can convince him, it's you," said Jason. "But Ethan does have a point. There's going to have to be some additional funding thrown in from another partner for his project to make financial sense. And giving up any of his riverfront property for a trail would make convincing another investor to sign on a more difficult proposition."

"You're not wrong there. I've been wracking my brain to see how to make this all fit together. In the meantime, now that you and Connie are here, we need to talk about how to reconfigure this condo for another staff member."

"Ya think?" came Connie's voice, laced with sarcasm, from across the room. "It's about time you hired someone to get us some help around here."

Ben rolled his eyes at her while giving her a warm smile. He was sure lucky to have her, as well as Jason. Hopefully Graham would be a good new addition to their team.

"Agreed," Jason said to Connie, chuckling at Ben and Connie's good-natured ribbing. "We've definitely got enough new work around here to support another full-time position. The challenge is going to be figuring out where to put another body inside this little condo."

CHAPTER 44

Open Water

IT'D BEEN A GREAT COUPLE OF WEEKS, THOUGHT BECCA. She'd missed Ben while he'd been away. But he was back—and he'd come to the group bike ride last Saturday. She smiled at the memory of Ben's jaw dropping when he'd seen both her and Carmen ride off along the trail, both on new bikes and both adept—well, sort of—at clipping in and out.

Sam had worked with both of them while Ben had been away, helping them perfect their clip-less pedal skills. And she hadn't fallen again; her knees were thanking her for that. After the practice with Sam, Becca had contacted Chad, who'd readily stepped up to switch out Carmen's pedals so they could practice together before their group ride last Saturday. She felt the pride she'd felt last week swell again in her chest at the memory. Both Ben and Chad had been right. Taking off on that beautiful midnight blue Contessa, with its sleek design and the extra power the clip-less pedals afforded made her feel on top of the world, as though she were flying through the stars on her own stealth flying machine. Ben had called her brave. And she'd felt brave, facing her fears—and the world—head on. And he'd be here again today for their first open water swim, she thought with a thrill of anticipation—and nerves.

"How are you doing with that wetsuit, Becca?" Ben asked,

approaching her where she sat near the water's edge of the lake they were to swim in today. Up to this point, the group had only trained in a swimming pool. But today was a whole new kind of swimming as they'd be swimming in a lake. And wearing a wetsuit. Her hands shook at the reminder, making pulling on the tight-fitting neoprene suit more challenging than it should be.

"Hey," Ben said. "Relax. You've got this. If you're brave enough to take on clip-less pedals, you're brave enough to get that wetsuit on for a swim in the lake."

Becca flushed at his nearness, her heart rate kicking up a notch. "I need to try you on for size," she said. The phrase Stacey had planted in her brain slipped out inadvertently, and she quickly corrected, "I mean, try *"it"* on for size—the wetsuit. It might be too big—too small, I mean!"

Ben laughed and sat down on the ground next to her, giving her a slow, seductive grin. That grin told her he knew exactly what she was thinking. She averted her gaze, not daring to look up again. She'd already caught sight of him in his own wetsuit. It fit snuggly, showing off his muscular build—as well as a bulge that seemed to have just grown larger, despite being crushed under that tight fitting neoprene. Maybe looking down hadn't been such a good idea after all, she thought, feeling the flush run further up her cheeks. She needed to get her own wetsuit on so she could jump into those frigid lake waters. She needed to cool off—and quick—before she gave away her thoughts any further. They were in dangerous territory, despite being outside amongst a large group of people in broad daylight.

Becca turned her body further away from Ben and continued to struggle with the wetsuit she'd been issued today. The suits were being provided for them by the Leukemia Society as a part of their training package. Thank goodness. The bike had been enough of an adventure in new equipment. But it also meant she hadn't tried the suit on yet—not even for size. Maybe it was too small? She couldn't even get it past her ankles.

"Let me help," Ben said, reaching toward the wetsuit she now at least had over both ankles but that she couldn't seem to get up any further. Now she just felt like a grounded whale as she tried in vain to get the rest of her body into the impossibly small heap of tight-fitting material.

Becca looked at Ben's outstretched hand and then up to his face. Their eyes locked, and her embarrassment intensified. "That's okay, I think I've got it."

Ben shrugged as he ran his hand through his hair, releasing a wisp of minty eucalyptus, making Becca already regret that she'd declined his offer. "If you say so. Just yell if you need me. Those things are hard to get on, especially when you've never done it before." Ben moved toward a couple of the other participants, who were also struggling to pull on their suits.

Becca continued to struggle, making little—make that no— progress. She looked up to see if Ben had noticed. Sure enough, just as she looked up, he swiveled his head toward her, and their eyes met again. He gave her a smirk, shrugged his shoulders, and turned toward another struggling participant.

"Anyone who is ready," Ben called out, "please go ahead over to the picnic table. Once everyone is suited up, we'll go over the items laid out on that table as well as some mechanics of this first open water swim."

Great, now she wasn't even going to be able to try the swim, as she wasn't making any progress with this wetsuit. Becca lifted her head and sighed in frustration, this time purposely looking toward Ben. She met his gaze head on and gave him, unfortunately, what she was sure came across as a damsel in distress appeal. She probably looked quite bedraggled at this point. Maybe even Ben couldn't help her with this predicament? There was no way this wetsuit was going to fit; it was simply too small.

"Stand up," Ben commanded.

Becca startled. She hadn't even seen him come over. Ben now stood over her, his shadow blocking out the rays of the sun. "I can't stand up," she mewled. "I'm stuck."

"Take the wetsuit all the way off and set it aside and then stand up," he repeated with a chuckle.

"It is not funny!" Becca pouted good-naturedly, her face now beet red with embarrassment, but she nonetheless heeded his command and stood up.

"I'm going to spray this on your legs and your body so you can more easily pull on your wetsuit," Ben said, showing her a small, silver colored metal bottle he held in his hand with the words *TriSlide* written across the middle.

As the cool spray from the bottle hit Becca's feet, then her calves, and then her thighs, she yelped in surprise, causing Ben's light chuckle to turn into a hearty laugh. Becca delighted in the sound despite it being at her expense. As the spray tingled across her limbs and nerve endings, her delight turned to desire. It felt like Ben was touching her with his fingertips—gentle and caressing. He continued to work the spray up her body, now reaching the bottom of her one-piece tri suit. As the spray hit the upper extremities of her long legs, she tried in vain to hold in the gasp that escaped her lips. Did he notice? She needed to keep things professional, between friends. She was brave, right? Ready for anything life had to throw at her—including Ben.

"There," he said. "It should be easier now to pull on the wetsuit. Go ahead and sit down and start by pulling it on over just one foot at a time, and then work it up just that one leg before attempting to pull it on over your other leg."

Becca followed his instructions as she tried to hide her lack of composure.

"Okay, good job. Now that you've got it up over most of your legs, go ahead and stand up."

Becca wobbled a bit as she stood. Ben quickly reached out to stabilize her just as she also reached out to stabilize herself, catching Ben's arm as she did so. She looked up at him, wanting to thank him. But no words escaped her lips. She really needed to jump into that cold water —and quick.

Finally, successful at getting the wetsuit on, Becca now realized the next step was going to be getting into the lake. Maybe getting the wetsuit on had been the easy part? She already felt like a giant whale in this suit. But now she felt like a giant whale that would surely sink right to the bottom of the lake as soon as she jumped in. She couldn't even catch her breath in this thing, it was so tight. Panic rose in her throat. Being on land was one thing, getting into water—and into water that would be over her head—was another. Great, she thought, she was going to drown on day one of their open water swim. And she'd been worried about the cancer. There were other ways to die.

Becca moved to stand with the other participants, all now clad in their new wetsuits, to listen to Ben as he reviewed the various endurance event items laying across the nearby picnic table's surface —timing chips, swim caps, chocolate Gu for fueling, goggles, and more.

"We've already talked some about alligator eyes, and today, you're going to get to practice them in open water," Ben said with delight. "You've all swum in the pool with goggles where you can follow the black line to make sure you swim a straight course and know when you're about to run out of room in your lane. It's rare in an open water swim that you'll be able to see to the bottom, or sometimes even your hand, in the water. Even if you could, there's no black line there to guide you. So, how do you swim the water portion of the course without getting off track? You don't want to have to keep slowing—or even stopping—to make sure you're on course. But you don't want to just keep swimming if you're not sure you're swimming in exactly the right direction. That's inefficient and could even cause you to end up with a DNF—that stands for 'did not finish', folks.

"There are time limits on the overall course as well as for each segment. If you don't finish each segment, including the swim, in under the allotted time, you won't be considered a finisher of the overall race. So, how do you swim the course without slowing when you don't have a line to guide you in the water?"

"Alligator eyes?" called out one of the participants.

"Correct," said Ben. "One technique for what we call 'sighting' in open water is alligator eyes. Ideally, you'll all be swimming freestyle in the race. You'll want to swim like you usually do in a pool, but for every three to five strokes, you'll push your chin slightly forward as you swim straight ahead, causing your head to lift. You do NOT want to lift all of your head out of the water. That will disrupt your stroke and slow you down. Just lift your head enough for your goggles to break the surface of the water.

"Picture an alligator as it smoothly glides forward, with only its eyes showing every so often to sight prey. That's what you want to emulate. Just like the alligator, as the top of your eyes—or in this case, your goggles—break the surface, take in your location in the water by quickly glancing at shore landmarks you've pre-selected before entering the water. You could also mark your sights on the next buoy in front of you on the swim course. Be sure when you lift your head that you only lift it slightly, and that your glance is quick and smooth and incorporated as a part of your swim stroke. Otherwise, you'll find your pace slowing significantly compared with what it is in the pool.

"You can also sight as you turn your head sideways to breathe. But it's the same thing—you don't want to disrupt your stroke by lifting your head out of the water. Just a small portion of your head comes out of the water when you breathe or when you sight forward using the alligator eyes technique. That's all you need, because—and this is the coolest part—your brain does the rest of the work. Once your eyes are back in the water, your brain fills in the missing pieces as an image in your head. Master this technique and you will find yourself able to stay on course without having to slow your pace. Sam and I will try to work with each of you one-on-one while you're in the water today. You can also, of course, practice alligator eyes while in the pool. Just shut your eyes when your head is in the water so you don't take in the line on the bottom of the pool—don't cheat, in other words. Just be careful you don't run into any of the other swimmers. It might be a little hard to explain why you're swimming with your eyes closed." He grinned.

"That is so cool!" said Carmen.

Ben gave Carmen a quick smile and a nod of appreciation. "Okay, everyone, go ahead and make your way into the water."

Becca stood, stock still, with the water only up to her knees, watching as the other participants swam alongside a rope about fifty feet out into the lake that Sam and Ben had set up to mark their practice course.

Ben came over to her. "Aren't you going to get in, Becca?"

Becca pursed her lips with a sideways glance at Ben. "I'll sink."

"You will not sink, I promise you. I already know you can swim. I've seen you in the pool. You're a good swimmer. And the wetsuit gives you added buoyancy."

"Maybe," she said uncertainly.

"How about we wade out together? I'll stay with you until you're comfortable. And if at any time you want to come back to shore, I'll help you get there."

"Maybe," she repeated, chewing on her bottom lip.

"Here," Ben said, taking her hands. He turned his back to the water just beyond where Becca stood. "Look me in the eye. Just follow me in," he said, and he gently pulled her toward him while he backed further into the water. "Just look at me. We'll make our way in slowly, and we won't go deeper than your shoulders. Once you're ready, we can swim along the shoreline, but you'll be able to stand up whenever you want."

"Okay," she said, following his lead into the water.

"That's it. Great job," he said gently, calming her nerves with that mesmerizing baritone. "You good?" he asked.

"Yes."

"You're doing great. Are you ready to try swimming?"

"I think so."

"Great. I'll keep holding your hands. I can stand here. I won't let go. Just let your body lie flat on the water like you would in the pool."

Becca did as he asked. "Oh my gosh!" Becca squeaked. "I can float!"

Ben chuckled. "Yep. The wetsuit helps you stay afloat. You still need to do most of the work, though. Are you ready for me to let go?"

Becca didn't answer, but she pulled her hands slowly out of his grasp. He stood to the side as she started her stroke. She was doing it! It wasn't scary at all anymore, she thought, as she stroked her way through the water. It wasn't really any different from being in the pool. It had been cold at first, but the wetsuit had almost immediately warmed her. She even felt faster than in the pool. The wetsuit was helping her swim faster! She turned to swim back the way she came, just like she would when swimming laps in the pool.

"Great job, Becca!" Ben called out. "Can you try the alligator eyes?"

She swam a couple more strokes as she worked through in her mind the instructions Ben had given them on the shore for the sighting technique. As she lifted her goggles just above the water in front of her, she caught sight of Ben up ahead. Now that was a good landmark. She was doing this, and Ben was guiding her, keeping her safe.

After several more laps that included practicing the alligator eyes technique, Becca swam toward shore. She stood with an enormous smile on her face. "Ben! I did it!" She ran toward him. "It was great! Thank you for teaching me!"

Ben grinned back at her and held his arms out to her. She ran into his arms and hugged him. "You're very welcome," he said.

Still held in his embrace, Becca looked at Ben. She wanted to kiss him. She wanted to be kissed. She tilted her head up but then realized that they were standing amongst all their teammates. Becca stepped away from him, flustered, but still feeling that triumphant grin on her face.

There was a smattering of clapping as her teammates congratulated her on her success. She took a slight bow. "Right back at ya," she said to several of her teammates standing nearby, all of whom had also successfully completed their first wetsuit swim. Becca took one more glance at Ben before turning to find where she'd left her dry clothes.

"Go on, kiss the girl," she heard Adam tease Ben under his breath.

"Are you going to break out into song now too?" Ben responded. But Becca could hear the grin still in his voice. "That wasn't what it looked like, ya know, Adam. She was just happy about meeting the challenge of that first open water swim."

"Yeah, but I'll bet there's no one she wanted to share that moment with more than you."

Becca looked back toward Ben and Adam, not even trying to hide that she'd heard that exchange. She grinned at both of them before turning away to find her belongings and peel off the still tight-fitting but now kinda comfortable wetsuit.

As Becca approached her car, now in her dry street clothes, she found Ben leaning against her car. "Good job today, Becca. I'm so proud of you."

"You and me both!" She laughed happily. "I really wasn't sure that wetsuit was going to work out. But it was amazing—you were amazing. Thanks, coach," she finished in a husky voice.

"Hey, I'm wondering if you would mind doing me a favor? Just as friends."

"Of course. What's up?"

"Well, there's this event coming up—a fancy gala type of thing. It's a fundraiser and a business networking meet and greet. Fischer Industries, my new client, is putting it on. It's next Saturday, a week from today. I should go, but I don't want to go alone and really should bring a plus one. Would you be willing to go with me? Just as friends," he quickly reiterated.

Becca felt a pang of disappointment at the 'just friends' part of that invitation. But it was for the best. It's what they'd agreed to. At the same time, she also felt a thrill of excitement about attending a dance with Ben. "I'd love to go—just to help you out, of course," she added shyly.

CHAPTER 45
Plus One Gala

BECCA WAS EXCITED ABOUT GOING TO THE GALA WITH BEN tonight. It was just a 'plus one' invitation and not a date. That was good. He was her coach, and neither of them were in the market for a relationship. They'd both made that clear, except she wasn't so sure that's how either of them was thinking anymore. Maybe she should have gone for that kiss last week after their swim... After all, she'd done nothing but think of that all week, including during their training this morning.

"Earth to Becca," said Carmen, interrupting her thoughts. "I love that dress you laid out for tonight." Carmen, clearly trying to be diplomatic, waved her arm toward the plain black dress lying on Becca's bed. "But, no offense, I think you should wear this one instead. It's perfect." Carmen held up a beautiful floor length chiffon dress. It was midnight blue with dark blue lace trim on the top and a split front that allowed for a length of leg to show with every step. It was sophisticated and demure yet sexy at the same time.

"Oh my gosh! I remember that dress." Becca took the dress from Carmen and ran her hand down the length of it almost reverently, lost in thought. "I bought it BC—before cancer," she said, more to herself than to Carmen. "But only just before. I got diagnosed before I even had a chance to cut the tags off." Becca turned to Carmen, still holding the dress. "Do you really think I should wear it?"

"Of course I do. There's no reason for that dress to hang idly in that closet. It was meant to be worn, and you'll look beautiful in it."

"Yes, it's perfect for tonight," Becca said with a smile. "Hand me those scissors, will you, please?"

Carmen opened the top drawer of Becca's bathroom vanity and handed her a small pair of scissors. "How come Ben isn't picking you up for this date tonight? You know I adore him, but I don't like that he's leaving you on your own to get to the gala."

"I told you already," Becca said, rolling her eyes. "This event is being put on by his new client. It's a pretty big deal. It's an influential firm and not just here in Pittsburgh. Ben told me they even have international dealings. One of the big-wigs asked Ben to come early and have a drink with him so they can discuss some potential ideas he has that go beyond the contract they just signed. Apparently it has something to do with projects his father worked on in Africa. Ben's excited about it. He wanted to talk more about it, but we haven't had time with work and training and all. I told Ben I would just meet him there. Plus, you know this is not a date. So, thank you again for offering to drive me there tonight. I'm still fine with getting an Uber if you've changed your mind and Ben said he will drive me home. You really don't have to be on point to deliver me to the door of the venue —or pick me up at the end of the ball." Becca grinned, loving to get to say the word 'ball.'

Carmen put her hands on her hips. "There is no way I'm letting you mess up this perfection we have obtained! You look beautiful, and I want you to stay that way. I'm taking you there myself to make sure you don't ruin your hairdo or wrinkle your dress. Or worse, decide after I leave that you're putting on that old black dress you've already worn way too many times. I'm not sure I trust you to take as good a care of yourself as I will. And you are my masterpiece tonight. So, no arguing."

Becca smiled. "Thanks Carmen. So, if we're doing this, let's do it. It's time for me to help our coach impress his new client."

∾

Becca waved goodbye to Carmen and walked up the front steps of the hotel where the gala was being held. A decorative sign pointed toward a hallway to her left that would take her to the ballroom. Becca immediately turned to her right, her nerves getting the best of her.

Why was she so nervous? She was just helping a friend. She hadn't been to a lot of events this fancy, but she'd been to client events before. It wasn't like she was completely out of her depth, Becca said to herself, as she snuck into the woman's bathroom and then into a nearby stall. Breathing in and out, she pulled herself up straighter. Okay, she told herself, you've got this. Becca ran her damp palms down the material of her dress, smoothing it out. It felt silky soft and gave her a measure of comfort. Releasing another breath, Becca squared her shoulders and left the stall to wash her hands, acting in front of the two women now standing at the row of sinks as though she had just used the toilet. After they left, she looked at herself in the mirror and gave herself a practiced smile. She was ready.

As Becca entered the ballroom, she scanned the large space, looking for Ben. There were at least twenty tables of eight carefully placed around the room, each with a vase at its center which overflowed with artistically arranged blue and salmon-colored flowers. Two open bars were placed in two back corners of the room. A podium stood just beyond the tables on a hard surface that would obviously become a dance floor later. A string quartet, situated in the middle of that area, played soft classical music, serving as a soothing backdrop to the conversations humming throughout the room.

When Becca moved her eyes to scan the crowd, she saw him. Ben was speaking with a nice-looking man of about fifty with distinguished silver streaks running through his dark hair and beard. The man looked somewhat familiar, but Becca couldn't place him. He probably seemed familiar only because he was one of many wearing tonight's requisite black tuxedo and bow tie. Ben also wore a tuxedo, his tall, muscled physique caged within smooth black fabric. She longed to pull the tailored coat off of him to free what she knew lay beneath. Even though Ben was similarly clad to the other men in the room, she felt drawn to him. Her body floated toward him as if pulled by an unseen force, her gaze never leaving his form.

She knew the moment he saw her. His head tilted up and away

from the man he was speaking with to latch onto her face. The room stood still as their eyes connected. Her tongue slid out of her mouth to moisten her lips and Becca felt a molten warmth sizzle within. She quickly averted her gaze, needing to regain her composure as the intensity of the moment became too much. But her body continued to float of its own accord across the intricately patterned carpet at her feet toward his compelling frame.

"Becca, I'm so glad you made it. You look gorgeous," said Ben, with a look in his eye that had Becca ready to swoon.

"Aren't you going to introduce me to your friend?" asked the man standing next to Ben.

"Of course. Pardon my manners," said Ben. "Jake, this is Becca. Becca, this is Jake Creighton, vice president of development and external affairs at Fischer Industries."

"It's nice to meet you, Becca," said Jake, holding out his hand.

"Oh!" Becca said, feeling her mouth turn up into a rounded circle of surprise as she shook his hand. "Mr. Creighton, I think we've met before. It's so nice to see you again."

"I'm sorry. Do we know each other? I'm sure I would have remembered meeting someone as beautiful as you." Jake smiled, still holding her hand.

Becca's checks reddened. "Yes, actually. It was a long time ago, so I wouldn't expect you to remember. You were putting up a new development of condominiums next to the Innovation Manufacturing Park, just east of Pittsburgh. I just drove by that development a couple of weeks ago. They turned out beautifully."

Jake looked more intently at her face, continuing to hold her hand in his, and then a spark of recognition entered his eyes. "Ah, yes! As I recall, you helped put the financial packet together for that project."

Becca nodded, pleased he'd remembered. As they exchanged pleasantries, a voice called out from the microphone at the podium, asking them to find their seats for dinner.

"Becca, it's so nice to see you again," said Jake. "I hope you'll save a dance for me later this evening. I hear that after dinner we're in for a treat as there will be a very good live dance band playing."

"Oh, yes, of course," Becca said politely.

"Jake," Ben said curtly. "Great discussion earlier. Thank you for taking the time. I'll think about the ideas, and maybe we can follow up again soon to see if we can flesh those ideas out more. I'm looking forward to our current project, but it sounds like we have some additional projects we might be able to work together on going forward."

Ben's face had lost some of its outwardly composed calm as he took Becca's hand, enveloping it in his much larger one now that it was free from Jake's grip. Maybe she should be offended as he all but demonstrated staking a claim over her. But, instead, Becca felt a sizzle of desire—and power—at the effect she was obviously having over Ben.

As they made their way to their assigned table, a woman sidled up to Ben. She had a sultry smile focused solely on the man at her side. A pang of jealousy ran through Becca's veins. The woman was tall and slender but with shapely curves around her hips...and cleavage that suggestively spilled over the top of her tightly cinched bodice. "Ben," she said, in a come-hither voice, "it's so nice to see you again. It's been a while. I should have known that if I were going to run into you again, it would be at a client event. When you're done with your client duties, I'd be happy to entertain you elsewhere. I miss our rendezvous," she whispered suggestively.

"Savannah," Ben said, nodding his head to her politely. "This is Becca. Becca, this is Savannah..." Ben hesitated before adding, "an old friend. Thank you for the offer, Savannah, but I'm pretty covered over with work these days. It's great to see you again, though."

Savannah sighed and gently shook her head. "Such a waste. I'll let you get to your table." She nodded at Ben and then at Becca, but before leaving, she took Becca's hand gently in her own and leaned in to whisper in her ear, "Good luck with that one. He's just not up for a relationship. Believe me, I've tried." With that, she walked away to rejoin a tuxedo-clad gentleman a few tables away.

As they reached their table and found their name placards identifying their assigned seats, Ben pulled out Becca's chair for her. There were already three other couples at the table. As Becca and Ben settled in, the conversations already in process subsided as everyone took his or her turn introducing themselves. All the couples were older and seemed to know each other already. As soon as introductions were made, the conversations easily picked back up, with the focus mostly on the antics of young grandchildren.

"So," asked the gentleman who sat next to Becca and who had introduced himself as an employee of Fischer Industries, "do you and Ben have children?"

"Oh...no," said Becca. "We're not married."

"Oh, I'm sorry. My mistake. You two make a good-looking couple, though," he said amiably.

As the man turned away, distracted by the need to make room for their server to place his salad in front of him, Becca turned her gaze to Ben, who simply winked at her. Fortunately, before Becca could react, the man seated next to Ben leaned over to ask him a question about his company, forcing him to turn away from her and giving her a moment to compose herself in time for a second server to place a salad in front of her.

Small talk continued throughout their meal regarding children and grandchildren, various projects in which each of them was involved, and even the weather. But mostly, the focus was on their speaker for this evening, the music, and the delicious dinner being put in front of them—prime rib, shrimp, a wonderful vegetable souffle, and finally, various selections of scrumptious looking deserts including chocolate cake, which Ben quickly commandeered for Becca. He held the plate out to her in question. Yes, she definitely wanted that chocolate cake. She smiled at Ben and he set the plate, as well as a fork, down in front of her. Ben then picked up a second fork and, with a challenging sexy smile, took a bite from her plate. She smiled back at him and moved her hand playfully to swat at his, but before she completed the motion, she noted the man sitting next to her watching them with an indulgent, fatherly smile. He probably thought he was watching a date in action. She wanted to dissuade him of that notion. This was not a date. But, instead, she tucked her head with a shy smile, picked up her fork, and took a bite of the delicious, rich chocolate cake as images of her and Ben's dinner at Tony's Restaurant flooded her memory.

With the meal finished, the band changed out from a string quartet to a dance band playing cover tunes.

"Would you like to dance, Becca?" Ben asked, holding his hand out to her.

Without saying a word and afraid that her voice would fail her, Becca took Ben's outstretched hand and let him lead her onto the dance floor. At the sizzle of desire that ran through her, she reminded herself that this was simply a client dinner Ben had needed a plus one for. Savannah had clearly misread them being together, as had the man sitting next to her. She wasn't looking for a relationship—and neither was Ben.

"May I cut in?" Jake asked, tapping Ben on the shoulder.

With Ben's back still to Jake, Becca saw his lips form into a tight line before he looked to her for permission to hand her off to Jake. Becca gave a slight nod, and Ben politely let go of her and stepped back, allowing Jake to step in. She and Jake danced to the end of the song that had been playing and then to the next. But as another song began, a slow song this time, Ben strode forward and tapped Jake on the shoulder. "May I?" he asked.

Jake smiled and stepped away. "Of course," he said. "Becca, it's nice to see you again. Hopefully we'll end up on another project one of these days. In the interim, keep me posted on the projects you're working on. Maybe there will be room for collaboration on one of them in the near future."

"Thank you so much, Mr. Creighton."

"Oh, please, call me Jake," he said, before turning to leave the dance floor.

Ben held her in his arms, and the lyrics from the song *I Hope You Dance* spoke to Becca as they swayed to the music. Maybe she and Ben did have a chance? Were the words in the song true? Would taking a chance be worth it? Is that what she wanted? What would that mean, though, for her move to D.C.? And how would Ben react to her cancer? It wouldn't be fair to him not to tell him about it. Maybe she should tell him tonight.... But how would he react? Maybe he wouldn't want her—and she wouldn't blame him. Living through cancer was hard. It was also unfair to put on anyone's shoulders who didn't need to bear that burden.

The song ended and a fast song started up. Ben reached out for Becca's hand and pulled her toward him as he led her with unexpected finesse through some intricate dance moves. Becca let out a soft squeal of delight. She would tell him, she told herself then—just not tonight. They were having too much fun. They continued to dance song after song. Jake and everything and everyone else in the room faded into the background as Ben swirled her around the room inside a bubble of ecstasy broken only when the band's leader called out the last dance. The band played one last slow song. Ben pulled her in close, and they swayed to the music, a bit of melancholy now clouding her brain as Becca knew the night must end.

They made their way back to their table to gather their belongings and say their goodbyes to those who remained. Becca spotted someone else she knew.

"Ethan!" she called to the man standing just across from their dinner table. "It's nice to see you here."

"Becca," Ethan said, a grin illuminating his face as he strode over, clasping her hand in his and pressing it warmly between his hands in greeting. "I wish I'd known you were here. I would've come over to claim a dance."

"Ethan," Ben said stiffly as he approached them.

"Ben," Ethan said with surprise, "I wanted to—"

Ben linked his arm through Becca's, causing her hand to slip from Ethan's grasp, and spoke before Ethan could finish his sentence. "Ready, Becca?" he asked. There was no inflection in his tone, his features schooled to give no hint of his sentiments. "We'd better get going. They're ready to shut the place down. Sorry, Ethan, maybe another time," Ben said, as he began to walk Becca toward the exit.

Becca looked apologetically at Ethan. He shrugged noncommittally but gave her a friendly smile, nodding for her to go ahead. She smiled curiously in return and then pivoted, allowing Ben to lead her away.

"How do you know Ethan?" Ben asked, now that they were out of earshot.

"Why?" she asked suspiciously. "Is there something going on with you two?"

Ben let out a discouraged huff of air. "He's the guy who stands in the way of the trail project that's part of the Marston revitalization. He owns a lot of land along the river between Marston and Pittsburgh and plans to build a large venue there. That's a good thing. But the way he wants to do it precludes us from being able to complete the trail as it leaves no pass through. He won't even meet to talk about the possibility," Ben said, clearly frustrated. "I'm sure there's a way to make this a win-win for everyone, including him, the community, and the region. If there isn't a way to do it that makes financial sense for him, I get it. But he isn't even willing to have the discussion." Ben's voice was laced with irritation. "Seeing him here just now really caught me off guard. I'm sorry, Becca, about dragging you away like that. I could have handled that better. Can you forgive me?"

"Of course. But, wait—a venue? Between Marston and Pittsburgh?"

"Yes, that's what I said. It's an amp—"

"An amphitheater?"

"Yes, how did you know that?" he asked with surprise.

"I'm on that project," said Becca, biting her lip. "I'm the one who is supposed to put together the pro forma. I'll be crunching those numbers."

"You've got to be kidding me! Why didn't you tell me?" Ben said, his face tightening.

"I didn't know. All I know about it so far is that it's an amphitheater project just north of Pittsburgh...along the river." She worried now that maybe she should have put two and two together. So much for her financial expertise, she couldn't even add two plus two. "My team has already had their first meeting on the project. But I wasn't able to stay for that meeting, and we've been so busy with other projects, including that emergency sewage project for the City of Allison that I haven't even looked over the amphitheater project yet, let alone started on the numbers," Becca said apologetically. But she knew how much Ben cared about Marston—even though he often dismissed it as not important. She knew it wasn't her fault but, nonetheless, she felt her chin tremble. She didn't want to disappoint him. "I'm sorry, Ben. I didn't know." She ducked her head so he couldn't see her face. Could nothing go right in her life?

Ben lifted his hand to Becca's chin and gently tilted her head up to look at him. "No, you have nothing to be sorry about. I'm the one who's sorry. How could you have known? And even if you had, you have a job to do. It's okay, don't worry about it." As he spoke, the valet arrived with his car. "Your chariot awaits, madame," he said gallantly while holding the passenger side door open for her and helping her into his car, an understated but elegant new-model Acura, she noted with surprise. This car was a far cry from his usual work truck. The thought distracted her, but only momentarily, as she dropped back into pondering the dilemma at hand.

"Becca..." Ben started, but then paused.

"Yes?"

"It's none of my business but, you don't have a relationship with Ethan, do you? I mean, he's not a past boyfriend or anything like that, is he?"

"No," she said, annoyed at the question. "I've only met Ethan once before. And it was at Patterson about one month ago and for all of about five minutes. And you're right," she said, "it's none of your business."

Silence descended upon them.

"I'm sorry. Again," Ben finally said, his voice sounding dejected.

Becca didn't respond and silence once again descended upon them.

Ben stared straight ahead, focused solely on his driving, his body rigid and his lips turned down in defeat.

She shifted her gaze to look at him. He looked so sad. He had that little boy look again. But this time there was no smile, only a frown and a sad, lost look in his eyes. "Ben, I'm sorry too. I don't mind you asking me, it's okay. There's nothing between me and Ethan, and there never has been."

He nodded slowly and then reached out and covered her hand with his, still looking straight ahead. "I had a great time tonight, Becca," he said softly. "Thank you for coming with me. I'm sorry I messed it up at the end."

"You didn't mess anything up," she said, squeezing his hand. "I had a great time too. It was another magical night," she teased, giving Ben a one-sided smile as they continued to hold hands, now in an amiable silence.

"I don't know what would convince Ethan to change his mind," Ben finally said, breaking their silence. "Or even if I can change it."

"There's got to be a way to make it all come together," she agreed.

"I've been working on that. But Ethan is a stubborn man; he won't even talk to me about it. I've heard through the grapevine that he believes there is just no way to make the amphitheater work financially without putting shops in to cover the entire section of land between the amphitheater and the river. I do think he needs more than just the amphitheater. But he's designing the project in a way that leaves no room for the trail. I don't know why he's dug his heels in so much. We could even do something as simple as sharrows painted onto the roadway for a small section of the trail. That could even boost business at those shops. I'm sure there's a way to work the trail in. But I need to convince him on that or this project is a no-go."

As they drove, the ideas started flowing from Becca to Ben and back as they talked it through, now both in full-blown problem-solving mode. This was fun, having someone to bounce ideas off, and someone who didn't shut her down at every outside-the-box suggestion. Maybe they could find a way, Becca thought optimistically.

"Do you want to come up?" Becca asked, as he pulled into the parking lot of her apartment complex. "I'm sure we can figure this out."

He looked at her with a smoldering gaze. "I'm not sure I can be trusted. Whirling you around the dance floor tonight and having to fight off other men vying for your attention did not leave me wanting to leave it at just friends. I would very much like to continue to work on finding a solution to this dilemma. But I don't know that I'm strong enough to do it in your apartment alone with you." He ran his hand through his hair and asked her in a tightly constrained voice, "Can you be strong enough for the both of us?"

"I don't know," Becca said in a whisper.

They stood in the parking lot at the entrance to her building, not making a move to cross the threshold. "Maybe," said Becca. "How about a cup of tea, though, instead of a glass of wine while we problem-solve?" Without waiting for his response, she reached out her hand to take his and pulled him along behind her through the door.

Ben groaned but followed along behind her more than willingly.

True to her word, when they entered her apartment, Becca went to the kitchen and put on a kettle to make some tea, something she had done many times during her cancer treatments. She found it was a good way to soothe her soul and settle her stomach. She also pulled out multiple pads of paper and pens and set them on her kitchen table.

They worked for several hours into the night. Becca was excited about what they'd come up with, and Ben had listened to her ideas and added to them and her to his. Ben was now sitting on the living room couch writing out some final notes while she cleaned up the kitchen. When she came back out to say goodnight to him, she found he was fast asleep with a pen still in his hand. Becca smiled down at him, wondering what in the world she should do now. She didn't want to wake him. He had to be exhausted, just as she was. They'd had a long work week, trained this morning, and then had danced the night away.

Becca went to her hall closet and pulled out a large soft blanket and gently laid it over Ben's sleeping form. She then went into the bathroom to brush her teeth, put on her pajamas, and crawled into bed, immediately falling into a deep sleep.

CHAPTER 46

Brunch with Ben

BECCA AWOKE TO THE SMELL OF COFFEE BREWING, AND HER lips quirked up in a smile. Ben was still here, in her apartment. She snuck into her bathroom and brushed her hair and her teeth and then washed her face. She was too excited to change out of her pajamas. They were decent enough, she thought, as she headed down the hall to her kitchen.

"Morning," she said shyly. "Sleep well?"

"Maybe too well," Ben said, rubbing his neck. "I think I could do without this crick in my neck. Other than that, I don't think I've slept that well in ages. Sorry I dropped off like that, and thanks for the blanket."

"You're welcome."

"I hope you don't mind; I took some liberties with opening some of your cabinets. I figured an offering of coffee was the least I could do to thank you for last night and for helping me to problem-solve on the Marston project. I was just about to cook up a couple of omelets." He pointed to a carton of eggs sitting out on the counter. "I found some eggs and cheese in the refrigerator. Not much else, though. If you'd rather go out, I'd be happy to treat you to breakfast. I owe you for all the ideas and hard work last night."

Becca gave him a smile. "Actually, I have a standing Sunday morning brunch date with my mom."

"Oh! Well then, I'd better get out of your hair." He handed her a cup of coffee and turned to gather all the notes he'd put together before falling asleep on Becca's couch last night.

Becca pulled her bottom lip in with her teeth. She didn't want him to leave, but she realized she needed to let him go. Was now the time to tell him about her cancer? How would he react? She didn't want him to look at her any differently. But if she really were going to ask him to stay—and blow off her mother—she needed to tell him and let him decide where this thing between them was going. "Ben, I should probably tell—"

"So," Ben started in a formal tone, just as Becca spoke. "Oh, sorry, go ahead."

"No, you go first."

Ben nodded. "I was just going to say that I'll pull our notes together into the start of a formal proposal with a mission statement, objectives, tasks, and timeline. I'll also put together some preliminary sketches that show where shops could go—both next to the amphitheater and the marina as well as further up the trail in Marston. I'll include in the drawing the existing Oaks Diner and the bakery next door to it as well as the lodging the bakery owner is putting in on his second and third floors. That'll be an asset. Your next step is to meet with your boss to show him our ideas to see if he would be amenable to you and him asking for a meeting with Ethan to run these ideas past him. I'll hold off on anything further until after your meeting with Nathan. Did I capture our agreed upon next steps accurately?"

"Yes, that's perfect."

"Are you sure you're still okay with this strategy, Becca? We don't need to do this, and I don't want you getting involved in this if you don't want to or if you don't feel absolutely comfortable with it."

"Are you kidding? Nathan has been fretting about the amphitheater project not having enough pizazz to leverage any external funding. And Ethan is going to need that funding for the numbers to work in his favor. There are literally millions of dollars in federal and state funding for public-private partnership projects—but only if they check all the boxes required by the funders. You saw how those numbers fleshed out last night. Ethan needs that seed funding, and he's not going to get it without something like this revitalization project to go with it. The amphitheater alone is not enough. Ethan would be crazy not to at least listen to the idea. At least, that's my opinion. But Nathan is good at all of this. I'll get his input before we go further." She thought for a moment, then added, "Maybe there's something we're missing, but I don't think so. Are you sure you don't want to come in for that meeting with Nathan? None of this is my idea and I don't want to short-change what you've put together."

"I'm sure. I don't want Nathan—or Ethan—to feel pushed. Run it by Nathan, and let him make the call on what he thinks should happen next. Are you comfortable with that?"

Becca nodded. "Yes. But can we go over the map we sketched out last night? It's a fabulous visual that will show how it would all fit together with the shops, amphitheater, marina, lodging, park, and the trail running through it all. It's a lot to present, and I want to make sure it's all clear in my head before I sit down with Nathan. And can we just jot down the top few talking points from all of those notes before you go?"

"Sure," said Ben, setting down the stack of papers he was holding to pull out the map and set it on her kitchen table.

Becca took a sip of her coffee and sat down next to Ben.

"So, here is where the amphitheater would go...."

"What time do you need to be at your mom's?" Ben asked, as they started in on their review of the map. "I don't want to cause a family rift."

Becca looked at her watch. "Not for another hour. We still have plenty of time." Then Becca started, and with excitement in her voice, said, "Hey!" But when Ben looked at her enquiringly, she ducked her head shyly and added, "Uh, never mind."

"What? Do you need to get going sooner? We can do this another time."

"No, it's not that. I was just going to ask if you want to come to brunch with me. Only if you want to, though. My mom makes great lattes and fantastic blueberry pancakes. She would love it if you could come." Becca sat nervously, waiting for Ben's response. Was she stepping too far into the personal again? For God's sake, she was inviting him to meet her mother. He would think she was crazy again, throwing herself at him. She really didn't mean to be doing that, but she just couldn't seem to help herself. Please, please, please want to come, she chanted to herself. Please, please, please say no, she chanted next.

"You mean Joan? Sure. But I think I'd need to get a shower first...and perhaps a change of clothes. She might wonder about me showing up in a tuxedo," he said with a grin. "I expect it's not your typical Sunday brunch attire at your mom's house."

Becca's cheeks turned crimson. "Good point. Maybe that was a bad idea."

"Actually, I love the idea. Blueberry pancakes sound great. I have a change of clothes in my car; just jeans and a pullover, though. Do you think that would go over okay? And would you be okay with me taking a quick shower here? That would give us a little more time to go over the sketches and hone the talking points before going to your mom's."

"Yes, that would be fine," Becca said, internally telling herself to be strong. "I'll give my mother a call to let her know you're coming, and then I'll get a shower and get dressed after you're done in the bathroom. Help yourself to whatever you need."

Becca headed down the hall to her bedroom and picked up her phone from her nightstand. She gently shut the door to her room, took a few deep breaths, and dialed her mother's number.

"Hi, Mom," Becca said, as her mother picked up her call.

"Are you coming for brunch, Becca? I'm looking forward to seeing you."

"Yes. But, I was wondering—would it be okay if I bring Ben, my coach?"

"Of course! I would love that. I know how much you're enjoying the triathlon training. And I didn't get to talk to him at all that day we saw him at Panera's. Please do bring him. Should I make anything special?"

"You already make everything special, Mom. Lattes and pancakes are perfect. We'll see you in about an hour, if that's okay? Oh, and Mom, I still haven't told Ben about my cancer," she said, lowering her voice. "So don't say anything about it. Okay?"

"Becca.... You really should tell him. He's your coach. What if something happens while you're training? He should know...."

"Mom," Becca said, agitated, "Carmen's there with me. She knows and will make sure I'm okay. And I will tell him. I plan to, but I need to do it when I'm ready. Can you do this for me?"

"Becca..."

"Maybe we should wait. I'm sorry, Mom. Maybe it's too soon, and we could come another time...after I've told him. Although," she said, her voice now thick with emotion, "maybe he wouldn't want to come after he knows...."

"Well, if that would be the difference between him wanting to come or not, he's not worth inviting," her mom said sharply.

"I'm just not ready yet, Mom. I don't want to be treated any differently than anyone else on the team. Not yet," Becca said, her voice cracking.

"Okay, honey," her mother said sadly. "I understand. I promise; I won't say anything. Bring your young man."

"Mom! He's not my young man—he's just my coach. Oh, and we're maybe working on a project together...maybe...we'll see. That we could talk about, at least. But only if Ben wants to. I'm not sure he will, though. Maybe we could just stick to only talking about the triathlon." Or about the foam on the top of those lattes, Becca thought with a sigh.

"I'm looking forward to whatever we talk about," her mother said firmly. "See you in about an hour, Becca. Love you."

"Thanks, Mom. Love you too."

CHAPTER 47
Opportunities

BECCA LEFT THE HOUSE AT EIGHT ON MONDAY MORNING. She was laden down with her usual work bag and purse but also with the sketches and talking points she and Ben developed over the weekend, as well as everything she'd need for today's workout—which included her running clothes and her bike. Well, not *her* bike exactly—the loaner bike, which was mounted and locked onto the bike rack on the back of her car. Good thing she'd splurged on that monthly parking pass for the garage. There was no way she could've gotten everything to work today via the bus, she thought, as she made her way across the two blocks from the parking garage to her office building and then to her desk on the fifteenth floor.

"Hi, Jenn," Becca said, sliding into her desk chair in front of her computer.

"Hi, Becca. Good weekend?"

"The best," Becca said with a smile.

"It sure is great to see you looking happy again," Jenn said, returning her smile. "And feeling well... You are, aren't you?" she asked with some concern, her lips twitching into a frown. "Feeling well, I mean?"

"I'm feeling great!" Becca laughed.

Jenn's lips twitched up again. "So, what'd ya do this weekend?"

"Actually, I'd love to show it to you," Becca said, her excitement growing. "I want to get your feedback on the sketches Ben and I worked on over the weekend. There are some ideas in here that might help the amphitheater project." Becca pointed to a stack of papers she'd just pulled from her bag. "And I think it could play off the Allison City infrastructure project we're working on too. But it goes even further than that. I'm really excited about it, and Ben is too. I want to show the sketches to Nathan and run the ideas by him to make sure he thinks it's worth pursuing. But would you mind looking at them first?"

"Ben? You mean your coach? The one who's an architect and developer? Interesting." Jenn smirked suggestively. "You've been mentioning his name a lot lately. Anything you want to share?"

"That's the one," Becca said with a happy nod of her head. "And nope," she added with a grin. "Nothing to share—at least not today."

Jenn laughed. "Do you want to go over those sketches now before we get immersed in everything else that's going on around here? We can grab a conference room if you like."

"That would be awesome. I'm excited to show you everything—but also nervous. I think what we've got here is really good. But you never know...maybe you'll hate it," Becca said, her voice laced with apprehension.

"Let's go find out," Jenn said, and she started down the hall toward an empty conference room.

Becca grabbed the large stack of papers she'd just set on the edge of her desk and hurried down the hall after Jenn.

"This is great stuff, Becca! I love the sketches. The design of—well, of all of it is amazing! The map you've drawn—"

"Ben drew," Becca corrected. "Ben drew all of that. Believe me, my artistry is not that advanced," she said, laughing happily at Jenn's positive reaction to their work.

"Okay—that Ben drew," Jenn qualified. "This map brings the entire area to life from Pittsburgh to Marston. And I like the way you—or he —have it color coded in sections so it's easy to see the overall vision but also how the project could be implemented in phases. That's really helpful. And I already can't wait to go there and hang out. Everything's here that anyone could want—the entertainment venue that Ethan wants to build, shops, eateries, lodging, the marina, the trail, the park—all of it. It's incredible. And these separate sketches of the infrastructure that would underlay it all are so detailed. It makes it easy to see the potential of the area as well as what's needed to make it a functioning reality. This is hands-down incredible, Becca."

"Do you think Nathan will like it too? And Ethan?" Becca asked hopefully.

"Absolutely, I'm sure of it. In fact, the sooner you show this to Nathan, the better. Let's go ask Frank if Nathan's got any time on his calendar today."

"Today?"

"Okay, well, this week sometime. But, believe me, Nathan is going to want to see this. I know he's got a busy schedule, but he and I have been beating our heads against the wall trying to figure out how in the world we're going to make Ethan Trapp's project work without additional outside capital. I don't even need you to crunch those numbers to see that. We have been tracking funding opportunities, and Ethan's project is an okay fit for some of them. But his current plans alone just aren't enough to be competitive. His project mostly consists of just a private developer wanting to put in a for-profit entertainment venue. That's great and all, but that rarely garners grant funding. Despite that, we've started to draft a proposal for funding for Ethan's project, even knowing that priority points go to projects that focus on just what you've got in these sketches: water and sewage infrastructure improvements, blight reduction and green space developments—just like the trail and park you've got drawn on this map. The competition's going to be steep for that funding and Ethan's project won't make the cut on its own, but with what you've got here, I think we might have a winner. However, closing dates are coming up quickly for proposals. So, time is of the essence. The sooner we get this on Nathan's radar and then on Ethan's, the better. Come on, let's go down the hall and see if Frank's in."

Becca gathered up the sketches and supporting paperwork and hurried to catch up once again to Jenn, who was already halfway down the hall, heading toward Frank's cubicle located just outside Nathan's office.

"Hi, Frank," Jenn said. "Becca has some great stuff here that Nathan needs to see ASAP." She pointed to the stack of papers in Becca's arms. "Does he have any openings on his calendar today?"

Frank gave Jenn a smirk and rolled his eyes. "Girl, you are too funny! That man is booked up every day, all day. He's got meetings heading north, south, east, and west. I can not keep up with the mess that is his calendar," Frank ended with a head wag.

"Please," Jenn said, putting on a sad puppy dog face. "There must be somewhere on that calendar you can find to tuck us in. If anyone can do it, you can. You're a magician at this stuff," she said, fluttering her eyelashes.

Both Frank and Jenn laughed. "Girl, you know that flattery and flirting won't get you anywhere with me. Well, maybe the flattery. Now, if you send that hunky Ethan Trapp in to ask, maybe I could find something," he teased.

"You are too much!" Jenn laughed. "How about for Becca? I know you can work miracles for her. And we won't need a lot of time. Becca's got it all neatly wrapped up and tied with a bow, ready to show Nathan. I'm sure all it will take is one glance from him and he'll be salivating."

"Well, now, that's a different story. Who would not want to do something for Becca?" Frank said, smiling at Becca. "Hmmm....let's see." Frank let out a dramatic sigh, taking another look at Nathan's calendar on his computer screen. "He did tell me to put a hold on his calendar from 4:00 p.m. to 5:00 p.m. today for a meeting with a potential new client. But, between you and me, I don't think that client is gonna show. Do you want me to pencil you in at four? If that client shows, it'll be a no-go. But, if he doesn't, ya'all might just be in luck."

"That would be great!" said Jenn. "Becca, is 4:00 p.m. today good for you?"

"Absolutely! Thanks, Frank."

Jenn and Becca excitedly chattered their way back to their cubicles.

"That was amazing, Jenn. Thanks for getting us on Nathan's calendar. You're coming too, right?" Becca asked.

"You really don't need me there. This is your show. You've done an amazing job on it, and I'm sure Nathan will love it right out of the gate."

"I think it would be way better to have us both there. You're project manager on both the amphitheater and the Allison City project. And this proposal incorporates elements from both of those projects. Please?" Becca asked hopefully.

"Well, sure. I'd be happy to come if you think it will help. But I think you should pitch it and I'll just follow your lead and lend moral support when and if needed. How's that sound?"

"Perfect. Thanks, Jenn."

They both settled back in at their desks. As Becca dove into another project, she rolled her shoulders back, trying to work out the tension in her neck. There were multiple stacks of paper neatly laid out across her desk, one stack for each project she was in the midst of working on. There was a lot to do here. Maybe she could skip today's workout—just this once. Going by her schedule, there just wasn't enough time to fit everything in, and she couldn't slack on her work. And she didn't want to, she thought, as her mind drifted to how cool it would be to get to work on a project that combined all the elements of the amphitheater, Allison City, and Marston. That would be something to be proud of! Okay, so it was settled. She'd skip her workout today.

Becca worked, head down, for another hour before a fissure of guilt crept its way far enough into her brain to distract her from her work. She really shouldn't skip her workout. How would that play out on race day? Life was always busy. And what about Ben? He had put so much into helping her and, of course, the other participants. She didn't want to let him down—or herself. She needed a lifeline, someone to help hold her feet to the fire so she wouldn't blow off this workout. Her mind immediately went to Ben...and then to Carmen. Yes, that would be better—and more appropriate, she thought, as she picked up her cell phone and texted Carmen.

Becca: You up for doing the workout together today? It's a run AND a bike ride. My resolve is weakening. I need someone to make me do it. You up for that?:):)

Carmen: Yes! I'm tempted to blow it off tonight too. Help me....

Becca: Do you have your bike with you?

Carmen: Yes. It's on my car in the parking garage.

Becca: 5:30 p.m.? Meet in the parking garage by my car? I already have my bike here too.

Carmen: Yes. See you at 5:30. I'll be dressed to run. I'll bring my cleats with me so we can go clip-less after the run!! That sounds so naughty, doesn't it:)?

Becca laughed and huffed a sigh of relief. She set her phone alarm for 5:15 p.m. She couldn't back out now. If she did, she'd be letting her friend down.

~

"Hey, Becca, you up for lunch? It's already 1:00 p.m.," said Jenn.

"Would you mind bringing me up a salad today so I can keep working while I eat at my desk? I've got to leave right at five fifteen tonight for my workout."

"You got it. I'll bring your usual. Don't work too hard, though. I worry about you, ya know. Are you sure you're okay?"

Becca shifted her eyes up to Jenn and gave her a smile. "Thanks, Jenn. No need to worry, I promise. I'm good right now. In fact, I haven't felt this great in ages. And I like this work and the training stuff too. It's just time consuming is all."

"You promise you're okay? You seem good these days...happy." Jenn smiled back. "But you didn't tell me about that last scare, and I felt bad you had to go through it all alone. Don't do that to me again." She pouted. "I want to help. Promise me you'll let me know—and let me help—if something like that happens again. Okay?"

"I promise. And, Jenn?"

"Yes?"

"Thanks. I'm lucky to have you as my colleague and my friend. Now, let me get back to work," Becca said in a firm tone, but with a warm smile still on her lips.

After Jenn left for their downstairs cafeteria, Becca got back to concentrating on the stacks of paperwork laid out along the credenza next to her computer. Even after Jenn dropped off her salad, Becca kept her focus, nibbling on her lunch absentmindedly as she worked.

"Becca," Jenn whispered some hours later.

Becca startled at Jenn's voice and her head lifted in question.

Jenn held her hand over the mouthpiece on her phone. "It's Frank," she whispered again. "He said come now!" She turned back to the phone. "Mmm hmm... Okay... Thanks, Frank. We're on our way!" Jenn hung up the phone and turned back to Becca. "I know it's only 3:45 p.m. and Frank said 4:00 p.m., but Frank told me that Nathan's in his office now with what looks like a free half hour. He said his calendar's changed up all over the place today, but if we get down there now, we should be good."

Becca immediately jumped up and grabbed the sketches off the end of her desk. "Ready as I'll ever be," she said to Jenn. "Lead the way."

"Hi, Frank, and thank you," Becca and Jenn said in unison as they arrived at his desk.

"You two are very welcome. Go on in and kill it—like I know you will," Frank said with another head wag.

Jenn lightly tapped on Nathan's half open office door as she and Becca crossed over the threshold.

Nathan lifted his head. "Come on in Jenn, Becca. What've you got for me? Frank said he was sure I was going to want to see it."

Jenn nodded at Becca, encouraging her to speak up.

Becca took a breath and steeled her nerves, offering Nathan a warm smile. "Thanks for seeing us on such short notice, Nathan. We have an idea of how to add some pizzaz to the amphitheater project in a way that would benefit several other nearby initiatives, making not only Ethan's project more competitive for funding, but also other projects already underway in the surrounding area. By pulling the projects into a collaborative, we think we could create an enticing, fundable, and exciting win-win situation for multiple parties— including Ethan Trapp. The idea came about through the triathlon training I'm doing. I don't know if you remember that I signed up for a race?"

"How could I forget?" Nathan laughed. "Craziness! But I admire you for it, Becca. Go on," he encouraged, swiveling his wrist to glance at his watch.

"The training has been quite a journey, there's no denying that," Becca said, ducking her head shyly. "It's really been an eye-opener. There are entire communities I didn't know about, and there's so much opportunity to intertwine those communities with the amphitheater project. Take boating, for example. There are marinas up and down all these rivers where people get together every weekend in the summer months to play together—swimming, waterskiing, tubing, barbecuing, you name it. A lot of those marinas have become their own little communities. The team also bikes and runs on the roadways and sidewalks through lots of little neighborhoods hidden throughout Pittsburgh.

"It's easy to get a variety of experiences just through one ride or one run, giving people a balance of small town and big city, and nature and cityscape, all in one go. Take this office building we're in right now, for example. It's a great building to work in. It's a sleek design but also has natural elements, like the cafe with the garden running through it. We envision intertwining those juxtapositions between city-scapes and nature-scapes on a grander scale. The amphitheater already incorporates design elements along those lines, just as this building does. But what if it could go much further? A friend of mine put some drawings together to make this project easier to envision. We also put some talking points together and ran some numbers. May I?" Becca motioned to a large table in the corner of Nathan's office.

Nathan nodded his head and Becca stood to lay the drawings across Nathan's meeting table.

"Here's where Ethan envisions building the amphitheater," Becca said, pointing to a marking on the map. "But if he moves it upriver just a bit, it would be positioned right here, next to this marina." Becca pointed to a small picture of a boat and docks on the sketches.

"There's a marina there?" Nathan asked in surprise.

"Yes. It's small, and it's pretty run down, but my friend docks his boat there and has already drawn up some plans for renovations. He's also drafted plans that would have a trail running from here," she said, pointing to a section on the drawings just above Pittsburgh that showed where the trail currently ended "to here, where this blue X is, right next to the marina. The drawings also show the trail being expanded north from the marina and into the heart of the City of Marston. My friend has met several times with the mayor and members of the city council as well as with some prominent business owners who are working to revitalize Marston—that's this town shown right here on the map. This includes one building owner who runs a bakery and is putting in a boutique hotel over the bakery right here." Becca pointed to another notation on the map. "With the trail coming through here, that brings an added cadre of people looking for places to stay, eat, and shop, as well as attend events at the amphitheater. Marston is a Rust Belt community, and there is specific funding for cities like Marston. If we could tie Ethan's amphitheater into this overall broader design, we think we would have a good case for bringing in several million additional dollars in federal funding in a way that the amphitheater project on its own would not. You can also see here on this separate drawing how we've brought in elements from the solution being crafted for Allison City to fix their sewage problem. That, and more, is depicted on this infrastructure drawing and aligns with the collaborative redevelopment shown on the map. As you can see, and as you directed us in our first meeting regarding the Allison City sewage problem, this is meant to be a proactive solution to a problem we already know is a disaster waiting to happen."

"This is great, Becca!" Nathan said in his booming voice. "And you're right. We've been missing that pizazz piece that would get us federal funding, and I don't think Ethan—let me rephrase that—I *know* Ethan doesn't have the capital to go it alone. But even with federal funding, and maybe even state and private funding invested, it's going to have to make longer-term sense economically once the seed funding is gone. Of course, I know you know that already. Have you thought about that aspect in any concrete terms?"

"Absolutely. We went ahead and ran some numbers. As you can see here," Becca said, handing Nathan a one-page summary of the financials, "Ethan would have a better chance of success by intertwining these additional elements and partners into his overall project, especially with the town of Marston already on board and wanting a partner. And, through our research here at Patterson, we already know this is something people are craving—developments that connect the larger city amenities to jobs, eateries, entertainment, and recreation with small town charm. And in a way that enhances those small communities rather than drains them."

"I like it! And these drawings are excellent. Who is this friend of yours?"

Becca kept her gaze on the drawings in front of them. She didn't want Nathan to see any of the emotion that surely must show on her face. "His name is Ben Morgan. He owns Morgan Designs and Development."

"That name sounds familiar. Why do I know that name?" Nathan cocked his head and pursed his lips in thought. "I know! Jake Creighton from Fischer Industries was telling me about him. They just signed a contract with him. He's really excited about this kid!"

The buzzer sounded on the phone sitting on Nathan's desk and he sighed, hitting a button on the phone's front panel. "What is it Frank? ...Okay, yeah, put the call through. Thanks."

Nathan turned back to Jenn and Becca. "I would love to hear more, but I just can't right now. I'll get in touch with Ethan and keep you posted. Good job, ladies!" Giving them a nod and a smile in farewell, Nathan hit another button on his phone's front panel, answering the call Frank sent through.

"Becca, this is so exciting!" Jenn said, as they made their way back to their cubicles. "I think all we have to do now is wait."

"It's killing me already!" Becca smiled. "Hopefully, with Nathan being the messenger, Ethan won't shoot it down right off the bat. Who knows why Ethan wasn't open to collaborating when Ben first approached him. Maybe it was just because the ideas weren't fleshed out enough yet, and there weren't any drawings to go with the concepts. At least, let's hope that's why."

"He'd be crazy to shoot it down," said Jenn. "It's too perfect."

"I hope so," Becca said, crossing her fingers. "Should I call Ben?" A moment later, she dismissed her own question. "Nevermind, I'm just going to text him. I don't want to interrupt his workday, and we really don't have any solid answers yet."

"Sounds good. I've got to get back to finishing up these client emails if I'm ever going to get out of here tonight. Yikes—look at the time!" Jenn said, settling back down in front of her computer.

Becca grabbed her cell phone and texted Ben.

Becca: Met with Nathan and my colleague, Jenn, today. They loved the proposal, especially the sketches! Nathan is going to try to meet with Ethan. I'll let you know when I know more.

She hurriedly turned back to her computer to follow Jenn's lead in getting some emails out before she had to meet Carmen. Phew!

There was lots going on, but it was exciting stuff, she thought happily.

~

"Oh—you scared me!" Becca smiled as Carmen walked up behind her and put her hands on Becca's shoulders. Becca stood next to her car in the parking garage, where she was changing into her running shoes. "You're right on time, Carmen—again! I'm impressed. Who are you and what have you done with my best friend?"

"Guess what?" Carmen said, interrupting Becca, clearly too impatient to share some news.

Becca felt her own impatience rise in anticipation. "What?" she returned, flashing Carmen an answering grin. "It must be something good. You're smiling ear-to-ear."

"Right after we texted today, my boss called me into his office. I was petrified. I was sure he was going to tell me I was one of the people getting laid off. But..." Carmen trailed off, raising her eyebrows with a leading smile.

"What?" Becca encouraged with a chuckle. "Come on, don't leave me hanging in suspense here! I can't stand it."

"My boss said they still want me in the marketing department, and they want me to continue as a graphic layout artist. BUT, they want to add photographer to my list of job duties. I'm so excited! I've taken some photos here and there for client marketing pieces but always simply because we didn't have just the right photo for whatever we were working on. A few of my pieces have even made the cut and gone to print. I always thought it was because they didn't have time to find something better and that it was just cheaper and easier when we were under a time crunch. But my boss said he thinks my photos are really good, and he wants to incorporate more of them into our client pieces and into my job description."

"That's fantastic, Carmen!" Becca said, giving Carmen a huge hug. "I knew there was no way they could let you go. You've got too good an eye for all that creative stuff!"

"Yeah." Carmen smiled shyly, clearly pleased. "The only thing is, my first photo shoot is on the last day of our training."

"Oh, no! Does that mean you'll have to miss it? I wouldn't worry, though, as long as they don't want you on race day."

"No way!" Carmen laughed. "I told my boss about the race, and he promised there was no way he would pull me away from race day. He thinks it's really cool that we're doing this race. And I should still be able to make it to the dress rehearsal training. The client shoot isn't until mid-afternoon. I might just have to leave a little early is all."

"I am so proud of you, Carmen."

"Thanks. Enough of that, though," Carmen said with another happy sigh. "You said you needed someone to make sure you got your workout in tonight. We'd better get a move on before we run out of daylight."

"Ready when you are."

As they made their way out of the parking garage to start their run, Carmen said, "By the way, I'm really glad you wanted to train together tonight. If you hadn't, I would've been texting you about going to Luna's to have a celebratory margarita. This is way better...although," Carmen dragged out suggestively, "as much as I'm glad you asked me to be the one to hold you accountable, I'm sure someone else we know would have come running if you'd just crooked your little finger at him."

Becca grinned. "He is still our coach, ya know. But..." she drew out teasingly, the top half of her body swaying happily now, "it is kinda going pretty great right now."

Carmen giggled as she mimicked Becca's happy dance. "Let's get running at our lolly-gag pace so we can talk while we run—just like we did back in junior high. I want to hear all about the gala and all about Ben at brunch with your mom yesterday. All I've gotten out of you so far are a couple of texts, and I want more!"

Carmen filled Becca in on the upcoming photo shoot, and Becca filled Carmen in about the gala, the brunch, and even the project sketches she and Jenn had pitched to Nathan earlier in the afternoon —all while they were running and biking. Okay, so their pace wasn't exactly up to par. And there were a couple of scares—just small ones— as they rode their bikes while trying to chat. But at least they hadn't blown off the workout altogether, Becca rationalized.

"Carmen," Becca said thoughtfully, as they changed out of their bike cleats and back into their everyday shoes.

"What is it? Are you okay?" she asked with concern.

"Yeah. It's nothing like that. It's just...I haven't told him yet."

"I know."

"Do you think I have to?"

"Well, yeah. I really think you do. Unless you want to keep it casual and end it before it really starts. But I don't think that's what you want, is it?"

"No. I really like him. But what if I tell him and everything changes —or worse, he decides he needs to treat me with kid gloves, tiptoeing around me and feeling sorry for me when all he really wants to do is dump me? I don't want him to feel trapped."

"Are you two officially a thing now? How can he dump you if he thinks you two aren't even dating?"

"Good point. I guess we are officially still just friends. That's what we agreed to, and we've been sticking to that—sort of, anyway," Becca said coyly.

"But there's more to it, isn't there?"

"I don't know what's going on. Ugh! I'm so confused. It's like there's a magnet under our feet that just keeps drawing us together. He's all I think about. And I know he's attracted to me, too. His eyes, his voice—they're mesmerizing, and I can see and hear the desire in them when he looks at me and when he talks to me, even when he's frustrated with me. And he was jealous when I danced with Jake Creighton at the gala. And then when we met Ethan Trapp. Ben looked like he wanted to punch Ethan and then pick me up and carry me out of there like a caveman. It was...well, I know I shouldn't feel this way, but it was awesome." Becca giggled. "It felt so good to be that desired," she added, looking up at Carmen uncertainly.

"Oh. My. God! Do you know how jealous I am of you right now?" Carmen laughed. "You have got to see where this is going—you've got to give it a chance. But you need to tell him about the cancer. You've got to be honest with him."

"You're right. And I need to be fair to him. I need to give him a chance to opt out. I mean, who wants to date someone who may or may not be in remission?"

"Stop that right now!" yelled Carmen. "You are in remission. End of story. And, just to play devil's advocate, let's say you aren't. The world could change for any of us at any moment. You've got just as much right to grab the life you want while you're here—and no reason to think right now that a long life isn't what's in store for you."

"I'm sorry, Carmen. I guess I'm just scared to tell him. But you're right, I need to tell him before this—whatever this is—goes any further." Becca reached over to give Carmen a hug, her eyes wet with emotion.

"I love you, girl," Carmen said, giving Becca an extra squeeze and handing her the towel she held in her hand. "Don't cry, you've got this. And I'm here for you whatever happens."

As Carmen rolled her bike through the parking garage to find her car, Becca secured her own bike on the back of her car. Then, before pulling out of the garage, Becca picked up her phone and texted Ben.

Becca: Hi! You up for dinner this week? I have something I want to tell you. I could make you a home-cooked meal at your house.

A beep came back almost immediately, alerting her to a new text.

Ben: That would be great! How about tomorrow at six? You don't have to cook, though. I can order something in.

Becca: Tomorrow at six would be great. Are you refusing my home-cooked meal? Don't you think I can cook?:) Oh...wait, I guess that's fair since all we've eaten together so far is pizza, lasagna, and my mom's cooking. At least give me a chance to prove you wrong....

Ben: I would love a home-cooked meal. See you tomorrow at six.

CHAPTER 48
Magical Angst

"HI," SAID BECCA, AS SHE STOOD AWKWARDLY OUTSIDE Ben's front door, laden down with shopping bags filled with the ingredients for the meal she'd promised him. "Thank you for letting me come over."

"How can I refuse a home-cooked meal? Here, let me help you with those bags," he said, reaching out to take them from her. "Right this way. We can set these on the kitchen counter, and then you can let me know what I can do to help."

"This is amazing, Ben. This house is enormous. And who are those two cuties that met me in the driveway?"

Ben laughed. "You mean Manky and Mel?"

"Uh…Manky and Mel? You named them? Aren't they ducks?"

"Yeah, but they seem to have adopted me. They just showed up one day about a month or two ago. They're here wandering around every day now. I'm figuring there must be a nest around here somewhere. I haven't found it yet, though, and neither of them is just sitting anywhere. So, who knows? They're here to greet me pretty much every time I pull up the drive. And they give me an excited waggle of their behinds in greeting." He flashed a grin. "Did you get a butt waggle?"

Becca raised a brow. "I did not. I must not rate yet."

"We can remedy that, I'm sure. Want a formal introduction?"

"Won't they just run away when we approach?" asked Becca doubtfully.

"They used to at first, but not anymore. I'm not sure how they'll react to a newcomer, though."

"Yeah, I want an introduction," Becca said, her eyes sparkling.

Becca followed Ben back down the front steps, stopping a couple of feet behind him as he crouched down near the ducks who were still about five feet from him. He put his hand out and gently crooned to them in his soft, soothing baritone, "Hi Manky. Hi Mel. Want to meet a new friend?"

One and then the other approached him, quacking and waggling their behinds in excitement until they stood only about one foot away from him. "Hi you two. I'd like you to meet Becca. Be nice to her." He cocked his head silently toward Becca, encouraging her forward.

Becca took a couple of steps toward Ben as quietly and as gently as she could, but the ducks just quacked more loudly in response and waddled away, back down toward the river.

Ben laughed. "Not today, I guess. You'll just need to come by more often so they can get to know you better. I'm always up for a home-cooked meal—from you," Ben ended in a sultry tone and giving her a smoldering gaze that set her heart to racing.

"Maybe you'd better try this first meal before you put that offer out on the table. You might not like what I cook tonight," Becca replied, trying to respond nonchalantly so as not to stoke the fire that was already burning between them. She needed to tell him tonight about her cancer—before this went any further. "Aren't you going to show me your mansion? This place is huge!" she said, changing the subject.

"It is that," he said with a laugh. "I apologize for it looking like a construction zone. The house was on its way to being torn down when I bought it. Believe it or not, I've made good progress where it matters most by fixing the roof, cleaning up the worst of the grime, and getting the most important living areas into semi-decent shape. I just haven't had time to do much more than that with work and all."

"And the triathlon coaching—don't forget that," said Becca. "I don't know how you're fitting it all in."

"The tri was an unexpected add-on," Ben admitted. "When Sam

called to tell me he'd gotten his dream job and asked if I could help, I didn't have the heart to turn him down. Who am I to stop someone from taking their dream job?" He gave her a thoughtful but pointed look before setting the grocery bags down on the counter and turned back to her. "I'm sorry about the kitchen. It's still mostly nineteenth century decrepit. It's got the basics, though."

"It looks just fine," Becca said, as she unloaded the groceries. "I hope you like pasta, because that's what we're having. The coach in you should especially approve of this one. It's loaded with healthy veggies and heart-healthy chicken. But I also brought dessert. It's a balance, right?"

Ben's smile was huge. "You really didn't need to go to all of this trouble. I'm happy to help you with whatever I can. I hope you know that."

"Yes. You've been a great coach—"

"Is there something wrong with the bike? Is that what you want to talk about? Are you having trouble with any of the trainings?" Ben interrupted with some concern.

"No, nothing like that," Becca said quickly, cutting him off. "The bike is amazing. And the trainings are going great, even though I didn't know what a triathlon was until Carmen dragged me to that info session. It wasn't anything I'd expected to be doing, not at all. That's sort of what I wanted to talk to you about...to tell you why I didn't expect to be doing anything like this."

"What's up?" Ben asked, clearly curious.

A waft of smoke slithered up between them from the frying pan sitting on the stove and Becca jerked into movement. "Oh, sorry! Could you please add those onions and garlic to the pan and give them a stir? That olive oil is clearly hot enough. I don't want to burn your house down," she said with a tinge of embarrassment. "So much for impressing you with my culinary skills!" She laughed self-consciously. "I guess I'd better pay attention to cooking before we get into any deep discussions."

"Sure," said Ben, stepping up to the counter next to where Becca now stood cutting up kale and carrots for the pasta. "Hey, where are my manners? Can I get you something to drink? I've got beer, wine, and water. I know you like wine, and it would go great with that pasta you're making."

"Sure," Becca said, remembering that night on the boat sipping wine with Ben, and then the night after their bike shop excursion at Tony's restaurant where they'd spent hours and hours talking and eating that delicious lasagna and chocolate cake while sipping red wine. A flood of heat enveloped her—and not from the stove. She quickly brushed those thoughts aside. She needed to tell Ben about her cancer before he found out from someone else. And she needed to tell him before either of them succumbed to whatever this was between them. Becca didn't want to lose her nerve again. She owed him that if things were going to go any further—and maybe even if they weren't.

"This one or this one?" Ben asked, holding out a bottle of merlot and another of cabernet. "Or would you prefer white?"

As Becca turned to inspect the labels, her eye caught sight of three large easels standing in the furthest back corner of the kitchen, each holding a vision board with paint colors and pictures of countertops, cabinets, and appliances. "Is that what you're working on for this house?" she asked in amazement. "These are beautiful."

"Yep, that's what this is supposed to look like eventually," Ben said, sweeping his arm around the kitchen. "I've got the renovations for the kitchen all mocked up and the materials on order. I'm not sure when I'm going to get to the install, though. Adam was a great help when he first arrived. He helped me pick things out for the kitchen and for some of the other areas of the house. But now that his summer program is in full swing, he's just as busy as I am, so it's now slow going."

Ben stepped up behind Becca and set down a glass of the cabernet on the countertop next to where she now stood, adding carrots, zucchini, baby heirloom tomatoes, and kale to the onions and garlic already sauteing on the stove. "I went ahead and opened the White-hall Lane Cab. I already know you're a fan of this one as this is the same one we had on the boat," he said, looking at her flirtatiously. "Here." He held out his hand for the spatula she was using to stir the vegetables. "Let me keep an eye on those so you can enjoy some of that wine."

"Thanks," she said, turning her body slightly to hand him the spatula. As she turned, her behind grazed up against him. She stilled, trying to hide the internal fissure of heat that ran through her. Taking a deep breath, Becca stepped away from Ben and reached out a shaky hand to pick up her wine glass.

After taking a sip to steady her nerves, she said, "Um, so, this pasta is almost ready to serve. Where would you like to eat?"

"How about in the living room? It's much more comfortable in there. I've been able to make a lot more progress with the renovations in that room."

Ben served their dinner and carried the plates while she carried the wine out to the living room. Their conversation was light and fun and soon morphed into sharing anecdotes about the various team members.

"Matt was amazing with the alligator eyes," Ben said with a laugh. "I'm so proud of him—and of you, Becca. You've both taken to the training incredibly well. Matt's even running some now. He's still a mixed run-walker but on day one, he told me he wasn't planning to run at all."

Becca shared a smile with Ben. "I love alligator eyes! It makes me feel so stealthy and accomplished. I love the clip-less pedaling as well, but that one's been a bit more painful to learn," she said, rubbing her knee where a scab still stood out with black and blue coloring over her otherwise unblemished and creamy skin.

Ben reached over and gently stroked his fingertips over her angry-looking, skinned knee. "I wish I could make it all better," he said, before quickly catching himself and pulling his hand back to his side. "That was delicious, Becca," he continued quickly, reaching over to pick up the still nearly full wine bottle and refilling her glass.

"Thank you. Before drinking that, I'll just take these plates to the kitchen and bring in the dessert."

Becca returned from the kitchen carrying two dessert plates, each laden with a decadent piece of chocolate cake reminiscent of what they'd eaten at Tony's Restaurant. She set them down on the coffee table and picked up her wineglass, taking a good look at the room before sitting. "This shelving surrounding your fireplace is gorgeous. Did you put this in yourself?" she asked Ben.

"Yep. I had to dust off my carpentry skills. It was fun, though. I used to do a lot of that with my dad when I was young. I've been so busy for a long time now on the business side of things with my company, that I was getting rusty. It felt good to delve back into it."

"I can see your commitment to your business from all these books on the shelves!" Becca said. She read aloud some of the titles as she ran her hand along them. *"The Language of Architecture; Architect and Entrepreneur; Architecture and Disjunction; Sustainable Community; Architecture: From Prehistory to Postmodernity; World Architecture: The Master Works; The Architecture of Community,* and look at all these awards!" she said with admiration. "Impressive."

Ben gave her a small smile at her praise.

Becca turned back to the awards and ran her hand over them, stopping at a framed picture pushed to the back of one of the shelves. She stared at it for a moment, taken in by the faces. "What a cute little girl! I recognize you and Adam, but who is the little girl?" Becca asked, turning to look at Ben.

Ben's face blanched, and his caressing tone turned strained as he started to answer her. "Ah, that is my—"

"Oh! I'm sorry, Ben, I'm being nosy. It's none of my business," Becca said, quickly putting the picture back down and returning to the couch. "No questions, right? Here you go. Are you ready for dessert?" she said, handing him one of the plates.

Ben took the plate from her outstretched hand but didn't pick up the fork or make any move to take a bite. He paused and then set the plate back down. "That's my sister," he said in a soft voice.

"Oh, she's adorable," Becca said hesitantly, sensing that something was very wrong but not knowing what Pandora's box she may have accidentally opened. "How old is she?"

"She would be twenty-three now. But...she passed away."

"Oh, Ben. I'm so sorry," Becca said, reaching a hand out to comfort him.

Ben covered Becca's hand, now resting on his arm with his own. "It's okay. It was a long time ago."

"Do you want to talk about it?"

There was a long silence before Ben answered in a gravelly voice laced with emotion, "It was cancer."

Becca moved closer to Ben as he spoke and put an arm around his shoulder. He leaned his head toward her and used his right arm to pull her in closer. A tear trickled out of the corner of his eye and his breaths deepened, escalating into a staccato.

"What was her name?" Becca whispered.

Ben just shook his head and held Becca tighter. No words came out of him now, just light sobs.

Becca reached over to hold his head between her hands and pulled his face closer to her bosom, holding him close as he released his grief. She stroked his hair and kissed the top of his head, offering solace in the only way she knew how, waiting on Ben to speak again.

"Her name was..." His words clogged in his throat, and he moved his head from side to side against her chest, not looking up, as though struggling to force the words out. He took a deep breath and said, "She had Leukemia."

Becca gasped—the same kind of cancer she has...or had. And his sister had died from it. She felt her heart wrench in anguish. Had his sister gone through all the chemo and radiation she'd gone through? Had she gone through the same pain? And had Ben had to sit on the sidelines, knowing there was nothing he could do to change the trajectory of whatever would be...just like her mother and her friends had?

How could she burden Ben with her own past now? How could she even think of being so selfish as to subject him to that kind of pain again? Becca felt her own tears fall down her cheeks and into the soft, dark auburn curls on the top of Ben's head that were still pressed against her chest.

"I was only fourteen and Adam seven when she was diagnosed," he continued quietly. "It went downhill quickly from there. She was in so much pain, but she always had a smile for me and Adam, and for Mom and Dad. Us kids were the three musketeers, and I was the big brother. I let her die. I couldn't save her...and I couldn't save Adam, not then." Ben's tears turned into gasping sobs. Becca held him more tightly and whispered words she didn't even know the meaning of, trying to soothe his pain.

After a moment, Ben lifted his head to look at her directly. "I'm sorry, Becca," he said. His eyes were full of anguish, making her gut twist in agony. "I didn't mean to fall apart on you like that. I'm so sorry. That's the first time I've spoken about her in a very long time." He suddenly pushed her to arm's length and peered at her closely. "Oh, Becca. I didn't mean to make you cry!"

Becca was pulled into his arms this time, held tightly while Ben rubbed her back, offering comfort to her now. "Thank you for listening to me ramble on. I don't know what it is about you. I don't feel quite as...as numb, when I'm with you. It's overwhelming. It's powerful. It's almost painful. But it's a good pain for a change. I'm sorry." He shook his head again, as though trying to clear the words he'd just spoken. "I don't mean to put that kind of pressure on you."

Ben straightened his body, leaning back from her again, and he pulled his hands away and back to his sides, an edge of embarrassment now tinging his cheeks. "That's not what you came here for tonight. As I recall, you said *you* had something to tell me. Please tell me what I can do to help," he almost pleaded.

Becca could see the sad little boy he must have been back when he lost his sister. She felt such a rush of love for him right then in that moment. No, that couldn't be right. It was just the emotion of the moment, she told herself. But Becca knew that wasn't the case. She loved him, really loved him, and she needed—no, *wanted* to protect him. "Nothing. It's nothing. It can wait."

"Are you sure?" Ben said. "If there's anything I can help you with, please tell me. I want to help."

"No...it's just that I wanted to tell you how grateful I am to you for the bike. It's amazing. And you're right, when I'm on that bike, I feel like I could fly. And thank you for allowing me to see your sketches for the Marston project and for including the amphitheater and the elements of the Allison City project. My boss loved what you put together. I really just wanted to thank you for that."

Ben didn't answer but instead reached out toward her, his hands now resting once again around her arms, this time lightly, as if in question. She felt her body lean in, drawn to him. She knew she should pull away. He needed her to be strong right now. She needed to be strong for both of them.

Then Ben leaned forward, his lips now just inches from hers. "Becca," he groaned. "What is this between us? I can't resist you." He rested his forehead against hers. "I've tried. I don't know what this is.

I don't know how it happened, but we have something here, don't we?" he whispered.

"I think we do," she answered huskily. "But, I don't want to cause you pain."

"It's the best pain I've ever felt," he said, and his lips gently touched hers.

Tears now streamed down both their faces as they pressed their lips together. Their arms tightly wound around each other as if of their own accord. Becca felt as though she wanted to crawl inside him. She wanted to give him her soul—anything he wanted.

He pushed her with more intention now back against the couch and coaxed her body into a prone position before moving his body to cover her own. Becca felt Ben's arousal and sighed, pulling him toward her more tightly and pushing herself up against the cloth covering his erection.

Ben responded by pushing his tongue into her mouth, exploring with abandon. Then he moved his lips to nuzzle her ear and then her neck, all while holding her arms captive above her head. He trailed kisses down over her shoulder and then moved his hands up under her blouse to cup her breasts. "Take this off for me, please Becca," he demanded huskily.

Without hesitating, Becca reached her hands down to lift her blouse up over her head, shutting her eyes gently to better take in the now familiar minty, eucalyptus scent, along with his deep, soothing, melodious baritone that sent a sense of calm through her while simultaneously throwing her into a delirious and wonderful storm of abandon...and magic.

Ben suddenly pulled away from her to look into her eyes. "Becca, will you stay with me tonight?" he pleaded.

Swirling storms of desire shown from the depths of his deep brown eyes. Becca felt her whole being melt as she nodded a breathless "yes."

With a sinfully delightful smile, Ben stood, taking her hand, and led her up the ornately carved circular wooden staircase to his large king-sized bed.

～

Becca awoke early on Wednesday morning. It took her but a moment to remember that she was in Ben's bed, in his house. Going by the light in the room, she knew she needed to get to work, but all she wanted to do was lie here, propped up on her elbow and watch him sleep. He looked so peaceful.

Neither of them had succeeded at being strong last night—and it had been wonderful. If only they could lie here forever in this bubble. But the real world was calling, and she needed to get to work. Becca realized that after last night, she couldn't just run out on Ben again with only a note, and she didn't want to. But more than ever now, how could she and Ben have anything deeper going forward? If he knew about her cancer, she would always be a painful reminder of his sister's death. She'd wanted to comfort him last night and she had. That was all there was to it, she lied to herself. Lust—they were just in a state of lust, and it would pass.

The lies fell flat, because Becca knew it was more than that. But she couldn't tell Ben about her cancer now—maybe not ever. How could she add that to what was clearly an already overwhelming burden for him? Feeling emotionally torn, Becca watched him for a few more moments before she couldn't sit there any longer.

"Ben, Ben," she said, gently nudging him.

"Hmm...Becca." Ben smiled. He wrapped his arms around her and gave her a kiss. She kissed him back. But she couldn't stay, she told herself as she struggled to pull her body away from him, when all that she really wanted was to stay here with him in this cocoon.

She tried again. "Ben, I need to get to work. Are you okay now?" Becca couldn't help stroking her hands over his deep bronze curls again.

He looked at her with a heated gaze. "Mmm, Becca, you are so beautiful. And no, I'm not okay, because we're not done here yet!" He kissed her again, deeply, and ran his hands over her breasts and then her hips....

CHAPTER 49

Bike, Run, Ick

BECCA WHOOPED AS SHE FINISHED HER RUN, FEELING A momentary reprieve from the angst she'd been feeling all week after her night with Ben.

"That was amazing," she said to Adam, as she joined him on the picnic bench he was sitting on next to the fuel table. I can't believe I just did another BRICK. Who knew? Maybe that wasn't exactly a BRICK, though. Didn't you and Sam and Ben say that stood for Bike, Run, Ick? What do you call it when you swim first and then run? Is it a SRICK?"

Adam laughed. "I really don't know, Becca. I'm just the wannabe coach. Remember, I didn't come by this triathlon coaching thing honestly; I just followed in my big brother's footsteps and everyone just kinda let me step into that role. I think you still call it a BRICK, though. It just means you've combined two of the sports into one training. And, by the way, you're amazing. You've really taken to this tri training. It looks like you're having a good time with it too." He smiled.

"I am!" she said proudly, helping herself to some Gatorade and a peanut butter, jelly, and banana sandwich from the fuel table. "Thanks for these snacks. Are these your doing?"

"Sam brought all of it, actually. I just set it out for everyone. Again, just the hanger on, remember?" he said self-deprecatingly.

"I'm not the last one in, am I? Are there still people out running?"

"Yep. And Ben's out there with them. I'm sure they'll all be in soon. In the meantime, help yourself to as many sandwiches as you want."

"Be careful; don't tempt me. I love PB&J—and banana, of course," she said, taking another bite. "How did you end up out here in Pittsburgh with your brother, Adam?" Becca asked curiously. "I know you moved here only recently for the summer program at CMU. Did you come out here because of Ben, or was that just a coincidence?"

"Kinda both, I guess. How about you? How did you end up here? Why this training?" Adam said, directing the focus back to Becca.

"It was Carmen who talked me into it. But...it's more than that. I need to talk to Ben about it," Becca blurted out. It was funny how much easier it was to tell a near stranger about her cancer than someone she cared so deeply about, she thought, deriding herself for being such a coward when it came to Ben.

"About what?"

"It's a long story. I was going to tell Ben earlier this week, but then he told me about your sister. I'm so sorry about your sister, Adam!" Becca said, feeling tears form in her eyes.

"He told you? Wow. He does not talk about that with anyone. I haven't even gotten him to open up to me about it yet."

"I'm sorry, I shouldn't have said anything."

"It's okay by me," said Adam. "It's just not okay with Ben...at least, I thought it wasn't. Maybe there's hope yet, though, if he told you about it."

"That's the problem," Becca said, as a tear escaped down her cheek.

"What is it Becca? Are you okay? What can I do to help?"

"I shouldn't be telling you this; I should be telling Ben. But that's just it—I tried to earlier this week...but then he told me about your sister, and I lost my nerve. I need to tell him, but I'm afraid. I thought I was getting braver...but maybe not so much where Ben is concerned," Becca said as another tear escaped.

"Tell me. What is it? Maybe I can help."

"I have leukemia. Or, at least, I had it. My doctor says I'm in remission."

"*What?*" Adam said. His mouth hung open in surprise.

"I'm sorry, Adam. Are you mad? I don't want to upset you."

"You're worried about upsetting me? Are you crazy? How could I be mad at you? But you're right. You really should tell Ben. He's crazy about you, ya know. It's obvious. But nevermind that right now. Are you sure you should be doing this training?"

"Yes," Becca said firmly, and with a tinge of irritation. "My doctor thinks it's great. She was a little surprised that I took on this much this soon, but she likes the idea. She said there's no reason for me not to do this as long as I pay attention to how I'm feeling and let her know if I end up with any concerns. So far, it's been great. Don't get me wrong, it's hard, but it's a good hard—a challenge, and something that makes me feel, well, alive again. It also takes me away from those months and months of treatments. The hardest part is getting up the nerve to try things like the clip-less pedals and the open water swims. Those are scary!" she said, hearing a smile now back in her tone.

"But they make me feel brave, accomplished, and part of the universe again," Becca continued. "I'm really glad Carmen talked me into it, and I'm really glad to have met you and Sam and Ben and all the other participants. I haven't wanted to share about my experience with everyone yet, though. I don't want people looking at me differently. I don't want to be coddled. I know that's a lot of what this whole thing is about—opening up and sharing and supporting each other. I'm just not ready yet as I'm still trying to figure out who the new 'me' is in all of this."

"Hey, guys!" Ben said, suddenly approaching the bench where Becca and Adam sat.

Becca immediately closed her mouth and turned to face Ben, feeling that sense of dread come over her again at the conversation she still had to have with him.

"Sorry to keep you waiting, Adam. I'll be ready to go soon by the looks of it." Ben turned to face her, his eyes raking over her body as he gave her a bright smile. "How'd it go, Becca?"

"Great," said Becca, returning his smile while her body instantly responded to him with a warmth that came from well beyond the run she'd just completed. She glanced over at Adam, who stood slightly behind Ben now. He gave her a gentle but encouraging look. Yes, she knew she needed to tell him. Becca quickly averted her eyes from Adam's piercing glance.

"Just about ten more minutes. Okay, Adam?" Ben said, pulling his eyes away from Becca.

"No problem; take your time. I'm just happy to have a ride home whenever you're ready."

"Do you mind loading up the table, coolers, and any remaining snacks for me?" Ben asked Adam. "Everyone's in now. I just want to check in with these last two runners before they leave."

"Sure thing."

"Thanks, Adam."

While Adam and Becca started packing up the fuel table and loading Ben's truck, Ben headed over to say his goodbyes and check in with the last of the runners.

"You don't need to help, Becca. I've got this. Besides, are you supposed to be carrying stuff?"

Becca rolled her eyes at Adam. "See what I mean? That's exactly why I don't want people to know. They will treat me differently and start coddling me and worrying. I'm training for a triathlon, you know. If I can't help load up the truck, I sure as heck shouldn't be doing this triathlon. But my doctor assured me this is exactly what I should be doing—getting back out there and exercising. It's a challenge, but I finally feel like my body is functioning again and like I'm actually living. It's a very good feeling," Becca said with consternation.

Apology was written all over Adam's face. "Sorry, Becca. You're absolutely right. My bad. It was just a knee-jerk reaction. I know you're fine—I can see it. You're also very brave, and I'm in awe of what you're doing. I wish I could have seen Sophia to this place. I know it just wasn't meant to be in her case. But in your case, you're clearly on the path you should be on. It's inspiring." Adam surreptitiously brushed his hand across his suspiciously moist eyes.

"Thanks, Adam," Becca said more gently now. "That means a lot to me, especially after all the suffering you and Ben have had to deal with. I'm grateful to both of you for pulling me through this far. The training helps—a lot. I must admit, though, I'm still having trouble sharing with people, partly because of exactly the reaction you just had. Even though it clearly helps me to listen to their mission moments."

"Sorry about that, Becca."

"No need to apologize. And, I know I owe Ben an explanation. I've been struggling with how to tell him. I will. I just have to figure out when. Until I figure that out, though, can you please not tell him? I need to tell him myself."

"Sure thing, Becca," Adam said gently. "I understand. But you'd better tell him soon. He seems to know something's up. And I know it will be better if he hears it directly from you than someone else. Don't lose your chance to tell him before someone else does."

"I will. Thanks, Adam."

"Go ahead and go Becca. I'll finish loading up the truck and I'll see you at the next training."

"Okay. See ya. And, Adam—thanks."

CHAPTER 50

Sweet Alligators!

"HEY, EVERYONE! GATHER ROUND, PLEASE," SAM CALLED out. "As you know, this will be my last group training with everyone."

A chorus of boos lifted from the group. "Don't leave us, Sam!" called out one participant, eliciting a laugh from everyone.

"It's all on you now, Ben. What can I say? Don't let 'em down," Sam said, clapping Ben on the shoulder and eliciting a cheer for Ben from the group.

"Go Ben, go Ben!"

"And don't forget Adam too," Sam said. "He started out as an honorary member, but I now officially promote you to assistant coach."

Everyone cheered as Adam grinned and bowed, his face crimson with pleasure and embarrassment.

"Fortunately, I get to be here for this training," Sam continued. "My last one before I fly out to California to start my new job. Luckily, it's one of my favorite trainings, because we're going to practice our alligator eyes, swim starts, and buoy turns—oh my!" Everyone laughed. "But first," Sam said, lifting his hand, "does anyone have a mission moment to share today?"

Elora stood and shared about her aunt's cancer. Everyone clapped in support and appreciation of her sharing once she finished her story.

"Okay," said Sam, "it's time to get your wetsuits on and head down to the lake."

~

"Great swim, everyone!" Sam said to the group that had regathered after their open water swim practice. "So, remember, next week is the last group training. Where did the time go?"

There was a commotion from within the group. "Go on, Adam. You do it," one participant whispered, pushing Adam forward.

Adam smiled and shyly ambled forward. "Sam, before we all break away for next week's session, we want to send you off in style. First, we have a card here for you signed by everyone," Adam said, handing Sam an envelope.

"Ahh, you shouldn't have," said Sam, opening the card.

"But wait, there's more. Ready, everyone?"

Carmen stepped forward and waved her arms like a symphony conductor, and everyone broke into song with a rendition of that old Roy Rogers's song, *Happy Trails to You*. Chuckles and giggles sprinkled the air as the excited group of participants belted out the lyrics. Sam stood before them with a happy grin. Mary sneaked up behind him, raising her eyebrows to cue the group in front of Sam. At her signal, they all yelled in unison, "Bon Voyage!"

Sam turned to see Mary behind him. She held a large cake with an alligator sitting on top of the frosting that had been made up to look like the surface of a lake. The alligator was wearing swim goggles and swim trunks with the team's Leukemia Society logo on it and Sam's name written across the alligator's snout. The message written across the top in orange and blue swirled frosting said, "See ya later, Alligator."

"I am humbled," said Sam with a laugh. "This is amazing, guys."

"Mary made the cake!" called out one participant. "Isn't it fabulous?"

"It's too beautiful to eat," agreed Sam. "We can't touch that cake, let alone eat it, can we?"

"We sure can!" said Mary with a grin. "To the fuel table, everyone! Sugar and carbs for all—coaches' orders!"

CHAPTER 51
Dress Rehearsal

"WELCOME TO DRESS REHEARSAL!" BEN SAID, AS HIS SIX-foot tall frame loomed over the soon-to-be racers. His deep voice called out expert tips and reminders, preparing the group for their final team training. In contrast to his imposing physique, his arms rested loosely at his sides, and his eyes sparkled, instilling a sense of well-being and confidence in Becca—and in the rest of the team going by their mesmerized expressions.

"Today, we get to put everything together—swimming, biking, running, and transitioning," Ben continued. "Remember that your transitions between swimming and biking, and then between biking and running, are important. They *do* count toward your overall race time. So, no dillydallying between segments," he admonished in a mock, hard-nosed tone while pointing his index finger at each team member. "I know some of you prefer to picnic along the way—Jennifer! Holly!"

His direct attention elicited giggles from the two women.

"Just don't forget this is a race," he said, now smiling warmly at them. Ben shifted his gaze back to the entire team. "We've talked about this many times. So, just a reminder: you don't want a DNF because you hung out after your swim to eat a peanut butter sandwich before jumping onto your bike. Who remembers what a DNF is?"

"Did not finish!" called out several voices.

"That's right," said Ben. "You're all aware of the cut-off times. And I assure you, you all can beat them—unless you dillydally. That's for my picnickers out there. For you competitive folks, I encourage you to get the best time you can. Just make sure it doesn't come at the expense of getting so serious about the race that you push yourself too hard, especially in the beginning. Save some energy for the grand finale, as you don't want to hit that proverbial wall and end up with no finish time at all. Whether you're fast, slow, or in between, remember to stick to *your* pace. What's our motto?"

"Run your own race!" sang out the group.

"Exactly! And, do not—I repeat, do not—decide to change things up on race day. No cute new shirt, Carmen." A wave of laughter ran through the group, including from Carmen. "That's a recipe for disaster. And, whatever you do, remember why we're here. This is more than just a race." Ben's voice had softened to just above a whisper and Becca noticed his lips flattened into a straight line. His gaze shifted to the ground as he added, "It's about so much more." Ben paused. Then, straightening his spine, he looked up at the group, his lips twitching back up into a smile. "It's also about having fun. It's a balance, right?"

"Right, coach!" called out Larry, an older gentleman, who'd been keenly taking in every one of Ben's words with such an intense look of determination that an onlooker might think he was preparing to charge into battle upon his leader's command.

"This is our last group training," continued Ben. "After today, you're officially in 'taper mode.' That means extra rest this week. You won't find much on your schedule in the way of swimming, biking, or running. Most important this week is to rest, hydrate, stretch, and visualize your race. Your orders are to stay relaxed and keep away from anything stressful, because, next Sunday, a week from tomorrow, it's showtime!"

"Woohoo!" called out one participant to the backdrop of a rousing round of cheers, applause, and excited chatter.

"Also," said Ben, his voice cracking uncharacteristically, "please know that I am so proud of all of you. You've put in a lot of effort, and

I'm grateful for your hard work and unwavering support for our broader purpose."

"Thanks, coach!" called out multiple voices.

"Any questions before we get started?"

The group remained silent.

Ben paused and took in a full breath before continuing, "Today is our last mission moment before race day." His arms tightened at his sides, and he swallowed noticeably. "My brother asked if he could speak today."

Ben looked over at Adam with a slight nod of his head while pressing his lips tightly together. Adam mimicked the gesture. Becca noticed the sad smiles they exchanged.

All eyes turned to Adam as he began to speak. "I just want to say," said Adam, tightly clutching his swim goggles, "that getting to be a part of this group has been amazing. I fell into it accidentally when I came to stay with my brother before starting my summer program at CMU. I think you all already know that piece about me. What I—we— haven't shared yet, is that our sister, Sophia, passed away from leukemia."

A collective gasp went out from the group.

"Oh my gosh, Adam, Ben, I'm so sorry," murmured Elora, with tears glistening in her eyes. She wiped away a tear that was about to fall, but said nothing further as Adam looked at her and mouthed a "thank you" through a small, tight-lipped smile.

"It was a long time ago. Ben and I were both just kids. We didn't know how to process what had happened—not back then and, unfor- tunately, I don't think either of us has fully processed it, even to this day. Perhaps we'll always be working through it, with some days good and some days not so good. Until I met all of you and heard your stories and your connections to this horrible disease, I didn't realize how far Ben and I still have to go to understand and deal with what happened. I guess I felt like our family was all alone in this. I realize now that's not the case, and I owe you all a huge thank you for your support, your caring, and your sharing. Today, I hope I can return the favor in at least a small way by sharing our family's story about our sister, Sophia."

He took a breath, closed his eyes for a moment, then reopened them and began, "Sophia was a happy child. She brought a lot of joy into our home. It wasn't until years after she passed that I started remembering so many of those wonderful memories. I'd dampened *all* those memories of her down as best I could into nothingness. Luckily, I've recently found those memories are still there within me. And as I've tentatively let them rise to the surface, I've found them bringing joy rather than pain. That's the gift you all have given me—the courage to let them rise. I admit, it's not a gift I've fully unwrapped," he said with telltale signs of moisture in his eyes. He gave a shrug of his shoulder. "It's a work in progress. It's just that when she died, it was such an awful and confusing time for our family. It left a horrible hole in our hearts. And, unfortunately, our once happy little family completely imploded. We—including, and even especially, our parents —didn't know how to let go or how to process what had happened, so we simply *didn't* process it. And we didn't have a group like this to help us through. If all of you had been around back then, perhaps it would have been just a little easier." Adam's face reddened as he shifted from one foot to the other.

"As hard as it was, though, it was Ben who gave me the beginning of a foundation I could use in later years to get my own life back. I'm embarrassed to say it took me a long time. And, believe me, I got into plenty of trouble during my junior high and high school days. I sure gave Ben a lot of crap. I was so angry, and I took that anger out on him. But, big brother," Adam said, turning to look at Ben, whose gaze was now steadfastly focused, unseeing, on the ground, "I want you to know, you really did right by me. You were only fifteen years old and yet you took care of your snotty little brother on those days when Dad was gone and Mom was a basket case."

Adam ignored the tear that ran down his cheek as he turned back to address the full group. "Don't get me wrong, our parents are good people. They just didn't know how to cope. I know it's hard to lose a sister. I can't even imagine what it must be like to lose a child. Luckily, Ben stepped right up and did his best to become the parent. He did a lot of grocery shopping, put meals on the table, washed my clothes, and I don't even know what else. I was only in elementary school. But, somehow, he made sure I got to school with breakfast in my stomach and a full lunch box in hand."

All eyes turned toward Ben with admiration, tears glistening in their eyes, and then they turned back toward Adam as he continued to speak.

"Thank you all for what you're doing—both on a grand scale and for me personally. From the bottom of my heart, thank you...and thank you, Ben."

The group broke into applause.

"Thank you for sharing, Adam," said Mary, swiping at the tears running down her cheeks. "And, Ben, we know you're an amazing coach, but we didn't know about your personal connection to this cause."

Ben gave a quick nod of his head but didn't make eye contact with anyone in the group. He stood with his arms crossed over his chest, his eyes focused on the ground, and his body rigid as he said, "Thank you, Adam. I couldn't have asked for a better group of people to train with, and I couldn't ask for a better brother."

No one pushed Ben for any further response. Raw emotion uncharacteristically showed on his partially hidden face, and the rigidity of his body betrayed the obvious effort he was making to hold his emotions in check to keep them from spilling over. His body language and the tone of his voice, deep and choked, revealed more than any additional words he could have uttered.

The clapping subsided as people approached Adam to hug him or pat him on the back. Adam looked at Ben to get them started on their training. Ben still stood as stiff as a board but looked at Adam with a glint of admiration in his eyes. Adam gave Ben a responding, shy smile.

"So, on that note," said Adam, "I guess we'd better put this emotional energy into getting our training in today. I know that's what I need right about now. Ben, are you ready to kick this off?" He shifted uncomfortably, waiting for Ben's response.

Becca looked from Adam to Ben, hoping Ben was ready to step in. While Adam had come into this group as a helper, he'd never coached before, and he'd never done a triathlon. He'd been a runner and clearly an excellent runner, but she wasn't sure he was ready to lead their dress rehearsal, especially not after his brave and poignant offering.

"Yep, you're right," said Ben after a long pause. Becca exhaled in relief, not even realizing she'd been holding her breath as Ben continued, "We need to get this show on the road. Actually, forget the road —it's into the water first. Let's go!" Ben called out to everyone in his melodious and soothing baritone that Becca loved so much—and which was now firmly back in place.

"I'm ready!" said a younger man.

"As long as there aren't any real alligators in that there lake," called out another participant, lightening the mood as they all jogged toward the water's edge.

CHAPTER 52

Encounters of the Worst Kind

"GREAT JOB TODAY, EVERYONE," SAID BEN. "I'M SO PROUD of you. And so is Sam. You'll be happy to hear he's doing well out in California in his new job. Just between you and me, though," Ben said with a wink, "I think he's a little jealous that I get to be here with all of you for our last training, and then again on race day, while he's stuck out on the west coast. He asked me to tell you he misses you, and he knows you'll all do great. I think his exact words were 'You are ready.' I definitely agree with him on that."

Carmen leaned over and whispered to Becca, "Gotta go. It's my client's photo shoot this afternoon and I'm on deck. Big afternoon for me! See ya."

"Break a leg. Call me when you're done. I can't wait to hear every detail," Becca whispered back. Carmen waved goodbye and silently slid away toward the parking lot.

"The next time we all see each other," Ben continued, "will be on Race Day. Any questions before we close out our last group training session?"

"Sam's correct," piped up one of the older participants. "I do feel ready. A big thank you to you and Sam for your great coaching. Of course," he chuckled, "we'll have to see how it goes on race day. Hopefully I'm not speaking too soon. I don't want to have to take back those words there, son." He gave Ben a smile.

"Me too," said another woman. "I've got butterflies in my stomach just thinking about race day. I'm feeling pretty proud of myself, though." She smiled, adding, "Even if race day doesn't go well, I sure learned a lot and loved getting to meet all of you."

"I just want to thank all of you for this wonderful opportunity," called out another woman. "I almost didn't make it past day one. A special thank you to Becca for helping me stay the course." She laughed. "Get that? Pun intended."

Becca looked at the woman with surprise, and then realized it was the woman she'd run with—or more like ambled along with—during their very first group training. What was her name? Becca reached into the depths of her brain—Gwen. Had she really helped Gwen? She didn't realize their conversation had made that much of an impression.

"I haven't made it to most of the group trainings because of my Saturday work schedule," continued Gwen. "But, Becca, you sure helped me on day one. I wouldn't have stuck with it if it weren't for you. I was ready to quit. But when you shared with me about your own cancer and talked me through some things I didn't understand about what my friend was going through—the chemo, the radiation, all the medicines—I realized I couldn't quit. I'm doing this with her in mind. It's one small way I can fight for her and with her. You're so brave, Becca. You've fought your own battle and come out the other side, willing to jump right into life again, still fighting. The least I can do is continue to fight for my friend. I'm glad you're here today so I can thank you. I wasn't sure you would be, as I know you'll probably be leaving soon for that Washington, D.C. job you have in mind."

Becca's thoughts whirled through her brain. She was glad she'd been able to help the woman. But she could feel the stiffness in her smile, and her body was trembling with shivers of fear as she tried to mouth out a responding "thank you." Blackness edged its way around the periphery of her vision, the Escher print coming to mind as her thoughts swirled uncontrollably, making it impossible for her to absorb fully what was happening. She hadn't seen Gwen since day one. Of course she would think Becca had already shared her situation with the group. Gwen had looked so scared and confused that first day, and Becca's words, in response, had uncharacteristically tumbled out, meant to comfort, soothe, and even educate. Sharing had come so easily with Gwen—a stranger—as they'd slowly jogged forward to cover that day's required distance. They'd barely even looked at each other as they moved forward, instead focusing on the ground in front of them as they spoke so as not to trip and fall or get off course. The emotional distance between them that came from being strangers— and from not looking directly at each other while they spoke—had made sharing so much simpler.

Becca looked toward Ben as another participant continued with the all-around thank you's and congratulatory comments. It should be a wonderful moment. But she could see the hurt on Ben's face. This was the first time he was hearing about her cancer. She should have told him. She meant to tell him. But she just hadn't been able to get the words out. She didn't want to be the cause of him having to relive Sophia's battle, and she didn't want him to look at her differently. It was one thing to help a stranger. It was a whole different ball game to share with someone she'd come to love.

"Okay, so...thanks everyone. I'm off. See you next week," Ben said gruffly, and he spun to face the parking lot and strode away toward his truck.

The group disbanded, some of them continuing with small talk while others gathered their belongings to head home or to whatever else they had in store for the rest of their Saturday. Adam stood perfectly still, not moving from his spot. Only his head moved as it swiveled from Ben to Becca and back.

Becca looked at Adam. He cringed and shrugged his shoulders. She could almost hear him talking to her through that shrug: "Told ya so; you should have told him." Or maybe she was reading too much into Adam's gesture? Maybe that was her own voice she was hearing in her head? Yes, she admonished herself silently, I should have told him. She'd made a mess of things.

"Ben!" Becca called. "Wait. I'm sorry. Let me explain."

Ben continued striding away as she ran to close the gap between them. A few of the participants who were making their way to their vehicles paused with invisible question marks etched into their faces.

"Ben," Becca called again. "Please—wait! I can explain. I didn't want to hurt you. I knew you were struggling with the pain of losing Sophia. I didn't want to trigger more pain by dumping my cancer on your shoulders. I should have told you."

Ben turned abruptly to face Becca. "And yet you didn't, did you?" he asked, his features no longer under control but instead creased with pain.

Becca stopped just short of slamming into Ben's body as his tall, muscled frame now stood stock still in front of her.

"Um, well..." Her body trembled, and no words formed in her brain. His voice, usually so composed and melodic, sounded cracked and broken.

"Yes? Cat got your tongue?" he asked, his pain now laced with anger.

As Ben stood, waiting for an answer, Becca fumbled for words. She hadn't known how to tell him. She told herself it was to save him from the pain. She knew telling him would be a trigger; it would be like poking a bruise that hasn't yet healed. You don't always remember the bruise is there—until you bump it against something or purposefully poke it. That angered bruise then triggers more pain, as the poke—innocent or not, self-inflicted or not, intentional or not—travels along the nerve system, radiating more pain throughout the entire body.

She knew, though, as a moment of clarity burst inside her brain, that her reasons were not just about not wanting to cause Ben more pain, they were selfish and cowardly. She didn't want Ben to see her as someone with cancer. She wanted to be normal—and she wanted a normal life with Ben. But that couldn't happen. Becca could see that all too clearly now. She was broken, and her cancer could return any day. Her doctor told her not to think that way. She'd told Becca she was officially in remission and to go forth and live her life, to enjoy it. But Becca knew she couldn't, and she wouldn't pull Ben into her daily personal reality.

She'd partly held off from telling him because, in her subconscious, she'd been holding on to that fantastical, magic-filled, romantic night they'd spent floating down the river. It had been an ethereal world filled with sparkling lights that had burst above them in colorful arrays against the stars. It was a world so close and yet so far from the reality of her life in downtown Pittsburgh. Becca knew that was also a part of why she hadn't told him. But the bubble of that fantastical dream had burst, as she knew it inevitably would.

"I'm waiting. I would think, knowing about my sister, you would be especially compelled to share your story rather than lie to me about it," Ben said.

"I didn't lie. I—"

"Oh, so you just forgot to tell me! It somehow slipped your mind?"

"Ben..." Adam said.

Neither Ben nor Becca had heard Adam approach or seen him standing just a short distance from them in the parking lot where they still stood.

"And you," Ben said, turning to Adam. "Did you know about this?"

"Well, I guess I did. I—"

"And you didn't think to tell me, either?" Ben's anger now focused on Adam.

"Dude, Becca was going to tell you. You don't exactly make it easy."

Ben turned back toward Becca, forgetting altogether about Adam. His typical calm facade was no longer anywhere in sight. Pain-filled, irrational words continued to spew from his mouth. "So, you and Adam teamed up together to keep me in the dark? To betray my trust? Is that what happened?" he asked.

"No, it wasn't like that," Becca insisted. "Adam asked me to tell you about my cancer. But, but...I wasn't ready. I love you, Ben. I didn't want to cause you more pain."

Ben's fingers trembled as he distractedly ran his hand through his hair in a gesture that usually had Becca melting with desire, but in this moment, it only heightened her anxiety. She knew that gesture. It was Ben's subconscious reaction to emotion—sometimes stress, sometimes frustration, and sometimes desire. She knew the emotion at this moment was not one of desire, but of hurt brought on by today's revelations. The news of Becca's cancer poked at that still not healed bruise, sending shock waves of pain through Ben's entire body, just like lava bursting from a volcano. It appeared that Adam's attempt to help had only stoked the flames.

"I should have realized it from that first day on the boat," Ben said. "You didn't even give me your last name. You had no intention of getting back in touch with me. But you had no choice once we were thrown together for this training, did you? You had me thinking you were this sensitive, shy—and even poor—little thing. I was so gullible; I even bought you that bike when you could easily have swung that purchase on your own. Are you even helping your mom out at all? I just don't understand!" he said, as barely coherent words continued to erupt from deep within his chest.

Becca flinched at his tone and his words. *What? He bought that bike for her?* Why would he do that? He'd told her it was a loaner. And what was he bringing her mom into this for?

"That was okay, though," Ben continued. "I wanted to buy that bike for you. I wasn't looking for a relationship with you or anyone. I have a good life and a great career, one I'm good at. But I wanted you to have that bike. I didn't mind sharing my money with you or with Adam. But my heart..." His words trailed off, and he sharply shook his head from side to side, looking as though he was trying to shake the thought loose and send it flying far and away. But he stopped and took in a deep breath, gathering steam toward another eruption of pain-fueled thoughts. "I thought maybe we had something here. That's on me. I know better than to trust with my heart. That always ends badly. Relationships, love, feelings—they're dangerous. This race can't come soon enough. Once it's over, we can be over, and we won't have to see each other ever again."

Ben had been looking right through her as he spoke, as if no longer seeing her standing right in front of him. His eyes made no connection with hers, now a molten shade of brown flaring with flecks of gold. But despite the lack of connection, his words slammed into her as though they were physical shards of glass aimed directly at her heart.

Becca stood, stunned. She knew he was hurting, and she knew she deserved some of Ben's anger, but he hadn't even let her explain. He'd heard nothing she'd said...*not even when I said I love you!* She wanted to scream and cry and pound her fists. She wanted to rail against...what? She didn't know. Who was she upset with? Ben? Herself? The world? Yes, all of the above.

Becca tried to make herself think rationally. Let it go; move on, she told herself. It had nothing to do with her anymore. She'd been right all along. Clearly, she could not have a normal life. She caused much of the pain the people she loved had to endure. Yes, she needed to put a stop to this dream right now. There would be no normal life or happily ever after for her. With that in mind, she pushed her feelings aside and said firmly, "Fine."

"Fine." said Ben.

And with those last words, each of them turned, marched off to their respective vehicles, and drove away.

Adam stood there, all alone, sadly shaking his head, and with no one left in the parking lot to drive him home.

CHAPTER 53

He Said What?!

BECCA PACED HER TINY KITCHEN. ROUND AND ROUND HER table she went. How had she gotten home, exactly? It didn't matter. She was here now and needed to figure out what to do next.

She attempted one of her breathing exercises, but only ragged sobs came forth. What should she do? She knew what she *wanted* to do— she wanted to throw all the dishes in the cabinets against the wall and hear them crash into pieces onto the floor, mimicking the shattering she felt in her mind and heart. At least she was rational enough to know that, while that would satisfy in the short run, in the long run, she'd just have to clean it up and then spend money she didn't have to replace the dishes. Not a good idea.

Try to calm down, she scolded herself. If the cancer taught her nothing else, it taught her coping strategies for moments of despair, just like this one. Life would go on—for the moment, anyway. So, what were her options? Take a walk, breathe deeply, meditate? *Yeah right*, meditate, she scoffed, shaking her head and trying to clear the foggy haze in her brain. The last thing she wanted to do was get more into her head on this thing—whatever it was—and Becca knew she couldn't sit still, even if she tried. Then she remembered about her best friend. Carmen always knew how to make her feel better.

Becca hit the speed dial button on her cell phone next to Carmen's name. No answer. That wasn't surprising; she would be at her big photo shoot right now.

Becca continued to pace, and then somehow found herself staring into her bathroom mirror. Her face showed the strain from the emotion heaving through her chest. She closed her eyes to shut out the image and tried, unsuccessfully, to will her breathing into a steady state. Her lungs still felt raw from her continued ragged breaths. She opened her eyes, contemplating the woman staring back at her. Frustration still oozed from every pore. It was no use, Becca thought, as she balled her hands into fists and a guttural cry escaped her parted lips.

Becca redoubled her pacing, feeling akin to a caged animal. Maybe a run? If she ran far enough and fast enough, she wouldn't have any energy to think—or throw the dishes against the wall. She stopped her useless pacing and leaned over the kitchen counter, pushing her forehead onto the cool, hard surface. She tried to calm her sobs with deep breaths. One deep breath in, one slow breath out. Again...and again.

Becca willed her entire body to turn into a rag doll in an attempt to eliminate the stress radiating through her rigid frame. She mentally pictured the stress leaving her head, then her neck, then her shoulders, and worked her way down to her toes before starting back up again, from her toes to the top of her head. She rolled her forehead from side to side over the countertop, feeling its cool surface soothe the heat of her skin as well as the fire raging within. Eventually, she felt her boiling emotions reduce to a simmer, enabling another intake of oxygen. Becca counted to five as she held her last breath in and then slowly exhaled the poisonous carbon dioxide and her traitorous emotions. Then, she stood up and went to find her running shoes.

"He said what!?" asked Carmen.

Becca relayed this morning's incident with Ben over the phone to Carmen, trying to keep the hysteria out of her voice.

"I'm on my way over," said Carmen. "Don't hang up; we can talk while I drive. And I will spend the night with you so you won't have to be alone."

Becca felt like Carmen had just slapped her. Those were words you said to someone who was suicidal. She was definitely not that. She had fought for her life, she wasn't going to end it now. Becca knew that wasn't how Carmen meant it, but it served to pull her out of her self-pity.

"No," Becca said in a strong and measured voice. "You don't need to come over. I'm going to go to bed. I'll be just fine."

"Should I come over tomorrow?"

"I'm going to my mom's for brunch tomorrow morning. I can already feel the craving coming over me for some of her pancakes," Becca said in a carefully measured tone.

"I'm worried about you, Becca."

"I know you are, but I'll be fine."

"Just promise me you won't make any big decisions right now?"

"I promise. The only thing I'm going to do tonight is crawl into bed and hopefully into a much-needed sleep. And the biggest decision I plan to make tomorrow is whether to put syrup or butter on my mom's pancakes."

"Okay, that's a good thing. I will sit tight. But you call me anytime, day or night, and I will come right over with whatever you need. Wine? Ice Cream? Something healthy, even? We could watch a chick-flick...no, wait, no romances. Strike that. We could watch a comedy."

"Thanks, Carmen. Have I told you lately that you're the best friend on the face of the planet? 'Cause you are, ya know."

"Of course I am! Although, maybe my idea of this whole triathlon thing wasn't such a good one. If I hadn't dragged you into it, you might never have seen Ben again, and none of this would have happened."

Becca yawned, now completely spent. She'd been up to the top of the roller coaster today, and then all the way back down again, and she was exhausted. "I doubt it. I think there's an invisible magnet pulling me toward him. But I need to stay away, Carmen. I need to."

"Okay, sweetie. Don't think about it right now. Are you going to be able to go to sleep? Are you sure you don't want me to come stay with you?"

"I'll be fine. I don't think I could keep my eyes open any longer even if I tried."

Becca and Carmen said their good-nights. And then Becca hung up the phone and crawled into bed and immediately fell into a deep but fitful sleep.

CHAPTER 54

Memories

"BECCA, WHAT'S WRONG? DID SOMETHING HAPPEN?" HER mom asked with concern.

Her mother was standing at her kitchen sink preparing lattes for their Sunday brunch. Buster, as usual, was the first to greet Becca when she arrived, running in crazed circles and barking with excitement. It did nothing to cheer her up today, though, and she'd dejectedly made her way into her mother's kitchen.

Becca knew her eyes were puffy and red. Her mother's question made her wonder if she looked as bad as she felt. She'd tried to wipe away the evidence of her tears. Clearly, she hadn't succeeded. In response to the concern in her mother's voice, her tears started gushing again with a will of their own. Becca had a fleeting thought of no longer being in control of herself, as her tears and then her words spewed from her body while her mind and her heart remained numb. "Ben found out about my cancer. He told me I betrayed his trust by not telling him. I told him I'd tried. I really did try, Mom. So many times. I just couldn't. And when he found out, I tried to tell him why I didn't. But he wouldn't listen. He was so angry. He said he'd see me at the race but that it couldn't come soon enough as far as he was concerned, because after the race, we wouldn't have to see each other anymore. Then he just stomped off and drove away. I don't know what I was thinking. I know I can't have a relationship with Ben. I'm not good relationship material. I'm broken."

"Oh, honey." Her mom closed the distance between them with two steps and wrapped her arms tightly around Becca, which only served to release more tears. "How can you say that? Of course you're good relationship material. Anyone would be lucky to have you in their lives. I know I'm lucky to have you in mine."

"But don't you see, Mom? The cancer could come back any day. I can't do that to Ben or anyone, but especially Ben. He's already had to suffer the loss of his sister. I can't make him go through that again."

"Becca, no one knows how long they have. Any of us could get hit by a bus tomorrow. You may have a good fifty, or sixty, or even seventy more years ahead of you. You no longer have cancer. And, even if you did, cancer is not who you are, it's just something you had. And it's something you fought through. You deserve a life just as much as anyone else, and you've been given that opportunity to live that life. That's not something everyone gets. Take it! Grab it!"

Becca startled at her mom's forceful delivery. "But, Mom, what about Dad? It's not just me I need to think about. Dad did so much for us. He worked so hard and, even when he was tired, he always came home to us and made time for us. I don't want all of his hard work to be forgotten. I don't want him to be forgotten. I need to honor his memory and make sure he would've been proud of me. That's the least I can do. I can't just selfishly go on and forget him, and that means I need to go to D.C. Don't I?"

Her mom continued to hold her and stroke her hair as she choked her words out between hiccuping sobs and while tears streamed down her face.

"I just don't seem to be able to keep everything together anymore," Becca continued brokenly. "It's been so hard keeping my focus all these years, first with school, and then with work. I was almost there —and then the cancer came. It derailed everything. And now I don't know what I want anymore. My boss keeps asking me when he should put the paperwork in for my transfer to D.C., and I keep putting him off. He's offering me just what I told him I wanted more than anything, and now that he's offering it to me, I'm not even sure I want to go. But how can I do that to Dad? I can't let him down. I can't let him be forgotten," Becca said through tormented, choking sobs.

"Of course he would be proud of you. And of course he's remembered. We're talking about him right now, aren't we? And we're nowhere near D.C., Becca. Work is important, but it's not everything. He worked hard to make sure he could provide for us. It's great that he enjoyed his job and found it fulfilling, but that's not why he worked so hard. He worked for those he loved—for us. And what he would want most is to make sure that you're happy. He would not want you to spend your whole life chasing his ghost to the point that you missed out on your own life.

"If going to Washington, D.C. is what makes you happy, then by all means, go. But don't do it through some misguided belief that going to D.C. will force people there to remember and love your father. They have their own families to think about. I'm sure that people who worked for your father day in and day out cared about him. But their focus wasn't on loving your father or making sure that he had a legacy. Their focus and their goals were to provide for their own families. To make sure their families were as happy as they could be, just like your father was trying to do for you and me. And besides, most of those people who worked with your father are probably long since retired. They won't even be there anymore."

"But, Mom, won't you be disappointed in me if I let go of Dad?"

"I could never be disappointed in you, Becca. And of course you aren't letting go of your dad. He'll always be with you. Just look at that necklace you're wearing. I remember when he gave it to you. He told you how strong you are. And he was right. You've been through so much and fought so hard your whole life to be there for others, even while fighting against the most evil of villains. And you beat it! What I want you to do now is be there for yourself. That's what would make me happy. And that's what would make your father happy—as well as proud."

Becca's sobs subsided, and she pulled away to look directly into her mother's eyes. "I'm so confused, Mom. I don't know who I am anymore. I was just Becca. And then I was Becca, the girl who lost her father. I found myself again after that, at least, I thought I did. But then the cancer hit. I had no energy to think about who I was during the treatments. It was all so exhausting. I tried to hold on through it all. I really did. But I don't know if I can anymore. I'm back to feeling good physically, even enough to do this triathlon. In fact, being a part of this triathlon training has been amazing—until yesterday. But who am I now? I don't think I'm the same person I was. But I can't find..." Becca groped for the words that would convey her struggle, "I can't find...*me*." Becca hiccupped out another sob, burying her face in her mother's neck and holding on tighter.

When Becca finally lessened her grip, her mother pulled away, guiding her to a seat at the kitchen table. She handed her a Kleenex from the box sitting across from where Becca now sat and held Becca's cheek in one hand and used the other to wipe her tears with a tissue. "I can picture your father looking down on you right now, Becca, with that special love shining through his eyes just for you. He would hate to know how you've had to suffer with cancer. But he would be so proud of how you've persevered through such adversity. And now a triathlon! What would your father say? He would be amazed. And who knows, he might've even signed up right along with you. Think of him when you're out there on race day. You know and I know that he'll be cheering you on. You are, after all, his little wonder woman. Right?"

Becca smiled and reached for the pendant hanging at her neck. Tears continued to fall down her cheeks, but she smiled, thinking about how her father would have loved this triathlon journey.

"Don't think I don't see you with that necklace on each and every day, young lady. You are clearly remembering your dad in everything you do," her mother said, wiping away the strands of hair sticking to Becca's wet face. "And right now, in this moment, you've been given a gift—a second lease on life. Not everyone gets that, Becca. You and I know that all too well. Your dad had a good life. He loved and was loved, but he didn't get that second go. You did. And, unlike most people, you now have a deeper understanding of what that really means. You've seen how close death can be, both with your dad and now with yourself. But you're fine right now. Embrace that.

"Yes, of course the cancer could come back. You've had a scare, for sure. Use that. Use that to help you think about what you want to do with the time you have. Life is not forever, and you don't know how long you have. That's how it is for everyone, not just you. Maybe you won't have a long life. Maybe you will die next year. But what if you have many, many more years? Do you want to spend all those years waiting for death, or do you want to live them loving those around you and making happy memories for the time you—and they—have?

"Think about what would make you happy and know that if you're happy, you will definitely fulfill your father's dreams and make him proud. Nothing else could say that more than his knowing he gave you a strong enough foundation to go forth and live your own dreams, along with the opportunity to love and be loved as fully as he did."

Becca sat in silence for a moment, absorbing her mother's words.

"Now," her mother said, this time cheerily, "let me get these pancakes finished up. Don't you need extra carbs for the race you're doing next week?"

Becca fidgeted with the tissues in her hand. Her tears had dried, and she sat there, contemplating, while shredding the tissues into little piles of strips in front of her. She looked up at her mother. "I love you, Mom."

"I love you too, sweetie."

"And thank you," Becca said. "Thank you for always being here for me."

"You're very welcome. Now, let's have some of those pancakes we both love so much. You just figure out what's most important to you, and know that I'm here to support you every step of the way, no matter what you decide."

"Hey Carmen," Becca said, as she drove home from her mother's house, "want to go for a bike ride this afternoon? Just a fun, easy one? I know we're not supposed to be doing much training this week— except for de-stressing. *So much for that!*" Becca said, letting out a gush of air into the phone's speaker. "But, hey, we're also supposed to be hydrating. We could drink some Gatorade along the way or, better yet, some non-training drink like lemonade. I haven't even heard about your big event yesterday. I'm sorry I didn't ask about it when you called last night. Did it go well?"

"It went great. But, more importantly, how are you doing? Are you okay?"

"I'm fine, actually. I had a good brunch with my mom this morning. We talked a lot about my dad."

"What? *Really?* That's awesome...and not at all what I expected you to say!"

"Yes, *really*. There are so many good memories and my mom is in a good place with those. I guess I thought she was still pining for him and that's why we didn't talk about him. But, I think it was more that she was trying to be protective of my feelings, so she just set up this perfect but surface-level existence for us, tiptoeing around me until I was ready to talk about him. I think we would have hashed this all out a lot sooner if the cancer hadn't hit. I'm not sure what to think about it all yet. It's still kind of new, all squishing around in my brain. It was great talking to my mom today, though. About everything, not just about my dad. I'm lucky to have her in my life. I mean, let's face it—her lattes, pancakes, and everything else, are the best!" Becca joked. "If I don't at least appreciate that about her, I'm an idiot."

"I have to agree with you there!" Carmen laughed.

"You would've been surprised today, though. She didn't mince her words, Carmen. She told me flat-out I was being an idiot."

"*Your* mom said that?"

"Well, maybe not exactly. She told me to quit chasing Dad's ghost."

"You have got to be kidding me? I mean, not that I disagree.... Well, I mean, are you okay with that?"

"Yeah, I am. In fact, it was a relief to hear her say it. *I think she might be right, Carmen!*" Becca said, as she reached for the pendant at the base of her neck and began rubbing the flat silver medallion between her thumb and forefinger, feeling the crevices etched into its surface. Those fissures made the pendant beautiful, she thought. Life was not perfectly flat. There were ups and downs. And maybe that was a good thing, because perfection was boring. It's the dents and scratches we earn along the way that make us who we are, and that make us interesting. Those etchings of our life journey form a beautiful picture, just like the one on her pendant. Becca took a deep breath and said, "Carmen, I don't think I'm going to go to Washington, D.C." Silence. "Carmen? *Carmen? Are you there?*"

"Whoa. Wow...Oh. My. Gosh!" Carmen squealed.

"Okay. So, can you maybe add a little to that? What do you think? Am I making sense?"

"Are you staying here for Ben?"

"No, silly, I'm staying here for you and my mom and for our Friday night happy hours with friends. How could I leave that?" Becca joked. "Seriously, though, Ben made it perfectly clear yesterday that he doesn't want a relationship with me. He's focused on his career, and that will probably take him away from Pittsburgh one of these days soon. And I've always made it clear to him that a relationship is not in my future."

"Yeah, but he thought that was because of D.C. He didn't know about the rest."

"And that's just it, isn't it? Ben's situation just makes our relationship that much more unrealistic. You should have seen the pain in his eyes yesterday—in all of him. Now that he knows about my cancer, every time he looks at me, he'll think of Sophia, and he'll feel nothing but pain. I can't burden him with that."

"I think he just needs some time to process this, Becca," Carmen said hesitantly. "I think both of you just need some time."

"After what happened yesterday, it's a moot point. He told me straight out that as soon as this race is over, he doesn't want to see me anymore," Becca said, sniffling into the phone.

"Oh, honey, you know he didn't mean that. That man is devoted to you. He's just too stubborn to give in to it. Aren't you two a pair? Or maybe that's just you, huh, chickie? You haven't even given him twenty-four hours yet to process what you told him."

"That's part of the problem. I didn't tell him. Someone else did. I know I should have. You know I tried."

"I know you did. But you can't beat yourself up over that forever. You—"

"But, Carmen, you should have seen him. Not just when he was angry with me—before that. He couldn't even look up while Adam was giving his mission moment about their sister yesterday. How can he ever look at me again? Now that he knows my story, every time he looks at me, he'll be reminded of his sister's death. And I'll know I'm just a source of more pain for him. I can't burden him, or even myself, with that. And if the cancer did come back, it would pull him into that cancer-filled world all over again and send him spiraling back into a world of pain. I don't know that either of us could recover from a blow like that."

"At least talk to him, Becca. You both deserve that. And you just said that talking to your mom about your dad was—."

"No," Becca interrupted. "I need to stay behind the scenes, Carmen. I think I can still help him, just not head on. Can we please let it go for now? I can't think straight anymore, and I need a distraction. Want to meet me for a bike ride? Please? How does 4:00 p.m. at the Pump House Trailhead sound?"

"*Fine,* I give. We won't talk about it—*for now.* But don't think I don't see what you just did there. I'm not done with you yet, missy. You are so stubborn; I'm going to talk some sense into you one of these days. And, yes," Carmen said on a huff of air, finally responding to Becca's invitation, "I would love to go for a bike ride. Ohh...wait! And can we get dinner at Primanti's afterward? I'm craving one of their amazing salads—covered in French fries, of course. We haven't been there in forever. And, ya know, we *are* supposed to be eating extra carbs. Isn't this whole being athletes in training stuff great? I've been eating everything in sight, and I've even lost a few pounds over the past couple of months."

Becca sighed, relieved that Carmen had been willing to go with her push to change the subject. "Absolutely. And, despite all this mess, I'm glad you talked me into the triathlon. See you at 4:00 p.m.," Becca said, hanging up the phone.

CHAPTER 55
The Transfer

"BECCA'S HERE," FRANK SAID, USHERING HER INTO Nathan's office.

"What's up, Becca?" Nathan asked. "Frank said you needed a quick minute with me. Good timing, because I need more than a quick minute with you. You first, though. What do you need? Is it about your transfer to D.C.? I hate to lose you here in Pittsburgh, but if you're ready for me to put the transfer paperwork in, just let me know," Nathan said with a dejected sigh. "You've had your heart set on this move for a long time and you certainly deserve it."

Becca watched him as he picked up a bottle of Advil from the edge of his desk and popped three pills. "Actually...that is what I wanted to talk to you about. I'm wondering if it would be okay if I stay here in Pittsburgh?"

Nathan's head tilted back and he sat up straighter, giving Becca a piercing look. Becca twisted her hands nervously in her lap. She knew Nathan wanted her to stay, but she wasn't sure how he'd react to her flip-flopping.

Then a big grin slowly slid up Nathan's face, and Becca felt her hands relax. "Hell yeah! You can stay," Nathan said in his usual booming voice. "That's one headache I can avoid. I haven't been looking forward to replacing you. Why the change of heart?"

"I just think this is where I belong—with my family and friends and my colleagues here in Pittsburgh. You've been a great boss—and mentor. Why would I want to change that?" she quipped, feeling a tinge of red creeping into her cheeks. "Don't get me wrong, I would love to get more involved in the federal aspects of our projects. I've just come to realize that maybe I don't need to move to D.C. for that. I think I can contribute just as well from here on the ground in Pittsburgh. In fact, maybe better."

"Oh, this is gonna be great," said Nathan, rubbing his hands together gleefully.

Becca gave him a huge smile. "Did you say you wanted to talk to me as well?"

"Yes. Glad you reminded me," Nathan boomed. "I met with Ethan Trapp on Friday. He's fully on board. Our next step is to run the ideas by Oscar out in D.C. He's been bugging me about setting a date for you to come to D.C. and about figuring out some way to make Ethan's amphitheater project stand out. When Frank said you were on your way down to see me, I asked him to get Oscar on the line. I can't wait to tell him about your ideas—and I really can't wait to tell him he can't have you," Nathan said, chuckling.

"Mr. Winslow," Frank's disembodied voice called out, "I've got Oscar Singleton on the line."

"Thanks, Frank," Nathan said, pushing the speaker mode button on his desk phone.

"Oscar," Nathan boomed. "How are you this morning?"

"Just fine. What's up? Your guy, Frank, seems to think this was important enough to interrupt me."

"My calls are always the most important part of your day," Nathan joked. "And I think you're gonna like what I have to say. Some of it anyway," he said, winking at Becca. "By the way, I've got Becca Clarke in my office here with me and on speaker phone. We, or Becca here, may have just what we've been looking for to get Ethan Trapp's amphitheater project through for some of that federal funding. Ethan's on board, and we want to see if you like the ideas too."

"It's about time," Oscar ribbed. "I'm all ears. Go."

"Becca, please fill Oscar in," Nathan encouraged.

Becca's eyes widened in surprise. But Nathan motioned for her to go ahead and speak while giving her a reassuring nod of his head.

Becca cleared her throat. "Hi, Mr. Singleton. Um...so...we've got some ideas about how to combine the amphitheater project with several other initiatives underway in our region. There's a small Rust Belt community about twenty miles outside of Pittsburgh called Marston. The town leadership and community members are working to revitalize important sections of the town, including a trail they're hoping to expand. Marston's mayor and council already have some funds set aside for its redevelopment, just not enough to build it out very far. The town is right on the water and only a few miles upriver from where Ethan plans to build the amphitheater.

"The idea would be to build that trail out all the way from Marston, past the amphitheater and into Pittsburgh. There are also some new shops, eateries, and lodgings in the works right next to that trail and by the river. There's also a marina close to where Ethan wants to put the amphitheater. If he moves that venue just a short distance away from where he's got it mapped out now, it could be right next to that marina so boaters could easily come and go to events, as well as people who come in via trail or by car. Our team here is also working on sewage infrastructure for Allison City.

"Like so many Rust Belt communities across the middle of the country, Allison City's infrastructure was in such terrible shape that they ended up with a catastrophic failure after a large deluge of rain. It left many of their businesses flooded along their main street—and not with rain but sewage. Marston isn't in much better shape, and the solution we're proposing for Allison City, with just some minor tweaks, could be implemented in Marston as well as further downriver as a part of an overall revitalization. That larger project, with multiple partners involved, could serve as a model for like communities across the country, which is something we know the funders are looking for." As Becca rolled on with her explanation, she found herself feeling more confident that this idea would work. Oscar interjected questions here and there, all of which Becca fielded easily. "....That's pretty much it in a nutshell," Becca ended.

Nathan looked at her proudly and gave her a thumbs up. "What do you think, Oscar?" he boomed out. "Pretty awesome, don't ya think?"

"I think it's good," answered Oscar. "I want to see those sketches and talking points ASAP, though. And you say you've got some connections already to the city's leadership and that they would be on board with this if we needed them to jump in quickly?"

"Yes, sir, Mr. Singleton," Becca said confidently.

"Good. Well, I'm going to have to look through what you've got and get my team on it to see what they think. We've got multiple projects in play right now, all of them, of course, looking for funding. I don't want to upset any applecarts. We need to step it up and take some risks on that amphitheater project, though, if we have any hope of beating out any of the competition. And I want that funding! Hold on just a minute...."

They could hear voices in the background talking to Mr. Singleton. In the intervening silence, Nathan looked at Becca and gave her a grin.

Then Oscar came back on. "Okay, I'll be right there. Nathan, Becca, I've gotta go. I like this. But I'm going to have to think on it and tee it up with a few people here to see what kind of reaction I get. Can you put together a pitch ASAP—the sooner the better? Something succinct and to the point that conveys vision and promise. Something that can easily be incorporated into what we've already put together. It needs to be ready to go at a moment's notice. I know we're going to get invited to make some pitches, I just don't know when. I want to have this one ready to pull out and pitch if and when we get the chance. And, Nathan, Becca, I agree with you. This is what's been missing. Oh, and hey, Becca, when are you coming out to D.C. to join my team? I'm eager to get you out here...." Oscar's voice trailed off and became muffled again as he spoke to someone else on his end. "I'm coming, I'm coming," Oscar said to whomever was there in D.C. with him. "Hold your horses."

"You wish!" Nathan crowed, smiling at the speaker phone. "She's staying right here!"

"What?!" Oscar said. But before he could say anything else, he was interrupted yet again by a voice from his end. "Okay, okay," he responded with a snap, before turning back to the bombshell Nathan had just delivered. "That's not good, Nathan. But we'll have to visit that news bomb another time. Gotta go." The line clicked and Oscar's voice disappeared.

"Good job, Becca," Nathan said, grinning at her. "It looks like we've got a shot at this. Let Jenn know what's going on and have her pull in whomever you two need to finalize that pitch you all have been working on. Good thing we've got a good start on it! Make it brief, but make it visionary. And you heard Oscar—we may not get to present, but we've got to be ready. Let me know if you run into any problems."

"Thanks, Nathan," Becca said, feeling her heart burst with excitement. "I'll get with Jenn right away."

"Don't thank me yet. This may go nowhere. It sure is nice to see a smile on your face, though. I haven't seen you smiling much over the past couple of years. Now, get outta here. I've got work to do," he said, as he picked up a sheaf of papers on his desk as well as his phone's handset, effectively dismissing her.

CHAPTER 56

Brotherly Love

BEN

BEN STOOD BEHIND HIS DESK POSITIONED IN THE BACK corner of his office condo when the buzzer sounded at the front door.

"I'll get it," he said irritably. He shifted his gaze to glance at his colleagues. Jason and Connie sat at the large conference table in the middle of the room, drawings and papers littered all around them. He caught their silent exchange of raised eyebrows. Ben's glance turned into a hardened glare that had them quickly turning their focus back to their paperwork.

Ben forcefully pulled open the door, which caused him to have to take a large step back so as not to lose his balance from the momentum. Adam stood on the other side of the door. Ben shook his head in surprise and released a heavy, audible exhalation of air between pursed lips. "What are you doing here?" he said shortly.

"I came to visit my big brother. Is that no longer allowed?"

"I thought you had exams this week. Shouldn't you be studying?"

"What are you doing, Ben?" interrupted Jason from across the room.

Ben turned angrily. "Stay out of this, Jason," he responded in a forceful staccato.

Jason held his hands up in front of him as though being held at gunpoint. "Whatever," he said derisively.

"Yes. I have exams," said Adam. "And, yes, I should be studying. But I figured I should at least come and check on you since you've gone and buried your head in the sand again."

"I don't need anyone to check on me, especially not you."

"Yeah, bro, I kinda think you do. Someone's gotta tell you to stop being an ass."

"What the hell? Where do you get off telling me to stop being an ass?" Ben said, heightening his stance and broadening his chest while taking a threatening step toward Adam.

"Whatta ya want me to call you? I came all the way out here to Pittsburgh, hoping we could reconnect. I shouldda known it wouldn't work. You ran last time and you're running again."

"Are you fucking kidding me? I was always there for you. And what did I get back? You treated me like shit. And you're doing it again. Only this time, you've teamed up with Becca."

"God dammit, Ben! Don't you think it's time you got outta your own way? You've got what most people only dream of right in front of you. But you've got your defenses up so high, and it's so ingrained in that psyche of yours, that you can't see the forest for the trees. Open your eyes and quit being such a damn fool!"

"What do you want from me? You're the one who pushed me away. You didn't need me in your life back then, and you don't need me in it now."

"Back when, Ben? Say it! Back when? You can't even say her name, can you? It's Sophia! Say it!" Adam yelled, taking a step toward Ben, their chests now just inches apart.

"Go study, Adam! Go make something of yourself. God knows you screwed it up enough in high school," Ben said, taking a step back and putting his hand on the door, readying to push it closed.

"Don't shut me out!" Adam yelled angrily, putting his hand on the door to keep Ben from closing it and taking a step inside, further lessening the gap between them. "And maybe if you'd stayed, I wouldn't have messed it up so badly. You think about that?"

"You made it clear you didn't want me there. Admit it! You were better off without me. I couldn't fix it!"

"Of course I wanted you there! But, dammit, Ben, I was all of eight years old when Sophia died. I was angry and confused. One minute we were one big happy family and the next it felt like everyone had left me. Dad flew off to Africa and Mom just shut down. You were the only one left standing. Where else was my anger supposed to go? You were the only target left. I get I fucked up by taking it out on you. I'll own that. But, dude, I was eight fucking years old!"

Ben could feel his anger rising. His ears thudded with the blood pumping through his veins, blocking out Adam's words. He just wanted to punch something, anything!

"Say it! Come on, say her name! She deserves that," Adam said, pushing Ben's blood pressure higher. "You can't do it, can you?" Adam challenged.

Ben growled. He raised his arms, palms open and flat out in front of him, and pushed. Adam fell backward onto the floor but quickly recovered his upright stance and moved forward to poke Ben's chest. "Her name is Sophia, and until you say it and let that pain out, we're never gonna be okay—and *you're* never gonna be okay."

Ben grabbed Adam's arm and twisted it toward his own chest, his elbow sticking out to slam into Adam's ribs.

Adam grunted as air escaped his lungs in a harsh, audible exhale. Adam used his full body weight to push Ben's arm away, knocking Ben sideways and off-balance as he gasped out, "And you're just that stupid to be doing it again with Becca! Get the hell outta your own way!"

Ben recovered his equilibrium, pulled his arm back, and with hand fisted, he struck, landing a blow just above Adam's chin.

Adam rubbed one hand over his fattening lip and danced away, quickly recovering to land a responding blow against Ben's nose.

Jason's arms suddenly appeared between them, trying to break up the fight. Both easily pushed him away as they struggled to gain the upper hand and wrestle the other into a weakened position. Ben pulled one arm back and pushed forward for another blow before Adam could gain the advantage.

"Ow!" said Jason, who had once again pushed in between them, still determined to stop the fight. "What the hell is wrong with you two?!" Jason yelled, as he pulled his hands up to his face to cradle his nose.

Ben startled and stopped, finally cognizant of Jason's presence between him and his brother. Blood gushed through Jason's fingers and onto the office floor. Adam, still in fight mode, leaned in to land another blow, but pulled back just before launching his arm forward. Ben took in Adam's widened and frightened eyes, remorse hitting him just as hard as Adam's blow surely would have if his brother had continued to propel his arm forward.

"Adam, I... Jason, oh my God, I'm so sorry," Ben said, as he grappled with which crisis to address first—the one between him and his brother or the one between him and Jason. Ben's instinct to help and protect kicked back in. He reached toward Jason, hoping somehow to staunch the flow of blood still gushing from Jason's nose and into the middle of their now motionless and silent circle. He wanted to help Jason as well as protect his brother from the gory sight in front of them.

Jason half-heartedly pushed Ben's attempt away. "I give up. This is ridiculous. Don't touch me. You've already done enough damage."

Ben pulled his hand back and reached up subconsciously to run it through his hair, transferring the wet blood that had fallen onto them from Jason's nose into his hair, leaving it oddly spiked in all directions. Ben continued distractedly clenching and unclenching his fingers as he grappled with how to rectify this mess. He rubbed his right hand over his nose and mouth, immediately wincing in pain. His tongue darted out to survey the damage done to his lip, but he quickly pulled his tongue back as another burst of pain radiated through him and the metallic taste of blood, dripping from his own nose, filled his senses. Adam had landed his blow, that was for sure, Ben thought with a surprising rush of pride in his little brother's abilities.

A hand snaked its way into the middle of their circle. "Maybe this will help," Connie said, three moistened towels clutched tightly in her hand. "Nice hairdo, Ben," Connie said dryly.

Adam and Jason looked up at Ben's comically spiked hair and burst out laughing. Ben responded with an embarrassed grin and lifted his hand to run it once again through his tousled and unruly waves.

"Nice punch, by the way, Adam. See what I mean?" he said with a sheepish grin. "You don't need me. It looks like you can take care of yourself pretty well, even in a fistfight."

"You didn't do too badly yourself. I'm sorry about your fat lip, though. And your nose. Ah, and your eye," Adam chuckled. "Just in case you haven't realized it, you're probably going to need a big, fat, cold steak not just for that fat lip but for that eye too. It's turning into quite a shiner."

"Hey!" Jason interrupted. "What about my nose, people? Is it broken? Don't I get some love here?"

Ben turned his focus back to Jason. "I'm so sorry, Jason. I didn't mean to hit you. Here, let me—"

Jason began shaking his head. "Uh ah, no way! Don't come near me. I forgive you—*maybe*. But no way are you getting anywhere near my nose again."

"Good grief—*boys!*" Connie said with exasperation. "Come here, Jason. Let me see to it. Ben, Adam, I'll take care of Jason. That okay with you, Jason?"

Jason stuck out his lower lip, his eyes watering, and nodded his head in assent to Connie, looking like a little boy whose mommy had just shown up to coddle him over a skinned knee. Jason turned his head away from Connie and stuck his tongue out at Ben and Adam—a wince quickly following as a result of the movement.

Ben and Adam laughed. Connie turned her head back toward Ben and Adam, giving them a suspicious, steely glare. They both gave her innocent shrugs but snickers continued to escape from between their lips as they tried, but failed, to curtail the spew of emotions bubbling out through their laughter.

Ben, at least, had the decency to compose himself enough to turn his gaze back to Jason with concern. Perhaps he should stay, he thought.

"What?" asked Jason. "You heard her. Go—git! Now that you two have vomited up all that toxic emotional baggage, go hash it out someplace else, and let me get a little tender loving care here from someone who isn't going to punch me. You wouldn't, would you, Connie?" Jason said with a bit of skepticism creeping into his voice.

Connie gave all three of them an exasperated look. "I'll take good care of you, Jason. God knows you're the only one here who deserves it today. Ben, Adam, you heard him—git. Now, Jason, sit yourself down at the kitchen counter and let me get some ice for that nose of yours. You're going to be fine, but it's going to be a doozy. I just hope you don't have a date tonight." She snickered.

"Come on, Adam. How about I buy you a beer? How about two? One for you and one for your lip?" Ben teased.

"Only if I can buy you three. You're going to need an extra one for that eye."

Ben grabbed a six-pack out of the refrigerator and put his hand awkwardly on Adam's shoulder to guide him gently toward the front door. "How about we take these down to the river?"

"Sounds good," said Adam, and the two of them made their way in an awkward silence out the door and to a bench by the river's edge, a few steps away from Ben's condominium office building.

"Thanks for coming to check on me, Adam," Ben said with an embarrassed sigh.

"I was getting kinda worried," Adam admitted. "Last time I saw you, you were tearing out of a parking lot looking mighty angry. I was kind of hoping you'd had enough time to cool off by now," Adam said gently.

"Why didn't you tell me about Becca's cancer?" Ben asked. "Why did she tell you and not me?" he asked, hurt dripping from his voice.

"It wasn't my story to tell. And I know she wanted to tell you. I think she tried a few times. She just didn't know how or when."

Ben thought back to that night at his house when Becca had cooked him dinner. She'd told him she had something important she wanted to tell him. But then she'd seen that picture of Sophia. Was that one of the times she was going to tell him? He realized he already knew the answer. He'd poured out his pain to Becca about Sophia that night. She'd been an amazing listener. No wonder. She knew almost exactly what he was going through—because she was going through it herself. He'd finally gotten around to asking her what it was she wanted to tell him, but she'd just shrugged it off. She'd held him and made love to him instead, he thought. A wave of tenderness flooded his system. He missed her so much. Ben shook his head, trying to clear the fog. But it was complicated; it was so complicated....

"She loves you. You know that, don't you?" Adam asked softly.

Ben didn't feel as though he could tackle that statement yet. After a moment of silence, he said, "I'm sorry I wasn't there for you, Adam."

"You *were* there for me, Ben. You were there for me for three long years at home after Sophia died. I'm the one who treated you like shit, and I regret it every day. I want to make things right. I came here for the summer program, yes, but I came here for more than that. I came to apologize. I came to get my big brother back."

Ben looked up, startled, and stared intently into Adam's eyes, a look of confusion on his face. "You have nothing to apologize for. Don't you know that? You did nothing wrong. I'm the older brother. I should've been able to fix it." Ben braced his elbows on his knees and ducked his head into his hands. "I'm the one who needs to apologize to you, Adam."

Ben looked back up at his younger brother. "When you called to say you were coming to Pittsburgh, I couldn't think of anything I wanted more. And now I've gone and messed it up, along with every-thing else."

"You didn't mess anything up, Ben. Not with me, anyway. You were always there for me, even when you were away at college, and then in that big job of yours. I know you checked in often over the years. And I knew you were sending money home to Mom and Dad. But, Ben, I didn't care about that money. Don't get me wrong, it was a big help in those days, but all I really wanted, and all I really want now, is my big brother. Please come back," Adam said, swiping his eyes with the back of his hand.

Ben reached over and grabbed his brother in a huge bear hug. "I love you, Adam. You're my baby brother. I've always loved you. Thank you for coming to Pittsburgh and beating some sense into me—*liter-ally*," he said, smiling and lifting his beer can up to cover and soothe his still fattening lip.

"I love you too, bro. And, you're welcome. Anytime you want a fist fight, just let me know," he said, grinning and lifting his beer can up to his own swelling lip.

Both men pulled away, sitting straighter now as they took in big pulls of air while chuckling, sniffling, and wiping their eyes all at once.

"So," Ben said, "care for another brewski?" He pulled another can from the plastic rings and held it out on offer to Adam.

"It's about time you let go of those beers," Adam said, accepting the outstretched peace offering.

"We're good now, aren't we, Adam?" Ben said, wanting the reassurance.

"We're good. I do believe we are better than good," Adam said, as his face split into a grin right along with Ben's.

They both sat silently for several moments. Adam took a long, slow pull of his beer before speaking again. "I don't think we're quite done here yet, though, do you?" he asked.

Ben didn't respond. He ducked his head and pressed his lips tightly together.

Adam didn't move or speak.

Ben finally looked up, directly into Adam's eyes, and whispered in a shaky breath, "What if she dies?"

"Then she dies," said Adam gently. "We're all going to die someday."

Ben sighed, his chest tight. "I really screwed it up, didn't I?"

"Yes, you did. But that's not the question. The question is 'what are you going to do about it?'"

"She said she doesn't want a relationship with me."

"Do you love her?"

"I love her more than anything."

"Then fight for her. Just like you and I just fought for our relationship. We're worth it—and so is she. But you already know that, don't you?"

Ben gave his brother a sad smile. "When did you get so smart? I'm proud of you, little brother. You have turned out to be one fine young man, haven't you?"

"Why, yes, thank you, I believe I have. It's about time you recognized that," Adam joked. "Now go get her!"

CHAPTER 57

Washington D.C

BECCA SAT WITH HER COLLEAGUES AROUND THE conference room table on the fifteenth floor of the Patterson Consulting office building. She glanced at her watch, anxious for their Thursday morning weekly check-in to start. She didn't want to think about Ben. But every spare moment she had, Becca found her mind betraying her and drifting to thoughts of him—and to that alternate fantasy universe she'd concocted for herself.

Becca tightened her lips, trying to tamp down her emotions as she felt a flush run up her cheeks. This meeting had better start soon, she thought, feeling tears prickle behind her eyelids and threaten to leak down her reddened cheeks.

Fortunately, since her meeting with Nathan on Monday, just four days ago, she'd been swamped. That was just fine with her. Becca wanted nothing more than to be buried with work right now. That was better than being buried in self-pity. Luckily, she and her team had been beyond busy from the moment she'd left Nathan's office on Monday. Now that Oscar—as well as Ethan—was on board and eager to turn Ethan's amphitheater project into a much larger collaborative with multiple partners, excitement about the project among everyone at Patterson had notched skyward, but so had the workload.

Nathan and Oscar really wanted this project to succeed and, for that to become a reality, seed funding was imperative. So, Nathan, as well as Oscar, had authorized their respective teams to double-down on their efforts and put together a pitch that incorporated all the elements in the sketches Ben and Becca had put together. They wanted something innovative—nothing run of the mill. They wanted a pitch that would catch the imagination of the funders out in D.C. and smoke the competition.

Despite all the excitement and extra work, Becca had found herself still with extra time across the week. That should have been a good thing. It was taper week, and she was supposed to be relaxing and keeping stress to a minimum so her body would be strong and healthy, rather than overtaxed, on race day. But she hadn't wanted empty time on her schedule this week. So, she'd looked for ways to fill it.

There were virtually no workouts on their training schedule for their last week before the race—now just three days away. Nonetheless, Becca had found herself out on a run on several occasions. She'd worked hours and hours in the office, but then as soon as she stopped working, her mind drifted to Ben and to the pain twisting her insides that had become both commonplace and unbearable. So, she'd laced up her shoes and ran; she ran until she was bone tired so she could fall into bed, completely exhausted and with no energy left for thoughts of Ben. But even after all that, it hadn't worked.

Becca looked at her watch again: 10:00 a.m. on the dot. Nathan was a stickler for starting meetings on time. But not only was he not here yet, not everyone from her team was here yet either. Becca sighed and kept her head down, pretending to be engrossed in her notebook where she sat at the conference room table. But the words kept swimming in front of her. *Come on, people, let's get this meeting started.* She desperately needed to dive into work. The last thing she wanted was someone noticing her reddened cheeks and puffy eyes and asking her if she was okay. That was likely to unleash the torrent of tears that constantly threatened.

The door to the conference room swung open, halting Becca's thoughts. Nathan surged across the threshold. "Hurry up, folks," he said, as Roger and Abbie rushed through the door behind him and dove into two empty seats at the conference room table. "We've got a lot to cover today. I just got a call from Oscar—we've got an invite from one of the federal agencies his team has been courting. Oscar said they were only getting hemming and hawing until they started floating the broader picture for the amphitheater that includes the Rust Belt community model revitalization.

"Here's the rub, though. The meeting is tomorrow at 11:00 a.m. That gives us about twenty-four hours to finalize our pitch. We need to be ready to hand them glossy one-page summaries as well as screen our video. And Oscar wants someone from our team out there in D.C. pitching with his team. Someone who knows what this project looks like on the ground first-hand. Becca," Nathan called, turning toward her, "I know it's last minute, but I want you there."

As all eyes turned to Becca, she felt her eyes dilate to the size of saucers. Thoughts skittered through her mind. *What about the race? It was only three days away. What about Ben? Shouldn't he be the one going to D.C., or at least one of the people going? Why not Jenn? She was project manager. How could I be the one going? I'm just Becca? What if I failed Nathan, my team—Ben?*

"I can't go," Nathan continued. "I'm booked solid today and tomorrow on other projects. Oscar and I agreed you're the one for the job, Becca. It was your idea—and your friend's. But he's not our client or even our partner—at least, not yet. Let's hope this meeting changes that. Plus, you're the one on our team who can best answer questions about the finances. That'll be a specific focus for this meeting. Also, there are likely to be questions about the community. You'll be able to answer those questions as well. Of course, there will also be infrastructure and other engineering-related questions. But Oscar's team has that covered. He's got some heavy hitters on that front. What he doesn't have is someone in that finance role. That position is currently vacant." Nathan looked at her pointedly. "Of course, I'm not complaining," he said with a chuckle. "I'm happy we get to keep you here. Just consider yourself out on loan this week. Don't let him weasel his way into talking you into staying out in D.C. I know you'll be able to do us proud. You up for it?" he asked rhetorically, clearly already having decided the matter was settled.

Nonetheless, all eyes remained focused on Becca, with the team anxiously waiting for her response.

"Uhhhh...yeah, sure," she said hesitantly.

An audible whoosh of air went through the room as the team relaxed. Nathan cocked his head, finally noticing Becca's tense facade and ghostly-white complexion. "I know it's last minute, Becca," he said, giving her a piercing stare, "but you've got this, right?"

Becca let a smile twitch up onto her lips and nodded her head, trying to look as confident as she could muster. It must have worked, because Nathan smiled broadly at her and turned his head back to take in the full team.

"Change of plans for today's meeting," he continued. "Instead of our round robin with each of you giving a quick update on all your projects, I want to see the video pitch and one-page handout you all put together. We'll need to get those out to Oscar for review by his D.C. team ASAP. And, Becca," Nathan said, turning to address her directly, "you'll need to get on the road right after this meeting. So," he boomed, rubbing his hands together gleefully, "let's get this show on the road! And, Becca, just in case you end up being the one in the hot seat tomorrow morning, let's have you give the presentation."

"Hey, Carmen. Yeah, so...there's kind of been a change of plans. I'm calling you from my car, because I'm on my way to D.C. right now."

"What?! Why in the world are you driving to D.C.? You can't be moving to D.C.—you haven't even packed! And what about the race? You promised me you wouldn't make any crazy decisions before talking to me," Carmen said, panic lacing her words.

"Of course I'm not moving to D.C. And don't worry, I still plan to be at the race. Nathan wants me in a meeting out in D.C. on Friday, so I'm driving out there now. He wants me to give a presentation at a HUD meeting tomorrow."

"A what?" Carmen asked.

"HUD. It's the United States Housing and Urban Development Agency. They have a lot of programs that provide grant funds for projects like the ones we work on at Patterson. He wants me to give the presentation. Can you believe it? Me! I'm petrified! But it's an amazing opportunity. And it could put Ethan's and Ben's projects on the map—literally! If we get a thumbs-up from the funders tomorrow, it means they'll be encouraging us to submit a proposal for funding and that we'd be pretty much a shoe-in."

Becca then filled Carmen in while steering her car onto the turnpike. "I should be able to head back right after the meeting tomorrow. The race isn't until Sunday, so that should give me enough time to regroup and maybe even get in a day of relaxation. So much for an entire week of tapering, though. At least I won't be doing any training today or tomorrow—there just won't be time. That's something, at least."

"Have you heard from Ben yet?" Carmen now asked.

"Not yet."

Carmen sighed. "Becca, why don't you just call him?"

"I can't, Carmen. Nathan told me in no uncertain terms I wasn't to talk to Ben about the collaborative between now and after that meeting tomorrow. And when someone does contact Ben about it, Nathan told me he wants it to be him. Until he knows how that meeting goes tomorrow, he asked me—*no, he told me*—to sit tight and let him drive that aspect of the project."

"Forget the project," said Carmen. "What about you and Ben?"

"He doesn't want to talk to me," Becca said, feeling those now ever-present tears threatening. But she couldn't let those tears fall right now, she told herself, lifting her virtual shield to try and protect herself from another onslaught of pain. Becca gritted her teeth and squeezed her eyes shut momentarily before focusing back on the road. She could do this. "He doesn't want to see me, Carmen, or even hear me. If he did, he would've called me. And if I call him, I'll fall apart. I can't let that happen. For one thing, I wouldn't be able to hold back from telling Ben why I'm going to D.C., assuming he even answered my call.

"It's already killing me not to tell him. I can't let Nathan down, though. He's the only reason we have this meeting tomorrow. And without additional players at the table—heavy hitters, who Patterson can deliver, and the funding this meeting tomorrow could tee up, Ben's project can't happen. I've got to let this play out over the next twenty-four hours before even thinking about calling him."

"Ugh!"

"Carmen, please understand; I'm barely holding it together. I can't fall apart right now. I need to make sure this meeting goes well, and not just for Patterson, but for Ben. Hopefully, Nathan will call Ben by this time tomorrow with good news. Do you understand?" Becca pleaded. "It's better this way."

"Maybe," said Carmen. "But I don't believe for a second that Ben doesn't want to hear from you." Carmen sighed. "Just please tell me you're not still planning to go to D.C. permanently. You're still staying here, right?"

"Yes. I'm staying in Pittsburgh. I told you about my meeting with Nathan on Monday. He was happy I want to stay. I won't be going to D.C. permanently, but I may do some back-and-forth like for this meeting tomorrow. It's the best of both worlds, Carmen. I just wish it weren't quite this crazy right now. I'm having trouble getting even a minute to think straight. One moment I'm excited about getting to stay in Pittsburgh *and* get to do some back and forth to D.C. The next, I'm freaking out. I want to be friends with Ben, but I doubt that can happen. I'm sure I'll always be a trigger for him. Maybe I should have told Nathan to put that transfer request in. That way I could move far away from Ben and just let him be happy." Becca sighed. "Either way, I do want to stay in Pittsburgh."

Becca waited for Carmen to say something. It wasn't like her not to interject with some dramatic declaration. "Carmen, are you there?"

"I'm here," Carmen said quietly.

Becca felt a fissure of doubt in the pit of her stomach. "Why are you so quiet, Carmen? What do you think? Wait! Don't answer that. I know what you think, but I can't travel down that path today. I've got to get through this meeting first, and then to the race, and then after all of that gets settled, maybe I'll be able to think straight without falling to pieces. Okay?"

Carmen ignored her question. "You know you're supposed to be relaxing, right?"

"Hah! That's real funny. Uh oh, I've got a call coming in from the office. Gotta go. Oh, and don't say anything to anyone about me going to D.C. Remember, this is a hush-hush meeting; Nathan would kill me if word got out about it. Right, gotta go!" Becca clicked onto the next call, effectively hanging up before Carmen could protest.

CHAPTER 58
Three Beers and a Plan

BEN

BEN STOOD OUTSIDE BECCA'S APARTMENT. HE HESITATED and then lifted his hand to ring the bell. No answer. He looked to the parking lot to see if her car was there. No car. That wasn't surprising, he thought, trying to reassure himself. It was only 4:00 p.m. She would still be at work.

Maybe he should call and invite her to dinner. Maybe he could offer to pick her up straight from work. *Slow down, coach,* he told himself. He needed to think this through. Maybe she wouldn't want to see him, or even take his call. He wouldn't blame her. He'd been an ass to her in that parking lot, he thought, anxiously running his hand through his hair. His fingers faltered as he felt the hardened crud clumping the strands of his hair together. He sighed, realizing he was a mess. He still had blood in his hair, a fat lip, and probably a black eye. It was just as well Becca was still at work. He'd already been an idiot and sent her running. He didn't want to add insult to injury by having her think he was some violent, crazed hoodlum covered in blood, bruises, and sweat.

Ben returned to his truck, pondering his options. He could call her and invite her to dinner. That way, he'd have plenty of time before she got off work to get cleaned up. He took in a deep gulp of air to settle his nerves and then dialed her number. It went straight to voice mail —again. He left another message.

"Hi, Becca. This is Ben. I, um, I just want to apologize. I had no right to treat you the way I did on Saturday. I hope you can forgive me. Can I take you to dinner tonight? I could swing by and pick you up from work. Anytime works for me. Just call me when you can. So...bye...."

Ben pulled out of the parking lot and headed to his house with his phone sitting right next to him in his truck's center console. He glanced at the phone intermittently while he drove, hoping for a text or return call from Becca. Still nothing. He'd just have to be patient. Or maybe he could give her a quick call at work? That wouldn't be such a bad thing. *But,* he thought with a sigh, *I don't have her work number.* Was that because she didn't want him calling her there? Just like she hadn't wanted him getting back in touch with her after their night on the boat? No, it wasn't the same thing, he assured himself. And it was different now. He wouldn't have to track her down. He knew where she worked, and he could easily look up the number.

Next thing he knew, his phone was ringing through to the Patterson Consulting office. A recorded message came on saying the office closed at four thirty. It was 4:38 p.m. Had he really just missed them? There was surely still someone there at the front desk. He could just drive over. *Stalk, much?* Yeah, maybe that wasn't such a good idea. He could just picture himself standing outside the building waiting for her and her coming out, and then there being a scene in front of the building because she wanted nothing to do with him.

Ben sighed again and instead steered his truck away from downtown and toward his house. As he pulled into his driveway, Manky and Mel came out from behind the trees to greet him. But not even their excited butt wags and quacking could drag a smile from him today. He struggled up the stairs, every step feeling like an impossible feat, and made his way into the shower. As soon as the water hit his face, he winced. Well, he deserved that, didn't he?

He hurried through his shower, wanting to check his phone again. Still no text or call. He pulled out the team paperwork and found Carmen's number.

"Hello, you've reached Carmen's answering machine. Please leave a message at the tone."

"Hi, Carmen. This is Ben. I'm wondering if you know where Becca is? I'm hoping to reach her. I...um...I need to apologize to her. So,...if you can, please... Please, can you call me or ask her to call me?"

Ben hung up the phone and dialed Adam's number. "I've lost her," Ben said into the phone as soon as Adam answered. "She's not answering her phone, and she isn't home, and her office is already closed for the day." He knew his voice sounded frantic and crazed.

"You don't know that yet. Did you leave her a message?"

"Yeah, but she hasn't called or texted. What should I do, Adam? I can't lose her. *I need her.* I don't care what the future holds—or about the past. I just need her in my life, beside me. How could I have treated her so poorly? She was hurting, probably is still hurting and I, of all people, should have some idea of what she's going through. I shouldn't have yelled at her and pushed her away. I should have taken her in my arms and comforted her. She deserves that and so much more. What should I do, Adam? You're good with people. Tell me. Anything. I'll do anything."

"Okay, let's think about this," Adam said in a slow, reassuring voice. "We need a strategy. Did you try Carmen? Maybe she knows where Becca is."

"I called her number too. I left her a message. She didn't answer. And I called Becca's work. Nobody answered the phone there, either."

"Okkaayy...let's not worry too much just yet," Adam said gently. "You only just called her this afternoon. Maybe she's still in a meeting or something. Or with her mom."

"Do you think I should call her mom?" Ben said in a slightly panicked voice but ready to hang up the phone and dial her mother's number—which, he realized, of course he didn't have.

"Maybe not just yet, Ben. You don't want to worry her mom. How about you give her till tonight to call you back? If she doesn't, you can try calling her office again tomorrow morning after they open."

After hanging up with Adam, Ben paced the house. He picked up a hammer—and then put it back down again. He didn't want to work on his house right now. He picked up his briefcase—and put it back down again. He couldn't concentrate on work. He made himself a sandwich and took a few bites—and then threw it away. Ben went back outside and found his axe. There was a fallen tree he'd been meaning to chop up for firewood. He made his way to where the tree had fallen. Manky and Mel reappeared and followed him into the woods. At least they were willing to keep him company, he thought with a sigh.

He chopped wood for a couple of hours, checking his phone in his pocket continuously until he finally gave up and made his way back into the house and into bed. He'd thought about taking another shower but just didn't have the energy to go through the motions, despite being covered in sweat again—and sore. Ben knew he'd pay for this tomorrow. Not only did his lip hurt, but his eye, his nose, and now his shoulder hurt from swinging that axe over and over.

Ben awoke, exhausted. He'd hoped to fall into a deep sleep, but he'd tossed and turned all night, simultaneously trying to make himself fall asleep while also listening intently for his cell phone to beep or ring. He'd finally fallen into a fitful sleep in the wee hours of the morning. When he awoke, the first thing he did was check his phone. Still no call or text from Becca.

He sighed and lumbered down his stairs and made a large pot of coffee, aware he'd need it to get any work done today. Ben looked at his watch. It was only 7:00 a.m.—two hours until Patterson's offices opened. He sat down at his kitchen table and pulled out the Fischer account drawings. He'd let Jason and Connie know he was going to work at home today. There was no need to drive into the office condo, and he knew he looked like hell. He'd be better off working from home today. Jason and Connie would probably thank him for that too, he thought, wondering with a shake of his head if Jason's nose was truly broken.

Finally, the clock ticked to 9:00 a.m., and Ben decided he'd call her cell phone first. And then, if he didn't reach her, he'd call her office. But his phone call clicked into her voice mail again.

"Hi Becca. It's Ben again. Sorry for another messages. I know you may not want to talk to me. But please just let me know you're okay. I'm worried about you. Please. I...I...well, I miss you." Ben hung up, trembling with worry, and dialed Patterson Consulting's main number.

"Hello, Patterson Consulting. This is Jenny. How may I help you?"

"Hi, Jenny. I need to speak with Becca Clarke. Is she available?" Ben asked with false confidence in his voice.

"Just a moment, I'll check for you."

Ben waited nervously. He hadn't given the receptionist his name. Maybe she'd just patch him through. If Becca knew it was him calling, would she answer the phone?

The woman came back on the line. "I'm sorry. She's out of town today."

His stomach fell. "Do you know where she's gone and when she'll be back?"

"Let's see.... The docket shows she's in Washington D.C. It doesn't show when she'll return. Would you like me to patch you through to her voice mail?"

"No. Thank you," Ben said. He hung up the phone and held his head in his hands with his elbows on the table. *Was she coming back?* Maybe he should go to D.C. But how would he even find her...and why would she want him to?

His cell phone, still in his hand, rang, startling him nearly out of his skin. Maybe it was Becca! He answered the call before looking at the screen. "Hello?" he said hopefully.

"Hi. Is this Ben Morgan?"

"Yes," he said, now looking at his phone and realizing there was no name attached to the number on the screen. It was a local number. But it was a number he didn't recognize. Probably a marketer, he thought, as he moved his finger toward the end button.

"This is Ethan. Ethan Trapp."

Ben stilled, his finger still in midair. "Ethan? What do you want?" Ben asked suspiciously.

"Well, first off, I owe you an apology."

"You do?" Ben asked, surprised.

"Yeah. I'm sorry I was so standoffish with you when we first spoke. I actually like your ideas—and I like them even more now that I've seen them fleshed out."

"Okay?" Ben said, still suspicious, but also too curious to hang up.

"It's just that I'd shown my designs to another local developer not long before you asked about them. The guy tried to sabotage me. I had an offer in on the final parcels of land I needed for my development. My offer was accepted but only verbally. We still had to do the closing on paper. But before that could happen, I got wind that the developer was trying to hone in and cut me out. It turned out the only reason he'd contacted me in the first place was to fish for information so he could buy the land for himself. Let's just say that when you called, I wasn't feeling too trusting of anyone. But, well, Becca convinced me you're a good guy."

"Becca? I thought you two didn't know each other. When we saw you at the gala, she said she'd only met you once for about five minutes," Ben said, his voice now laced with steel.

"That's right. And we still don't know each other well. But, since that gala, I've gotten to see her a couple of times in her team meetings at Patterson. Nathan called me in to look at the sketches you two put together to see if I'd be interested in collaborating. At first, I told him no way. But then Nathan talked me into sitting in on one of their team meetings. It was amazing. A lot of talent, a lot of energy, a lot of innovative ideas. You name it, they've got it. On one break, Becca and I got to talking. She couldn't stop singing your praises. I've got to admit, I got a little jealous. I'd love to have a woman talking about me that way." Ethan laughed. "She said all the ideas were yours—the sketches too. I was impressed. Anyhow, I thought it was about time I apologized. And since the Patterson team is out in D.C. right now pitching our ideas, I thought maybe it was about time you and I met."

"What do you mean they're out in D.C. pitching our ideas?" Ben interrupted, his voice hard and low as he reeled from Ethan's words, both about being jealous of him and then about Ethan knowing the team was in D.C. Is that where Becca was? And why hadn't she told him?

"Didn't you know?" Ethan asked with surprise. "Patterson got a call yesterday, inviting them to pitch to HUD this morning. Nathan called me. He was excited, but he also sounded pretty harried." Ethan chuckled. "It sounded like that call sent everyone over at Patterson into overdrive. Nathan said he didn't have time to give me any details but that he'd call me—and hopefully you if we get good news—after the meeting. I haven't heard anything yet. Have you?"

"Nope."

"Oh...well, sorry about that. I didn't mean to catch you off guard. Maybe I should have waited until after the meeting today to call you. But the call from Nathan last night got me kind of excited. And even if

HUD nixes the idea at today's meeting, I still think there are ways you and I might be able to collaborate. Are you interested in having lunch today—my treat?"

"Is Becca there? In D.C.?"

"I don't know. Nathan didn't say exactly who was going. He just told me they got a slot and that he'd keep me posted."

"Hmm." Ben grunted, wondering why she hadn't called him. And then he answered his own question—the better question was why would she call him. But did he trust her? He knew the answer to that one too. Of course he did. She might not have told him everything, but she'd kept him in the loop about Nathan and about Ethan. She'd gotten his project through not only Patterson's gates but HUD's. That was amazing.

"You still there, Ben? If you let me treat you to lunch, I promise to listen to your ideas this time—maybe without a scowl on my face," Ethan joked.

"I could eat," Ben answered. "Where to?"

"I know a great place downtown—best lasagna you've ever eaten. It's called—"

"Tony's restaurant?" Ben said, before Ethan could get the word out.

"How'd you know?"

"Let's just say it's one of my favorites. I'll see you there in an hour."

"Done," said Ethan.

Ethan took another bite of Tony's lasagna and groaned. "Hmm...that is so good."

Ben eyed Ethan contemplatively as he took another bite off his own plate. "I brought the sketches with me if you want to go over them," said Ben.

Ethan chuckled. "Me too," he said, as he pulled a stack of papers out of his briefcase. "I really love this section here," he said, pointing to the shops next to the marina. "And here," he said, pointing to the Oaks Diner further up the trail.

Ben gave Ethan a thoughtful look. "That's my favorite section, actually," said Ben. "And that diner. The mayor owns it. She's a great lady, and she has lots of good ideas that she's not afraid to put into action and get some muscle behind."

"Becca told me you were friends. I can't wait to meet her," said Ethan offhandedly. "And what about here?" he continued, pointing to another marking on Ben's map, their comments now ricocheting off each other's at a quickened pace. Their conversation built increasingly positive energy as they shared their respective thoughts across the full spectrum of ideas laid out before them.

"I really think this is great stuff, Ben. I say we meet again after we hear from Nathan, no matter whether it's good news or bad from HUD."

"I agree. There's a lot we can do on this together. How about we meet early next week at my office?"

"Done," said Ethan, gathering the papers he'd brought that were now strewn across their table. He stuffed them back into his briefcase as Ben did the same.

"How are two of my favorite guys doin'?" asked Tony in his thick Italian accent as he stopped at their table.

Ben looked at his plate and realized he'd polished off the entire large helping of lasagna. "Now that we're eating your lasagna, we couldn't be better," he lied. Tony's lasagna always tasted amazing, melting in his mouth with gooey melted cheese and freshly made marinara sauce. He realized now, though, that he hadn't really tasted what he'd eaten today. Yes, it melted in his mouth, but every bite tasted like sawdust as worry and guilt overwhelmed all of him, including his tastebuds.

Tony smiled at the compliment, not noticing Ben's distress. "I didn't know youse two were acquainted," he said. "How come I haven't seen you in here together before?"

Ethan looked at Ben, waiting for him to answer first.

"We haven't actually known each other long, but maybe you'll see us in here together again one of these days," Ben hedged, shrugging his shoulders.

"I hope so," said Tony. "Let me know if you need anything else."

"Just the check," said Ethan, before Tony turned and started toward another table of diners.

"So, Ben, how did you and Becca meet?" Ethan asked, as he took a sip of his iced tea and waited on the bill.

Ben felt his left eye begin to twitch and his face redden. "It's a long story," he said, his voice coming out in a flat monotone with no infused emotional inflections. "Fate, maybe?" He shrugged. "Anyhow, I'm her triathlon coach now. We've been training for a sprint tri for a few months. The race is Sunday."

"No shit? Becca said something about being busy because of a race coming up. But there was so much going on that day when I was in the office that I didn't get a chance to ask her any more questions. And you didn't know her before that?"

Ben squirmed in his chair uncomfortably. "Uh...well, we met before that actually...."

"How'd you meet the first time?"

"It's a long story."

"From the look on your face," Ethan said, smiling gently, "it's a good one. Care to share?"

"Not really."

"Oh, so it's like that," Ethan said, cocking his eyebrows. "Are you two a thing?"

"No. Yes. Maybe...."

Ethan's lips twitched up. "That sure of yourself, huh?"

"Like I said, it's a long story."

"I think I get it. No wonder you were so cold to me that night at the gala. I was mad at first, but then I remembered what a jerk I was to you when we first talked. So, I figured I probably deserved it. But it wasn't that, was it? It was about Becca. There's something between you two."

"Actually, I kinda blew it," he blurted out, no longer able to hold on to his composure. As his emotions bubbled up, crumbling the protective shield he'd so carefully built around himself, Ben's words tumbled out, and he filled Ethan in on their story.

Ethan must think he was a nutcase. And he'd be right. Ethan was still mostly a stranger, and here Ben was, pouring his heart out to him. But, somehow, he knew Ethan was a good guy...just like he knew

Becca wouldn't betray him. And if he and Ethan were going to be partners, he might as well lay it all out there.

Ben rubbed his hands over his face, trying to wipe away the tension. See what she'd done to him? His heart had cracked wide open and left him vulnerable. But he didn't care anymore. The risk was worth it.

He poured out his story while Ethan listened, finishing with, "So, that's about it. I don't know if she'll ever forgive me."

"Maybe I can help," Ethan said thoughtfully.

"Yeah? How?" Ben asked hopefully.

"I don't know exactly, but if we put our heads together, like we are now about the revitalization, I bet we can think of something."

Ben gave Ethan a grateful but brittle smile. "How about you just help me not think too much about Becca right now, and instead we talk more about how we can make these projects work—with or without that federal funding? The phone stays right here, though," Ben said, pointing to his phone sitting next to his water glass. "Just in case she calls or texts."

"Yeah, you've got it bad, don't ya?" Ethan said. He motioned Tony over to their table, ordering a beer for each of them in place of the iced teas they'd been drinking. Three beers later, they'd synced up their ideas, both of them excited about the possibilities.

Ethan motioned Tony over again and asked for the check. "We're really ready to go this time, Tony," Ethan said. "I've got to get to my dad's birthday party. My sisters and my mom will be furious with me if I'm late."

When the check arrived, he and Ben both reached for it at the same time. "Oh, no you don't," said Ethan. "This is part of my apology, remember? And it's the least I can do to try to cheer you up. Hang in there, man. Believe me, I don't see how you don't at least have a chance with Becca. Not with the way she went on and on about how amazing you are. That woman isn't interested in anyone but you, least of all me," he joked. "Sorry, too soon?" he asked, making Ben realize his face had momentarily turned thunderous.

Ethan laughed. "Chill, dude. I already have a girlfriend. And, no matter what happens, Becca is clearly interested in you. You are a lucky man."

Ben sighed. "Let's hope so. Thanks for lunch, Ethan, and for trying to help me drown my sorrows," he said, pointing to their empty beer glasses. "Have fun at your dad's birthday party. You're a lucky man, too, ya know. Family can be a good thing. I didn't get that until recently. I just hope it isn't too late."

CHAPTER 59

Traveling Woes

It was late Saturday, and Becca was only now—finally—on her way back to Pittsburgh. It'd been a hectic couple of days, and she'd been without her phone for most of it, losing it almost immediately upon arriving in D.C. She'd finally found it this afternoon, now with a dead battery. It had been sitting on a chair tucked under a conference room table where she'd been meeting with Patterson's D.C. team this whole time. Who knew how many messages she'd missed, she thought, as she made her way down to Patterson's parking garage, found her car, climbed in, and plugged her cell phone into the car's charger.

As it powered up, Becca felt a wave of anxiety wash over her when she saw the phone's screen. She'd missed multiple phone calls and texts—way too many to look at now. She needed to get on the road if she had any hope of getting at least a bit of rest and her gear gathered in time for the race tomorrow morning. Becca took a deep breath to calm her nerves and then set her GPS for home and her phone messages to auto-play through her car's speakers. At least she could listen to them while driving. Who knows, she thought, maybe that would help keep her awake for at least a portion of the long four-hour drive ahead of her.

Thursday, 4:20 p.m.: "Hi, Becca. This is Ben. I, um, I just want to apologize.

I had no right to treat you the way I did on Saturday. I hope you can forgive me. Can I take you to dinner tonight? I could swing by and pick you up from work. Anytime works for me. Just call me when you can. So...bye...."

Thursday, 8:00 p.m.: "Hi, Becca. It's Carmen. I just got home from work...long day. Anyhow, there's a message on my machine from Ben. He called me at about 5:30 p.m. asking if I knew where you were. Glad I didn't answer that call! I would not have known what to say. I feel bad, though. He sounded worried. He asked me to tell you to call him if I hear from you. You really should, you know. Call him! Okay, that's it. Call me too. Bye."

Thursday, 9:00 p.m.: "Hi, Becca. This is Adam. Are you okay? Please don't be upset with Ben. I know he loves you. And he's worried about you. Sorry to butt in. I know it's not my place, but I'm worried about you and Ben both. Please call me to let me know you're okay. Or, better yet, please give Ben a call. I know he wants to hear from you."

Friday, 9:00 a.m.: "Hi, Becca. It's Ben again. Sorry for another message. I know you may not want to talk to me. But please just let me know you're okay. I'm worried about you. Please. I...I...well, I miss you."

Friday, 3:00 p.m.: "Becca, this is Carmen. Just checking in to see how it's going. Did your meeting go well? Did you call Ben? I hope so, and I hope you're on your way back home, because we have a race to get ready for! And why aren't you answering your phone? Call me!"

Saturday, 10:00 a.m.: "Becca! This is Carmen. Are you home yet? Where are you? Call me!"

Saturday, 11:00 a.m.: "Hi, Becca. This is your mother. Just checking in. I know your race is tomorrow. I'm excited for you and your friends. Don't be too hard on that coach of yours. I can tell he cares about you—and that you care about him. Call and check in if you get a chance. Love you."

Saturday, 1:00 p.m.: "Becca! It's Carmen. Where are you? Ben called me again. This time I got the call, and I had to hem and haw about what I know and don't know. I don't know what I'm supposed to say! I told him you are coming to the race and that you're fine. You are, aren't you? Please call me ASAP. We're doing our last photo shoot later this afternoon, and I probably won't be able to answer my phone from about 2:00 p.m. until we're done. If you call after that, just leave me a message so I know you're fine."

Saturday, 3:23 p.m.: "Hi, Becca. This is Ben. Your office said you're in D.C. I met with Ethan. We had a good meeting. He said he'd be hearing from Nathan after your meeting and that I would be too. I haven't heard from him yet—or *you. Is everything okay? I'm worried about you. Please come back. I'm sorry about last week. I know you must have been hurting—and that you are probably still hurting. I'm so sorry. Please give me a chance to make it right. And please don't miss the race on account of me. Please call me and let me know you're coming and that you're okay."*

Becca's hands tightened on her steering wheel as another rush of anxiety coursed through her. She couldn't listen to her messages anymore. She'd screwed up—again. She'd caused her family and friends, including Ben, to worry. She needed to let everyone know she was okay. But what could she say to Ben? She'd always be a cause of worry for him—and pain—no matter what she did. Becca knew she couldn't put him in that position.

But she did need to let him know she was okay. But what if she called him and he wanted to know about the HUD meeting? Their meeting had gone well, but she, and even Oscar and Nathan, didn't have any answers for anyone yet. Instead, HUD had asked for some modifications. Maybe Nathan wouldn't mind if she told Ben that much? And she really owed that to Ben. Their pitch had included lots of his ideas.

First, though, she'd call her mom and then Carmen. Maybe she could ask Carmen to relay the message to Ben that she was okay and that she'd be at the race? Maybe Carmen could also let him know that she was still tied up with work. Because Becca knew that if she called him herself, she would cave and tell him everything—maybe even that she loved him. And that was the worst idea ever.

CHAPTER 60

Race Day

BEN

IT WAS A PERFECT MORNING FOR THE RACE—SEVENTY degrees and sunny, with no rain in sight. Ben watched as participants, excited and nervous, checked in. An anticipatory energy filled the air, from the gathering area near the race check-in table to the finish line all the way to the water's edge.

Ben kept a smile plastered on his face as he fielded question after question from his own team, as well as from the larger field of racers. He enjoyed helping everyone, especially the first-timers, whose questions provided a much-needed distraction that he needed today. His own nerves simmered barely beneath the surface, hopefully well-hidden under his mannequin-like smile. Everyone from his team was here now—all except Becca.

"Ben," called out Holly. "Could you please help me with my wetsuit?" She was sitting on the ground next to a nearby picnic table with one leg of her wetsuit pulled up over her ankle, attempting to inch the tight-fitting neoprene further up her leg. "It's so hard to get this thing on." She giggled nervously. "Could you please hand me that bottle of TriSlide? If I try to stand up, I'm sure I'll just tip right over." She giggled again. "Maybe if I spray a bit more of that TriSlide on my calves and thighs, I'll be able to get this thing on before the race starts."

"No problem," said Ben, and he took a couple of steps toward the picnic table where Holly had laid out her belongings.

"Thank you so much," she said, as Ben handed her the bottle. "I hate getting this thing on. But I'm sure glad it didn't end up too hot today to wear our wetsuits. I need the extra buoyancy." She giggled again nervously. "You're sure I'm ready for this race, Ben?" she asked apprehensively.

"Absolutely. You're going to be great. Just think about dress rehearsal last week. You were done with that swim and out of the water in no time. I was so impressed. If you have any doubts during the race, just remind yourself that you've done it all before. No big deal. Just do the same thing you did last week. You've got this," he reassured her.

"Hey, Ben, can you please zip up my wetsuit?" asked Elora, coming over toward them. When he nodded, she put her back to him and futilely tried to grab hold of the long cord tied to the end of her zipper pull.

"Which leg do I put my timing chip on again, Ben?" called out Matt nervously. Matt had come a long way since their first training when he'd informed Ben he saw himself as only a walker, and Ben had encouraged him to finish a fourth lap around the track to complete their one-mile distance that day. Matt would likely run most of the run portion of the course today, thought Ben proudly.

"It's best to wrap the timing chip around your left ankle," he called back. "That way, when you get on the bike, you don't have to worry about your timing device getting caught up in your derailleur. That's not likely to happen, but it's better to be safe than sorry. Remember too, Matt, that while the Velcro on that anklet is unlikely to come loose, it's a good idea to add a safety pin as an extra precaution. You don't want that anklet falling off and getting lost somewhere out on the race-course. If that happens, the computer will think you're wherever your anklet is rather than wherever you are. That Velcro is strong stuff. But, I've known people to lose their timing chip mid-race, especially during the swim. It's not unheard of for someone to accidentally kick your ankle as you pass each other rather than having every kick hit the water."

"Thanks, Ben. How did you know I was going to forget about the safety pin? There's a lot of new stuff to remember. This is so exciting, though! And, by the way," Matt said to Ben with a sheepish grin, "do you happen to have an extra safety pin?"

Ben reached into his pocket and pulled out a handful of safety pins. "Of course. Here you go. I may not be able to find you a safety pin on just any day. But, on race days, I always have a pocket full of them. And quit your worrying; you're going to be great. Although, there's nothing wrong with a few nerves. They trigger your fight-or-flight response and can give you an extra boost of energy. Just don't let those stress hormones take over your entire brain. Remember, the race is just as much mental as physical, more so even. You need to keep your wits about you so you can keep on pace. If you go out too quick, you'll struggle later in the race. Remember to go out gentle like we practiced. You've got this. You've done it before so you already know you can." Ben gave Matt a pat on the shoulder.

Ben loved this part of coaching. The training was done. His role today was mostly about reassuring people they would be fine and helping them keep their nerves in check so they did nothing stupid. Thank goodness for the distractions. His team might not know it, but their questions were the only thing keeping him sane—and keeping him from doing anything stupid.

He scanned the pre-race-course area, yet again looking for Becca. He ran his hand through his hair. Was she going to show?

"Hey, Ben," said Adam. "Settle in there, dude, or you won't have any hair left by the end of the day."

"It would serve me right," muttered Ben.

"Don't be so hard on yourself. She'll show."

"I don't know," said Ben. "It's only about ten minutes until the first swimmers enter the water. You haven't seen her yet, have you?"

"Not yet. I'm sorry, Ben. But you said she sent you a text last night saying she'd show. But...well...there's nothing we can do about that now. We've got to focus on who's here. There are one hundred and fifty racers today—and twenty-three of them are yours. Just focus on that right now. Let the rest play out and let's see what happens. It'll be okay."

"Yeah, sure, I guess...."

"Hey, Ben," Larry said, as he approached Ben and Adam. "Are you coming down to the water? I think they're about to call up the first swimmers. Will you walk down with me? First, though, could you please hold my water bottle? I've got to adjust my goggle strap."

"Sure thing," said Ben, and he took the bottle Larry held out to him. While he waited on Larry, Ben glanced over at Adam. He knew Adam was right. He needed to focus on the racers in front of him, and he had no one to blame but himself if Becca didn't show. "Here. Let me help you with that," Ben said, as he watched Larry fumble nervously with his goggle strap. "There, how does that feel? Is it a good fit now?"

"Yes. Thanks! It's perfect. I'm so nervous, my fingers aren't working anymore." Larry smiled with a hint of embarrassment. "I hope they work okay once I hit the water."

"Believe me, you're not alone. It happens to everyone. And you'll be fine once you get started. Come on, I'll walk down with you. Ready?"

"Ready as I'll ever be," Larry said, grinning at Ben and giving him an excited but nervous smile.

As Ben and Larry approached the water's edge, they joined a mass of neoprene clad people of all shapes, sizes, and ages, chattering excitedly. Varying colors of swim caps dotted the landscape, adding an air of festivity. Today's race was a deepwater start, meaning each group of swimmers—by gender and age group, with each group identified by different colored swim caps—would start their swim from behind the first swim buoy rather than from the beach. The colored caps would make it easier for the course staff and safety team—some of whom were already out in the water on kayaks and paddle boards—to monitor the swimmers.

"Hey, Ben," said Diana, the racecourse director. "It's just about showtime. You ready to help me get these swimmers in the water? If you're ready, I'll start calling out the groups. John over there," she said, pointing to a man about ten feet away with his feet already in the water, "is going to keep count of the swimmers as they enter the water. Can you serve as gatekeeper for each group? Just keep them corralled while they wait for their group to be called and field any questions anyone has as they wait their turn. You know we're going to have some nervous nellies out there, and at least one person is going to get confused about where they're supposed to be and when they're supposed to enter the water. It doesn't seem to matter how many times we go over the logistics," she said good-naturedly. "Once race day hits, those nerves have people's brains turning into mush—at least until they settle into the swim and let their training kick in. Well, that's if they had a good coach, of course," she joked. "Although, I understand you're one of the best!" She smiled at him.

Ben could barely concentrate on what she was saying. He looked around one last time. Still no Becca. He wanted to tell Diana they needed to wait. "Hold up!" he wanted to yell. But they couldn't wait any longer.

"Am I forgetting something?" Diana asked with concern.

"No, not at all. You've got everything running like clockwork. And you're right, it's time to get started. Let's get 'em in the water." He smiled. "I sure love this part—nerves and all. If we can get 'em into the water calm, it usually bodes well for a smooth rest of their race. I'll do my best to steer them right. Start callin' whenever you're ready."

A huge grin split Diana's face, and she turned back toward the crowd. "Swimmers!" she called out through a bull horn she held in her right hand. "We're ready to get started. Make sure you're standing with your cohort. As I'm sure you all know, the swim is a deepwater start—not a beach start—and it's a wave start, meaning you will go in with your age and gender cohort. Each cohort is identified by a different colored swim cap. Be sure you're wearing the swim cap that was provided to you at check in as that cap matches your age and gender. First up, we have men, aged nineteen and under. You should be wearing a blue swim cap. Women, aged nineteen and under..." Diana continued to call out each group along with their corresponding color of swim cap, and people started organizing themselves into their cohorts.

"Please look around," she continued, "and make sure you're standing with your group. If your swim cap is not the same color as those you're standing with, you're in the wrong place. If you have any concerns or last minute questions, Ben's the guy to ask." She motioned toward Ben, who held his hand up and waved.

~

"Last group, you're up! In ten, nine, eight..."

Becca hadn't made it. Her group was already in the water. Some swimmers were even already out of the water and onto the bike course. Ben felt a heaviness in his heart. He wanted nothing more than to slink away and lick his wounds....

"Ben! Ben!" called out one of the course volunteers as she ran toward him. "Can you please come help? One of the swimmers just got pulled from the water. He was panicking and put his hand up, asking to be pulled out. The safety crew just brought him to the medic tent. They think it's just a panic attack, but they're checking him out just in case. He's pretty distraught. The medic asked me to see if I could find you and bring you over. He said you're the best at calming people down. Can you come? Please?"

Ben was already hurrying alongside the volunteer as she explained the situation. He could see a man sitting near the beach in the medic tent, his elbows leaning on his knees and his hands holding either side of his head. "No problem," said Ben. "Thanks for volunteering today and thanks for coming to get me. Do you know his name?" Thoughts of Becca disappeared as Ben went into autopilot and triage mode.

As the safety team had thought, the man, Walter, was fine. They'd just needed to help him get his breathing and his heart rate under control. Ben had talked him down, telling him it was common for someone to get panicked in open water. That didn't mean he couldn't compete in another race on another day. He'd just need to use what he'd learned today to better prepare for the natural reaction that came from entering water that was over your head while surrounded by others thrashing all around you.

Ben had laughed with Walter at the absurdity of even thinking about entering the water under those conditions. Walter admitted he'd only trained in a swimming pool and that this was the first time he'd tried an open water swim. Ben encouraged him not to give up; there would be other races. They'd had a few sips of Gatorade together before Ben left him in good hands with his family, who had come over to cheer him up.

As soon as Ben left the medic tent, thoughts of Becca rushed back into his head. But, next thing he knew, he was getting another request to help with a racer who'd wiped out on the bike course. The accident wasn't serious. Just some road rash that the medics were cleaning up with some antiseptic and bandages. The man was out of the race for today, though, and he'd have some bruising for sure but, luckily, no broken bones or anything serious. He appeared more disappointed than anything else from knowing he wouldn't finish the race today.

So far, Ben hadn't heard of any problems with his own team members. Let's hope it stays that way, he thought, as he helped the safety team get the biker and his bike to the staging area next to the finish line so he could watch the rest of the race from there. At least he'd be able to cheer his friends and the rest of the racers over the line.

As soon as Ben left him, his mind turned back to Becca. Where was she? Was she okay? Her text last night had come in late. But she'd written that she'd be here.

"Ben!" Adam yelled, as he came running up the hill toward the finish line where Ben stood. "She's here! She's in the water!"

"What?! How can she be in the water? I saw all the racers go in. She wasn't with them."

"She got here late—right after you got called away. Diana let her go in. There were still plenty of people in the water, including the safety team. So there really wasn't any reason not to let her go in. Her personal time will start from the moment she enters the water, so Becca will have as much time as everyone else to complete her swim. She'll just need to beat the cutoff time for the overall race. That might be tough, but she just might be able to do it if she stays focused. She may cross the finish line last, though." Adam grinned.

Ben reached over and hugged his brother, lifting him off the ground.

"Hey, put me down!" Adam laughed.

"I need to go and watch her! Want to come with me?"

Adam glanced at his watch. "Yes, but she's probably out of the water by now and already on her bike. You should be able to catch her in the transition area before she starts on her run, though. By the way, all her friends are here, including her mom—and even Ethan Trapp,"

Adam gave Ben a quizzical look. "You okay with that? I'm not sure why he's here."

Ben smiled. "Yeah, I'm good with that. It's a long story. I'll fill you in later."

"You know, Ben, everyone's rooting for you—and I'm not talking about the race. You two belong together. Everyone knows it—just maybe not Becca. Carmen said Becca's standing firm. She doesn't think you two have a future together. She thinks it would be too painful for the both of you. And Carmen said Becca can be pretty stubborn about changing her mind once she gets something into her head, especially since her cancer diagnosis. I guess she's had to be quite the fighter, and it's taken a lot of determination to keep her life on track. You're just going to have to convince her to let her guard down. You both deserve to be happy, and I think this is your shot at that—no matter what else comes."

"Thanks, Adam," Ben said. "Thanks for the warning and the pep talk. And thanks for beating some sense into me—literally." He smiled, touching his still swollen lip. "I'm going to do my best to break through that protective shield she's erected for herself. I love her—no matter what. I've just got to make her see that. Right?"

"Right!" Adam encouraged, slapping Ben on the back.

Ben made it to the transition area just as Becca was coming in. She looked beautiful with her hair flying behind her as she rode in confidently on her midnight blue bike that was sparkling in the sunlight filtering down through the trees. Ben watched her, mesmerized, as she expertly unclipped and quickly changed into her running shoes with an intense look of concentration on her face. She was in the zone, Ben thought. She hadn't seen him yet, and he didn't want to rattle her. He waited until she was through transition and out onto the run, before he caught up to her and yelled, "Becca! You're doing great!"

She looked up, startled. "Oh my gosh! Ben! Your lip! Your eye!"

"Oh, this," he said, reaching up to touch his lip. "No, this is good," he said, smiling broadly at her—and wincing at the pain from the movements in his face muscles. "This woke me up...to all the good stuff around me already in my life—to you!" He looked around them, gesturing to her race clothes. "Look, now isn't the time but I'll tell you all about it once you finish this race. I don't want to get in your way. I'll see you at the finish line."

As much as Ben hated to pull himself away, he knew he needed to get out of her way and let her focus on finishing this race. She was breathing heavy, and she had little time left. But she still looked strong and beautiful. Nothing could change that in his mind. Nonetheless, his insides twisted with angst. Could she pull this off? Even after getting such a late start?

CHAPTER 61
The Finish Line
BEN

BEN MADE HIS WAY TO THE FINISH LINE AND STOOD anxiously with two of the race course volunteers. Becca was still out on the course. All the other participants were in and accounted for, with most of them now standing in the staging area, gobbling up slices of watermelon, pulled pork sandwiches, and cookies from the buffet table sitting under a large outdoor open tent.

He couldn't hear what anyone was saying from here, but he was sure he could guess pretty accurately. They were discussing every inch of the course and sharing their experiences. They were feeling proud and, although exhausted, feeling ecstatic. They had accomplished a large and scary goal—most of them, anyway. They had finished and had the proof of it when a volunteer draped their finisher's medal around their neck and congratulated them on their accomplishment. It was a heady experience, especially for first-timers. But the feeling never got old. He'd completed many races, and not a single one of them had left him without that feeling of giddy accomplishment. He wanted that for Becca.

"Are there any more racers out there?" asked one of the two volunteers standing next to him. "We're almost at the cutoff time. Are we ready officially to close the course?"

"There's still one more coming," Ben said anxiously. "She'll be through any minute. She'll make it."

"Should I run out and check on her?" asked the volunteer.

"No need, I already did," said the second volunteer. She's doing fine. She's got some friends out there running alongside her and cheering her on. She's real close. I think she'll make it. Wait...do you hear that? She's coming in now," the woman said excitedly, as the sound of cowbells and kazoos wafted over the breeze to them.

Ben heard the cheers coming from just beyond the trees around the bend, not far from where he and the two volunteers were standing. He knew Diana, the race course director, was probably wondering where he was. She'd be up on the awards platform by now, waiting for him to join her so she could start calling out the awards. She'd asked him to join her for that so he could personally hand out any awards to his own team.

Ben squinted into the sun to see if he could see Becca yet. Where had he put his sunglasses? He looked down and pulled them off his t-shirt and put them on before looking back to the course. "Becca," Ben whispered to himself.

"What was that?" asked one volunteer.

"Becca!" Ben yelled, and a grin consumed his face.

The first volunteer shifted her eyes sideways to look at Ben and then toward the other volunteer. No, he wanted to tell her, I have not lost my mind. I'm in love with the most amazing woman...and she's about to become a triathlete for the first time!

Becca's face was beet red and covered in sweat. But she had a smile on her face as she proudly crossed the finish line and leaned her head down so the course volunteer could drape a finisher's medal around her neck. She didn't stand back up straightaway, but put her hands on her knees while she took a moment to catch her breath. Ben didn't wait for her to stand fully before rushing up to her. "Becca!" he said, picking her up and twirling her around. "You did it! I am so proud of you! You're a triathlete!"

Becca looked up at Ben and grinned. Carmen, Eileen, Stacey, Anna, Natalie, Jenn, and Adam all stood behind her, having run right alongside her for the last quarter mile. Ethan and Becca's mom stood just a few steps behind them.

Ben didn't let her go. "Becca, please forgive me. Please forgive me for being such an idiot," he begged.

"I forgive you, Ben," she said. "And you're not an idiot. Well, except for maybe hugging me when I'm dripping with sweat," she huffed out, still trying to slow her breathing and recover her voice.

Ben felt a wave of elation, and he could barely hear the next words she uttered until the last five caught his attention.

"...but as your friend, Ben."

His stomach dropped. "Becca. No! We're more than friends. I want us to spend the rest of our lives together, no matter how long or how short that is. I love you, and I want to be there right by your side through all life's up and downs."

"It will be too painful, Ben." She shook her head and sighed. "I can't do that to you."

"You're right," he said firmly. "There will be pain. But there will also be joy. We aren't meant to live our lives with no highs or lows. You've taught me that. You've all taught me that," he said, sweeping his arm to encompass those who still stood nearby. "Love and loss are the realities of a life well-lived. I want to experience all of it with you, Becca. The joys—and even the pain."

"But what if I get sick again? I can't put you through that. You don't want that."

"You don't get to decide what I want," he said, frustrated. "I know what I want. What do you want, Becca?"

"But...your sister...what you went through with her...."

"Look, I know how I feel, and I know what I went through with my sister—with Sophia," he said, clearly enunciating her name. "I know the risks. And I don't give a damn! I know it's worth it. So, Ms. Wonder Woman, that's my truth! You're worth it!" he choked out.

A voice came over the loudspeaker, interrupting his appeal. "Will Ben Morgan please come to the awards platform," came Diana's voice. "We are ready to announce our winners!"

Ben looked up at the platform. He could see Diana looking expectantly at him from across the expanse between the finish line and the awards platform. Adam, as well as all of Becca's friends, her mother, and Ethan, still stood silently off to the side—now with awkward expressions on their faces but also, like Diana, looking expectant.

Ben swiveled his gaze back to Becca. "Becca, please..." he said, his heart twisting and feeling torn. He needed to make her see that they belonged together. But he didn't want to ruin this race experience for her or for any of the other participants by making a scene. He looked into her eyes to see sadness emanated from their depths. His gut wrenched.

"Go on," she said gently, giving him a thumbs up and waving him off toward the podium.

"Just please don't go yet, Becca. This conversation isn't over. Just think about it. I'll be at the finish line—today, and every day if you'll let me." When she gave him a small sad smile, he turned to make his way toward the podium.

CHAPTER 62
Highs and Lows

BECCA WATCHED BEN AS HE MADE HIS WAY TO THE STAGE, her body motionless but her mind swirling with confusion. Which way was up and which way was down? And where was she in this moment on that roller-coaster ride? She felt herself soaring to the top, euphoric. Had she really just completed a triathlon? And then plummeting to the bottom in despair. Had she really just sent Ben away? Her mind ricocheted along that track, up then down, up then down.

Maybe Ben was right. Maybe life was continually made up of ups and downs and everything in between. Maybe you didn't always get to choose when they came or which way they went. Maybe you just had to hang on for dear life and ride out those lows and soar with those highs. But did she, or anyone, have any control over their direction and when they came or went?

Yes, came her answer. She'd trained for this triathlon. She'd worked hard, and the payoff was exhilarating. And she'd done it with the help of her friends and her family...and her coach, making it all that much sweeter. She, just like everyone else, didn't have control over everything, though. She couldn't have predicted her father would die so suddenly and so young, and she couldn't have predicted she'd get cancer. It was up to her, though, Becca realized, as to how she reacted to those blows. That was her choice; no one could make that decision for her. Just like Ben had told her that she couldn't decide for him what he wanted in life.

"Becca?" Stacey said gently.

She turned, startled, forgetting her friends still stood nearby. Becca took in their uncomfortable expressions and their rigid posture. Their faces were etched with sadness and concern as they looked at her and waited for her to respond. She didn't know what to say. Her mind was still spinning, and she couldn't seem to find that stable portion of the roller-coaster track she knew was there somewhere—the place where we live most of our lives. The place that allowed for the processing of our ups and downs.

"Becca," Stacey said again, this time with a gentle but awkward smile. "I think you've tried him on enough. I think it's high time you buy him."

Eileen, Natalie, and even Anna jerked back in surprise, their bodies becoming even more rigid as they stood with their eyes wide and their lips pursed together, waiting anxiously to see how Becca would respond. Adam, Ethan, Jenn, and Becca's mom just looked at Stacey in confusion.

As Becca watched their faces, an indescribable calm come over her. Her breathing evened out and the swirling of the Escher print, along with her roller coaster ride, stabilized. A clarity filled her brain unlike anything she'd ever felt before and Becca felt a smile quirk up on her lips. "I've been an idiot, haven't I?" she asked them.

There were careful nods all around. But no one said a word.

She sighed, then conscious of the commotion behind them, said, "We'd better get over to that awards ceremony, don't you think?" Her smile grew wider, as she turned to make her way to the stage area. The entire group fell in line behind her, following, just as Manky and Mel followed Ben around his driveway—not sure where he was going, but nonetheless following loyally behind.

CHAPTER 63
Awards

"THAT'S THE LAST OF OUR AWARDS," SAID DIANA TO CHEERS from the crowd. "Congratulations to our winners! I also want to especially thank all our course staff and volunteers. We couldn't put on a race like this without all of you helping to get everyone checked in or constantly monitoring the course from start to finish. A special thank you to all of our kayakers, paddle boarders, bike course volunteers, and run course volunteers; and to all of our sponsors who provided the food and hydration for our fuel stops and for our after-race buffet. Please join me in thanking them." Catcalls and cheers went up.

Diana continued, "And a very special thank you to Coach Ben Morgan and his team, who not only took part in the race today but also raised several thousands of dollars to help raise awareness and fund the fight against cancer." The sound of cowbells ringing and kazoos added to the cacophony of cheers as Becca and her teammates, family, and friends, standing in front and just below the stage, hooted and hollered. "So, with that—"

But before Diana finished her next sentence, Ben interrupted her by leaning over and whispering in her ear.

She pulled back and looked at him. "Of course... Hold on a moment, folks. Ben has something to add." She handed the microphone to Ben.

"If you'll all bear with me a moment," Ben said, fumbling with the microphone and nearly dropping it as he shifted from one foot to the other. "I want to—no, I need to—send out some special thank you's. First, to my team. You all have made this an incredible journey. I can't thank you enough for all you've taught me and for how much you all have given me. I know I'm the coach and I'm supposed to be the one giving to you, but you all have done so much more for me than I ever could for you.

"And to my brother, Adam, thank you especially for helping me come to terms with the loss of our sister—Sophia—and for helping me remember all the good times with her. I know she's looking down on us now and cheering us on—both in terms of the race and in life."

Ben paused and looked toward his team standing in a pod amongst the larger crowd, a pod that now included Becca and all those who had been standing with her only moments ago at the finish line. Tears leaked out of the corners of everyone's eyes, especially Adam's, Ben noted, as Adam lifted a hand to wipe his eyes, trying to hide his emotion but not succeeding very well.

He turned his gaze to Becca, and she felt herself hold her breath. "And one participant in particular has brought acceptance and love back into my life," he announced. "Becca, you are so strong, so brave, and so beautiful in everything you do. Your determination, your fight, and your spirit are amazing, and I can't imagine living without you." The microphone wobbled precariously in Ben's hands, causing a collective cringe to distort the faces in the crowd. But not a sound could be heard, not from Ben and Becca's team or from anyone else as they all waited to see what the outcome of Ben's speech would be. Becca felt just as captivated as the rest of them, waiting with bated breath for Ben to continue.

Ben swallowed, as if forcing his nerves aside, and said, "Will you forgive me for how long it's taken me to come to my senses? I love you, Becca, and I want to experience all of life with you, day in and day out—both the joy and the pain. And today is a day filled with joy. I am so proud of you. You are now officially a triathlete!" He looked at her proudly as a tear trickled, unchecked, down his cheek. "But, I promise you, I will also be there for you through life's challenges and for every-thing in between."

Becca felt spellbound at Ben's public show of emotion. Her body, her mind all felt glued to his.

"Go on up," Carmen said from beside her, giving her a light push in the back.

Becca looked at Carmen, who nodded her head encouragingly. Becca then looked at Adam, her mom, her friends, and her teammates, seeing nothing but smiles and encouragement. Becca felt a profound sense of love for everyone there, but most especially for the man on the podium. She took a tentative step forward and reached her hand up to Ben.

The crowd cheered and hooted and hollered as Ben reached down to grasp her hand and pull her up onto the stage. Becca fell into his arms as he pulled her in close. She wrapped her arms around him just as tightly and lifted her face to his. Ben ran kisses along her hair and over her eyes and cheeks. Both of them now had tears streaming out of their eyes but huge smiles on their faces.

She tilted her head up to look into his eyes. Eyes that shone with love just as she knew hers did. Ben gently grasped both sides of her cheeks, running the pads of his thumbs along her cheekbones to wipe away her tears, and then brought his lips to meet hers—for one of the best kisses of her life.

Amidst the cheers and catcalls, Ben pulled away and whispered for her ears alone, "I love you, Becca. You are and always will be my Wonder Woman."

"I love you too, Ben," she said, then leaned in for another kiss.

Epilogue

One Year Later

BECCA STOOD NEXT TO BEN AND ETHAN, WAITING
expectantly amidst a handful of dignitaries behind a long red ribbon
strung from a newly installed swing set to a large and intricate sculp-
ture of a beautiful butterfly emerging from its cocoon. Rose stood
front and center with them.

"As Mayor of Marston," announced Rose, "I now proclaim the
Marston Marina Park and Playground open for everyone to enjoy!"

Ben, Becca, and Ethan together ceremoniously passed an enormous
pair of oversized scissors to Rose, who took them and cut the ribbon
in front of her, eliciting a huge round of cheers and clapping from the
celebrants standing throughout the newly renovated park.

Becca thought back to the dilapidated Sutter Street Park that sat on
this spot just one year ago. Gone were the cracking concrete walk-
ways, the weeds, and the precariously leaning fence and sign. In their
place was a garden blooming with spring and early summer flowers, a
swing set, a slide carved to look like a rope snaking down the hillside,
and a merry-go-round. Seating areas dotted the park, encouraging
people to sit awhile and enjoy the outdoors, including two beautifully
designed benches, one of which was dedicated to Sophia Morgan and

the other to Noah Clarke. There was even a new ice cream store across the street.

The sign at the entrance to the park welcomed everyone—both children and adults. Another sign next to it informed the public that the park was largely funded through grants from the United States Housing and Urban Development Agency, among other contributors. Prominently included in that list were Becca and Ben and many of their friends, family, and colleagues. Four large eye-level billboards lined the western edge of the park, depicting more to come, with artistically drawn maps—thanks to Ben—that highlighted the phased revitalization plans for the park and for the surrounding area. Included on three of the billboards were the plans for the marina, the trail extension, the amphitheater, and additional shops, eateries, and lodging. The fourth displayed the planned infrastructure improvements.

Included among the revelers here today were multiple community members who had helped make the park a reality, as well as the mayor, council members, all of their happy hour friends, many of their triathlon teammates, and a multitude of family members. Jake Creighton from Fischer Industries was there as well, having helped with the design of the planned infrastructure improvements. Even Sam had flown in from California for the celebration.

With the formal ribbon cutting ceremony completed, the revelers peeled off into various groupings to view the grounds, partake of the delicious delicacies laid out in the center of the park on tables draped with festive tablecloths, and catch up with old and new friends.

Becca flitted happily from one conversation to another, feeling a heady sense of accomplishment along with a deep sense of contentment, landing now with a group of celebrants that included Jason, Connie, and Graham from Ben's office, as well as her mother.

"Will you look at that!" Becca said, pointing to the now busy playground. "Thank you for all you did to make that playground so extraordinary, Mom. It really pops!" She gave her mother a grin and a hug. "Your students did a great job drawing out their ideas for the playground. The parks and recreation committee loved getting to look through all of their great ideas. And it obviously appeals to them." She laughed as a squeal of delight and the sound of small running feet drifted across the breeze to where they stood.

"What a wonderful event!" Rose exclaimed as she approached their group. "Thank you for everything all of you did to make this place a reality, especially you two," she said, reaching over to give Ben and then Becca a hug. "You two did a great job and I, along with many others, will be forever grateful to you both."

"We're the ones who should thank you, Rose," said Ben. "None of this could have happened without your leadership—and perhaps not without those wonderful burgers and caramel pretzel milkshakes of yours," he joked. "Becca and I never would have gotten to know each other without those. That was our first date." He turned to give Becca a wink.

"And the first-time we put on our rose-colored glasses," Becca added. "We needed those to see past the dilapidation to this," she said, sweeping her arms around her. "At least I did. I never would have seen it if it weren't for Ben."

"I think we've all outdone ourselves," said Rose. "You two should feel very proud of this accomplishment and of all that's still to come. I know I do. Even the event today went perfectly, with every detail seen to from the design of the park to the installation and even now to the grand opening. And look how long people stayed today! Goodness, we're about two hours past our end time."

"I suppose it is time to clean up," said Ben. "I've already got my truck loaded, but I can take this stuff up to the house and then come back for another load."

"Oh, no, you don't. You two go on now," said Rose. "You've done too much already, and we've got a great crew out here to help us. Even my nephew, Nick, here." She gestured to the young man approaching their group. "Of course, you two know him well—he's from the U-Haul store," Rose said with a sly grin.

"Hi, Mr. Morgan, Ms. Clarke—I mean, Becca," he said with a smile. "I'll be happy to help."

"See? You two go on and enjoy yourselves now," said Rose. "We can handle this cleanup. You've got enough to deal with already with that one load. Go on," she urged, smiling at them and giving them each another hug.

∽

Becca now stood on the back patio of Ben's no-longer-dilapidated mansion—and now her home too—reveling in this beautiful day. The river glistened in the distance, peaking through the trees full of spring and early summer leaves. Sunlight filtered down through those leaves, and the sweet smell of honeysuckle wafted on the light breeze that brushed across her cheeks.

Becca took in a deep breath and closed her eyes, lifting her face to the warmth above her. "Hey, Dad," she said, opening her eyes and looking up into the expansive blue sky dotted with puffy white clouds. "It's me, Becca. As you can see, I'm not in D.C., but I think you'd be happy about where I ended up. I'm truly happy here. I followed in your footsteps, and I get to spend my time doing financial analytics, just like you did and in a way that helps people here where Mom and my friends are. And just like you, I get to do it surrounded by people I love and who love me. It just turns out that place isn't in Washington, D.C. as I thought it would be. It's in a little town in the Midwest outside of Pittsburgh, Pennsylvania. Who knew? I sure didn't."

"Becca?" Ben called out with a frantic chuckle. "Manky's getting a bit too excited here. Do you think you can come save us?"

Becca turned her head to see Ben. He had his arms full of supplies from their celebration this afternoon, which were held precariously in his arms and threatening to fall while Manky waddled in and out between his feet, risking getting stepped on but quaking incessantly for attention.

Becca grinned at the ridiculous sight. "Be right there," she called out before looking back up into the sky. "See what I mean, Dad? It's crazy around here—but it's a good crazy. Yep, I'm home. I'm definitely home," she said, before making her way toward Manky.

"Here, boy, I'll give you some attention!" Becca reached into her pocket and gave Manky a piece of a cookie. "Now leave poor Ben alone, silly," she said, shooing him away and then turning to help Ben get the rest of the supplies into the house.

As Becca put away the unused supplies in their kitchen's new, expansive pantry, she felt the warmth of Ben's body envelop her from behind as his arms wrapped around her in a protective embrace. She leaned back into him with a sigh of contentment, luxuriating in the feel of his lips as he kissed her neck, sending shivers up her spine.

Becca clasped his hands in hers and grasped them tightly in front of her waist, pulling him in closer behind her. "You'd better be careful with those kisses. They're pretty potent. I can't promise you I'll be able to stop myself from dragging you upstairs to have my way with you," she teased.

Ben rubbed his hands up and down her arms, eliciting another happy sigh from her. He kissed her neck again and then leaned in to whisper in her ear, "There are fireworks over the river tonight. Want to go for a boat ride?"

～

Thank you for reading The Metamorphosis of Becca!

I hope you enjoyed reading this book as much as I enjoyed writing it. If you did, please consider leaving a review. Reviews are very important for authors as they ensure increased visibility on Amazon, making it easier for readers to find the books they enjoy reading. This author, and readers everywhere, will thank you for it!

～

Click below to sign up to receive updates and *Bonus Content!*

Join Jocelyn's newsletter to be among the first to get announcements about upcoming books, and to receive FREE Bonus Content.

https://www.jocelynkraemerbooks.com/

About the Author

Jocelyn Kraemer lives near Pittsburgh, Pennsylvania, with her husband, two boys, and a menagerie of wild pets, including two ducks, who keep her entertained every morning over coffee. Jocelyn enjoys boating, endurance events (especially triathlons), and a great glass of wine (or two) with amazing friends and family.

She believes in happily ever afters and, when she doesn't get one immediately, she writes one! Pick up one of Jocelyn's books, sit back, and relax. Even when grappling with difficult subjects, Joycelyn's got you covered with a guaranteed happily ever after.

Please visit Jocelyn's website for more information. While you're there, sign up for her newsletter and access bonus content!

Website: https://www.jocelynkraemerbooks.com/
Facebook: https://www.facebook.com/JocelynKraemerBooks
Email: JocelynKraemerBooks@gmail.com